A SEDUCTIVE GAMBLE

Suddenly Christine knew she was going to seduce Chad. The thought shocked her. Not because she felt it was wrong, but because she still doubted she could do it.

She stripped off her clothes and slipped on the daring green nightgown. Her heart pounding with fear and anticipation, she walked down the hallway and knocked softly on Chad's door. The door swung open and Chad, seeing her standing there in her flimsy nightgown, gasped in surprise. He pulled her roughly into the room and slammed the door.

"What the hell are you doing here?" he demanded, feeling the heat of his desire rise at the sight of her. Doesn't she know what she's doing to me? he thought.

Christine looked up at him, her eyes pleading. She leaned into his strong chest, and slipped her arms around his waist, whispering, "Love me, Chad. Please, love me."

Chad's control shattered. His mouth crashed down on hers in a bruising, demanding kiss as his arms pulled her into a fierce, savage embrace. And the time for hesitation was gone. . . .

EXCITING BESTSELLERS FROM ZEBRA

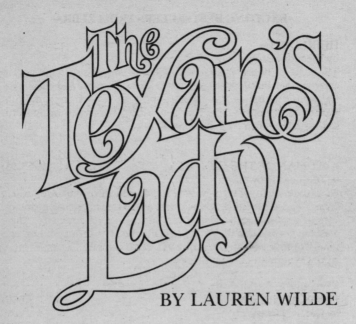

The Texan's Lady

BY LAUREN WILDE

ZEBRA BOOKS
KENSINGTON PUBLISHING CORP.

ZEBRA BOOKS

are published by

Kensington Publishing Corp.
475 Park Avenue South
New York, N.Y. 10016

Third printing: February 1986

Printed in the United States of America

For Neil, my husband, who believed in me and wouldn't let me give up.

ACKNOWLEDGMENT

I would like to take this opportunity to give special thanks to Gwen for all of her patient help and for being my second pair of eyes.

Chapter One

Christine Roberts stood in the middle of the dusty street and stared at the squat adobe building before her, totally oblivious to the hot sun that beat down on her head, the stench of rotting fish and raw sewage that rose from the river beside her, the braying of burros and the laughter of half-naked children playing nearby, the buzzing of flies around her, and the curious stares of several Mexicans who leaned listlessly in the doorways of their miserable huts in the hope of catching a breath of cool air. Her full attention was riveted to the sign above the doorway of the building, a sign that read in sprawled, uneven letters, Rosita's Cantina.

Yes, this is it, she thought, her heartbeat accelerating with excitement. This was the place where the hotel desk clerk had told her she would find him, the man she was searching for, the man she prayed would agree to help her, perhaps the only man who could help her.

She frowned. She had no idea what a *cantina* was. Judging from the bawdy laughter coming from inside the building and the two intoxicated men who had just staggered from the door, she assumed it was the Mexican version of a saloon, no place for a respectable woman, certainly not a socially prominent New York heiress. Normally she would never dream of entering such a low, disreputable establishment. But then, during the past month, she had done many things she had never dreamed of doing: first defying her domineering uncle; then traveling alone over thousands of miles to cross the dangerous Texas frontier; braving the scorching sun, the hot wind, and the possibility of Indian attack; and enduring the jolting, bone-shattering stagecoach ride, the rancid, inedible food and filthy, bug-infested beds of the stage inns. She had gladly paid the "flood rate," the extra five cents a mile, for the privilege of sitting inside the coach when it rained, instead of getting out to help push the heavy stage through the deep mud bogs and swollen creeks.

Now she stood in the middle of a dust-choked street in a foreign country, a country torn apart by war; a backward, underdeveloped country, the majority of its people poverty-stricken and illiterate; a barely civilized country whose native tongue was only a confusing mumbo jumbo of sounds to her ears. What am I doing here? she asked herself.

Her eyes drifted southward, squinting in the bright glare of the sun, to scan the foothills of the Sierra Madre, an awesome, gigantic upthrust of

8

almost solid rock, torturous and forbidding. Somewhere in those rugged, barren mountains, the only person she had ever deeply cared for was being held hostage. And if her mission today was unsuccessful, he would die.

This realization gave her the impetus she needed. With renewed determination, she turned back to the cantina. She really didn't have any choice. Even if it was the devil's own lair, she had to go into the building. She had to find *him*.

She knew that he was her last hope. She had already exhausted all other possibilities. She had gone to the Mexican Consulate in Washington, the army, even the governor of Texas. Upon hearing her story, they had all expressed concern and then, regretfully, told her there was nothing they could do to help her.

Her search would have ended there had not the governor referred her to a former captain of the Texas Rangers. It was from him that she had obtained the name of the man she was now seeking, and information on where to locate him—but not until after the captain had ranted, long and bitterly, about the stupidity of the Reconstruction government that had disbanded the Texas Rangers, the only body of men capable and experienced enough to deal with the Indians and the Mexican bandits that terrorized the western part of the state and the entire Texas-Mexican border.

Christine had been shocked to learn that these lawmen had, in the past, swept down into Mexico in pursuit of raiding Indians or Mexican bandits, crossing the Rio Grande as casually as if it were just another river, instead of an international border, and administering justice, often without benefit of judge or jury. She had asked whether the Mexican government had not objected to the rangers trespassing into their territory and acting in an unofficial capacity. The captain had replied that the Mexican government had probably been glad the rangers had taken care of the problem for them, since they had been too preoccupied with revolutions and wars to control the bandits that plagued the border and the entire country.

But regardless of what Christine thought of the Texas Rangers' tactics, she was grateful to the captain for giving her Chad Yancy's name, her last possible hope. No doubt, Mr. Yancy would be as disreputable as the cantina she stood before and that disgusting hotel she had checked into, the hotel where the captain had told her she would find him. But then what could she expect of a mercenary, a gunslinger? Undoubtedly, he would be crude, ruthless, uneducated, and . . . certainly dangerous. She shivered, both in revulsion and fear.

She hesitated, wondering if she should have taken the desk clerk's advice and waited for the gunman to return to the hotel in El Paso. In the safety of that respectable building and surrounded by fellow Americans, that might have been a safer place to approach him than this deserted cantina on the Mexican side of the border, a place that was probably a den of thieves and murderers. After all, he was a hired gun, a professional killer, probably just as savage as the Apaches that roamed this inhospitable land, ravishing and plundering.

No, Christine told herself firmly, she couldn't wait any longer. Time was running out. There was no telling when or if the gunman would return to the hotel today, especially if he had been drinking. She couldn't take the risk of missing Chad Yancy again.

She took one last look at the dusty Mexican street and the adobe huts huddled against the muddy river twisting beside it. Then squaring her shoulders and taking a deep, ragged breath, Christine stepped into the cantina.

Chapter Two

When Christine stepped from the bright light of the sun and into the dim interior of the cantina, she was temporarily blinded. One sense gone, her remaining senses sharpened. She heard the mournful twang of a guitar, the tinkle of glass hitting glass, and then the distinct sound of cards being shuffled. The smell of the cantina assaulted her nostrils: a mixture of tobacco smoke, stale liquor, unwashed bodies, spicy cooking odors, and the musty smell of the adobe building itself. The odious smells mingled and, combined with her apprehension, brought on a sudden wave of nausea.

Once her eyes had adjusted to the darkened room, she looked about her anxiously. The cantina was crowded with low tables and rickety chairs. Three Mexican peons, dressed in their traditional white tunics and loose-fitting breeches, sat at one table, their wide-rimmed sombreros tossed carelessly on the dirt floor beside them. At yet another table, four rough-looking, bearded men sat; Christine recognized them as Americans by their slouch hats and the inevitable guns strapped low on their hips. All of the men stared at her with stunned looks on their faces.

Christine was very aware of their stares. She wondered briefly if their shocked looks stemmed from surprise at finding a lady standing in the middle of their all-male domain or from her appearance itself.

Christine was used to being stared at by strangers. Her unusual size made her outstanding. At five foot, ten inches tall, she towered over the other members of her sex and, in an age when the average height of a man was five feet, eight inches, over a good deal of the men also. The fact that her framework matched her height, that her shoulders were as broad as many men's, only added to her impressive measurements. Not that she was fat. To the contrary. She was perfectly proportioned. She was simply a lot of woman.

Surprisingly, in a day and age when daintiness was associated with femininity, an age when most women would be horrified to be as big or bigger than a man, Christine wasn't in the least disturbed by her unusual height and dimensions. On the contrary, she was delighted she was a tall woman. To her, her size was a boon, her secret weapon against men. Combined with a carefully developed haughty attitude, her imposing figure made it all the easier to intimidate men, to keep them at bay. And for Christine, keeping the men away was a necessity. She wanted nothing to do with men. She didn't trust them.

Ignoring the men still gawking at her, Christine turned and walked to the small bar, addressing the Mexican bartender standing behind it. "Excuse me. I'm looking for a man. A Mr. Chad Yancy. Can you tell me if he's here?"

The man looked at her blankly, saying, *"No comprendo inglés."*

Tears of frustration rose in Christine's eyes. It seemed that everywhere she turned, she was blocked by someone or something. Now would she be unable to find Mr. Yancy simply because she couldn't speak Spanish? Maybe if she spoke slower.

Without realizing it, Christine raised her voice, carefully enunciating, "Mr. Yancy? Chad Yancy?"

The bartender stared at her, shaking his head mutely.

"I'm Chad Yancy," a deep, male voice said from behind her.

Christine whirled and looked at the table where the Americans sat. Was one of those rough-looking men Chad Yancy? But the four men stared back at her, their looks almost hostile.

Had she only imagined the voice? Or were these men playing some kind of game with her? Suddenly she remembered where she was and that these men might well be murderers or thieves. A shiver of fear ran through her.

"I'm over here," the same husky voice drawled.

Christine's eyes flew to the darkened corner of the room from which the voice had come. She was barely able to distinguish a figure sitting at the table against one wall. Her heart pounded in her chest from both fear and anticipation as she wove her way through the crowded tables, only too aware of the other men's smirks and snickers.

A man sat behind the table in one corner. His chair was tilted backward, so that his broad shoulders rested against the wall behind him. With his arms folded across his chest and his battered hat pulled low on his forehead, one might think he was dozing. But Christine was not fooled by his casual, almost indifferent air. She could feel his eyes following her as she threaded her way through the tables. That, combined with the feeling of unleashed power he seemed to exude, like a coiled-up snake about to strike, did nothing to allay her apprehension. By the time she stood before him, her legs were shaking badly.

She licked her lips nervously before asking, "Are you Chad Yancy?"

"That's right," the man answered in a cold, flat voice.

Christine quickly scanned what features of his face she could see, the strong, cleanly shaven chin, the rugged planes of his lower face, the deep lines on each side of his mouth, a mouth that, even with its mocking tilt, was strangely sensual. She shivered. Despite his surprisingly rugged good looks, good looks that should have reassured her, there was something about him that disturbed her, disturbed her deeply. Was it that sense of unleashed power, that aura of danger that seemed to surround him? she asked herself. No it was more, much more. He possessed a virile mas-

16

culinity so profoundly male that it seemed to radiate from him in powerful waves, threatening to engulf her. Never in her life, had she met a man so totally and irrevocably male, his sexuality stamped on his every feature, every fiber of his being, his every motion and gesture. And never before had Christine felt so threatened by a man's sensuality. It seemed to overpower her, frightening her with its intensity.

Quickly Christine brought up her defenses. With her haughtiest voice, she said, "My name is Christine Roberts."

Chad Yancy's only acknowledgment of her words was a curt nod. Despite his indifferent appearance, he had been aware of Christine from the minute she had stepped into the cantina. Born and raised on the wild, west-Texas frontier, where survival was the name of the game, Chad's senses had developed until they were razor sharp. There wasn't a second that ticked by that he wasn't aware of everything and everyone around him. He heard the slightest sound, saw the smallest movement. The men who had served under him in the war had sworn he had eyes in the back of his head. And when those failed, he put out invisible feelers that could sense things an ordinary man couldn't.

But even if Chad hadn't had such finely attuned senses, he would have noticed Christine. And no wonder. She was a woman it would be impossible not to notice. Like the other men in the cantina, he had been stunned by her size. He had never seen so much woman. For a brief minute, he had

17

thought a magnificent Viking goddess had been dropped into their midst, a beautiful, silver-haired warrior-woman, standing tall and proud and fierce-looking, bigger than life itself.

After the initial impact of seeing Christine had worn off—Chad had to admit that Christine's first impression packed a tremendous wallop—he had calmly assessed her. While he could appreciate her unusual beauty, he wasn't particularly attracted to her. That didn't surprise him. He was a man who had very definite tastes when it came to women. He liked small-statured women; big-hipped, full-busted, voluptuous women; soft cuddly women. And he had never been attracted to blondes. He preferred women with vibrant coloring and dark, flashing eyes, eyes that seethed with promised passion, a passion to match his own. One look at Christine's eyes was all it had taken to convince him. They had a hard, cold glint about them. Yes, he'd been correct in his estimation of blondes. They were cold, frigid, passionless women.

But despite the fact that Christine wasn't his type, Chad hadn't been able to take his eyes from her. In some strange way, she fascinated him, seemed to draw him to her.

Why? Chad had asked himself. Was it her proud carriage? The way she seemed to be throwing her body out like a challenge, as if she were saying, here I am. Am I too much woman for you? Are you man enough to take me on? And since he was never a man to turn his back on a challenge, was that what drew him to her?

18

Or did his fascination with her stem from simple curiosity? She was obviously a lady, a lady of high quality. Good breeding fairly oozed from her. What in the hell was a high-class lady like her doing in the middle of this dirty, stinking cantina?

When she had asked for him, Chad had been stunned, his curiosity even more aroused. But when she had used that haughty tone of voice on him just now, he had been angered. It had set his teeth on edge. No woman trampled him under her boots, and certainly not some rich, spoiled bitch!

Chad stared at Christine coldly. The silence hung heavy in the air. Well, he certainly isn't going to make it easy for me, Christine thought bleakly. Gathering her courage, she said, "I have a business proposition to offer you, Mr. Yancy."

Chad smiled smugly. Here was his opportunity to bring her down a peg or two.

Christine felt, rather than saw, Chad's eyes boldly rake her body from head to toe. She had been stared at all of her adult life, but she had never been looked at like that! She felt as though his eyes had stripped her totally naked. The look left her feeling weak-kneed. She clutched the back of the chair sitting in front of her for support.

She could barely see Chad's mocking smile as he drawled lazily, "Sorry, ma'am. I'm not interested."

Christine was momentarily stunned, wondering how he could refuse her offer when he hadn't even heard it yet. Then suddenly she realized what he was thinking. My God! He thought she was a prostitute! She blushed furiously. Then indignation replaced embarrassment, and she snapped, "I'm not talking about *that* kind of a proposition, Mr. Yancy. I want to hire you."

The chair slammed to the floor, and Christine jumped in surprise. The battered hat was removed to reveal a head of thick, wavy black hair. And when Chad Yancy looked up at her, she gasped. A pair of deep blue eyes, startling in the deeply tanned face, gazed into hers.

"Sit down, Miss Roberts," Chad said in a deep Texas drawl as he carelessly tossed his hat to one side of the table.

It took a minute for Christine to recover from those eyes. She had never seen such a deep blue in her life. Only when she realized he was still sitting did she come to her senses. Well, for all of his rugged good looks and sexual magnetism, he's certainly no gentleman, she thought angrily. First he ignores me, then he rudely stares at me, and now he refuses to even pull the chair out for me. Thinking to put him in his place, she drew herself up to her full imposing height and looked down at him coldly.

At six feet, four inches and two hundred ten pounds, all sinewy muscle, Chad Yancy wasn't intimidated by anyone's size, man or woman. He smiled up at her blandly.

Christine was taken aback. What had gone wrong? That usually brought the men scurrying to their feet. Yet there he sat, grinning at her as if he didn't know what she expected him to do. Angrily Christine jerked the chair away from the table and sat down, glaring at the man sitting

20

across from her.

"Now, Mr. Yancy," she said in a biting voice, "about my business. . . ."

"Just a minute, lady," Chad interrupted in a hard voice. "It just so happens, I was fixing to eat. And I make it a point never to discuss business on an empty stomach."

Chad sat back, enjoying the surprised look on Christine's face. He hadn't missed her little display of temper, and he didn't like it any better than her haughty attitude. He couldn't imagine what she wanted to hire him for, but if they were going to do any business together, he was going to let her know who was boss from the very beginning.

"Would you like to join me?" he asked with a small, mocking smile. "The food here is not half bad."

Christine was totally frustrated. She fought back the urge to scream. Here she had finally found Chad Yancy, and now she would have to sit and wait for him to eat before she could find out if he would help her or not.

"No, thank you, Mr. Yancy," she replied stiffly, struggling to keep her temper down. "I'll eat when I get back to the hotel."

A dark eyebrow arched. "Oh? Which hotel are you staying at?"

"The Longhorn Hotel, just across the river in El Paso."

The eyebrow rose higher. Why in the hell was she staying at that dump? Chad wondered. Only whores went to the Longhorn Hotel. Surely she could afford a better hotel than that flea-bitten place.

He shrugged, saying, "You must have just arrived in El Paso."

"Why do you say that?"

"Because if you had been here any time at all, you'd know none of the hotels in El Paso have dining rooms," Chad drawled lazily. "Now on this side of the river, Rosita's is the only place you can find something to eat. Of course, there are some good restaurants in the downtown area."

Christine was aghast. No place to eat except here or downtown El Paso? She looked about the dim, dirty cantina with disgust. Then she remembered her harrowing drive from the stage depot to the hotel.

She had hired a Mexican boy to carry her and her trunk on his wagon. The dusty, narrow street had been crowded with traffic, people ambling from one side of the street to the other, horses and their riders weaving through the press of Mexican carts pulled by shaggy burros, and wagons driven by surly, rough-looking men.

The noise in the street had been almost as bad as the traffic, saddles squeaking, harnesses jingling, wagon wheels creaking, whips cracking, flies buzzing, men yelling and cursing at one another and their oxen or horses. Christine had blushed, having never heard such obscene and abusive language in her life.

By the time the traffic had thinned out, Christine had been totally unnerved. Her hair was plastered to her head from sweating in the hot

22

sun; her eyes were watery from the acrid dust. She had just expelled a sigh of relief, only to be frightened half out of her wits when two men, swearing and swinging at one another, had exploded from a saloon beside their wagon. She had sat, stunned, as the two men had thrown themselves into the street before them, rolling in the dirt, viciously kicking and slamming their fists into each other's face and body. When the two combatants, still engrossed in their bloody battle, had finally rolled to one side of the wagon, the Mexican boy, totally unperturbed by the disturbance, had calmly urged the mules forward. By the time they had finally rolled up to the Longhorn Hotel, she had had a splitting headache. No, she couldn't take that trip twice in one day.

"Maybe I'll join you after all, Mr. Yancy," she said.

"Fine," Chad answered lazily. "What would you like to eat?"

Christine looked about the table, then asked, "Where's the menu?"

Chad laughed harshly, saying, "I'm afraid we're not dining at the Menger Hotel in San Antonio. This is just a Mexican cantina, and they don't have menus."

Menger Hotel. The words brought back memories to Christine of the only really pleasant experience she had had since leaving the steamer at Corpus Christi. She remembered how shocked she had been to see the elegant hotel, laced with fine wrought-iron grillwork, sitting right next to the crumbling walls of the chapel of the Alamo and surrounded by chili stands and dilapidated saloons. And the food, she thought, her mouth watering in remembrance. She had never tasted such delicious food in her life: the rich turtle soup—the hotel's specialty, made from turtles caught in the San Antonio River—ham, venison, quail, delightful vegetables, and exotic fruits. They had even served an excellent table wine. She groaned silently, wondering if she would ever eat that well again.

Chad cleared his throat and said in an impatient voice, "Well, are you going to order or not?"

Pulled from her pleasant memories and resenting his tone of voice, Christine snapped, "Well, how do I know what to order if they don't have menus?"

Chad smiled, enjoying her frustration. "The menu's listed on that sign over the bar," he said calmly, pointing to the sign.

Christine peered across the smoky room at the small sign. It was covered with cobwebs and . . . "But it's in Spanish!" she cried.

"Of course, it's in Spanish," Chad said sarcastically. "We're in Mexico. Or have you forgotten?"

Christine was seething. She had never met such a rude, arrogant man in her life! And to make matters worse, he seemed to take perverse pleasure in taunting her. "I'm afraid I don't read Spanish, Mr. Yancy," Christine replied curtly. "Would you be kind enough to read it to me?"

Chad sighed, wondering if putting her in her place was worth the trouble. "Well, the first thing listed is *cabrito*."

"What is *cabrito*?" Christine asked.

"Goat meat."

"Goat meat!" Christine gasped, her nose wrinkling with distaste.

"It's not bad."

Well, Christine thought ruefully, she had probably eaten much worse than goat meat at the last few stage stops. At least, she knew she had eaten buffalo at one. And this was the first time she had had any choice of what she would eat since she'd left San Antonio. Maybe they had something better.

She gazed at the sign and asked, "And the second item?"

"Frijoles," Chad answered. "That's beans. Dried beans. They're the Mexican's staples, that and corn."

Christine was well acquainted with the beans he was referring to. She had been served them at every stage inn since the old Moor's Ranch outside of San Antonio. Except at the last stage stop, she remembered with disgust. There, they had tried to serve her mesquite beans, and Christine had positively balked at that. No, she was sick and tired of beans.

She looked back up at the sign and smiled, grateful for the first time in her life for her geography lessons. "Chili?" she asked.

"Yes," Chad answered, "but I wouldn't advise that unless you're used to hot, spicy food."

Christine sighed in exasperation. This could go on all day, she thought with disgust, and she wasn't even hungry. She turned to the big, dark-haired Texan, saying, "Tell me, Mr. Yancy, what are you having?"

"*Criavillas*, with a side order of frijoles," he answered.

Christine wondered what criavillas were, particularly since she had noticed a glimmer of amusement in the Texan's eyes when he told her what he planned to order. Well, she'd be damned if she'd give him the satisfaction of asking. "Then that's what I'll have too," she said decisively.

Chad smiled smugly and said, "Fine. Now, what would you like to drink?"

Oh no, here we go again, Christine thought in disgust. She sighed wearily and said, "What are you having?"

"Beer."

"Beer?" Christine asked, surprised.

"Yes, Mexican beer. It's not as good as the Menger beer, but it's passable."

"Don't they have anything to drink but beer?" Christine asked.

Chad shrugged. "Sure. There's tequila and pulque."

Christine knew what tequila was. But *pulque*? Well, it sounded innocent enough. "What is pulque?"

"It's a fermented drink the Mexicans make from the maguey plant."

"It's intoxicating?"

Chad grinned, saying, "Very intoxicating."

26

Christine sighed in exasperation, then said, "I'll just have water."

Chad's look turned serious. "No, lady. Water is one drink I'd definitely not advise in Mexico. It might make you sick."

"You mean, I can't drink any water in Mexico?" Christine asked in a shocked voice.

"Not unless you're positive of its source, or that it's been purified," Chad replied. "Spring water and well water are usually safe. But the Mexicans get most of their water from the rivers and creeks, and they don't bother to boil it. Typhoid is a very serious problem down here."

"Well, for heavens sake," Christine said irritably, "don't they serve anything besides alcoholic beverages?"

Chad shrugged, saying, "There's coffee. It's certainly been boiled long enough to be safe."

Christine glared at the Texan. Why hadn't he just said they served coffee in the first place? "I'll have a cup of coffee," she snapped.

Chad motioned to a Mexican girl standing by the bar. Christine watched as the pretty girl approached them, her hips moving in an exaggerated provocative sway, her lips smiling seductively at Chad. She gasped when the girl plopped herself in the big Texan's lap, wrapping her arms around his neck possessively, snuggling against him suggestively. Christine had never been so shocked in her life. She sat stiffly, blushing furiously, as the girl pulled Chad's head down, practically burying his face in the deep cleavage of her big breasts and whispering something in his ear.

Chad laughed softly and pulled the girl's arms from around his neck. Pushing her gently off his lap, he said, "Not now, Theresa. Maybe later. Right now I want to eat. Be a good girl and bring us two orders of *criavillas* and frijoles. I'll have a beer, and the lady"—he motioned to Christine—"will have coffee."

The Mexican girl turned to Christine, her look one of pure hate. Christine gasped in surprise. I wonder what's wrong with her? she thought in astonishment as the Mexican girl flounced away angrily.

"What part of the country do you come from, Miss Roberts?" the Texan asked.

"I'm from New York City," Christine answered in a disinterested voice.

Chad wasn't surprised, having noticed her clipped Yankee speech. There were a lot of Yankees down here since the war, but they were mostly men. In fact, his last two jobs had been escorting Yankee speculators down into Mexico to investigate mining prospects. Yes, Chad thought bitterly, as soon as the French vultures pull out of Mexico, the American ones will be there to take their places, every one anxious to get a piece of the Mexicans' natural resources. Well, what the hell, Chad thought, he didn't care what they did as long as he got his money. In this world, it was every man for himself.

Christine looked on silently as the Mexican girl, smiling sweetly, placed the plate, eating utensils, and bottle of beer in front of Chad, openly taking every opportunity to brush her body against his. Well, she's certainly not very subtle, Christine thought with disgust. She jumped when the girl slammed her own plate in front of her, practically throwing the knife and fork at her, and dumping the coffee cup down, half of it spilling over.

Christine glanced at her plate, surprised to see it actually looked appetizing. She took a bite of the frijoles and smiled. They were much better seasoned than the beans she had been served before. She looked warily at the *criavillas*, their appearance reminding her of small pears. Gingerly, she cut off a piece and put it in her mouth. The meat had a consistency much like liver. She chewed slowly. Why, it's delicious, she thought with surprise.

She looked up, intending to comment on the good food, and saw the Mexican girl placing another platter on the table.

"Pancakes?" she asked in disbelief.

Chad chuckled, saying, "No, they're tortillas. They're made from a cornmeal dough and patted into that shape. Then they're baked on an ungreased griddle. The Mexicans use them in place of bread. Watch, this is how it's done."

Christine watched as he picked up one of the thin, round tortillas and rolled it deftly between his fingers. Then he used the tortilla to push his frijoles onto his fork.

Christine picked up a tortilla and tried to imitate his action, but the finger movements were strange to her, and the tortilla plopped down in the middle of her plate. She looked up with embarrassment to see Chad watching her, his brilliant blue eyes glittering with amusement. Resolutely she picked up the wayward tortilla and finally managed to awkwardly fold it.

Christine was disappointed in the taste of the tortilla. To her, it was rather bland tasting and papery. But the other food was delicious, and as she ate, she realized with surprise that she was ravenous. By the time she had eaten her third tortilla, she had decided she liked their taste after all.

Chad sat across the table and watched Christine as she ate. At least she's not coy about eating, he thought with relief. Nothing disgusted him more than a woman who toyed with her food, pretending disinterest. It was a pleasure to see a woman who honestly enjoyed her meal and ate with a healthy appetite.

And Christine did thoroughly enjoy her meal. She had been aware of the Mexican girl standing by the table, impatiently waiting for her to finish so she could remove her dishes, but Christine had refused to be rushed through the best meal she had had in over a week.

Placing the fork back down on her empty plate and totally ignoring the Mexican girl's angry stare, Christine said, "That was delicious, Mr. Yancy. Tell me, just what kind of meat is *criavillas*?"

"Beef," Chad answered, trying to hide a small smile playing at his lips.

"Bull's balls," the Mexican girl said loudly,

30

then giggled, her dark eyes glittering maliciously.

Christine looked up at her, thinking at first that she was making some obscene exclamation. But upon seeing the girl's silly smirk, Christine realized she had meant the words literally. Christine's stomach lurched, her face colored hotly.

The Mexican girl snickered, one hand on her broad hip. Christine knew she was enjoying her discomfiture. For some reason or another, the girl had taken an instant dislike to her and was taking every opportunity to embarrass her in front of the Texan. Christine was sick and tired of it. It was time to give her a dose of her own medicine.

Raising her head proudly, Christine said in her haughtiest voice, "Really? How interesting. When I was in France, I ate frog legs and snails."

The girl's smile froze, her dusky face turned pale.

"Oh, they're really quite tasty," Christine assured the girl, a sickening sweet smile on her face. "And then for dessert, we had fried ants coated with sugar."

The Mexican girl's eyes were round with horror. She whirled, one hand clutching her stomach, the other over her mouth, and stumbled from the room.

Christine was ashamed of herself. After all, she was a lady, and ladies didn't lower themselves to verbal spats with serving girls. Of course, the whole story was an out-and-out lie. She had never been to France in her life, much less eaten those horrid things. From the corner of her eye, she could see Chad Yancy watching her, his eyes gleaming with amusement. *Does he know I lied?* Christine thought with panic. *He couldn't possibly know that. Or could he?*

Chad had been amused by the confrontation. Theresa could be a little bitch when she wanted to, and she'd deserved what she got. What had surprised him was the crafty way the Yankee woman had put her in her place. But had the prim, haughty woman sitting across from him actually eaten snails and frog legs? He doubted it. Somehow, despite her obvious good breeding and expensive clothes, she lacked the sophistication of a true woman of the world.

Chad pushed the empty dishes away, took a small Mexican cigar from his pocket, and lit it. Casually leaning back against the wall, he took a deep drag, his eyes boring into the woman across from him. "All right, lady, let's talk business," he said. "Just what did you want to hire me for?"

Christine suddenly felt nervous. The time she'd been awaiting anxiously had finally arrived, but she didn't know how to begin. "I understand you hire out as a guide for people who want to go into the Mexican interior," Christine said in a tentative voice.

"Yes, I'm a guide and a *pistolero*," Chad answered.

"*Pistolero*?" Christine asked, having never heard the term before.

Chad smiled mockingly, saying, "*Pistolero* is what the Mexicans call a man who hires out his gun. I'm a hired gun, lady. But surely, whoever

32

sent you to me, must have told you that."

Christine stared at him, her revulsion showing clearly in her face.

Chad saw her disgusted look and laughed harshly. "Look, lady, the men who hire me to take them into the Mexican interior aren't only interested in someone to guide them. They want protection too. In case you don't realize it, there's a war going on down here right now. It's not exactly the safest place in the world. And then, there's the Indians and Mexican bandidos too."

Chad's last words drew Christine's attention away from her disgust. Despite what she thought of him personally, she needed this man desperately, and she couldn't afford to alienate him. Smiling nervously, she said, "I'm sorry, Mr. Yancy, I just wasn't familiar with the word, that's all."

Chad nodded curtly, knowing damned well she was lying. God, it galled him to have to make money this way. But hell, if that was what it took, he'd sell his soul to the devil himself to get his ranch back.

Christine fidgeted nervously and then fumbled in her reticule for the letter. Handing it to him, she said, "Maybe, you'd better read this first."

Frowning, Chad opened the battered envelope and saw that it was a personal letter. "You're sure you want me to read this?"

"Yes," she replied. "It might help to explain things."

Chad looked down at the letter and read:

Dear Chris,

I hate to send you this letter, but I have gotten myself in a jam. I got drunk one night in a cantina, and like a fool, I started bragging about how rich I was going to be when I came into my inheritance.

The next thing I knew, I'd been knocked over the head, blindfolded and carried off. Chris, I don't even know for sure where I am. Somewhere in the Sierra Madre, I'd guess. To make matters worse, I'm not sure whether the Mexicans holding me hostage are Juaristas or just bandidos.

The Mexicans are demanding a twenty-five thousand dollar ransom, or they will kill me. Chris, you've got to convince Uncle William to pay the ransom. Tell him I'll pay him back with any amount of interest he demands when I get my inheritance.

The Mexicans want the money delivered on the eighteenth of July, three months from today. They said to send only *one* man with the money to the Los Gallos Cantina in Sarita, a small Mexican town in the mountains just north of the city of Chihuahua.

Chris, get that ransom money down here and follow these instructions to the letter. These men are desperate, so please, don't try anything foolish, or they'll kill me for sure.

I'm sorry about this, Chris. Please try not to worry about me. I love you.

Charles

Chad looked up from the letter, saying, "Who is Charles?"

"My twin brother," Christine answered.

"Twenty-five thousand dollars," Chad said, whistling in awe. "That's a hell of a lot of money. Are you sure you'd trust me with it?"

Christine looked up, startled. "What do you mean, trust you with it?"

"Well, that's what you want to hire me for, isn't it?" Chad replied. "To take the ransom down and bring your brother back from Mexico."

Christine swallowed hard, fighting back the tears threatening her eyes. "There isn't going to be any ransom, Mr. Yancy," she muttered.

The big Texan looked at her, stunned. Then his eyes narrowed. "Look, lady," he said, his voice biting, "your brother is right. Those bandits are desperate and won't hesitate to kill him. So don't try any cute tricks. The safest thing to do is pay the ransom."

"I know that!" Christine cried. "But there isn't any ransom money."

"Why not?" Chad retorted. "From your brother's letter, I got the impression that money wasn't any problem. He said something about his inheritance."

Christine struggled for composure. "That's true, Mr. Yancy. Next year, when my brother is twenty-five, he will inherit a quarter of a million dollars. But until then, my uncle, as executor of my father's will, controls his money. And my uncle refuses to pay the ransom!"

"Why?" Chad asked, thoroughly puzzled.

"Your brother said he'd pay him back with interest. Hell, that letter is as good as any contract."

Christine sighed deeply, saying, "My uncle said he wouldn't bow to extortionists, that the bandits were only bluffing, that they wouldn't dare kill an American."

Chad leaned across the table, his look hard. "Lady, those bandits aren't bluffing," he said in an ominous voice. "If you ever want to see your brother alive again, you'd better convince your uncle to pay that ransom!"

"I know that, and my uncle knows that!" Christine cried. "But my uncle won't pay the ransom because he *wants* them to kill my brother!"

Chad sat back, shocked at her accusation. Why? he asked himself. What possible reason could the uncle have? He looked at the trembling pale woman and the wild look in her eyes. Had the shock of her brother being captured by bandits deranged her?

Christine saw the look on Chad's face. "I'm not crazy," she said. "If you'll just be patient, I can explain."

"Sure, lady, take your time," Chad said in a placating voice. Hell, he thought, the last thing I need is a hysterical woman on my hands.

Christine took a deep, ragged breath to calm herself, then said, "When my uncle refused to pay the ransom, I tried to raise the money myself, but my uncle knew what I was going to do and blocked me." She laughed harshly, saying in a

36

bitter voice, "My uncle is a very powerful and influential man, Mr. Yancy. All he had to do was let it be known that he would look unkindly upon anyone lending me money. No one had the courage to defy him. But I did find out something very interesting, something my brother and I never knew."

"What?" Chad asked, a wary look in his eye.

"One of the men I approached for a loan had been my father's personal lawyer. He didn't have any money he could loan me, but he did tell me something about my father's will that my uncle never told my brother and I. We always knew we wouldn't inherit until we were twenty-five, but neither of us knew that if something happened to us before that age, our inheritance would revert back to my uncle. That's why my uncle refuses to pay the ransom." She leaned forward over the table, her eyes boring into Chad's, her look intense. "Don't you see? He wants my brother killed so he can get his inheritance!"

Chad frowned, saying, "That's a strange will. You'd think your father would have written it so the inheritance would revert back to your mother or either of you."

"My mother is dead," Christine replied in a flat voice. "She died when my brother and I were four years old."

"But why your uncle? Why not you? You're your brother's closest kin."

How could she explain about her father and her uncle? Christine wondered. She hated to tell this stranger that her father had deserted her and her

37

brother after their mother had died, and left them in the care of his older brother, a cold, insensitive, brutally domineering man who made no pretense of having any feelings for the two children suddenly thrust into his keeping. She and her brother had been shocked and bewildered by their father's sudden disappearance from their lives, but because she was the more sensitive, intense child, one of those people who had a deep need to love and be loved in return, she had been more deeply hurt by her father's rejection. It had left an ugly wound on her soul, a wound that had never healed, a deep distrust of men.

And so, she and her brother had been raised in the lap of luxury, denied nothing except that which they needed the most, someone to love them. They had turned to each other for this need, forging an even deeper bond than being twins had already given them. To Charles, Christine had given all of her adoration and affection. He was the only male she had ever trusted, for she knew he wouldn't hurt her, and for that reason, he was different, he was special.

By the time she had grown into adulthood, Christine had vowed she would never fall in love or marry. Never again would she be put into a position where she could be hurt by a man, never again would her heart be vulnerable. Nor would she allow himself to be dominated by a man, as she had been by her uncle all those years.

But why had her father written his will that way? Christine wondered, her mind returning to Chad's question. Had it been to ease his conscience for dumping his children in his brother's lap? But if her father had wanted to pay her uncle back for raising his children, why hadn't he just left the money to him in the first place? Christine shook her head in exasperation. She had no idea why her father had written such a strange will, any more than she knew why he had deserted her and her brother. Why had he walked out on them that way, without even saying goodbye, with no explanation? And all those years with no word—nothing. After five years had passed since his disappearance, they had assumed he was dead. And then three years ago, his lawyer had shown up with his will. It seemed her father had discovered gold in California and had amassed a neat fortune of his own, a cool half-million dollars that he had left to his children. All those years, he had been alive, yet not once had he sent his children a present or even a letter. If he had been a failure, Christine might have understood his reluctance to come crawling back. But he had been a success. And then to leave everything to them. To Christine, that had added insult to injury. Did he think his money could make up for all the pain his rejection had caused them, for all of the long, lonely, loveless years she and her brother had had to endure with their hateful, domineering uncle? All of the old pain came welling back, stunning her with its intensity. Damn him, she swore silently. And damn this man sitting across from her for probing, for bringing it all back!

Chad had sat and watched the emotions

flickering across Christine's face. A less sensitive man might not have noticed, but Chad was as attuned to another's feelings as he was to his surroundings. At that minute, he sensed her vulnerability and it touched a chord deep inside him, arousing a strange, protective urge that surprised and puzzled him.

Christine didn't realize that her defenses were down, that there was a chink in her armor that allowed Chad to get a glimpse of her inner self, something she had never allowed anyone but her brother to see. She saw his puzzled look and, having no way of knowing what he was thinking, misinterpreted it. He expects an explanation, she thought. She hated to tell him about her father. She longed to scream in his face that it was none of his damned business! But she knew she couldn't. She needed this man's help desperately. He might well be the only man who could find and rescue her brother. She'd have to set her pride aside.

In a carefully controlled voice, she said, "I'm afraid I can't offer any explanation for why my father wrote his will the way he did, Mr. Yancy. You see, I never really knew my father. When my mother died, he sold his interest in the family business to his brother and went west, leaving my brother and I in the care of my uncle. We never saw or heard from him again. In fact, until his lawyer showed up with his will, we presumed he was dead."

Chad was just a little shocked at Christine's tale. Having grown up in a warm, loving family,

40

he couldn't imagine any man abandoning his children, walking out of their lives without so much as a second glance, as apparently Christine's father had. But he was even more shocked by Christine's apparent unconcern over her father's desertion. And to think that just a few minutes ago, he had had that ridiculous urge to take her in his arms and comfort her. Christ! What in the hell was wrong with him? Why, she was just as cold-hearted as her father!

And as for the rest of her story, Chad didn't know what to think. Did her uncle really want her brother killed so he could claim the inheritance? A man would have to be pretty desperate for money to sit back and let another man be murdered for it.

"You said your uncle was a powerful and influential man," Chad remarked. "I got the impression he was a wealthy man himself. What makes you think he wants that money that badly?"

Christine's eyes glittered. "I don't think he wants that money, Mr. Yancy. I *know* he wants it! You see, when I was trying to borrow money, one of the bankers I approached let it slip that my uncle was trying to borrow money too. Oh, he tried to cover up his slip quick enough, but it made me suspicious. I hired a private investigator, who discovered my uncle had made several bad investments over the past few years. He is in deep financial trouble, and he needs my brother's inheritance desperately if he's to save his manufacturing business."

"And your uncle? Is he aware you know about the will and his financial status?"

"Yes. I confronted him with everything. He admitted that what the lawyer said about the will was true, but naturally, he denied that he wanted my brother killed. He insisted that he felt the bandits were just bluffing, that it would be a waste of money. I considered going to the police, but I realized it wouldn't do any good. I had no proof of what my uncle intended. I knew it was hopeless to fight him, and that's when I decided to come down here myself."

"And your uncle didn't object to that?"

"No, he just laughed and said if I was crazy enough to throw my money away, he wouldn't stop me." Her eyes took on a hard, determined gleam. "But even if he had, I wouldn't have let that stop me."

Chad sat back, thinking. The more he thought about it, the more convinced he became of her story. But a question had been nagging at the back of his mind ever since he'd read the letter.

"Just what was your brother doing down here in Mexico, anyway?" he asked.

"He came down here to get a story. You see, Charles has always had a secret ambition to be a journalist. When he graduated from college last year, he told my uncle he wanted to get a job as a reporter, preferably a foreign correspondent. Naturally, my uncle didn't approve. He felt journalism was below the dignity of a Roberts. So my uncle blocked him, much as he did me when I was trying to raise the ransom money. But Charles was determined and he finally found an editor who wasn't afraid of my uncle. The editor told him if he would go down to Mexico and send him back some good stories on the war down here, he would hire him. That's what my brother was doing down here, looking for a story."

Well, that answers that question, Chad thought. But it still didn't explain what she wanted to hire him for.

As if reading his mind, Christine leaned across the table, a profound look on her face. "Mr. Yancy, I have five thousand dollars that I inherited from my mother. If you can go down into Mexico and rescue my brother—that money is yours!"

Chad sat back, astonished. Five thousand dollars? Why, it was a gift from heaven, the answer to all his prayers. With five thousand dollars, he could pay off the back taxes on his ranch. Hell, he'd even have some left over. And with that and what he had been able to save this past year, he'd be able to rebuild the burned-out buildings and restock.

Then he remembered what he would have to do to earn the money, and his dreams crumbled. He didn't even know for sure where the brother was being held hostage, and the Sierra Madre covered a hell of a lot of territory. Besides, even if he could find him, he couldn't possibly sneak him out from under the bandidos' noses. No, the whole idea was impossible, crazy. Hell, it would be suicide!

He sighed deeply, saying, "Sorry, lady. No deal."

"But five thousand dollars is all I have!"

"Miss Roberts," Chad said gently, "money isn't the issue."

Christine stared at him, desperation written all over her face.

"Look," he said, trying to reason with her, "July eighteenth is just five weeks away. Now, Mexico is a big country, and the Sierra Madre stretch for hundreds of miles. In mountains like that, it would take me months, maybe years to find your brother. Besides, that whole damned area is crawling with Indians and bandidos. Chances are I'd be killed before I even got a hint of where your brother is being held hostage."

"But I think I know where he is!"

Chad looked across the table at the young woman, her eyes bright with excitement. His brow furrowed. "Why do you say that?"

"Mr. Yancy, have you ever heard of a man called El Puma?"

Chad's dark eyebrows rose a notch. "Yeah, I've heard of him. He's the leader of a Juarista guerrilla band down in the mountains of northern Mexico. The Mexican people consider him a kind of national hero."

Christine smiled smugly. "Well, I think he's the man that's holding my brother hostage."

"El Puma?" Chad asked incredulously. "Where did you ever get that idea?"

"About six weeks before I received this last

letter from Charles, he wrote me saying he was going into northern Mexico to try to find this man, this El Puma. He wanted to interview him and write a story on the war from the Mexican guerrilla's viewpoint. So you see, he must be the man that's holding him for ransom."

Chad shook his head, saying, "No, lady, I doubt that. El Puma isn't a bandido. Sure, he's dangerous, fierce and crafty. That's why the Mexican people call him El Puma, the mountain lion. But he's a true Juarista, a patriot." Chad looked thoughtful; then he said, "No, from what I've heard of El Puma he wouldn't capture a man and hold him for ransom. It's just not his style."

Chad looked at Christine sitting across from him, her shoulders slumped with disappointment, her eyes glittering with unshed tears. She looked so dejected, so miserable. Again, he had that strange urge to take her in his arms and comfort her. He shook his head in self-disgust, then said, "Miss Roberts, the best thing you can do for your brother is scoot back East and try to raise that ransom money. That's the only way you're going to save him."

Christine felt numb, all of her hopes shattered. She pushed away from the table and rose wearily. She looked down at the big Texan once more, her eyes pleading. "You're sure you won't change your mind?"

Chad smiled apologetically and shook his head, saying, "Sorry, lady. The answer is no. I'm afraid I like living too much."

Chad watched Christine as she walked away,

feeling like a heel and cursing himself for it. He fumbled in his pocket for a cigar and then noticed the letter still sitting on the table. "Damn," he muttered, picking up the envelope. He looked up, but Christine was gone. Shoving the letter into his shirt pocket, he rose to follow her.

Christine had been walking in a daze, her mind preoccupied with her plight. She was totally unaware that she was standing in the middle of the street, nor did she hear the cries of warning or the horses hooves behind her. Suddenly a pair of big strong hands grabbed her shoulders and slammed her into the adobe wall of the building beside her, knocking the wind out of her. A hard male body pressed her into the wall, shielding her from the runaway wagon.

Christine barely got a glimpse of the wall-eyed, galloping horses and the wildly careening wagon as they rushed past her. The realization that she had almost been run over made her feel weak. Her knees buckled.

"You crazy, little fool! Why in the hell don't you watch where you're going?"

Christine recognized that deep husky voice. Oh no, she thought. If anyone was going to rescue her, why did it have to be *him*? She forced her knees to straighten and raised her head, expecting to look into Chad Yancy's face. Instead she found herself staring dumbly at a muscular, deeply tanned neck. Christine was stunned, for she hadn't had to look up at anyone since she had reached puberty. The realization that she was going to have to look up to the arrogant Texan totally unnerved her.

A rough, warm hand gently lifted her chin, and Christine's eyes rested on Chad Yancy's ruggedly handsome face. "Are you all right, lady?" Chad asked in a concerned voice.

This time it was Chad's turn to be stunned. In the dim interior of the *cantina*, he hadn't noticed Christine's eyes. Large, almond-shaped, they were a pure golden-green, curiously lacking the blue or brown flecks usually seen in green eyes. He stared at them in amazement. Why, they're beautiful, he thought. The same color as mesquite leaves in the spring.

Christine saw his stare. Honestly, he's the rudest, most insolent man I've ever met, she fumed silently. Hadn't anyone ever told him it was impolite to stare at people like that?

Angrily, she pushed away from him, snapping, "I'm fine, Mr. Yancy." Then she added, coldly, "Thank you."

Typical rich, spoiled bitch, Chad thought with disgust. Oh, she can talk nicely enough when she wants you to do her dirty work for her. But otherwise, she won't even say thank you civilly. He knew all about rich, spoiled women like her. All they were interested in was using you. Well, he wasn't through with her yet!

He reached into his pocket and pulled out the letter, saying, "You forgot this."

Christine looked at the letter in dismay and reached for it. Chad pulled it back from her reach. She glanced up at him in surprise and saw him smiling mockingly.

"Say please, lady," Chad said, his voice a low, menacing purr.

Christine gasped with indignation and started to snap some retort, but the dangerous gleam in the big Texan's eyes quickly changed her mind. She ducked her head and mumbled, "Please."

"My pleasure, lady," Chad drawled sarcastically, handing the letter to her.

Christine glared at him, snatched the letter from his hand, and whirled away. She marched angrily down the dusty Mexican street, the Texan's insolent laughter ringing in her ears.

Chapter Three

Chad returned to the Longhorn Hotel in El Paso that night in a foul mood, having spent the entire evening at the cantina brooding darkly. The rich Yankee woman had somehow reminded him of Anne and brought back painful, bitter memories.

He remembered traveling to Galveston to pick up a load of furniture for the ranch. The man he had done business with had invited him to a dinner party at his home that evening, and that's where he had met Anne.

Anne, beautiful and sensuous, with her fiery red hair, flashing black eyes and soft luscious curves, had left him stunned at first sight. At twenty-four, Chad had not been inexperienced with women, but he had never known a woman like Anne before, the epitome of genteel Southern womanhood, petite, soft spoken, gracious, teasingly flirtatious. He had fallen head over heels in love with her that night. When Anne returned to her father's Louisiana plantation the next week, Chad had sent the furniture back west with his Mexican vaqueros and followed her. He had courted her fast and furiously, with dogged determination, and within a month, they were engaged to be married. That's when Anne had started to weave her soft, silky web of treachery.

At that time, the Civil War was in its second year. A west Texas man without slaves, Chad had paid little attention to the war that had split his country in two. The people in west Texas had been too busy struggling for survival, fighting Indians and drought, to pay much attention to politics. So despite the fact that Texas was part of the Confederacy, Chad had never considered it his war. But Anne's family had been fiery Southerners, and Anne had used her soft voice and tempting body to persuade Chad that it was his duty to fight for the South. She had waved him off gaily, telling him how proud she was of him and promising to wait for his return.

And so, like a fool, Chad had gone off to fight in a war to which he felt no commitment. It was a long, ugly, bloody war. But Chad had survived it, not because of his belief in its cause, but because of his proficiency with a gun and his sharpened instincts from living on the dangerous Texas frontier.

After the war was over, he had headed for New Orleans, to Anne and his reward for doing his "duty." He had arrived in the city half starved, battle weary, sick to death of killing, and still limping from the wound he had received in his leg.

It was then that he had discovered Anne's treachery.

For Anne was a survivor too. After the fall of New Orleans, she had quickly forgotten her promises to Chad and had married a man with known Union sympathies and connections. When Chad had heard the shocking news, he'd realized that Anne had never really loved him, that she had only used him.

He had returned to west Texas hardened, bitter, and disillusioned, vowing never to trust another woman or to fall in love again. But when he stood on his ranchland, staring dumbly at the blackened building that had once been his home, he realized the real price he was going to have to pay for his foolish infatuation with Anne. For while he had been away, fighting Anne's war, his mother and brother had been killed in a Comanche raid, their buildings burned and their cattle stolen. The bank that held their mortgage had foreclosed for back taxes, and Chad had been left with nothing. Nothing, and all because of Anne and her treachery.

That day, Chad had sworn he'd get his ranch back. His land became an obsession with him, his only reason for living. He had gone to the bank that held his mortgage and talked to the banker. The old man had known Chad all of his life and, only for this reason, agreed to hold back on selling the ranch for a year, while Chad tried to raise the money to pay off the back taxes. In three more months, the time would be up, and Chad would still be a long way from collecting the sum.

God, how he hated the way he was forced to earn his money. He didn't mind being a scout and guide. He had earned extra money doing that for the Texas Rangers before the war. But with the rangers, it had been different. As rugged, proud, and independent as he, they had accepted him as an equal. Everyone had pulled his own weight. But not those damned Yankee speculators. They not only wanted a guide and someone to protect them, but apparently a nursemaid and servant too. He remembered them sitting on their fat behinds at night, whining about how sore they were, while he took care of the horses, set up camp, and cooked the meal. And the days had been even worse. As if he hadn't had enough problems in trying to watch for Indians and bandits, one of his charges had always been doing something stupid like getting lost, falling off his horse, or shooting his own foot trying to kill a harmless grass snake. God, the whole thing disgusted him, but it was the only way he could make large sums of money, short of out-and-out robbery.

And that damned five thousand dollars the Yankee woman had offered him this afternoon! That hadn't helped his mood either. The thought of the money had flickered in and out of his mind all evening, teasing and taunting him. Several times, he had caught himself reconsidering the proposition; then with disgust, he had pushed it out of his mind.

But even now, as he slowly climbed the rickety hotel stairs, his mind was toying with the proposition. Maybe I was too quick to discredit the idea that El Puma was holding her brother, he thought. Chad knew the Juarista leader operated from out of the foothills of the Sierra Madre just northeast of the city of Chihuahua. And Sarita, where the Mexicans had said to deliver the ransom, was in that general area. The two just might be a coincidence, but the more Chad thought about it, the more he wondered. True, El Puma was a fierce patriot, but the Juaristas were in a tight spot right now and getting desperate. And sometimes desperate men did crazy things, things they would not ordinarily do. Yes, I should know all about desperate men, Chad thought ruefully as he placed a foot on the last step of the stairs.

Chad was shocked from his musing by a woman's shrill scream. His big body tensed; then realizing where he was, he grinned and shrugged. Another scream followed, and Chad was immediately alert. That was no scream of ecstasy, he thought, moving to the door at the head of the stairs.

He rattled the door handle. It was locked. He could hear the sounds of a struggle behind the door and the muffled voice of a woman pleading for help. Without hesitating, he slammed his broad shoulder into the panel and, with the sound of splintering wood in his ears, plunged into the room.

In the dim light cast from the hallway, he saw two figures struggling and twisting frantically on the bed. The blade of a knife flashed momentarily, and Chad lunged for the man that held it. Twisting the man back from the woman, Chad ducked as the knife swung in a wide arc and barely missed his face. Chad's fist slammed down on the man's wrist. The man grunted in pain, and the knife fell to the floor with a metallic clatter. Then, before Chad could grab him, the assailant ran from the room and stumbled down the stairs.

Chad started to follow, but a small whimper from the bed stopped him. He looked about the darkened room, found the lamp, and lit it. Turning, he looked at the terrified woman cowering on the bed before him.

Christine sat huddled against the head of the bed, her long hair wildly tangled about her pale face, her body trembling visibly.

"Well, I'll be damned," Chad muttered to himself.

Then noticing the crowd of curious onlookers standing at the doorway, he scowled. Walking to the door, he said in a hard voice, "Show's over folks. Now get! Vamoose!" The men and women scattered as he slammed the battered door shut.

Chad turned back around and looked at Christine, noticing that she had pulled the sheet up and was clutching it tightly under her chin. Her modesty amused him. Yep, she was a true-bred lady all right. As if he could see anything through that ridiculous granny gown she was wearing.

He bent and picked up the chair that had been turned over in the shuffle. Placing it in front of the bed, he lazily threw one leg over it and sat leaning forward across its back, his brilliant blue eyes still glittering with amusement. "Lady, you sure have a way of attracting trouble," he drawled.

Christine gasped. She had just gone through the most terrifying experience in her lifetime, and now this big, arrogant Texan calmly sat before her acting as if he thought the whole thing amusing. She completely forgot her fright and glared at him.

But Chad was unaware of her hot look. His attention was on the fluttering curtains at the open window, the window he knew the man must have used to gain entrance to the room. Then he gazed about, noting that nothing seem disturbed, before his eyes swiveled back to Christine. "What happened?"

"I don't know," Christine answered in a trembling voice. "I woke up suddenly, and the man was bending over me with a knife. I screamed and started struggling with him and you came in."

Chad nodded. Then looking her directly in the eye, he said, "Did he try to rape you?"

The blunt question shocked Christine. She flushed hotly and looked away, muttering, "No."

"You're sure?" Chad asked calmly.

"Of course, I'm sure," Christine snapped.

Chad shrugged and looked about the room thoughtfully. "Then robbery must have been the motive. You'd better look and see if anything is missing."

Well, Christine thought, that was the most reasonable suggestion he'd given. Careful to wrap the sheet around her, she rose and searched the dresser and her trunk. She found her jewelry, her money, even her brother's letter. Everything was there.

She walked to the bed and sat on it, feeling weak with relief. "Nothing is missing."

The glimmer of metal on the floor caught Chad's eye. He leaned over and picked up the knife he had knocked from the man's hand. A switchblade? he thought. Hell, men in these parts didn't carry switchblades. They carried hunting knives or Bowies. And something else was rattling around in the back of his head, something that he'd noticed from his peripheral vision, a faint glimmer of a scene buried in his subconscious. Then the picture cleared, a man jumping from a wagon thundering wildly down a dusty, narrow street. And suddenly he knew, without a shadow of a doubt, that the runaway wagon that afternoon hadn't been an accident. It had been a deliberate attempt on Christine's life. An ugly suspicion began to grow in his mind.

He frowned, saying, "Lady, let me get this straight. Did you say you were due to inherit some money too?"

Christine looked up, surprised by his question. "Why, yes I am. My brother and I share equally in the inheritance."

"And if something happens to you, your inheritance also reverts to your uncle?"

Christine nodded, wondering what he was leading up to.

Chad leaned forward, saying, "Lady, I hate to tell you this, but that runaway wagon this afternoon wasn't any accident. And someone tried his damnedest to kill you tonight." He rubbed his chin thoughtfully and then said, "Greedy man, your uncle."

Suddenly Christine realized what he was thinking. "You think my uncle has hired someone to kill me?"

"That's what it looks like to me," Chad replied.

"He wouldn't dare!" Christine cried.

"Wouldn't he?" Chad asked. "Maybe not in New York. Too many questions might be asked. But, lady, when you came out here all by yourself with no one to protect you, you were playing right into his hands. A lone woman comes out to the wild, lawless Texas frontier and has an unfortunate accident. Now who could connect that with your uncle way back in New York?"

"I'll go to the law!" Christine replied indignantly.

Chad's eyebrows rose. "The sheriff? And what will you tell him? That you suspect your uncle has hired someone to kill you? Can you identify the man or describe him?" Chad shook his head. "I can't. It was too dark for me to get a good look at him. And, lady, without that man and his confession, you don't have one shred of proof against your uncle."

Christine realized what he said was true, and she was terrified. A man was stalking her, trying to kill her; yet she had no way of proving her uncle had hired him. "I think he's tried it before," she said in a trembling voice. "On the ship, I was almost killed by a falling crate."

Chad nodded, not surprised by her revelation.

Then looking at the sheet balled up in Christine's lap, his eyes narrowed. Seeing his look, Christine glanced down and stared dumbly at the big bloodstain on the sheet.

"What the hell?" Chad muttered, rising from his chair.

Before Christine realized what he was going to do, Chad yanked the sheet away and her gown up to her thigh. Christine stared down at a jagged, two-inch cut on her leg, a cut that was bleeding freely.

"Why didn't you tell me you were injured?" Chad asked in a voice that was almost accusing.

"I . . . I didn't notice it."

Chad wiped the blood away with the sheet. "Well, I don't think it's very deep. But we'd better get it cleaned up and bandaged." He rose and walked to the door, saying, "I'll be right back."

After he had left, Christine realized both her legs were exposed. Quickly she pulled her gown back down.

Chad returned, carrying a bottle of tequila. He set the bottle down on the dresser while he poured water into a basin sitting there. Then, carrying both the basin and the tequila, he knelt on one knee before Christine, placing the bottle down on the floor.

As he reached to pull her gown back up, Christine gasped, "No," and caught his hand.

"Cut it out, lady," Chad snapped. "I've seen a woman's legs before, and I'm sure there's nothing special about yours."

He pushed her hands away roughly and pulled

the gown back up. But as he wiped the blood from her thigh and cleansed the wound, Chad reluctantly admitted he had been wrong. Incredibly long and well-shaped, Christine's legs were undoubtedly the most beautiful he had ever seen. And the texture of her skin, Chad thought in amazement, so firm, yet soft, almost silky feeling. To his surprise, he felt his heat rising. What's wrong with you? he asked himself. Hell, she isn't even your type. Reflex, he told himself. Just sheer animal reflex.

Christine sat and blushed furiously as Chad's eyes examined her naked leg. But when he gently washed the wound and Christine felt his warm slender fingers brushing her thigh, the peculiar feelings his touch stirred in her overrode her embarrassment. She had never been touched so intimately by any man. A warm, tingling feeling washed over her. When he poured the fiery tequila over the cut, Christine was actually grateful for the distraction of the burning pain. Only when he pushed the gown back down did she relax. She sighed deeply, not realizing she had been holding her breath.

Chad straddled the chair beside her again, his arms crossed casually over its back. "Now, lady, let's talk business."

Christine looked at him in surprise, saying, "What do you mean, talk business?"

"I mean I've changed my mind about taking that job of yours."

Christine felt her spirits soaring. "You mean you'll take the job after all?"

"That's right," he answered, grinning.

"When do we leave?" Christine asked in an excited voice.

Chad's head snapped up. "We? What do you mean, we?" he asked warily.

"Well, I'm going with you, of course," Christine replied.

Chad frowned. "I don't remember you saying anything about going along."

"Of course not!" Christine snapped. "You never let me say anything at all. If you'll remember, you refused me outright."

Chad pushed himself from the chair, saying, "Deals off, lady."

"But why?" Christine cried.

"Why?" Chad asked incredulously. "Do you actually think I'd even consider taking you with me. Lady, I might be crazy, but I'm not *that* crazy!"

"You told me yourself that you take people down into Mexico all the time," Christine retorted. "Why not me?"

"Because you're a woman that's why! And a greenhorn to boot. Hell, lady, going into Mexico to rescue your brother won't be any picnic, you know. That's mean country down there. I'd be going through scorching deserts and rugged mountains, dodging Indians and bandits the whole time. I'd be lucky to get back with my own skin, much less having to worry about yours too." Chad walked to the door, saying, "Forget it, lady."

"Well, that's just fine with me!" Christine

screamed to his back. "I have another man I'm going to hire, anyway."

The Texan turned, a surprised look on his face. "Another man? Who?"

"Jack Harris," Christine answered smugly.

"Jack Harris?" Chad asked in a shocked voice. "Who gave you his name?"

"The desk clerk," Christine answered. "I asked him this evening after I came back from talking to you."

Chad's eyes narrowed. "Lady, do you have any idea what kind of a man Jack Harris is?"

"Why, yes," Christine replied haughtily. "He's a guide and a *pistolero* just like you."

"The hell he is!" Chad yelled. "Jack Harris is a half-breed renegade. He's a thief and a murderer. Why, he's a bigger cutthroat than those bandits holding your brother. He'd just as soon kill you as look at you. And you're going into Mexico with a man like that? Hell, lady, you're not only crazy, you're plain stupid!"

Christine was furious. She jumped from the bed and cried, "I don't care who Jack Harris is! I don't care if he's the devil himself!" Her chin rose stubbornly. "If Jack Harris will take me with him to rescue my brother, I'll go with him."

Chad looked at the woman standing tall and proudly defiant before him, her hands on her hips, her green eyes flashing dangerously, once again reminding him of a fierce Viking goddess. He had never felt so frustrated in his life. Damn it, he wanted that five thousand dollars so bad he could taste it. And if it wasn't for this obstinate

61

woman insisting on going along, he'd take the job at the drop of a hat, regardless of the risks. Didn't she have any idea of what traveling in Mexico would be like? Why, she was spoiled and pampered, used to all of the comforts of life. Hell, she wouldn't last a day. A sudden glimmer lit in Chad's eyes.

"Have you ever ridden a horse, lady?" he asked.

Chad's unexpected question took Christine aback. "Why . . . why no."

"Did it ever occur to you that horseback is the only way you'd be able to travel in the Sierra Madre?"

Christine's one and only thought had been to rescue her brother. She had never stopped to consider what traveling in Mexico might entail. "Well, no," she admitted, and then added stubbornly, "But I'm sure I can learn."

Just what I figured, Chad thought smugly. She has no idea of what she would be getting into. Let her spend a couple of hours on horseback, and she'll be whining just like those Yankee speculators. All he'd have to do was give her a taste of what she'd be getting into, and she'd back out quick enough. Then he could go on down into Mexico, do the job, and collect that five thousand dollars. Chad almost laughed out loud at the simple solution. "All right, lady. I'll take you down into Mexico with me. But on my terms."

Christine was wary. "What terms?"

"First, if you plan on traveling with me, you'll have to go disguised as a boy. You'll have to dress like a boy and act like a boy. I'll have enough problems without having to worry about protecting you from rape."

Christine flushed hotly. There was that ugly word again. Honestly, did he have to be so crude?

Chad ignored her reaction to his blunt words, saying, "That's the only way I'll agree to take you along. Do you understand?"

As much as Christine disliked the idea of disguising herself as a boy, she had to admit she could see the wisdom of it. She nodded her head curtly in agreement.

"And another thing," Chad continued. "You'll have to pull your own weight. That means you'll have to take care of your own horse and equipment and do your share of the camp chores. You're not hiring me to be a damned servant."

Christine didn't know a thing about horses, much less how to care for one. Nor did she have any idea of what camp chores were. But she wasn't going to let that stop her from going.

"Agreed," she said calmly.

"And let's get something else straight from the very beginning," Chad said in a hard voice. "I'm the boss on this little expedition. You'll do anything and everything I tell you to, when I tell you to do it. And no back talk!"

Anything and everything? That was an awfully broad statement. Christine started to balk and then noticed the hard, determined look on Chad's face.

"I understand," she snapped.

Chad grinned. "Well, lady, now that we've got that problem straightened out, I can start making some plans. I've a friend who has a small ranch just south of here. We'll go over there tomorrow and pick up a horse for you. I'm sure he won't mind if we stay around there for a couple of days while I give you a few riding lessons."

A couple of days? Again, Christine started to object and then remembered their agreement. "Whatever you say, Mr. Yancy," she said tightly.

Chad nodded. "Okay, let's get your things together and go to my room."

Christine's head snapped up. "To *your* room?" she gasped.

"Lady," Chad said with an exasperated sigh, "have you forgotten about the man that tried to kill you? What's to keep him from coming back tonight for another try?"

Christine had forgotten about the attempt on her life, but she couldn't sleep in a hotel room with a man. Then she thought of the obvious solution. "I'll just ask for another room," she said.

Chad groaned. Now how was he going to tell her that there wasn't a vacant room, that at this time of the night every available room was taken by some cowpoke and his whore? Hell, the only reason he stayed at this dump himself was because it was the cheapest hotel in El Paso, and he was trying to save money.

"There aren't any vacant rooms," Chad blurted.

"But I don't understand," Christine said. "The desk clerk said there were plenty of rooms this afternoon."

"There aren't any vacant rooms," Chad repeated stubbornly.

"But I can't spend the night with you!" Christine cried.

"Look, lady," Chad said, trying to hold his temper down, "if you're worried about me trying something, forget it! No offense meant, but you're just not my type."

Chad frowned at his own words. He wasn't too sure about Christine not being his type anymore, not after the way his body had responded to the sight and feel of her long, luscious legs. And then there was that strange fascination he had felt from the very first and those crazy protective urges he had felt too. The last was a complete puzzle to Chad, those protective urges. If she was one of those little, meek, defenseless-looking women, he might have understood. But there was certainly nothing little or meek about Christine. Christ, when she got her temper up, she wielded that big body of hers like a broadsword. And he had never met such an obstinate, stubborn woman in his life.

But whatever it was that was drawing her to him, Chad was determined he wasn't going to succumb to it. Their relationship would have to be strictly business. He needed this job badly to get his ranch back, and he wouldn't take any chance on jeopardizing it. No woman was worth losing his land over, and certainly not some strong-willed amazon!

Christine was having her own reaction to Chad's words. She had felt them like a slap in the face. Then he was one of those men who found her

65

big body offensive, distasteful, she thought. Yes, she had noticed that big men seemed to prefer small, dainty women. Apparently that old adage that opposites attract was true. She should be relieved that he wasn't attracted to her. Wasn't that what she wanted? To keep the men away? Then why had the words stung so badly?

But even if he wasn't the least bit interested in her—she wasn't his type as he so bluntly put it—she couldn't stay in a room alone with him all night. She was a lady, and that simply wasn't done.

She raised her head and said primly, "Nevertheless, I can't stay in a room alone . . ."

Chad was at the end of his patience. He didn't even wait for Christine to finish her sentence before he exploded. "Goddamnit, I'm not going to stand here arguing with you all night!"

Before Christine realized what was happening, Chad swooped her up in his arms and carried her out the door. Christine was stunned. She had always assumed, as big as she was, that no one could possibly lift her. And yet, this Texan was carrying her as effortlessly as if she were a mere babe. My God, he must be as strong as an ox!

But as Chad carried her down the hall, his mouth tight-lipped with grim determination, Christine became acutely aware of the rippling muscles on his broad shoulders, his hard chest, his powerful arms around her back and under her knees. His hand, resting just below her right breast, seemed to burn even more than the fiery tequila had on her open wound earlier. Only when he roughly deposited her on his bed, did she realize that she was trembling violently, and not from fear.

Chad looked down at the trembling woman on his bed, her golden-green eyes wide with shock. For the second time that day, he stared into those remarkably beautiful eyes, eyes that sent his senses reeling. He shook his head as if in a daze, then turned and stalked from the room.

Christine lay sprawled on the bed, stunned more by Chad's touch than his audacious action. Not until he returned to the room and dumped her trunk in one corner, did her senses return, her muscles jumping at the sudden thump as the heavy trunk hit the floor.

Chad walked to the bed and glared down at her. "Look, lady, if you're going into Mexico with me, you and I are going to be spending a lot of nights together. So you'd better decide right now if you trust me or not. Because if you don't, you'd better walk out that door right now and we'll forget the whole thing."

Christine stared up at him mutely. Trust him? Why, of course she didn't trust him. She didn't trust any man, particularly this man whose touch did such strange, peculiar things to her.

"Now, what's it going to be, lady?" Chad demanded. "Are you going or staying?"

Christine glanced about the room nervously and then back up at Chad looming over her. She fought back the urge to run, remembering that this man might well be the only man who could find and rescue her brother. Of course, there was

67

still Jack Harris. But the Texan had said he was a murderer and cutthroat. Besides, he might not agree to take her along and the Texan had.

She swallowed hard and managed a strangled, "I'm staying."

Chad nodded curtly in acknowledgment of her words. He picked up one of the pillows, saying, "You can have the bed. I'll sleep on the floor."

Totally ignoring Christine, Chad threw the pillow onto the floor and blew out the lamp. Christine watched him warily in the dark as he sat down and removed his boots and gunbelt, tucking the gun under the pillow. Then he rolled over with his back to her.

Christine lay back, still trembling, her fear of the Texan having nothing to do with his being a *pistolero*. No, she was much more frightened by her strange reactions to his touch. I won't let him touch me again, she vowed. And I won't close my eyes for a minute.

But Christine was physically and emotionally exhausted. Only minutes later, she drifted off into slumber, her last recollection the deep, baritone voice of the big Texan saying softly, "Night, lady."

Chapter Four

By the next morning, Christine had regained her composure, having decided her reaction to the Texan's touch the night before had been nothing but a case of bad nerves. She stood to one side of the buckboard as Chad loaded her trunk, admiring the big stallion tied to the back of the wagon. The horse was big chested and powerfully muscled, his coat sleek and shiny in the morning sun.

"Is that your horse, Mr. Yancy?" she asked.

"Yep, that's my bay, lady," Chad drawled lazily.

Christine cringed and gritted her teeth. His habit of calling her lady had become an irritant to her. It grated on her nerves.

Chad took her arm and started to help her up into the buckboard. "We'd better get started, lady."

Christine jerked her arm away and cried, "Don't call me that!"

"What?" Chad asked, surprised at her outburst.

"Lady!" Christine snapped, her eyes glittering. "I don't want you to call me that anymore."

"Why not?" Chad asked, a small mocking smile playing at his lips. "I thought that's what you are, a lady."

"I am!" Christine retorted. "But the way you say it, it sounds so insulting . . . so unladylike!"

Chad grinned. He had to admit that he had been ridiculing her. "All right, Chris, I'll try not to call you lady anymore."

Christine gasped. Chris? No one but her twin brother ever called her that. It had been his personal pet name for her, and for that reason Christine considered the name to be intimate. "No, don't call me Chris."

"What, then?" Chad asked.

"Why, Miss Roberts, of course," she replied indignantly.

Chad looked exasperated. "Look . . . lady," he drawled sarcastically, "you and I are going to be in each other's company for the next month or so, day and night. Now don't you think it would be a little ridiculous for us to traipse all over Mexico calling each other Miss Roberts and Mr. Yancy?"

"Then call me Christine."

Chad's wide brow creased as he thought; then he said, "No, I think Chris would be better. Chris can be either a man's or a woman's name. And since you'll be disguised as a boy, Chris would be ideal. Yes, you'll be Chris, my younger brother," he ended decisively.

Christine knew it was futile to object any

further, besides what he'd said made good sense. "All right, Mr. Yancy," she agreed reluctantly.

"Chad," he corrected her. "After all, my little brother would hardly call me Mr. Yancy."

Christine nodded curtly, climbed into the buckboard, and watched as Chad jumped easily onto the other side. Strange how gracefully he moves for such a large man, she thought.

As they drove into El Paso del Norte, the dusty road became more crowded with people on their way to the marketplace. Most of the Mexicans walked, others rode on rickety carts pulled by shaggy burros, the backs of the carts piled high with fresh produce and goods they were taking to the market to sell.

Several times, Chad and Christine were forced to stop on the narrow road and wait for the cart in front of them to move again. The cart was pulled by a particularly intractable burro, a stubborn animal more interested in nibbling on the shrubbery beside the road than pulling a cart heavily loaded with melons and yellow, crooked-neck squash. At these times, the Mexican driving the cart would have to get out and pull and shove at the burro, his angry frustration bringing laughter and jibes from the Mexicans on foot.

At one such time when they were forced to a standstill, three young women passed Chad's and Christine's buckboard. All three girls cast ad—miring glances in Chad's direction. The looks, followed by flirtatious smiles, irritated Christine. Knowing that Chad was aware of their interest only served as a further irritant. The big, arrogant

71

ox, Christine thought hotly. As if *his* ego needed any boosting.

Christine was astonished when they drove into the sun-splashed plaza a few minutes later. Having grown up in New York City, she had never seen an open marketplace before. The plaza was crowded with people, and their buckboard had to travel at a snail's pace. As they drove along, Christine marveled at the merchandise in the hastily constructed stalls the Mexicans had thrown up at random. There were woven baskets of every shape and size; colorful, hand-painted pottery; beautifully tooled, broad-skirted saddles; embroidered rebozos and colorful serapes; bushels of fresh vegetables and fruits and dried corn and beans; delicate silver jewelry studded with turquoise and brilliant fire opals; crates of squawking chickens and squealing pigs; lacy mantillas and broad-rimmed sombreros.

Christine would have dearly loved to stop and buy some things. Why, she could spend hours browsing through all of the lovely merchandise. But she knew this was not the time. Perhaps on the return trip, once Charles was rescued and safe.

An old Mexican woman, carrying a huge bouquet of flowers, approached their wagon and held up a flower to Christine. Creamy white, its petals velvet-textured, its leaves a deep, glossy green, the flower was almost the size of a saucer.

"Oh, stop," Christine begged Chad. "I want to buy that flower."

Chad had been chafing at the delays and the slow pace at which they had been forced to travel.

"Why?" he asked irritably. "It's just a gardenia. They grow like weeds down here."

"I don't care. I think it's lovely and I want to buy it," Christine retorted.

Chad brought the buckboard to a halt, and Christine fumbled in her reticule, saying, "Ask her how much it costs."

Chad restrained her hand with his, saying, "No, Chris. It's not done that way. You'll have to haggle for it."

"Haggle? You mean bargain? Don't be ridiculous! I'm willing to pay what she wants for it."

Chad shook his head, saying, "You don't understand. Down here, the Mexicans expect you to haggle, particularly when you buy something at the market. You see, they're not just interested in buying and selling. To them, the market is a social event too. Haggling over the price of something gives them the opportunity to socialize. Often, they'll stop right in the middle of the bargaining to visit or gossip." Chad nodded to the old woman standing by the wagon, her black eyes bright with anticipation. "She's going to be sorely disappointed if you don't haggle with her."

"But I can't speak Spanish," Christine objected.

"I'll take care of it," Chad replied.

He turned to the old woman, saying, *"Buenos días, señora."*

The woman grinned, causing her leathery face to wrinkle even more. *"Buenos días, señor."*

Christine watched as the old woman and Chad argued in Spanish, alternately scowling and

73

shaking their heads. But she could tell the Mexican woman was enjoying the verbal tussle immensely, for despite her fierce disapproving looks when Chad made his bids, her eyes were twinkling merrily. After what seemed a ridiculous length of time to Christine, the bargain was finally made, and she watched as Chad paid the woman and she handed him the flower, her dusky face once again creased with a broad grin.

Chad handed the flower to Christine, and as they drove away, she remarked, "Well, she may have enjoyed it, but all that haggling seemed like a waste of time and energy to me."

"That's the difference between the Yankees' and Mexicans' natures," Chad answered. "We're always hustling and bustling about, rushing here and there. The Mexicans approach life in a more leisurely manner. They never do anything in a hurry. At least, not if they can help it."

Christine glanced about the plaza. What Chad had said was true. The plaza was crowded with people, but no one was hurrying. The Mexicans strolled lazily, often stopping to visit and chat with one another, acting as if they had all of the time in the world to do their shopping. Suddenly Christine noticed a change in the crowd; a sudden excitement seemed to stir the air.

Then the Mexicans seemed to go berserk, jumping up and down and running across the plaza, shouting, *"Viva Juárez! Viva Méjico! Viva Juárez!"*

The crowd's abrupt change of mood alarmed Christine. She remembered her brother saying the

Mexicans were a volatile people, their hot Latin blood often making them subject to sudden and sometimes violent eruptions. What had happened? Had they stumbled right into the middle of a riot or something?

Chad saw the frightened look on Christine's face and said, "Relax, Chris. There's no need for alarm. They're just excited because Juárez is passing through the plaza."

"Benito Juárez? The President of Mexico?" Christine asked in astonishment.

"Yes," Chad replied calmly. "That's him up there in that little black buggy of his."

Why, of course, Christine thought. Now that El Paso del Norte is the capitol of Mexico, naturally its president would be here. She sat up and craned her neck, trying to see over the Mexicans who were racing behind the buggy, many throwing flowers at it. She was anxious to get a glimpse of the man her brother had written her so much about.

She had been surprised to learn that Benito Juárez was a full-blooded Zapotec Indian, a man born in abject poverty who had pulled himself up from his humble beginnings to become President of Mexico. His fierce dedication to the rights of the common man had earned him the love of the Mexican people and the title of "the Thomas Jefferson of Mexico."

But despite the Mexican peoples' adoration, Juárez had not found his tenure as president an easy one. When he had come into office, Mexico had been in dire financial trouble, caused by the lavish spending of his predecessor, Santa Anna. Hoping to put the country on its feet, Juárez had passed a law suspending the payment of all foreign debts for two years.

That was when Napoleon had stepped into the picture. For years, the ambitious French emperor had wanted to get a foothold in the Americas. Using Mexico's delay in paying France the money it owed as an excuse, and knowing that the United States was too busy fighting its own bloody civil war to enforce the Monroe Doctrine, Napoleon had seen his golden opportunity for conquest in America and had declared war on Mexico.

But Napoloen had underestimated the Mexicans. He had expected his army, the largest and most powerful in the world, to quickly defeat the miserable, ragtag Mexican army. But the Mexican forces had given the French a merry chase all over Mexico. Even when the French finally pinned Juárez and his army down in the northern provinces, the war had been far from over. Then the Mexican people had taken up the fight. It had become a war of guerrilla fighting, and the French army, trained to conventional warfare, had been unable to deal with the Mexicans' hit-and-run tactics.

For four long years, the Mexicans had held out against the French. When the Civil War ended in the United States, President Johnson had issued France an ultimatum: Get out of Mexico or else. Then, to show he meant business, he had sent General Sherman down to the Mexican border with an army of one hundred thousand well-armed men.

And now what would happen? Christine wondered. With Juárez standing with one foot in Mexico and the other in the Rio Grande and the American army poised on the border at his back, would the French continue to advance, or would they withdraw from Mexico as President Johnson had demanded? If the French refused to withdraw, would the American army actually cross the border to force them out? She shivered. That would be no hit-and-run war. The American army was well armed; its men, fresh from the Civil War, battle seasoned. No, it would be a full-fledged confrontation between two powerful armies, and all of northern Mexico would become one big bloody battlefield. Would she get caught in the middle of it?

Maybe she should have done as the Texan suggested, waited in El Paso while he found and rescued Charles, then brought him back. But she couldn't do that. She didn't trust the Texan. What if he couldn't find Charles right away? If he got discouraged, what would keep him from giving up the search and just taking off? Or if he didn't find him until after the deadline and discovered that Charles had been murdered, would he even bother to come back to the border to tell her, knowing that he had lost his chance to earn the money? And there was always the possibility that the Texan might be killed himself on the way down, or he and Charles both in the rescue attempt. If Chad Yancy didn't come back, she'd never know what had happened. Besides that, she couldn't just sit in El Paso, waiting and wondering what was going on. She'd go crazy! No, she had to go along, not only to see that the Texan stuck to his job, but for her own peace of mind.

The sudden lurch of the buckboard snapped Christine from her musing as their wagon was brought to an abrupt halt by the crowd surrounding Juárez's buggy. She looked up to see that the buggy was stopped in front of a government building, from the roof of which the green, white, and red Mexican flag fluttered in the early morning breeze. Again she craned her neck to get a glimpse of the President of Mexico as he stepped from his buggy, but when he alit, he was swallowed up by the crowd of Mexicans.

Christine stood up to get a better view and then realized why she hadn't been able to see Juárez for the crowd. Dressed in a black suit, his white shirt a startling contrast to his dark bronze skin, he couldn't have been much over five feet tall. She felt a twinge of disappointment.

She sat back down, saying, "So that's the President of Mexico. He's not very big, is he?"

"No, he isn't," Chad agreed. "But don't let that stubborn, little Indian's size fool you. Remember, he's managed to keep Napoleon at bay longer than anyone else has." Then he chuckled, adding, "But then, I've heard Napoleon is a small man himself. Maybe they were equally matched."

That's true, Christine thought. Strange how often small men were overly aggressive and fired with ambition. Was their size a contributing factor? Did they feel the need to prove to the world that they were just as manly as larger men? Did they compensate for their lack of stature by overdeveloping their other masculine characteristics?

While Christine was musing over this, Chad spied a break in the crowd and took quick advantage of it, skillfully and deftly easing the buckboard through it and down a side street. Within minutes, they were away from the plaza and on the outskirts of the city.

As they drove away from El Paso del Norte and into the open countryside, Christine was once again stunned by the vastness of this land. Having grown up in New York City, where one's vision was blocked by tall trees and buildings, she was utterly amazed at being able to actually see from horizon to horizon.

Her eyes drifted over the sweeping panorama. Dotted with an occasional mesquite tree, sagebrush, and clumps of cacti, the landscape looked like one enormous, almost empty room, its ceiling the clear blue sky stretching across it, its walls the mountains shimmering in the sunlight far in the distance. It was a desolate, strangely silent land that seemed endless, stretching into eternity itself; and to her, its sheer size and loneliness were awesome, almost frightening.

As they drove, Christine watched a dust devil dancing across the road and scattering tumbleweeds before it. Then her eyes widened in surprise. "I didn't know cacti bloomed," she remarked.

"Yes," Chad answered, glancing toward the

nopal cactus at which she was looking. Its paddlelike leaves were topped with delicate yellow flowers. "The bloom on that particular cactus turns into a fruit resembling a small pear called a tuna. The Mexicans eat both the fruit and the leaves."

Christine looked down at the cactus they were passing. Its pulpy leaves were dotted with vicious thorns.

Seeing her look, Chad laughed and said, "After they've been peeled, of course."

Christine looked around her and noticed that there were other species of cacti. "But why aren't the others blooming?" she asked.

"Some cacti only bloom after it rains," Chad explained. "The Spanish dagger, while not a cactus, only blooms once a year or so. The century plant"—he pointed to a tall, greenish-gray plant, its huge, broad leaves bending to the ground—"only blooms once in a lifetime and then dies. But personally, I think the Spanish dagger has the most beautiful bloom. It puts up one big spike right in the middle of the plant, covered with clusters of small, creamy, bell-shaped flowers that have a sweet odor, much like that of the gardenia. I've often wondered if the plant knows its bloom is particularly spectacular, and that's why it puts out those swordlike leaves, to protect its beautiful bloom."

Christine frowned at his words. She wouldn't have thought a hardened gunslinger would pay any attention to flowers. She glanced up at him curiously. He sat hunched over slightly, his alert blue eyes scanning the horizon. At a casual glance, he looked completely relaxed. But Christine could feel the unleashed power in him, that same frightening power she had felt the first time she had met him. At that minute, a vision of him standing in the middle of a dusty Western street, slightly crouched, his eyes boring into his adversary, his hand hovering over his gun flashed through her mind. She shivered despite the hot sun beating down on her.

They rode in silence for a while, with Christine marveling that any plant could survive in this hot, arid climate. Several times she noticed Chad glancing back over his shoulder. The next time he did it, Christine looked back too. She scanned the landscape, but she couldn't see anything unusual.

Seeing her baffled look, Chad said, "I'm just checking to see if he's still with us."

"He? Who are you talking about?"

"See that dust cloud back there?" Chad said, pointing off into the distance behind them.

Christine had to squint to see it. "Yes."

"Well, it's been there ever since we left El Paso del Norte. Someone is following us."

"An Indian?" Christine asked in an alarmed voice.

"No. Indians usually ride in groups. That's one man back there, and he's deliberately hanging back far enough so we can't see him. And I'll bet my last dollar he's your friend from the hotel last night."

Christine breath caught in her throat. "You mean the man who tried to kill me?"

"Yep."

Christine's heart raced in fear. "Maybe it's someone else," she said hopefully.

"Nope, I don't think so. Anyone else would have passed us long ago at the pace we're traveling."

The memory of her struggle with the assailant the night before returned in vivid, terrifying detail. Christine had never been as frightened in her life as she had been when she had fought so desperately for her life. Only too well, she remembered the knife looming over her and then plunging downward with deadly menace, barely missing her chest as she had twisted away at the last minute. Raw panic rose in her. "But we've got to do something!" she cried.

"Calm down, Chris," Chad said in a firm voice. "He's not going to try anything now. If he was, he would already have made his move."

"But if he follows me to the ranch, he'll know where I am! He'll kill me!" she wailed. She caught Chad's arm and shook it, a wild look in her eyes. "Do you hear? He'll kill me!"

Chad stopped the buckboard, dropped the reins, and grasped her shoulders, shaking her so roughly her head bobbed. "Cut it out!" he barked.

Shocked by his abrupt action, Christine sat, stunned and blinking.

"Now listen to me," Chad said in a hard voice. "That man isn't going to try anything as long as we're at the ranch. There'll be too many people around, and he doesn't want any witnesses. No, Chris, he'll wait until we leave the ranch. Then he'll follow us and try to find someplace to ambush us."

"But . . . but . . ." Christine sputtered.

"And that's just fine with me," Chad continued. "If that man followed you all the way from New York, like you said he did, that means he's a greenhorn. He doesn't know a damn thing about this country and probably even less about tracking. Once we're on horseback, we'll lose him so fast it will make his head spin. Believe me, Chris," Chad added in a low, deadly voice, "no man tracks me if I don't want him to."

The tone of Chad's voice calmed Christine somewhat, but she was still visibly shaken. Chad looked down at her pale face and trembling lips, suddenly very aware of how close she was, of her soft shoulders beneath his hands. He gazed into her beautiful green eyes, still wide with fright, and felt his senses reeling. Totally forgetting his vow to keep their relationship strictly business, he drew her to him, his head slowly descending.

Nothing in Christine's past experiences had prepared her for Chad's kiss. She had been kissed by several men, men who had been drawn by her unusual beauty and hadn't been intimidated by her size and icy disdain. She had found their kisses wet and messy, repugnant, before she fought them off. But there was nothing repugnant about Chad's kiss. His lips were incredibly warm and sensuous as they moved over hers, softly testing, seeking, tasting. She had never known another's lips on hers could feel so wonderful, be so exciting. When Chad's tongue brushed across

83

her lips, then flicked at the corner of her mouth, her defenses crumbled, a sudden weakness washed over her. She caught his broad shoulders for support, her body swaying before she melted into him.

Chad felt Christine's soft, full breasts pressing against his hard chest and tightened his embrace, crushing her body against his. Her scent, sweet and womanly, filled his nostrils as he savored the sweetness of her lips and felt himself drowning in sheer sensation. The feel of her soft thigh against his was like a burning brand, igniting his passion even further.

Chad's lips left hers to drop a trail of feathery kisses over her temple, forehead, and eyes as his hands roamed urgently over her back and the curve of her hips. He nibbled at the long column of her throat and then felt Christine tremble as he gently probed her ear with his tongue. And then as his mouth returned to capture hers in a demanding, possessive kiss, his tongue sliding into her mouth and dancing sensuously around hers, his hand rose to caress her breast, cupping its fullness, his long fingers teasing the hardening bud through the material of her dress. It wasn't until Chad heard Christine's throaty moan that he came to his senses and finally heard the warning signals his brain had been desperately trying to send him. Christ! What in the hell was he doing? he asked himself. He was jeopardizing everything!

Chad tore his mouth away from Christine's and released her so abruptly she almost tumbled backward in the buckboard. "There's nothing to be afraid of, Chris," he said in a roughened voice. "We'll be at the ranch in a few more miles."

He picked up the reins and viciously snapped them at the horses, barely able to contain his anger at himself for breaking his vow. Deliberately he kept his eyes on the road ahead of them, holding his breath as he waited for Christine's reaction to his impulsive action. What in the hell had gotten into him? He had promised her he wouldn't try anything and then, like a damned fool, he'd gone and kissed her. But once she was in his arms, he hadn't been able to help himself. Kissing her had seemed so natural, so right. And now because he had let his passion rule his mind, would he lose his chance to get his ranch back because of it? He waited, every muscle in his big body tense, expecting any minute that Christine would announce she had decided to hire Jack Harris instead and to indignantly demand he turn the buckboard around and take her back to El Paso.

But Christine never even thought of Jack Harris. She was reeling, from the strange, wonderful sensations Chad's sensuous kisses and caresses had aroused in her and from her confusion at his abrupt withdrawal. She clutched the sides of the buckboard weakly for support, wondering what had happened? Why had he stopped kissing her so suddenly, practically throwing her away from him, as if he couldn't get away from her fast enough? Was it when she had slumped into him and pressed herself to him that he had seemed to change? Had the feel of her big body against his repelled him? Was that when he had lost interest?

But you should be glad he stopped kissing you, Christine reminded herself firmly. You don't want to get romantically involved with him. Or with any man, for that matter. Have you forgotten your vow never to give your heart to any man? Do you want to be hurt again? Besides, he's nothing but a hardened, cold-blooded pistolero, a crude, hired gun, a man with no roots, no future. No respectable woman would get involved with a man like that.

But strangely, Christine didn't feel in the least reassured. A little pain, caused by Chad's sudden rejection, still lingered. Combined with that was a keen sense of disappointment. Both disturbed her deeply, and she was still engrossed with her thoughts when they turned from the main road and drove up to a sprawling adobe building, one of its walls covered with a riot of purple-blooming bougainvillaea.

It wasn't until Chad stopped the buckboard beneath the shade of a small huesache tree and jumped down, that Christine finally became aware of her surroundings. As he turned to assist her, she noticed the petals scattered over his thick, black hair and across his broad shoulders. She glanced up at the tree, seeing the delicate yellow blossoms for the first time.

When she looked back down, the buckboard was surrounded by Mexicans, everyone talking excitedly at once. Then she heard a high female squeal and turned her head to see a pretty, young woman running from the house, her black pigtails flying behind her. The girl threw herself into Chad's arms, and Christine watched as Chad twirled the girl around, kissing her soundly on her rosy cheek.

"Margarita!" a plump, older woman standing by the buckboard cried in an admonishing voice.

Chad chuckled and gently set the girl aside. Then he turned back to Christine to help her from the wagon, his eyes searching her face warily for any signs of anger at his kiss. Seeing nothing, he relaxed, relieved that she was willing to overlook it and vowing that he would never pull a fool stunt like that again. No, he'd keep it strictly business from now on.

After Chad had helped Christine down from the wagon, he said, "Chris, I want you to meet the Morales family. This is José Morales and his wife, Consuelo."

José Morales bowed politely, saying, "My pleasure, *señorita*."

"This is their son, Pablo," Chad continued, ruffling the small boy's hair affectionately. The boy grinned up at him with adoration.

"And this," Chad said, turning to the pretty girl, "is their daughter, Margarita."

Christine smiled at the Mexican girl. Margarita looked at her resentfully, her dark eyes brooding, her pretty mouth pouting.

Chad drew Christine's attention to three men standing at the back of the group. "That's Juan, Roberto, and Tomás. They're José's cousins and help him on the ranch."

The three men grinned broadly, nodding their heads vigorously.

"I'm pleased to meet you all," Christine said with a smile.

All of the Mexicans, except Margarita, smiled back and then watched her mutely, their looks obviously curious.

"This is Miss Christine Roberts," Chad said to José. "She's hired me to take her into Mexico to meet her brother."

Well, that's not exactly the truth, Chad thought. But it wasn't a lie either. He didn't want José to know about the harebrained rescue he was going to attempt. He knew his friend would try to talk him out of it, and Chad didn't feel like arguing.

"I'm afraid I have a favor to ask of you, *amigo*," Chad said. "You see, Miss Roberts doesn't know how to ride a horse. I was wondering if we could stay here for a few days, while I give her a few riding lessons?"

José smiled broadly. *"Sí, amigo. Mi casa, su casa."* He turned to Christine, explaining, "My home is your home."

"Gracias, amigo, gracias," Chad said, bowing slightly.

Christine stared at him in amazement. Well, she thought ruefully, it seemed Chad Yancy could be very charming—when it suited his purpose.

José turned and spoke in Spanish to his wife. Chad leaned over and said in a low voice to Christine, "He's explaining everything I said. Consuelo doesn't speak English."

"And the others?" Christine asked.

"Pablo and Margarita speak a little," Chad replied. "But not the rest of them."

Christine walked between Chad and José as they made their way to the house. "I've known José all of my life," Chad explained as they walked. "He was one of my father's best and most trusted vaqueros. In fact, my first recollection of sitting on a horse was on his saddle in front of him."

Christine had no idea what a vaquero was, but this was hardly the time or place to ask, nor did Chad give her the chance, for he continued, "When I was thirteen, José moved back to Mexico and bought this ranch down here. I didn't see him again until last year when we met by chance in El Paso. It was like old home week, wasn't it, José?"

José grinned, saying, "*Sí, amigo.* But if you hadn't recognized me, I would never have known you. You see, *señorita*, he was quite a bit bigger than the last time I saw him."

Christine smiled and then glanced up at Chad. He seemed to tower over her. Just how tall is he, anyway, she wondered irritably.

Chad laughed softly at José's remark about his size, then continued. "José insisted that I come out to the ranch for a visit, and that's when I discovered he raised a few horses besides his goats. That's when I started renting my horses from him for my trips down into Mexico."

"Goats?" Christine blurted. "This is a goat ranch?" Immediately Christine regretted her rash words. She glanced over at José, hoping she hadn't offended him, but he was grinning proudly back at her.

"You can't raise cattle on this land," Chad explained. "Not unless you've got a big spread. And only the Creoles own that much land in Mexico, most of them old Spanish land grants. Now, goats can survive on land that larger animals can't, and goats will eat vegetation that cattle won't eat. And there's a good market for goat meat in Mexico. In fact, many Mexicans prefer it to beef."

"And don't forget the cheese, *amigo*," José said.

"That's right," Chad agreed. "Consuelo makes a cheese from the goat milk. She probably makes the best goat cheese in all of Mexico. In fact, the people of El Paso del Norte consider the Morales' goat cheese the best there is. José and Consuelo can't keep them supplied with enough."

José looked down at his wife, walking beside him, his eyes full of pride and love. Christine was deeply touched by his look. I wish someone would look at me like that, she thought, and then recoiled from the thought. What's the matter with you? Have you forgotten that men can't be trusted?

Later, Christine stood by, feeling awkward and useless, while Consuelo and Margarita prepared the evening meal. She would have offered to help, but she didn't know the first thing about cooking. Why, she had never been in the kitchen in her uncle's home. That had been the servant's domain.

She gazed about the small kitchen, looking at the small open fireplace, the colorful pottery cookware and dishes, the pots of fresh herbs sitting in the window sill, the string of garlic bulbs, green and yellow banana peppers, and red chilis hanging on one wall, thinking it very clever how the Mexicans had managed to use the string as a colorful wall decoration too. Despite its simplicity, there was a coziness and warmth about this home, one that her uncle's lavish home had never had. She found herself almost envying the Mexicans.

After they had sat down to eat, Margarita placed a glass of water next to Christine's plate. Remembering what Chad had told her about drinking water in Mexico, Christine looked up at him with questioning eyes.

Chad caught her look, nodded slightly, picked up his glass, and drank from it. Christine sighed in relief. She would have hated to have had to ask if the water was safe in front of the Morales family.

The food was delicious, even better than in the cantina the night before. Christine ate with a hearty appetite that brought a look of pride to José's eyes and nodding approval from Consuelo.

"About those horses," Chad said, turning to José and speaking in a low voice Christine couldn't hear.

Christine looked up from her plate and caught Margarita staring at her, her black eyes once again brooding, her mouth tightly set. Then the girl smiled sweetly and offered Christine a bowl. Christine looked down at the bowl, wondering what it was.

"Sauce for the meat," Margarita said.

Christine put a large spoonful of the sauce on her meat and then took a bite. She gasped and swallowed quickly, reaching frantically for her water glass as her eyes filled with tears and she started to cough. Everyone at the table looked at her strangely, including Chad.

Chad glanced down at her plate and muttered, "My God, I should have warned you. That's Mexican hot sauce. Even I won't eat that."

After Christine had controlled herself, she apologized profusely. Blushing furiously, she said, "I'm sorry. I must have choked on a piece of meat."

Chad interpreted, and everyone at the table looked relieved.

"Are you all right now, *señorita*?" José inquired with concern.

"Yes, I'm fine," Christine said and then added, "*Gracias*."

Chad's eyebrow rose at the last word. The Mexicans smiled in return, pleased with her use of their native tongue. Christine looked back down at the hot sauce and then, through lowered lashes, at Margarita across from her. The girl was smiling smugly. Why is it that all of these Mexican girls seem to dislike me so much? she wondered.

That night, when Christine was alone in her room, she heard a knock at her door. She opened the door to see Chad standing in the hallway, holding a package in his hand.

"This is for you," he said, handing her the package.

"What is it?" Christine asked.

Chad leaned casually against the doorjamb and drawled softly, "Your new clothes. I'm not sure if the pants and shirt will fit. I had to guess at that. But the boots should fit. I took the liberty of borrowing one of your shoes. You'll find it in there too." He pointed at the package.

Christine had completely forgotten about her promise to dress as a boy. The thought that he had bought the clothes for her, without even asking for her opinion, infuriated her. "The least you could have done is let me buy them myself," Christine snapped.

"Why?" Chad replied, maddenly calm. "Clothes are clothes. What difference does it make who bought them?"

"Well, at least I could have gotten the right size."

Chad's eyebrows rose; he smiled mockingly. "You would have tried men's clothing on at the store?" He shook his head, clucking softly. "For shame, Chris. I thought you were a lady."

Christine was furious. Angrily, she slammed the door in his face, Chad barely having time to step back out of the way. She flung the package on the bed, muttering curses.

The door slammed open, startling Christine. Chad stood in the doorway, his look murderous, his blue eyes glittering. "Let's get one thing straight—lady," he said in a hard voice. "That's the last temper tantrum you pull on me. The next time you act like a two-year-old, I'm going to throw you over my knee and give you a good paddling. Is that clear?"

Christine was truly frightened of the big Texan looming over her. At that minute, he looked very dangerous and menacing. She ducked her head and muttered, "Yes."

"Now, tomorrow," Chad said in a steely voice, "we're going to see if I can teach you how to ride a horse. I'll expect you up bright and early, and dressed in those clothes I bought you. Understand?"

Christine stared at the floor and nodded mutely.

Chad looked at the meek, subdued woman standing before him and felt strangely disappointed. He hadn't realized it before, but he enjoyed their skirmishes, their little contests of wills. Most of the women he knew were too malleable, too passive, too eager to please. He found Christine's spirited obstinacy refreshing, exciting.

He turned and walked from the room, throwing over his shoulder, "And cut your hair!"

Chad heard Christine's angry gasp, and he grinned with satisfaction, shutting the door softly behind him.

Chapter Five

Christine frowned at the mirror. The image that frowned back at her looked more like a tall, gangly youth than the Christine she knew. The man's pants and shirt, still stiff with sizing, were too large for her and bagged at the waist and shoulders. Christine squirmed uncomfortably under the scratchy material of the shirt, wishing she had washed it first.

She bent and studied her hair closely in the mirror. She had angrily sawed at her long tresses with scissors, cutting them off just above the neckline. Now her silver hair hung lankly against her head, its edges ragged and uneven. I look like a street urchin, a big, overgrown street urchin, she thought, fighting back tears.

She lifted her head resolutely and awkwardly walked from the room, the stiff leather of the new boots pinching her toes and rubbing her heels. When she entered the Morales's kitchen, she heard the gasps of the Mexican men, their faces registering horrified shock. From the corner of her eye, she saw Consuelo shaking her head in mute disapproval. She glanced about the room and saw Chad watching her with amusement. Then she heard Margarita's giggle and she fervently wished the earth would open up and swallow her.

Christine sat through breakfast feeling miserable, acutely aware of everyone staring at her. This must be how the two-headed cow at the circus feels, she thought, struggling to force her food down.

When they had finished eating, Chad rose and said, "All right, Chris. Let's get to work."

José looked up from the table and smiled at Chad, saying, "*Ah, amigo*. I wonder if Margarita could show you the horse I picked out for Señorita Roberts? You see, I promised Consuelo I would take the cheese to the market today, and already I am late."

"That will be fine, José," Chad replied. "You go ahead and do what you need to do. Don't worry about us."

Totally ignoring Christine, Chad walked from the room and out into the yard, Margarita clutching his arm and skipping to keep up with his long strides. Christine followed glumly behind them, stumbling in the awkward boots as she tried to keep up. She watched Margarita smiling flirtatiously up at the big Texan, chattering in Spanish, an obvious attempt to make Christine feel even more left out.

As they walked into the ramada, Margarita

pointed at one of the horses standing in the open-sided shed.

"That black stallion?" Chad asked.

"*Sí, señor*," Margarita answered, smiling sweetly up at him.

Chad looked at the horse, saying, "Well, he certainly is a good-looking animal."

He walked up to the stallion and ran his hands over the horse's sleek legs, checking each hoof carefully. He eyed the animal's deep chest, nodding in approval, and looked into his mouth.

"He seems healthy too," Chad remarked, stroking the horse's neck absently.

"*Sí, sí, mucho* good horse," Margarita replied, throwing a smug look in Christine's direction.

Christine saw the look and wondered at it. She had not forgotten the Mexican girl's trick the night before with the hot sauce. Immediately, she was wary.

"Chris, come here," Chad said in a demanding voice.

Christine bridled at his tone of voice, but walked up to him and the horse.

"This will be your horse," Chad said. "He's a good-looking animal, and I'll expect you to keep him looking that way. For that reason, you're going to learn how to care for him, how to feed him, how to rub him down, how to saddle him, everything. Do you understand?"

Christine nodded curtly, resenting his dictatorial attitude. He's just like my uncle, she thought. Bossy and domineering.

Chad reached for a bridle hanging on a post

near him, saying, "We'll use this bridle with the plain bit. I prefer them to those Spanish bits that butcher a horse's mouth. Now watch how I do it."

Christine watched as Chad effortlessly slipped the metal bit into the mouth of the horse and deftly drew the bridle over the animal's head. That doesn't look hard, she thought.

Chad slipped the bridle off and handed it to her, saying, "Now you try it."

Christine took the bridle from Chad and tried to slip the bit into the horse's mouth, but the animal's jaw seemed glued shut. She prodded at his teeth with her fingers, trying to force his mouth open.

"Come on, Chris," Chad said impatiently. "We haven't got all day."

"He won't open his mouth!" Christine retorted.

"He'll open it," Chad replied. "Force his mouth open if you have to, but get a move on."

Margarita, sitting on a bag of corn and watching, giggled. Christine glared at her, saying resentfully, "Does she have to be here?"

Chad's dark eyebrows arched in surprise. "Margarita?" Then he shrugged, saying, "Why not? She's not bothering anybody."

Christine saw Margarita's self-satisfied smile and suppressed the urge to slap her. She turned back to the horse and pushed and shoved at the bit until the stubborn jaw finally gave and the metal bit slipped into place. Then she lifted the bridle over the horse's head, but the ears, made of flexible cartilage, seemed to have grown solid bone to resist her efforts. Muttering darkly to herself, Christine persisted until the bridle finally slipped over the horse's head. She stood back, sighing in relief.

"Okay," Chad said lazily, "take it off and do it again."

"Again?" Christine gasped.

"Yes," Chad said firmly. "You're going to practice doing it until you can do it in the dark if you have to."

Christine groaned. She turned and pulled off the bridle and repeated the procedure. She did it over and over, noting with relief that it became easier each time and finally monotonous.

"All right, that's enough," Chad said. "Now we'll try the saddle. Watch closely."

He bent, picked up the saddle blanket, and tossed it over the horse's back. With one easy movement from Chad, the saddle followed. Christine watched carefully as he tightened the cinch and girth.

Chad turned, saying, "Got it?"

Christine nodded confidently.

"Okay," he said as he removed the saddle and blanket. "Now you try it."

Christine picked up the saddle blanket and placed it over the horse's back. Then she bent to pick up the saddle. It was much heavier than it looked, she discovered. She grunted as she picked it up and, summoning all her strength, threw it over the animal's back. The saddle and blanket both slid off the horse's back and fell into a heap on the ground. Christine stared at the animal's back in disbelief. Chad shook his head in disgust.

Christine quickly scampered to retrieve the blanket and saddle. When she threw the saddle on the second time, it stayed in place. Christine buckled the cinch and girth and stood back, proudly admiring her work.

"Better tighten up that cinch," Chad remarked.

Christine ground her teeth angrily, then tightened the cinch. She turned to face Chad, waiting for his approval. The big Texan sat on the ground, leaning his back against a post, his long legs leisurely crossed in front of him. Christine watched impatiently as he calmly tapped tobacco into a brown paper, deftly rolled it, and twisted both ends. Placing one end in his mouth, he lit the other and then looked up at her, one eyebrow arched.

Christine didn't even bother to ask. Muttering very unladylike words, she jerked the saddle off the horse. Not until she had saddled the horse five times, did Chad finally stop her.

"Okay, Chris," he said as he rose and walked out of the ramada and into the adjoining corral, "bring him out here."

Christine took the horse's reins and led him into the corral. She frowned when Margarita climbed up and perched atop of one of the twisted mesquite limbs that formed a fence around the area.

"Do you think you can get on him?" Chad asked.

"Why yes," Christine replied hesitantly. "I suppose I can."

Chad nodded curtly and Christine walked to

the side of the horse.

"What do you think you're doing?" Chad barked.

"Why, I'm going to get on the horse!" Christine snapped back.

"From the right side?" Chad asked in disbelief. Shaking his head, he said, "No, Chris, you never mount a horse from that side, only from the left. Go to the other side."

Christine sighed in exasperation and started to walk around the rear of the horse. Chad pulled her back roughly, yelling, "Do you want to get your brains kicked out? Even an idiot knows better than to walk behind a horse."

Christine's temper flared. "Stop yelling at me! How should I know that? I've never been around any horses."

"Didn't your uncle own any horses?" Chad asked.

"Yes, carriage horses. But I was never allowed in the stable."

Christine walked in front of the horse and approached him from the left side. Holding on to the middle of the saddle, she started to put her foot in the stirrup.

"Not that foot, Chris," Chad said, trying to be patient. "The other one."

Christine lowered her right foot, hating her own stupidity. Why hadn't she just admitted she really hadn't the faintest notion of how to get on a horse? Back east, her only exposure had been to carriage horses. True, she had been in Texas for weeks, but she had been too preoccupied with her worries over Charles to pay any attention to how the men out here mounted their horses.

She put her left boot in the stirrup and started to push up, but her foot slipped and she fell back down, painfully hitting her chin on the saddle. Chad groaned in disgust, and Margarita giggled.

Christine shot the girl a heated look. She placed her foot firmly in the stirrup. Holding on to the saddle, she pushed herself up and started to swing her leg, but realized with dismay that with both hands in the saddle there was no place to sit.

Chad mumbled darkly to himself and pulled her back down. "Hold on to the saddle horn, Chris. Pull on that horn as you push with your foot and then just fling your leg over. Hell, anyone with legs as long as yours shouldn't have any trouble getting into a saddle."

Christine bristled indignantly at Chad's remark about her legs, but Chad ignored her.

Placing her left hand on the saddle horn and her left foot in the stirrup, he said, "Now, up you go!"

Christine gasped in shock as Chad's large hand cupped her bottom and pushed her upward. She had no choice but to fling her leg over and straddle the saddle. But the second she hit leather, she felt herself flying through the air.

Chad's big body broke her fall. He grunted with exasperation as he set her on her feet firmly and said sarcastically, "Well, Chris, I can see I'm not going to have to worry about you falling off your horse. At this rate . . . you'll never get in the saddle."

102

Christine snatched her arm away angrily, thinking, if he hadn't have touched me so intimately and made me so nervous, it wouldn't have happened. "Just don't help me!" she snapped. "I can do it myself."

Chad shrugged indifferently and stepped back. "Suit yourself."

Christine grabbed the saddle horn firmly and placed her boot carefully in the stirrup. She pulled herself up and flung her leg over, instinctively feeling that this time it was right. She felt herself land firmly in the saddle—and then the emphatic buck of the horse's back. Again, she flew through the air, this time bumping her head against Chad's as he tried to catch her.

"Goddamnit, lady, can't you do anything right?" Chad roared, rubbing the knot on his forehead.

"I did do it right!" Christine retorted, rubbing her own head. "The horse threw me!"

"The hell he did! Why don't you just admit you can't get in the saddle?"

Margarita laughed outright from the corral fence. Christine glared at her and then back at Chad. "I did get in the saddle! I tell you, that stupid horse threw me!" Christine insisted.

A pair of deep blue eyes challenged a pair of green eyes, and Christine's didn't waver. The two stood glaring at each other, each refusing to yield. Fortunately, Pablo ran into the corral, calling something to Chad in Spanish.

"All right, Chris," Chad sighed. "We'll forget it for now. Pablo says it's time to eat, so take the

103

horse back into the ramada and unsaddle him."

"Unsaddle him? Why? We'll be right back out," Christine objected.

Chad clenched his teeth. Did she have to argue about everything? Struggling to control his temper, he said, "No, we won't be right back out. Not for several hours. After lunch, we'll take a siesta."

"Siesta? What's that?"

"In Mexico, after the noon meal, everyone takes a nap," Chad explained.

"A nap?" Christine said in disbelief. "Why, I haven't taken a nap in the daytime since I was five years old."

"You don't necessarily have to sleep," Chad replied wearily. "Just rest. In this climate, it's downright foolish to do any kind of activity in the noonday heat unless it's absolutely necessary."

"But . . ."

"Damn it, Chris. Stop arguing with me and do what I said!" Chad thundered, his eyes flashing warning signals, his jaw tightly set.

Christine felt a flicker of fear. She might be hardheaded, but she wasn't stupid. Silently, she led the big stallion back into the ramada and unsaddled him. But her mind still raged. I know I didn't fall out of the saddle, she thought insistently. That damned horse threw me!

After lunch was over, Chad went to his room and lay down on his bed, smoking and thinking. One more day like this and Chris will give up her stupid idea of going with me, he assured himself. He knew she felt humiliated wearing the men's clothing. And that haircut! God, he'd never seen anyone look so bedraggled. Or anyone as stupid about horses either, he added with disgust. Yes, give her another day or two and she'll be begging to stay behind, he thought smugly.

He rose from the bed, ambled out of the house, and headed for the ramada, intent on selecting the bridle he would use for his packhorse. As he walked toward the shed, he saw Pablo standing behind the thick mesquite that lined one side of the corral.

The little Mexican boy stood, peeking through the brush and shaking his head, mumbling, "*Loca gringa.*"

Chad walked up behind the boy and asked curiously, "What are you looking at, Pablo?"

The boy turned, a surprised look on his face. Then he frowned and pointed through the brush, saying, "Ah, *señor*, three times, the crazy *gringa* get on the black horse, and three times, *uno, dos, tres,*" he counted solemnly on his fingers, "he throw her. She *mucha loca.*"

Chad peered through the brush. Christine stood in the corral with the big black stallion. She was just fixing to mount him.

Chad turned to the Mexican boy, saying, "Pablo, let me get this straight. Are you telling me the *señorita* has fallen off that horse three times already?"

The little boy looked up at him, his black eyes wide, saying, "Oh no, *señor*. She no fall. The horse, he throw her."

"Threw her?"

"*Sí, señor*," Pablo said. "Three times, she climb on the horse. Three times, he buck his back." He shook his head gravely. "Crazy *gringa!*"

At that minute Chad and Pablo heard a sickening thud. Both winced at the ominous sound.

"*Cuatro*, four times," Pablo muttered.

"That crazy, little fool! She'll break her neck!" Chad whirled and headed for the corral.

Christine lifted her face from the ground, spitting dirt, her head spinning dizzily. She looked up at the black stallion above her through blurred eyes. Angry and frustrated, she struggled to her feet and stumbled to the head of the horse.

At this very minute, Chad strode from behind the mesquite brush. But when he saw Christine approaching the horse's head, instead of his side, he stepped back, curious.

Christine stood defiantly before the big horse. Half sobbing, she said, "You big, ugly brute! If I don't learn how to ride you that damned Texan isn't going to let me go into Mexico with him." She raised her chin stubbornly. "And I am going with him!"

The horse drew back his lips in an ugly snarl and lashed at her with his big teeth, barely missing Christine's cheek. Without thinking, Christine balled up one fist and slammed it into the sensitive muzzle of the animal. The stallion whinnied shrilly and stepped back, shaking his head, blinking his eyes in disbelief.

Christine leaned into the horse's face, her hands on her hips, her green eyes flashing. "Now you

106

listen to me you big, black devil! I'm going to ride you if it's the last thing I do. I'm going to ride you if it kills me—or you!"

The stallion stood perfectly still, his ears twitching, a wary look in his eyes, while Christine mounted him. As Christine landed in the saddle, she automatically clenched her knees, anticipating the horse's buck. For a minute, she sat in stunned surprise as the horse stood meekly beneath her. Then her face broke into a wide grin.

For several minutes, Christine sat and savored her victory. Then she picked up the reins, saying, "All right, boy, let's go."

The horse stood quietly, his tail switching lazily at the flies that buzzed around them.

"Come on, move!" Christine cried.

The stallion stood as motionless as a statue, as if he had suddenly turned to stone. Christine frowned, wondering if there was some magic, unknown word that would make the horse move. Without realizing it, she nudged his flank with the heel of her boot, and the animal started forward in a subdued walk.

Christine sat on the back of the horse, feeling a momentary thrill at her success. But as the stallion circled the corral for the third time, she began to worry. How was she going to get down?

"Stop!" she commanded.

The horse plodded doggedly on, and Christine fought back tears of frustration, having visions of her and the stallion going round and round in the corral for hours in the hot sun until someone finally came out and found them. She strained her memory and recalled what she had heard the stage driver call.

"Whoa, horse . . . whoa!"

The stallion trudged on lazily.

Christine jerked on the reins, more to attract the animal's attention than anything else, and called, "Whoa."

The horse stopped and Christine quickly scampered off. As her feet hit solid ground, she sighed in relief and then limped to the horse's head. She stroked the stallion's neck, saying, "That's a good boy. You and I are going to do just fine together. Why, we're going to be good friends. Just you wait and see."

Chad stood, still concealed by the mesquite brush, and watched as Christine, limping badly, led the horse back into the ramada. He ran one hand through his thick, dark hair and shook his head, muttering, "Crazy *gringa*." But as he walked back to his room, he found himself again admiring her spirit and determination.

When Christine emerged from the house an hour later, Chad chuckled to himself. She looked awful. Her new pants and shirt were crumpled and filthy, her face still smudged with dirt. Her hair hung in damp, ragged tendrils around her face and neck, and she was trying very hard to hide her limp.

Taking her arm and leading her away from the house in a smattering of small mesquite trees, Chad said, "I've decided you've had enough riding for one day. This afternoon, I'm going to teach you how to shoot a gun."

Christine was too shocked by his announcement to wonder over his reference to riding. Shoot a gun? But guns were dangerous. Why, a person could get killed fooling around with a gun!

"You didn't say anything about learning to shoot a gun," Christine objected.

"Didn't I?" Chad asked, then shrugged. "Well, you're going to be carrying a sidearm, and if you're going to carry one, you're going to know how to use it."

"But why do I have to carry a gun? You're the *pistolero*, not me!"

Chad struggled for patience. "Listen, Chris, we're going to be traveling in dangerous country. Every gun helps. A bandit might not think twice about attacking a man with a gun, but two men with two guns? Besides, the way I have it planned, if we can find El Puma, we'll try to infiltrate his camp on the pretense that we want to hire out as mercenaries. Now, did you ever hear of a hired gun, who didn't carry a gun? I may be the *pistolero*, Chris, but you're going to pretend to be one. And you're going to know enough about guns to give a convincing act."

By this time, they were standing under a gnarled mesquite tree. Chad picked up a gun sitting on a tree stump and handed it to her. Christine accepted it reluctantly, her nose wrinkling with distaste.

"That's an Army Colt," Chad said. "It holds six shots." He pointed to the handle saying, "You hold it here, and the ball comes out there," he motioned to the muzzle of the gun.

"I know that!" Christine snapped.

Chad grinned. "Well, considering what happened with the horse this morning, I decided not to assume too much."

Christine bristled at his sarcasm. Chad ignored her reaction to his jibe. Taking the gun from her hand, he said, "The first thing you're going to learn how to do is load it."

He walked to the tree stump and picked up a small metal object, about the size of a match head. "This is a percussion cap. It fires the powder. Now watch while I place it."

Christine watched as Chad placed the hammer at half-cock, and then cradling the gun in his left hand, pressed the percussion cap snugly over the small cone at the back of the cylinder. He rotated the cylinder, exposing the next chamber, and pressed another percussion cap in place. When he had positioned all six percussion caps, he squatted and fired the gun at the ground.

Christine cringed, expected to hear a gunshot, and watched with surprise when no noise came from the gun except the metallic click of the hammer. Six puffs of air stirred the sand below the ground.

"That was just to clear the oil and dust from the gun. It prevents the gun from jamming on you later. One thing you don't want is a jammed gun, particularly when you've got it pointed at a bandit or an Indian," Chad said.

Christine nodded in understanding.

"Now for loading it," Chad said as he rose. "Watch closely. I'll load the first chamber, and then you can do the others."

Chad placed the hammer at half-cock and cradled the gun with his left hand, its muzzle pointed upward.

"The ball and powder are loaded from the front of the chamber. Hold the muzzle up to keep the powder from falling out." He picked up a powder horn from the stump, saying, "This is a measured flask. That means that you can't pour too much powder with it."

He placed the flask into the exposed chamber and poured in the black powder. Then he picked up a ball and placed it firmly over the powder. He rotated the cylinder forward, placing the loaded chamber at the bottom of the gun.

"Now you force the ball solidly against the powder with this loading lever," Chad said, pulling back on the lever under the muzzle of the gun and ramming the ball home.

Christine watched as he dipped his finger into a tin sitting on the stump. "This is bear grease," he said, generously smearing the grease over the ball. "That prevents the powder flash in one chamber from jumping to the other and causing multiple discharges. It also acts as a lubricant."

Chad handed the gun to Christine, saying, "Now let's see you load the other chambers."

Christine was awkward in loading the first chamber. Chad stood beside her, offering additional instructions and helpful hints. By the time she got to her fourth chamber, she was much more adept. She rotated the cylinder and started to load the last chamber.

"No, don't load that one," Chad said.

"Why not?"

"Because we'll leave it empty to rest the hammer of the gun on. A good jolt or jar can accidentally fire one of these guns, Chris. I've known more than one man who has accidentally shot himself or his horse because he was either too stupid or too hardheaded to leave one empty chamber for his hammer to rest on."

"But that means there will be only five shots in the gun," Christine pointed out. "That's not very many."

"That's right, Chris," Chad agreed. "That's why you'll always carry an extra, loaded cylinder on your belt. Now see if you can place the percussion caps."

Christine picked up the small cap and started to place it on the nipple at the back of the chamber.

"Keep your gun pointed down, Chris," Chad instructed. "In case of accidental firing."

Christine nodded nervously and smiled weakly. She placed the five percussion caps firmly in place.

Chad nodded his approval and said, "All right, now we'll see if you can shoot it."

Christine felt her knees shaking, her mouth suddenly turned dry.

"That's an 1860 Army Colt," Chad drawled. "That revolver was the most widely used sidearm in the Civil War and prized for its reliability. But it's over a foot long, has a barrel length of eight inches and weighs two pounds, nine ounces. So it's a good-size gun for a woman to handle. And although you're bigger than most women, I still think you're going to have to use both hands to fire it."

Christine colored hotly at his remark about her size. Oh, he just had to keep throwing it in her face, didn't he? She whirled, intending to ask him a question, and inadvertently pointed the gun right at him.

"Damn it, Chris!" Chad yelled, pushing the gun away from his chest. "Watch where you point that damned thing!"

"I'm . . . I'm sorry," Christine stammered. "I didn't mean—"

"Chris," Chad interrupted, "*never, ever* point a loaded gun at someone. Not unless you fully intend to shoot it."

"I understand," Chris said. "It's just that I'm so nervous."

"Not near as nervous as I am," Chad said with a groan.

Christine couldn't help but smile at his candid admission. Chad shrugged and said, "All right, we'll forget it happened. Just be more careful from now on."

Christine waited while Chad positioned the big gun in her hands. "Now hold the gun out straight, look down the barrel at the sight, and pull the trigger," he instructed.

"What should I shoot?"

"Aim for that big mesquite stump over there," he said, pointing into the distance.

Christine pointed the muzzle of the gun at the stump and pulled the trigger, grimacing and squeezing her eyes shut in expectation. A deafening roar followed and the gun seemed to leap out of her hands. She opened her eyes to find herself surrounded by orange-white smoke.

"What in the hell did you drop the gun for?" Chad yelled.

"I didn't drop it!" Christine retorted. "It jumped out of my hands."

"That's recoil," Chad said in a disgusted voice as he picked up the gun. "Every gun has it. That's why you've got to keep a tight grip on the handle. Now try it again." He handed her the gun.

Christine accepted the gun reluctantly, pointed it at the stump, and fired, this time holding the gun tightly as it snapped upward in recoil. She opened eyes. The acrid smoke from the gun stung her nostrils and made her eyes water.

"Did I hit it?" she asked, squinting through the thick smoke.

Chad stood, shaking his head in disbelief. "No, but you hit that tree over there." He pointed to a lone hackberry about twenty feet to the right of the mesquite stump. Christine stared at the tree in dismay.

"I've seen wide shots," Chad said, "but that's ridiculous." He sighed in exasperation, saying, "All right, Chris, try it again."

Christine aimed the gun, determined that this time she would hit her target. She carefully sighted the mesquite stump. As she pulled the trigger, she squeezed her eyes shut in anticipation of the gun's roar.

"Damn it, you're closing your eyes!" Chad

roared over the noise of the gunshot.

Christine opened her eyes to see the big Texan looming over her, his eyes glittering angrily. With the smoke swirling around him, he looked like the devil himself.

"I can't help it," Christine said. "The noise, the smoke . . ."

"Chris," Chad said, trying hard to curb his temper, "you can't shoot with your eyes closed. Keep your eyes on your target, even after you've fired. You'll get used to the noise and smoke."

Christine turned back to the stump, acutely aware of the sun beating down on her head and Chad's eyes boring into her back. She aimed and fired, forcing her eyes to stay open even after the gun roared and she felt its recoil. She peered into the thick, orange-white smoke, unable to see a thing.

"Did I hit it this time?" she asked in a small voice.

"No, but you came a lot closer," Chad said. "You'll get better with practice."

And practice she did. Chad kept her out there in the hot sun all afternoon, reloading and shooting. Most of the time, he was amazingly patient with her. Even when Christine repeatedly missed the stump, he continued to teach her, offering her hints on how to correct her mistakes.

When they walked back to the house that evening, Christine felt dispirited. She ached all over, but particularly in her wrists and shoulders. Her nose and her eyes still stung from the black powder smoke. And I never did hit that damned stump, she thought, feeling pure hatred toward the inanimate object.

"Tonight after we've eaten, I'll show you how to clean your gun," Chad said.

Christine's shoulders slumped, a small groan escaped her lips. Chad smiled knowingly.

That night when they were all seated at the table, Señor Morales said to Chad, "Ah, *amigo*, the *señorita* liked the mare, *si*?"

Chad frowned, saying, "Mare? What mare?"

Pablo, his black eyes bright with excitement, interrupted. "*Padre*, she no ride the mare. She ride Diablo."

José Morales's face paled. "Diablo?" he muttered. Then his dusky face colored, and he said something to his daughter in Spanish, the tone of his voice angry.

"But, *Padre*," Margarita cried, her voice full of innocence, "I thought you meant the black horse." She ducked her head, wiping an imaginary tear from her eye.

José stared at his daughter in frustration and then turned to Chad, his look apologetic. "*Amigo*, there has been a terrible mistake here," he said gravely. "Diablo is not the horse I picked for the *señorita*. He is still half wild, half broke. I am very sorry."

Chad looked at Margarita suspiciously. She sat with her head meekly averted, still dabbing her eyes. Then he turned to Señor Morales, saying, "Don't worry about it, José. There's no harm done."

Christine's head snapped up. She stared at

116

Chad in disbelief. No harm done, she thought, hardly believing her ears. Why, every muscle in her body ached, and she was covered with bruises and scrapes. Why, she could have been killed! And he says there's no harm done? Her anger rose. Then she remembered that Chad knew nothing of her escapade with the horse that afternoon. She would either have to expose herself or keep quiet. She chose to do the latter.

Señor Morales looked at Christine, saying, "I am very sorry, *señorita*." His face brightened. "But you will like the little mare. She is very gentle."

Christine glanced across at Margarita before answering. She had not been fooled one minute by her innocent act. Her desire for revenge against the Mexican girl overruled her good sense.

Christine smiled at Señor Morales and said, "Thank you, *señor*, but I think I would prefer to keep Diablo."

José looked aghast. "But, *señorita*, Diablo is still half wild. He is dangerous!"

Christine lifted her chin stubbornly. "Still, I'd like to keep him."

José looked to Chad for support. *"¿Señor?"*

Chad shrugged his broad shoulders, saying, "If that's what the lady wants, it's fine with me."

José stared at him, open-mouthed, totally dumbfounded at his words.

Christine looked back down at her plate, sneaking a glance in Margarita's direction. The Mexican girl was wide-eyed, her look one of utter disbelief. Christine smiled smugly, savoring her revenge. Then she frowned, wondering why Chad hadn't tried to talk her out of keeping Diablo. Somehow, his unconcern for her welfare robbed her of the pleasure of her revenge and left her feeling strangely depressed.

That night, Christine washed out both pairs of pants and her shirts, having decided that even if the clean pair didn't need it, they would be much more comfortable if they weren't so stiff. Wringing them out, she carried them out of the room and headed for the small fence of mesquite limbs at the back of the house, thinking to dry them there overnight. But as she stepped out of the back door, Christine realized with dismay that the fence was already occupied.

Chad stood, leaning casually across the upper crossbar of the fence, smoking. Margarita stood beside him, hugging his arm possessively and smiling up at him flirtatiously, her curvaceous body pressed close to his.

Christine stopped abruptly, momentarily perplexed. Then realizing Margarita was talking about her, she stepped back into the shadows, listening.

"I do not like the yanqui woman," Margarita complained petulantly.

Chad chuckled, saying, "How can you say that, Margarita? You don't even know her."

Margarita looked up at him, her eyes narrowing. "You are taking her with you into Mexico?"

"That's right," Chad replied. "I'm taking her to

meet her brother."

"And you will be alone with her all that time, even at night?" Margarita asked.

Chad frowned, saying, "Now, Margarita, that's none of your business."

"She is too big. As big as a man. A giant!"

Chad saw no reason to comment. Christine was as big as a lot of men, even taller than many others. He shrugged.

Margarita backed away from him, her dark eyes flashing, hissing, "She is a *puta*! An ugly *puta*!"

Chad was shocked at Margarita's vicious attack on Christine and her use of the ugly word, *puta*. He turned to her, saying, "You should be ashamed of yourself, Margarita. Your mother would wash your mouth out with soap if she heard you talk like that."

The Mexican girl blinked back tears. "I hate her! I hate her!" she screamed, whirling and running back into the house.

Christine stepped further back into the shadows, terrified that Chad would discover her presence. She couldn't possibly face him now, knowing that Margarita had just brutally pointed out all of her faults. No, she was too humiliated.

Well, at least she knew now why Margarita disliked her so much. She was jealous of her. Christine could understand why the Mexican girl was so drawn to the tall Texan. With his rugged good looks and magnetic masculine sexuality, what woman wouldn't be attracted to him? Even she had felt the effects of his devastating

119

sensuality, she admitted reluctantly, remembering her almost violent reaction to his casual touch in the Longhorn Hotel and the strange sensations his kiss had invoked.

The memory of that kiss flooded over Christine, and with it, the pain of Chad's rejection returned. How silly of Margarita to be jealous of her. Why, she meant nothing to Chad. At best, he was indifferent to her. She wondered what the Mexican girl would think if she knew Chad had told her she wasn't his type from the very beginning, that he had brutally proven it when he had recoiled from her when she had pressed her body against his when he'd kissed her. Undoubtedly, Margarita would take smug satisfaction in that knowledge.

A fresh pain tore through Christine's heart. Sudden tears filled her eyes. The realization that the Texan thought her unattractive hurt, more deeply than she was willing to admit. Angrily, she wiped at the tears, then turned and rushed back into the house.

When Christine reached her room, she was surprised to see Consuelo standing before her door, her plump face smiling broadly. Christine was besieged with a flurry of Spanish words, none of which she understood. She shook her head mutely in reply.

Señora Morales held up a scissors and pointed to Christine's hair. Christine laughed in relief. All she wanted to do was cut her hair. Well, maybe she can even up the edges, Christine thought. At any rate, it certainly couldn't look any worse.

"Sí, señora," Christine agreed.

Christine allowed the Mexican woman to position her on a stool and sat patiently as the woman snipped away busily. But as more and more hair fell to the floor, Christine became alarmed. My God, she's scalping me, she groaned silently.

When Consuelo had finished, she beamed proudly at Christine and handed her a small mirror. Christine looked into it and caught her breath in surprised amazement. Her silver hair hung in soft curls around her face, the hairstyle much more becoming than the one she had worn all of her life. She couldn't believe her eyes.

She looked up at Consuelo, tears of gratitude in her eyes. *"Gracias, señora, gracias."*

"De nada," the Mexican woman replied softly.

After Consuelo had left, Christine sat for a long time admiring her new hairstyle, turning her head this way and then the other. Her pretty mouth curved into a soft smile, her eyes sparkled. I wonder what Chad will think of it? she thought.

Chapter Six

Christine was up bright and early the next morning and rushed to the ramada before Chad had even appeared for breakfast. She had misgivings about her rash words the night before and wanted to reaffirm her position with the big black stallion before Chad arrived on the scene.

As she entered the ramada, Diablo lifted his head, his brown eyes flickering with recognition. Christine smiled nervously at the horse and stroked his neck, saying, "You remember me, don't you big boy? We're friends, remember?"

She pulled out the pilonce she had bought on her trip to Texas and offered the horse a piece of the brown sugar candy. Her hand shook as the horse lowered his big mouth.

She felt weak with relief when Diablo nibbled gently at the candy and she sighed, crooning, "That's a good boy. You see, if you'll be nice to me, I'll be nice to you."

When Diablo had finished eating the candy,

Christine slipped on his bridle and saddled him. She was standing, smiling proudly, when Chad entered the shed a little later.

Chad's long strides came to a complete halt. He stared at Christine, feeling as if he'd been kicked by a mule, his reaction having nothing to do, as Christine thought, with the fact that she already had Diablo saddled and waiting.

In fact, Chad had never even looked at the horse. His eyes were locked on Christine's body. The shirt and pants had shrunk from being washed and clung to every luscious, magnificent curve, the sight taking his breath away. How in the hell can she look more feminine in men's clothes? Chad puzzled.

His eyes narrowed as he studied her closer. The shirt clung to her high, proud breasts, and at the vee, he could see a tantalizing glimpse of cleavage. His eyes drifted downward over the soft swell of her hips to her incredibly long, beautifully shaped legs, legs that were clearly outlined in the skin-tight pants. Chad's mouth suddenly turned dry, his heart accelerated.

Christine smiled smugly, still thinking that his gaping at her was due to his surprise that she had managed to saddle Diablo by herself. And she could hardly wait to mount Diablo and surprise him again when she stayed in the saddle. In fact, she couldn't even wait until he saddled his own horse. She'd show him right now.

She turned and placed her foot in the stirrup, and Chad found himself staring at her well-shaped buttocks.

"Wait a minute!" Chad barked.

Christine turned to face him, startled by his sharp words. Then seeing the strange look on his face, she asked, "What's wrong?"

"Walk up and down," Chad demanded.

Christine started to object to his strange demand. "But—"

"Damn it, Chris," Chad roared, "do what I told you to!"

Christine was just a little frightened by his peculiar behavior. She turned and walked as he had commanded.

Chad watched Christine as she walked, his eyes glued to the graceful sway of her hips. Because of her unusual height, Christine's hips didn't look as full as a shorter woman's, and yet, their movement was more sensuous, more arousing than the provocative twist of lusher hips. To his chagrin, he felt a familiar stirring in his loins.

"Stop walking like that!" he demanded.

Christine turned, saying in bewilderment, "Like what?"

"Like a woman, damn it!"

"But I am a woman!"

"But you're not supposed to be a woman! Or have you forgotten? You're supposed to be a boy. So walk like one! Hell, one look at the way you walk would give you away in a minute."

"I'm not sure I know how to walk like a boy," Christine admitted.

"Lenthen your stride, keep your hips still, and tuck in your ass," Chad instructed.

Christine blushed hotly at his blunt reference to

her bottom. Indignantly, she turned and tried to walk as he'd instructed her. Lengthening her stride was easy for Christine with her long legs. She had to concentrate, however, on pulling in her buttocks. But Christine had a woman's pelvic girdle. Her bone structure dictated her walk, and despite her effort, her hips swayed.

For the life of him, Chad couldn't keep his eyes off her hips. He groaned, saying, "You're still doing it! You're still swinging your hips."

"I am not!" Christine retorted hotly, glaring at him.

Chad sighed in a mixture of frustrated arousal and exasperation. He still had hopes that Christine would change her mind about going along with him to rescue her brother, but after seeing her determination to stay on Diablo yesterday, he was beginning to accept the possibility that he might have to give her more than just a taste of what traveling in Mexico would be like. He might have to actually take her with him for a few days and let her really experience some of the trip. After being in the saddle from dawn to dusk, riding over that tortuous terrain in the hot, blazing sun, eating camp food, sleeping on the hard ground at night, and going without a bath, she'd change her mind. Then he'd bring her back to the border, drop her off, and go on down and do the job. But he couldn't take her into Mexico, even for a few days, looking like that! No one was going to mistake her for a boy, not with those skin-tight clothes and that seductive walk of hers.

"Look, Chris," Chad said, trying to be patient,

126

"I'm only telling you this for your own good. Now a woman walks with her hips, but a man walks with his shoulders. Try to keep your hips still and swing your shoulders instead."

Christine gave a little snort of disgust and squared her shoulders, causing her proud, full breasts to strain even more arrogantly at her shirt. Chad stared at those soft twin mounds, breasts that looked to him as if they were just begging to be touched. And his hands were itching to do just that!

He forced his eyes away from her breasts and studied her walk critically. Her stride and the swing of her shoulders were a good imitation of a man's. But after one look at her shapely legs and her breasts, no one was going to mistake her for a boy, not up close anyway. Hell, looking the way she did, she just invited trouble. He wished the clothes hadn't shrunk. Now he'd have to worry about disguising her again. But how?

His eyes fell on an old serape folded over a spare saddle. He picked it up and tossed it to Christine, saying, "Here, try this on. Let's see if it will cover your hips."

Christine looked down at the dirty garment in her hand with disgust.

"Put it on, Chris," Chad said in a low, warning voice.

Christine shot him a quick, heated glance and donned the smelly garment.

"Now walk," Chad said.

Christine sighed deeply and walked back and forth in front of Chad, feeling ridiculous. The serape fell almost to her knees, concealing her breasts, the sway of her hips, and most of her legs.

Chad nodded in approval. "Yes, the serape hides the sway of your hips." He decided not to mention the breasts and legs. "You'll wear it too."

Christine stared at him in dismay. "But it's filthy, and it smells awful."

"You can wash it," Chad replied calmly.

"But I'll burn up in it," Christine objected.

Chad had to admit she was right. The serape would be entirely too hot in this heat. "All right," he said, "you don't have to wear it when we're by ourselves, but anytime we ride through a town or we're around other people, you'll have to wear it."

Christine accepted the compromise reluctantly, knowing if she tried to argue it would be just like him to make her wear it all the time just for spite. Damn him, she thought hotly, he's the most obstinate, arrogant, and domineering man I've ever met!

She stripped off the serape and tossed it aside, waiting impatiently while Chad saddled his horse. She was eager to see the expression on his face when she mounted Diablo and stayed in the saddle. When Chad was mounted, she swung on the big stallion's back and smiled smugly, waiting for Chad's look of surprise.

But Christine was sorely disappointed. Instead of the look she was expecting, his face was closed, totally void of all expression.

"All right, Chris," Chad said, "we'll take the riding lessons in steps. First a walk, then a trot, then a canter, and finally a full gallop. Okay?"

Christine fought back her disappointment. Just once, she wished he would praise her. When I do something wrong, he's awfully quick to let me know, she thought ruefully. But she nodded her head curtly in agreement to Chad's plan.

"Now follow my instructions closely," Chad said. "Because the first time you fall off that horse, you're staying behind."

Christine started to retort, but she saw the adamant look in Chad's eyes. She nodded, praying silently, please, Diablo, don't try anything funny.

As they walked their horses from the ramada, Chad explained the use of the reins, and Christine realized how stupid she had been the day before. He gave her pointers on how to use her knees and heels to help guide the horse and spur him on.

When they broke into a bone-jarring trot, Christine gasped. Chad, riding easily beside her, chuckled and said, "Stop fighting the horse, Chris. Move with his movements instead of against them. Try to catch his rhythm."

Easier said than done, Christine thought glumly, wincing at each jog.

"Raise your body out of the saddle and let your weight fall on the stirrups," Chad instructed.

With Chad beside her, giving her instructions, she finally got the feel of it. And when they broke into a full gallop, she felt a brief twinge of fear and then laughed with sheer pleasure at feeling the powerful muscles of the horse between her legs and the wind whipping at her face.

At the sound of her laugh, Chad glanced across

at Christine. Her green eyes were sparkling with excitement, and the wind was ruffling her short curls about her face. Chad stared at the curls in renewed surprise. Where in the hell did they come from?

Chad had never even noticed Christine's new haircut, having been distracted by the sight of her magnificent body in the snug clothes and then preoccupied with teaching her how to ride. He frowned at the silver curls framing her face, puzzled as to why the shorter haircut disturbed him. Lots of men had curly hair. His own had a tendency to curl when it was damp. But on Christine, the soft curls accented her beautiful green eyes and softened the feminine contours of her face. I wish she had left it alone, he thought irritably. She looked more like a boy when it was longer and ragged. Now, I have to figure out some way to hide that too!

Well, she'd just have to wear her hat all the time too, Chad decided. And keep it pulled down low to hide her face. Hat? Hell, he'd completely forgotten to buy her a hat. And she would certainly need one, not just to cover her hair and hide her face, but to protect her from the sun, particularly once they were on the trail and riding all day. Well, if she didn't change her mind about going along in the next few days, he'd just have to ride back into El Paso and pick her up a hat before they left. Damn, she was more trouble!

As they rode into the corral later that morning, Christine said, "That was fun. Can we ride again this afternoon?"

130

Chad looked at her face, flushed with both excitement and a hint of sunburn. He frowned. Hell, she wasn't supposed to like it. How come she wasn't complaining about how sore she was? "No," he answered. "We'll practice some more shooting this afternoon. Come on, I'll teach you how to rub down your horse."

Christine pouted and followed him into the ramada. Shooting, she thought with disgust. That's no fun at all. She'd much rather ride Diablo.

But when Christine lay down for her siesta that afternoon, she was grateful for Chad's edict. Being caught up in the excitement of the ride, she hadn't realized how sore her muscles were. That, compounded with her bruises from the day before, made Christine wonder briefly if it was all worth it. She groaned in pain as she rolled to her side. But with renewed determination she vowed, I'm going with him! As she fell asleep, Christine smiled smugly, thinking, and I didn't fall off the horse—not once.

Chad was waiting for Christine, holding a rifle in his hand, when she walked from the house later that afternoon. He smiled knowingly when he saw her limping painfully toward him. He waited for her to voice her complaint and frowned with disappointment when she smiled up at him.

"I'm ready for my next lesson," Christine said cheerfully.

Chad looked down at her, feeling frustration rise. What in the hell does it take? he wondered. She must be covered with bruises from those falls she took yesterday, and now today, after four hours in the saddle, she was limping badly. Anyone else would have backed out by now. She was the most obstinate woman he'd ever met!

"You're going to learn to shoot a carbine today," Chad growled at her.

Christine's eyebrows rose in surprise at his gruff manner. Goodness, he's cranky this afternoon, she thought.

Chad led her to the clump of mesquite trees and handed her the rifle, saying, "That's a Spencer repeater carbine. It holds seven shots."

Christine looked at the rifle curiously. "How do you load it?"

"It's loaded through a trap in the butt plate," Chad replied. "It's slow to load if you only use one cartridge at a time. That's why I use the seven shot tubes of cartridges." He reached for a tube and slipped it into the trap.

"You mean I don't have to load it with black powder and balls like I did the pistol?"

"That's right."

"Well, if it's so much easier to load, why don't you get a pistol that loads like that?" Christine asked irritably.

"Because they don't make one!" Chad snapped back.

"Oh," Christine replied.

Chad put the carbine in her hands and then stood behind her, placing his long arms around her as he positioned the gun butt against her shoulder. Christine suddenly found it difficult to breathe, and not because of her fear of the gun.

She could feel the hard length of the Texan's body behind her, his muscular thighs pressed against her own, his powerful arms around her, his chin resting lightly on her head, almost caressingly. She became acutely aware of the heat radiating from his body and of his masculine scent, not unpleasant, but strangely exciting. Her knees seemed to turn to rubber. In fact, she felt weak all over. She seemed to be drowning in a warm vortex of sensation.

"Chris, are you listening to me?" Chad asked in a demanding voice.

Christine fought her reeling senses. "Yes, I'm listening," she muttered.

"Stop trembling, Chris," Chad said. "This is no worse than shooting a pistol. There's nothing to be afraid of."

Chad stepped back from her. Christine felt strangely bereaved, disappointment replacing all those pleasant sensations she had just experienced.

"Now look down the muzzle and sight the tree trunk," Chad instructed.

Christine looked down the muzzle of the gun and struggled to control her arms, still shaking from her reaction to the feel of Chad's body against hers. She sighted the stump and pulled the trigger. The carbine slammed hard into her shoulder, and Christine staggered back into Chad's body.

With Chad's arms locked around her once again, the same warm, pleasant sensations engulfed Christine, feelings that frightened her with

133

their intensity. Frantic, she scampered out of his arms.

Mistaking her pale face and trembling for fear of the gun, Chad said, "I should have warned you. The carbine has a more powerful recoil than the pistol. You'll have to learn to absorb the shock with your shoulder."

Christine nodded her head mutely, her knees still shaking, her heart still racing.

"Try it again," Chad said, after he had shown her how to discharge the empty cartridge. He stepped up behind her to position the gun again.

"No!" Christine shrieked. "I'll do it myself!"

Chad frowned, puzzled by her strange behavior. Then he shrugged and moved back.

All afternoon, she practiced with the carbine, and by the time they walked back to the house, Christine was exhausted, her shoulder aching from the rifle repeatedly slamming into it. But Christine's mind wasn't on her many and various aches and pains. She was still puzzled by her strange, almost violent reaction to the big Texan's casual touch. Why did this man's touch send her senses reeling, while other men's had only left her cold, even repulsed? Did he hold some strange power over her? Christine's mind recoiled at the thought. Oh, no! No man would hold her in his power! Never again! And certainly not *this* man!

The next day when Chad was giving Christine her riding lesson, she couldn't resist sneaking glances at him. He rode with his battered hat pushed to the back of his head, and Christine gazed into his brilliant blue eyes. Her brother,

Charles, had blue eyes, eyes that Christine had always thought beautiful. But Chad's eyes were a deeper shade of blue, so intense her breath caught in her throat everytime she looked directly into them.

She glanced at his face, comparing it to her brother's. Both men were handsome, but Chad's good looks were much more rugged, more masculine, the planes of his face harsher, his jawline stronger, his skin deeply tanned. For the first time, she noticed the bump on his nose and wondered if it had been broken at some time. Strangely the imperfection didn't detract from his looks, but added character to his face.

She glanced down, admiring the way he sat his horse. He rode with a graceful ease, a fluidity that made man and horse appear as one. Her gaze dropped to his powerful thighs, the sinewy muscles straining against his pants, and then, as if they had a will of their own, her eyes locked on his crotch. The tight pants and straddled position left nothing to the imagination, and apparently, Chad was just as well endowed in that area as he was in the exceptional breadth of his shoulders.

Shocked at her own boldness, Christine jerked her eyes away guiltily, her heart pounding furiously in her chest, her breath suddenly ragged. What's wrong with you? she asked herself. Why, you're no better than those Mexican girls devouring him with their eyes and panting after him. The next thing you know, you'll be throwing yourself at him!

Christine was so disturbed by her own shocking

behavior that she didn't notice when Chad's horse veered to avoid a clump of cactus. Her thigh brushed Chad's, and Christine felt a sudden electric shock run up her leg, stunning her.

Suddenly, Chad's presence was overpowering, frightening her in its intensity. Christine turned her horse sharply away from his, fighting for composure, her heart pounding in her ears.

Chad had not been unaware of the brief contact of their bodies. He had felt the same thing Christine had felt . . . and had been just as stunned. Once more, he knew Christine had felt something too. His sharp eyes had not missed the jerk of her leg or the sudden flush on her face.

But what had it meant to Christine? Chad wondered. For himself, he had recognized it as a sudden, unexpected flare of passion. Had the brief, intimate touch excited her as it had him? Or had it embarrassed her? And why had she moved away from him so suddenly, almost as if his touch repulsed her?

Then Chad remembered other times Christine had acted strangely when he had touched her. The thought that his touch repulsed her infuriated him. Well, she didn't have to worry about him making any unwanted advances, he thought angrily. There were too many willing women around, hot-blooded women. No, he certainly didn't need this cold-blooded bitch riding beside him. To hell with her!

Chad spurred his horse and rode in front of Christine. The rest of the morning, he kept his distance. Even when he gave her her shooting lesson that afternoon, he was very careful not to get too close.

That night when Christine took her clothes to hang them out to dry, Chad was again leaning against the fence and smoking. He stood with his back to her, his attention apparently on something in the distance. She glanced around quickly, wondering where Margarita was and surprised that she wasn't hanging on to him possessively, as she usually took every opportunity to do.

She hesitated, remembering her body's reaction to the accidental brush of their legs that morning. She had finally admitted to herself that Chad did hold some sort of strange power over her. But it wasn't the same kind of power her uncle had held. It was something different, something she had no defenses against. And for that reason, it was all the more frightening. Maybe she should go back in before he noticed her. She could come back later after he had left.

But before she could retreat, Chad turned from the fence and squinted into the darkness. "Is that you, Chris?"

Christine suppressed a gasp. Ridiculously she felt as if she had been caught. But how silly, she thought, wanting to turn and flee like some frightened rabbit just at the sight of him. Gathering her courage, she forced herself to walk to the fence, saying, "Yes, it's me. I just came out to hang up my wet clothes."

Christine walked to the fence and draped the dripping wet shirt and pants over the crude rails, very aware of Chad's gaze on her and her trembling hands. Damn, why did he have to stare at her like that? It made her so nervous. She turned and started to walk back into the house.

"It's a beautiful night, isn't it?" Chad commented.

Small talk? Christine thought in surprise. Why, that certainly wasn't like him. Usually he was all business. She turned and looked about her, for the first time aware of her surroundings.

The night sky was filled with a million glittering stars, and Christine gazed at them with wonder. For some reason, they looked bigger and brighter than they ever had back in New York. "Strange," she muttered half to herself, "the stars never looked that large or close before."

Chad glanced up at the stars. "It's a combination of a lower latitude and the drier air that makes them look that way."

Christine nodded silently, her attention drawn to the full moon that was just rising. She had never seen a moon like it. It was enormous, its color almost blood red before it faded to a fiery orange.

Seeing her look of awe, Chad said, "That's what we call a Comanche moon out here. It's beautiful, isn't it?"

"Yes, it is," Christine barely breathed. Then she turned to Chad, saying, "But why do you call it a Comanche moon?"

"Because the Comanches make their raids across the border when there's a full moon like this one."

Christine's eyes flew back to the barren

landscape, now bathed in soft white moonlight. Were the Comanches out there somewhere? She could almost see them racing their horses across the flat land, then up and down the twisted arroyos, the moon casting an eerie light before them, their minds intent on plunder and rape and murder. Maybe even now they were surrounding them, crouching behind the cactus clumps or lurking behind the mesquites, creeping closer and closer.

A coyote howled in the distance, a low, mournful wail, and Christine jumped back in fright. It took a minute for her to recover, and when she did, she realized she was in Chad's arms.

Feeling very foolish, she muttered, "I'm sorry. I was just thinking about the Indians and then . . ."

Christine's voice trailed off as she watched Chad's eyes darken with passion and then his mouth slowly descend to cover hers. For a brief minute, she was stunned by the suddenness of the kiss, but as Chad's sensuous lips moved softly over hers in an achingly sweet kiss, she trailed her hands over his broad shoulders to tangle her fingers in the soft curls at the nape of his neck, pulling him even closer. When Chad's mouth left hers, she whimpered in protest, afraid he was leaving her, afraid he would stop kissing her and rob her of all of these warm, wonderful sensations she was feeling.

But Chad left a trail of fiery kisses over Christine's face and temple before his lips returned to claim hers in a deeply passionate kiss that left Christine's senses reeling and made her knees buckle. Still locked in that searing kiss, Chad drew her to the ground, and Christine made no protest. She was whirling in a warm vortex of sensation, weakly clinging to Chad's broad shoulders as if her life depended on it.

Chad half covered Christine with his body as his lips nibbled at the long column of her throat, then traced the outline of her shell-like ear with his tongue. Christine shivered with delight, drawing him even closer, then gasped as she felt Chad's warm hand slide inside her bodice and caress her breast. But as his nimble fingers flicked across, then gently rolled the sensitive nipple, all thought of protest vanished in the warmth curling deep in her belly. Then Chad's mouth was covering hers again, the tip of his tongue brushing hers, following their outline before he pressed insistently against her teeth, demanding entrance. She opened to him willingly, her heart pounding in her ears as his teasing, probing tongue searched the warm recesses of her mouth. She arched her body into his, seeking to get closer to that heat that threatened to consume her, and when Chad shifted his weight, pressing that long, hot, throbbing proof of his arousal against her thigh, she felt a momentary pang of fear, followed by a thrill of incredible excitement, the warm coil deep in her spiraling outward, leaving the very core of her womanhood throbbing with need.

Under Chad's searing kisses and sensuous caresses, Christine was drowning in a sea of feverish heat. All restraint flew as she instinctively pressed herself against Chad's rock-hard erection, her body aching for release. Totally aroused, she started kissing Chad back, her tongue at first meeting his tentatively, then more boldly and urgently, performing an erotic dance as it flicked around his. Through her dulled senses, she barely heard Chad's sharp intake of breath and then his tortured groan as he pulled away abruptly, breaking the impassioned kiss.

Christine looked up in a daze to see Chad gazing down at her, his breath coming in ragged gasps, his look intense with some emotion she did not recognize. And then she plummeted to earth as she watched Chad's expression turn to a frown and his lips tighten into a hard, taut line.

Chad pushed her away and stumbled to his feet. Then he muttered in a half-choked voice, "Good night, Chris," before he whirled and strode rapidly away.

After Chad had rushed away, Christine lay reeling in a mixture of confusion and thwarted desire. Finally she pulled herself up and weakly clung to the fence railing, feeling a profound loss, her lips still throbbing from Chad's fiery kisses, her body still aching with need. Why had he rejected her again? A small tear trickled down her cheek as she fought back a painful sob.

Chapter Seven

Chad's eyes narrowed as he watched Christine walk across the yard toward him the next morning. He was deeply troubled. He could no longer deny his sexual attraction to Christine. He had wanted her last night, still wanted her. He had been amazed at how well their bodies had seemed to match, mouth to mouth, breast to chest, thigh to thigh. And he was no longer worried that his touch might be repulsive to her or that she might be angered by his advances. No, Christine had been more than willing, almost eager. It would have been so easy to have taken her. And he almost had. Christ! He had been on the verge of making passionate love to her right there in the wide open, right there in the middle of the Morales's yard.

But it wasn't the realization of where they were that had stopped Chad from making love to Christine. He had found he couldn't do it to her, for he had sensed that Christine was particularly vulnerable, and over the past few days, he had come to respect her too much to take advantage of her weakness just to satisfy his needs. She wasn't some cheap tramp to be taken for a quick tumble and then tossed aside when his lust was sated. No, Christine deserved better than that. She was a lady and, undoubtedly, a virgin. She was the kind of woman for whom sex and commitment went hand in hand. And Chad wasn't about to make any commitment, nor was he in the position to, having to make his living the way he did.

He had tossed and turned half the night, cursing himself. Once more, he had renewed his vow that it wouldn't happen again. If it killed him, he'd keep their relationship strictly business.

As they rode that day, Chad was careful to keep his instructions to Christine brisk and impersonal. Christine was very aware of his change of attitude, an attitude that bewildered her and made her even more miserable. She would almost think that his kisses and caresses the night before had been a figment of her imagination, except that the feel of his warm lips and of his body against hers was much too vivid in her memory. Chad had awakened the woman in Christine and left her aching for a fulfillment that, in her innocence, she couldn't understand.

As they rode, she told herself that she preferred his crisp, businesslike manner to his bursts of anger and his taunting, but that wasn't true. Even his taunts had had a teasing quality about them, and his anger had seemed human. But this cold, insensitive, unapproachable man riding beside her didn't seem human at all. In fact, he reminded her of her uncle, making her even more acutely uncomfortable in his presence.

A little later in the morning, they met the Rio Grande and followed the muddy, sluggish river downstream for several miles. When they stopped for a brief breather beside the stream, Christine was acutely aware of the uncomfortable silence between them. She looked about her, trying to find something to say to break the awkward tension between them.

Her eyes fell on the river, a bare trickle of water at this point. "Whoever named the Rio Grande must have been blind. From what I've seen of it, there's certainly nothing grand about it."

Chad glanced at river and then, to Christine's relief and delight, chuckled and said, "We Texans have a saying about the Rio Grande, Chris. It's a mile wide, a foot deep, too thick to drink and too thin to plow, always flooding and always changing its course."

Christine sensed the tension easing between them and laughed, partly from relief and partly at what Chad had said.

Chad was startled by her laugh, a laugh that was delightful to his ears. It wasn't timid or simpering like many women's. She didn't giggle or titter. It was a robust laugh, a spontaneous burst of joy, a clear tinkling sound that pleased his ears and lifted his spirits, a sound that made him want to laugh right along with her. He frowned, realizing that he had only heard her laugh twice and wishing that she would do it more often. He was so distracted by this thought, that it took him a minute to realize that she was saying something.

"What did you say?" he asked.

"I said, I can see the Rio Grande being a foot deep. But a mile wide? That's ridiculous!"

Her beautiful golden-green eyes were sparkling with mirth, her mouth, still curved with a smile, soft and inviting. Chad stared at those lips, remembering only too well what they had felt like pressed to his own the night before. God, he wanted to kiss her again, so badly he could taste it.

He tore his eyes away from her face and forced himself to concentrate on the river beside them, saying, "You can't judge the Rio Grande by what you've seen of it, Chris. It's a mighty long river, traveling over nineteen hundred miles from where it starts in the Continental Divide to where it empties in the Gulf of Mexico. And it's a river of many faces and moods. In the spring, when all those millions of tons of water comes thundering down out of the mountains, this river turns into a wild, rampaging monster. That's why the Mexicans call it the Rio Bravo del Norte, the Bold River of the North."

Chad's eyes continued to scan the river, its bed cracked and peeling from baking in the hot sun. "At this time of the year, the river is muddy and sluggish. In some places, you can actually walk across it without even getting the soles of your boots wet."

Chad's voice lowered as he drawled softly, "But

in other places, it's beautiful. Up in the mountains, where it begins, the water is crystal clear, bubbling and dancing over the rocks, and it is surrounded by tall, graceful aspens. In some places, it's wide and deep, ambling slow and serene through big cottonwoods. Farther south, it narrows and tumbles through big black canyons, turning pure white with dangerous, wild rapids. And down by Brownsville, near the mouth of the river, it's wide and deep, and surrounded by coconut palms. That's why the Spanish, who first discovered it in the 1500s, named it 'Rio de Las Palmas.'"

Christine shivered. The soft sound of Chad's husky drawl had been almost caressing, and she hadn't missed the hint of pride in his voice as he described the river, an almost poetic description. Why, he loves this land, she thought in amazement. Somehow this deep love of the land didn't fit in with the image of a cold-blooded *pistolero*. Again, Christine had caught a glimpse of the inner man, and to her surprise, she longed to know him better. She wished she had the courage to ask him why he made his living by hiring out his gun. Surely something must have forced him to his way of life. But Chad had never discussed himself, his past, his dreams for the future, and Christine sensed he would resent her intrusion into his personal life.

That afternoon when Chad had finished giving Christine her shooting lesson, she asked, "When are we leaving?"

"When I think you're ready," Chad replied.

147

"But I'm ready now," Christine objected. "I can ride, and I know how to shoot. We're just wasting time."

"Chris, we leave when I say so and not one minute sooner," Chad replied adamantly.

Christine sighed in frustration and snapped, "Oh, all right!"

She turned and walked angrily toward the house. Chad called after her, "Don't forget to clean your carbine."

Christine bristled and mumbled hotly to herself, "Do this, do that, don't do this, don't do that! Why, he's nothing but a big, bossy bully!" She slammed her bedroom door and then stopped, frozen in terror.

A grotesque, foot-long monster lay on her bed, its gray body topped with a ridge of spiky, pointed scales from neck to tapered tail. The horrible-looking monster stared at her with beady, black eyes, the pouch below his head and neck swinging loosely.

Christine watched, too frightened to scream, as the monster scuttled off the bed on his short, squatty legs and headed toward the window on one wall. Without thinking, Christine raised her carbine and fired at him. The shot was wide by five feet and hit the wall, the adobe crumbling and falling to the floor in a large crash.

The frightened reptile tried frantically to crawl up the wall as Christine discharged the cartridge and fired again. Hearing the metallic click of the hammer, she remembered that that was her last bullet and grabbed the carbine by the muzzle, intending to club the monster to death with the carbine's butt.

The door crashed open as Chad rushed into the room. He wrenched the gun from Christine's hands and threw it on the bed, yelling, "What in the hell are you doing?" He swung her around roughly. "Have you gone completely crazy?"

Christine looked up at the big Texan and sighed in relief, her knees buckling weakly beneath her. Chad caught her arm, steadying her. Making incoherent sounds, she pointed with a shaky hand to the monster, still clawing frantically at the wall and trying to get away.

Chad frowned, saying, "Chris, that's just a desert iguana. He's perfectly harmless."

"Harmless?" Christine's voice squeaked. "But . . . but he looks like . . . like a prehistoric monster," Christine stammered.

"He might look like a monster, but he's just a harmless lizard," Chad replied. "As a matter of fact, the Morales family keep him around here as a sort of pet."

"Pet?" Christine croaked.

"Yes, he eats flies and insects."

Chad looked at the gaping hole in the wall and shook his head in disgust. "Well, I guess this is one time I should be glad your aim is lousy, but did you have to shoot up the Morales's home?"

"Oh, Chad," Christine said, fighting back tears of humiliation. "I feel so foolish."

Chad looked down at her in surprise, realizing that this was the first time she had used his first name. Strangely, it pleased him. He smiled down

149

at her, saying, "Don't worry about it, Chris. I'm sure they can fix the hole."

Señora Morales and Margarita rushed into the room, their faces anxious. Señora Morales looked at the hole in the wall and gasped in shock. Margarita ran over to the lizard and picked him up in her arms, crooning over him, looking at Christine reproachfully.

At that minute Christine felt she could have died from embarrassment. "I'm sorry. I didn't . . . I didn't realize he was a pet. He looked so dangerous," she said, her face blushing furiously.

"Let me explain, Chris," Chad said. He spoke to Señora Morales in Spanish, motioning first to the lizard and then to Christine. When he had finished, Señora Morales smiled at Christine in forgiveness, but Margarita's eyes glittered with hate.

"You are a stupid *gringa*!" the Mexican girl hatefully spat out and left the room, rocking the hideous lizard in her arms.

Christine shuddered, more at the thought of Margarita actually holding the grotesque lizard than her words. She turned back to Señora Morales and smiled nervously. The plump, kindly woman smiled back and reached for Christine's hand to reassure her, but when she touched it, Christine jerked the hand back in pain.

Chad took her hand and held it palm up. Big blisters were already forming on it. "My God, Chris, didn't you realize that rifle barrel was hot? Look at that burn!"

Christine was as shocked as he. She had been

150

too frightened to even notice her hand was burned. "I guess I didn't realize," she muttered. feeling even more stupid.

Señora Morales looked at the burn with concern. She mumbled something to Chad in Spanish and left the room.

"Sit down, Chris," Chad said firmly. "Señora Morales has gone to get something for that burn."

The Mexican woman returned and quickly applied a clear, viscous substance to Christine's hand. Almost immediately, the pain subsided. Christine smiled up at her gratefully.

"*Gracias, gracias, señora*," Christine said.

"*De nada*," Señora Morales answered, patting her cheek affectionately.

After Señora Morales had left, Chad said, "Chris, you've got to be careful down here. In Mexico, things that often look the most dangerous are the most innocent. And things that look the most innocent are often the most deadly. For example, the coral snake has a lethal bite, but because it's small, children often think it is harmless and pick it up, attracted by its bright yellow, red, and black bands."

"You don't have to worry about that," Christine said. "I'm not about to pick up *any* snake."

Chad grinned at Christine's frank admission. Then he noticed someone walking down the hall. "Pablo, come here," he called.

The little Mexican boy ran into the room, his face inquisitive, his black eyes twinkling. "*Sí, señor.*"

Chad said something to the boy in Spanish.

The boy's face broke into a broad smile as he rummaged in his pants pocket, saying, *"Sí, sí, señor."* He held his hand out proudly for Christine to see.

Christine looked down at a squat, brownish, toadlike creature, its body covered with horny spikes, especially around its head.

"It's a horned toad," Chad said. "And like the iguana, it's perfectly harmless. Some people think they spit blood, but actually they eject it from their eyes."

Christine turned pale.

Chad chuckled. "It's a harmless protective mechanism they use to frighten off their enemies. Actually, they're helpful to have around. I've never seen anything that can eat ants like a horned toad. And I'll bet every kid in west Texas and Mexico has had one for a pet at some time or another. I did myself when I was a boy. Called him Sam."

Pablo grinned, saying, "The *señorita*, she would like to hold it?"

Christine's stomach felt suddenly queasy.

"No, I'm afraid not Pablo," Chad said. He pointed to Christine's hand. "You see, she burnt her hand."

Pablo bent and looked at Christine's hand sympathetically. He rose, smiling down at the horned toad in his hand, stroking it affectionately. Then he shoved his hand in his pocket, horned toad and all, and skipped from the room, calling, *"Adiós."*

Chad turned to Christine, saying, "You see,

looks can be deceiving down here. You'll have to be careful."

"But how will I know what's dangerous and what isn't?"

"Ask before you touch," Chad replied. Grinning, he looked pointedly at the hole in the wall. "Or shoot."

Christine averted her head in renewed embarrassment. Chad walked from the room, still grinning.

Then he stopped at the doorway, all signs of humor gone from his face. "And, Chris, I'd better not catch you using your gun as a club again. That carbine cost forty bucks, and it's not made to take that kind of abuse. Repeater carbines are hard to come by in Mexico, so you had better take care of it."

Chad turned and walked down the hallway before Christine had a chance to reply. As he ambled down the narrow corridor, his mood was thoughtful. Chad knew the Morales family never allowed the iguana in the house. Then how had the lizard gotten in Christine's room? Chad strongly suspected Margarita, remembering her outburst a few nights before. He wondered now if that bit about Diablo hadn't been intentional too.

Chad sat down on his bed, disgusted with the whole thing. He was just as anxious as Christine to leave, and he was wasting valuable time. Obviously Christine hadn't changed her mind about going along. No, he was going to have to give her more than a taste of what traveling in Mexico would be like. He was going to have to take her with him after all, at least for a few days until she discovered what the trip would really entail.

He still didn't like the idea of taking her along, not even for a few days. True, she could ride passably well, as well as most of those Yankee speculators. And although her aim was lousy, she had proved today that she wasn't afraid to use a gun if she had to. He had to admit he admired her courage. If she had really been as frightened of the iguana as she appeared to be, it had taken guts to attack him. Most women would have screamed bloody murder or fainted. But still, taking a woman into Mexico, even for just a few days, was a crazy, fool thing to do. That whole territory was swarming with Indians and outlaws, not only Mexicans, but Americans who had slipped across the border to avoid the law.

And Christine was a woman. And what a woman! He was still amazed that she could look more feminine, more alluring in pants than a skirt. Just thinking about that seductive walk of hers made his heat rise. And remembering the feel of her soft body against his, her sweet, warm lips opening to him, sent his senses reeling. Hell, even after his renewed vow to keep it strictly business this morning, he hadn't been able to keep his eyes off her. She was beginning to get to him. Being alone with her on the trail and keeping his hands off her was going to be sheer hell.

What in the hell's the matter with you? Chad asked himself. You're not some callow youth in the first throes of passion. Surely you can control yourself better than that? Besides, once you get on the trail, you'll be too damned busy tracking and watching out for Indians and outlaws to even notice Christine's charms.

He forced his mind back to his main problem, that of getting Christine to change her mind about going with him on the rescue attempt. He still felt sure once she was actually on the trail and found out how rigorous it was, she'd cry off. But how long on the trail would it take before she changed her mind? A few days? A week? If it took as long as a week, he'd be in serious trouble. By the time he brought her back to the border, he'd never have enough time to reach her brother before the ransom date. Damn it, what was he going to do?

A plan began to form in Chad's mind. He could travel southeast, following the Rio Grande. That way, they would be moving gradually southward, and when Christine changed her mind, he could drop her across the border at the nearest Texas town and head directly west. It was a roundabout way of reaching his destination, but it was better than sitting around here wasting time.

Yes, that was the best thing to do, Chad decided firmly. Besides, if they stayed around here much longer, there was no telling what Margarita might try next. Chad frowned, puzzled by the girl's vindictiveness. He had always thought her such an innocent, sweet girl. Chad rolled to his back and drifted off to sleep, thinking that just goes to show you, all women are bitches at heart.

That night at the dinner table, Chad announced his decision to leave in the morning. Christine wondered at his abrupt change of mind. But if Christine was surprised, Margarita was thoroughly crushed. At Chad's announcement, the Mexican girl rose from the table and ran crying from the room.

Later, Chad knocked on Christine's door and, when she opened it, handed her a pair of saddlebags.

"Here are your saddlebags," Chad said. "I've already loaded one side with your ammunition. You can use the other for your clothes."

Christine looked at the small bag in dismay.

As if guessing her thoughts, Chad said, "All you need to take is an extra change of clothes, a couple of pair of socks, a comb or brush and some soap. Anything else is just extra weight and unnecessary." He handed her the filthy serape. "You can hang this over the back of your saddle, but I thought you might like to wash it tonight."

Christine took the smelly garment, her nose wrinkling from its strong odor.

Chad looked at her, a hopeful gleam in his eyes. "You're sure you don't want to change your mind?"

Christine lifted her head stubbornly. "No, of course not."

Chad gave her a hard look and growled, "I'll see you in the morning."

After Chad had left, Christine packed the saddlebag. She rummaged through her trunk, wondering what else she could take that wouldn't be too bulky. Her eyes fell on the soft, green nightgown she had bought several months before.

Distracted from her packing, Christine picked up the gown and held it against her. It was sheerer than her other gowns and cut low at the neckline, with tiny puffed sleeves. Its bodice was gathered below the breasts, Empire style, a style that somehow made her appear shorter and smaller. Christine had tried it on only once and then was too embarrassed to wear it, realizing that it wasn't a gown for sleeping in, but for seduction. She wondered what Chad's reaction would be if he saw her in it?

A knock sounded on the door, and Christine, thinking it was Chad returning for some reason, blushed furiously at her own thoughts and guiltily shoved the gown into her saddlebag to hide it from his prying eyes.

She opened the door to see Consuelo standing in the hallway. The Mexican woman pointed to her burned hand and held up the jar of burn medicine.

Christine smiled and held out her hand. After Consuelo had rubbed the medicine on the burn, she smiled, saying, *"Gracias."*

Consuelo smiled back and rummaged in her pocket, pulling out a bar of scented soap. She handed it to Christine, saying carefully, "A gift for you, Miss Roberts."

Christine was deeply touched, not so much by the simple gift, but by the knowledge that Consuelo had taken the time and effort to learn the English words for her benefit. She blinked back tears, saying, *"Gracias, señora."*

After Consuelo had left, she sat on the bed and held the bar of soap to her nose, drinking in its sweet scent. She was so appreciative of the Mexican woman's gift and of her thoughtfulness that she completely forgot the gown she had hastily shoved into the saddlebag.

Chapter Eight

Christine was up bright and early the next morning, hardly able to contain her excitement about starting their trip into Mexico. They were finally on their way to rescue Charles.

After she had saddled Diablo and thrown her saddlebags and serape over his back, she turned and looked impatiently about for Chad. Her eyes fell on his horse standing off to one side, already saddled and waiting patiently. I wonder where he wandered off to? she thought irritably. Then she saw him ambling across the yard, with that long-legged, lazy swagger of his, leading the packhorse behind him.

When he walked up to her, Chad commented, "Well, I see you're mighty anxious to get started."

"Yes, I am," Christine admitted.

He turned and took a hat that was dangling from the pack on the horse and held it out to her, saying, "Here's your hat."

Christine looked down at the hat in his hand,

wondering why he hadn't given it to her before this? She could have used it on their rides in the hot sun. Already her nose was peeling from a slight sunburn.

"Why didn't you give it to me before now?" she snapped.

"Because I didn't have it before!" Chad snapped back. "I forgot to get the damned thing when I bought your other clothes. I had to ride into El Paso last night and pick it up."

Christine took the hat and looked down at it, realizing for the first time that it was battered and dirty. She knew her saddle, saddlebags, and gunbelt were secondhand, their leather water-stained and nicked. But the thought of wearing a secondhand hat, something that had touched someone else's skin, was repugnant to her.

"Well, at least, you could have bought me a new one!" she said irritably.

Chad snorted, saying, "Now that would have been downright stupid."

"Why? Surely they're not that expensive."

"Cost has nothing to do with it, Chris. Out here, a man might buy a new pair of boots, or saddle or gunbelt every now and then, but the one thing he doesn't buy is a new hat. Not unless he loses his or gets it shot off his head. No, the only people out here that wear brand-new hats are greenhorns. And a bandit or Indian can spot a new hat a mile off and knows the man wearing it is easy pickings." He shrugged, saying, "Why advertise your vulnerability? Now put it on, Chris."

160

Christine placed the hat on her head, her nose wrinkling with disgust. The strong odor of stale sweat wafted down to her nostrils.

Chad looked at her critically. The hat hid her silver curls and threw her face into shadow. "That's better," he said, thinking out loud.

"It stinks of sweat," Christine complained.

"Yeah?" Chad said with a sneer. "Well, so will you after today's over. Then you won't notice the smell of the hat so much."

Christine shot him an indignant look, but the effort was wasted on Chad. He was taking something else from the packhorse.

He turned and said, "Here's your gun and gunbelt. Put it on."

Christine placed the gunbelt around her waist and buckled it tightly.

"No, Chris," Chad said, "drop the gunbelt. Let it ride over your hips so that the gun rests against your thigh."

Christine rearranged the gunbelt and tied the rawhide string around her leg. The gun felt peculiar to her, its weight making her feel lopsided.

"Okay," Chad said, buckling his own gunbelt. "Let's get going. I want to get some distance in before the heat gets too bad."

Christine moved toward her horse, but stopped to stare at the gun hanging from a saddle holster on Chad's horse. She had never seen such a massive pistol. "What kind of gun is that?" she asked.

"That's a Walker Colt," Chad replied. "It's one

161

of the first six-shooters made. Colt designed it for the Texas Rangers back in the thirties. In fact, he named it after the captain of the rangers at that time. That's who I got it from, the Texas Rangers, when I used to scout for them before the war."

Christine thought the gun lying heavily against her thigh was big, but the Walker Colt was twice as big. "But doesn't it weigh you down?" Christine asked.

"You don't wear it on your hip," Chad replied. "That gun weighs over five pounds. It's designed for saddle holsters. The rangers usually carried two, one on each side of the horse. But with the new repeater carbines, the Walker's becoming obsolete now. The only reason I'm taking it is because I already have it, and where we're going, you can't have too many guns."

Well, we certainly have enough guns, Christine thought. Two pistols, two carbines, and the massive Walker. As she mounted, she wondered wryly, if the Texan had a cannon, would he drag that along too?

Christine followed Chad as he rode off, leading the packhorse behind him. After they had covered some ground and the sun had become hotter, the hat became more and more of an irritant to her. The heat seemed to intensify its offensive odor. Furthermore, the hat seemed to hold the heat, causing the top of her head to feel as if she had stuck it in an oven. Finally, Christine pushed the hat off her head, letting it hang down her back.

Chad, riding across from her, frowned and said, "You'd better keep your hat on, Chris."

"I'll put it back on later," Christine answered. "When it gets hotter."

God, she was the most stubborn woman he'd ever met! Chad thought irritably. All right, let her get a good sunburn. And with that fair skin of hers, it wouldn't take long. Then, maybe she'd learn to listen to what he said.

Shortly after they had left the ranch behind, Christine noticed Chad looking back over his shoulder. Chad caught her questioning look and said, "It's just like I figured. Your friend is back there, following us."

Christine's heartbeat quickened with fear. She had completely forgotten about the man who had tried to kill her. Her face turned pale as she muttered, "What are we going to do?"

"There're some canyons up ahead," Chad replied calmly. "We'll lose him there."

But despite Chad's confident manner, Christine didn't feel reassured. She kept glancing back apprehensively, thinking he might not be so easy to lose. Hadn't he followed her all the way from New York?

When they reached the floor of the canyon, Chad said, "All right, Chris, stick with me. This is where we shake off your friend."

Chad urged his horse into a hard gallop, and Christine followed. Had Christine not been so frightened of becoming lost herself, she wouldn't have been able to follow Chad's wild, erratic course. They veered right and then left into side canyons, up the steep sides of one canyon wall and then down the sides of another, rocks

163

scattering and sliding beneath the horses' hooves. They twisted and turned down one gorge after another, crisscrossing; careening one way and then shifting direction, up and down and around in the maze of canyons.

Christine raced behind Chad, reeling dizzily from the twisting and turning, holding on to Diablo's reins for dear life as the walls of the canyon rushed by her, her heart pounding in her chest for fear she would lose sight of the horse before her.

Then Christine froze in horror as Chad raced into a solid rock wall at the end of the canyon, seemingly headed for a disastrous collision. She blinked in disbelief when the massive rock seemed to swallow him and the horses. Only when Diablo followed in a perilous lurch around the flat rock that hid the narrow opening, did Christine realize that yet another canyon lay beyond.

As Diablo and Christine finally surfaced from the depths of the canyon, her horse scrambling madly up its steep, rocky walls, Christine saw Chad patiently waiting for them at the top.

He sat on his horse, casually looking over the rim of the canyon, smiling in self-satisfaction, saying, "I guess that takes care of him."

Christine looked at him in amazement. She and the horses were gasping for breath, drenched in sweat, their hearts still pounding from their exertion. Chad sat calmly in the saddle, looking as if he had just taken a leisurely stroll instead of a frantic, breath-taking ride.

Christine looked down at the maze of canyons

and knew that her assassin would never be able to follow their trail. She found herself almost feeling sorry for the man, picturing him wandering, lost, in the canyons for days or more until he finally died from lack of water.

"What if he never finds his way out?" Christine asked.

Chad shrugged, saying, "That's tough."

Christine stared at him, shocked at his cold-blooded attitude.

Chad saw her look and said, "Have you forgotten that that man tried to kill you, not once, but three times?"

Christine felt mixed emotions, pity for the man and fear for her own life. "No, but . . ."

"Chris," Chad said firmly, "if that man down there dies, we didn't kill him. His own greed killed him."

Chad whirled his horse and trotted off, and Christine had no choice but to follow. As the morning progressed, she found she had little time to worry about the man lost in the canyons. All of her concentration and energy were expended on keeping up with Chad.

When they finally stopped for lunch, Christine slumped to the ground in relief. Her hair was plastered to her head with sweat, her face wind- and sunburned, her lips dry and cracked. She took her canteen and gulped down the warm water greedily.

"Go easy on that water," Chad said.

"Why? Don't we have enough?" Christine asked, feeling panic rise.

"That's not the problem," Chad replied. "In this heat, the more you drink, the thirstier you get. You'd do better to limit your water to a swallow or two at a time."

He handed her a piece of cheese and a couple of tortillas.

"Is that all we're going to eat?" Christine asked in dismay.

"Trail food isn't fancy, Chris," Chad said in a hard voice. "You eat to survive, not for pleasure."

She took a bite of the goat cheese and almost choked on its strong flavor. She slumped wearily against a rock and nibbled with disinterest at the tortilla. What did it matter? she thought. She was too hot and tired to be hungry anyway.

When Chad rose and started putting the remnants of their meager lunch back in his saddlebag, Christine looked up at him with disbelief.

"We're not leaving already?" she asked.

"Yes," Chad answered. "We've been here for an hour. That's long enough for the horses to rest up."

Long enough for the horses, Christine thought. What about her? But then she remembered that Chad had not wanted her to come along, had even warned her, and Christine was much too proud and stubborn to ever give him the satisfaction of saying I told you so. She climbed wearily back into the saddle.

Chad drove them hard all afternoon, unmercifully. Christine followed, at first mumbling darkly to herself, then calling him every dirty, ugly name she could think of—a considerably long and sometimes shockingly obscene spate of words. Then, when even cursing him became too much of an effort, she rode with her eyes boring pure hatred into his back. And finally as the sun dipped low in the west, she stared at him with dull, lifeless eyes.

When Chad stopped beneath a whispering cottonwood, it was almost dark. Christine paid little attention to the lazy, muddy river beside them. She was too numb to even notice her surroundings.

She slid from the saddle and gasped as pain stabbed up her hips. Her legs seemed to be permanently bowed. With a supreme effort, she straightened them, her sore muscles screaming a protest. For a long minute, she clung weakly to the saddle.

"Better get that saddle off Diablo and rub him down," Chad said.

To Christine, his words seemed to come from a long way off. With mechanical movements, her mind detached from her body, Christine unsaddled Diablo and rubbed him down with grass. Then she staggered to the fire and collapsed, exhausted.

She watched, totally numb, while Chad prepared their meal. When he handed her a tortilla wrapped around a thick piece of fried bacon, she accepted it dumbly and raised it to her mouth. But chewing and swallowing were too much for Christine. Her exhausted body simply refused to expend one more ounce of energy. She fell asleep with the tortilla still in her hand.

Christine never knew when Chad picked her up and laid her in her bedroll that night. She didn't even awaken when he took off her boots. As he covered her with a blanket, she was dead to the world.

Chad looked down at Christine, her face fiery red from sunburn, her lips cracked and bleeding from exposure to the hot wind. Lines of exhaustion were etched on her face even as she slept. A wave of deep regret for what she was forcing him to do washed over him. He knew he was deliberately pushing her past the limits of her physical endurance to break her spirit, the same spirit he had come to admire.

Christine's proud spirit reminded him of the wild mustangs that roamed the Texas prairies. He had, on occasion, broken them too. Rode them down, pitting his own brute strength and will against their's to break their fierce spirits, until they were finally docile beneath him. Some men found breaking a wild mustang a challenge, feeling euphoric when it was done. But not Chad. He only did it out of necessity, and when it was done, he felt a deep regret, knowing that he had destroyed a thing of rare beauty.

Christine shivered in her sleep, and Chad crouched down beside her, pulling the blanket closer around her shoulders. He gazed down at her face for a minute; then he felt a sudden tenderness for her welling up in him.

Without even thinking, he bent and softly kissed her forehead, gently smoothing the curls back from her face. "I'm sorry to have to do this to you, lady," he said in a husky voice. "But it's for your own good."

Christine awakened the next morning totally disoriented. She lay looking up with confusion at the cloudless sky and then down at her dirty clothes.

"Come on, Chris," Chad called across the campfire. "It's time to get up."

Christine looked at him, only vaguely remembering where she was and not remembering bedding down at all. She moved and then groaned in pain. Every muscle in her body ached, her shoulders, her back, her legs. She felt stiff all over and doubted if she could ever move again.

"I can't move," she groaned.

Chad chuckled knowingly. "Come on, Chris, get going. What you need to do is get up and move around. Walk the soreness out of your body." His voice was totally devoid of any sympathy.

Christine rolled from the blanket, grimacing. She struggled to her feet and took a tentative step. Involuntarily, she cried out at the burning pain radiating from inside her thighs. Her eyes filled with sudden tears.

Only then did Chad take pity on her. He walked to a small twisted tree, bent, and cut off a leaf from the plant growing at its base. He handed the leaf to Christine, saying, "This is aloes. It's the same thing Señora Morales put on your hand when you burnt it. Go down to the river and rub this on that chafed area inside your legs. Put some on that burn on your face too."

Christine accepted the leaf gratefully. She limped painfully down to the river and hid behind some bushes. She smeared the slimy cut end of the leaf over her face and then on the raw area inside her legs, sighing with relief as the pain began to ease.

She walked to the river's edge and knelt, washing her face, neck and arms, wishing that she had time for a complete bath. She looked down at her filthy, smelly clothes and wondered if she should put on her clean shirt and pants this morning or wait until evening when she could wash her dirty ones.

Chad made the decision for her, impatiently calling, "Come on, Chris. What's taking you so long?"

When she entered the camp, Chad handed breakfast to her. Christine sat gingerly down on her blanket, asking, "What river is that?"

"The Río Bravo," Chad answered indifferently.

"The Río Bravo?" Christine exclaimed. "Isn't that the same as the Rio Grande?"

"Yes," Chad answered calmly. "Except on this side of the border, it's called the Río Bravo."

Christine glanced quickly at the sun, saying, "But the Rio Grande flows east."

"No, south, southeast," Chad drawled lazily.

"But we should be going directly south!"

Chad's look was hard, his jaw bunched with anger. "I know what direction to take, Chris. I'm the scout, remember? And I choose the route. In

Mexico, it's a good idea to stick close to water as long as you can. We'll follow the Rio Grande down to Ojinaga, opposite Presidio, and then we'll follow the Río Concho directly west."

"But that's the long way around. We'll be losing time!"

Chad shrugged. "We'll lose a couple of days."

"But . . ."

"Damn it, Chris! If you don't like the way I'm running this show, you can either go back to Texas and wait, or find yourself another man! Now what's it going to be?"

To Christine, there really wasn't any choice. She wouldn't do the first and couldn't do the second. "I'll stay," she mumbled.

"All right, Chris. But if you stay, I'm the boss. That means I make all the decisions. If you give me any more trouble, I'm turning around and going back. Do you understand?"

Christine dropped her head, mumbling reluctantly, "Yes."

"What?"

"Yes!" Christine cried, her eyes shooting green fire as she reached for her boots.

As she started to pull on a boot, Chad stopped her, his voice urgent. "No, Chris! Don't put on that boot yet."

Christine looked up, surprised at his tone of voice. She looked at her boot bewildered, saying, "Why not?"

"Give it here," Chad said, taking the boot from her.

He shook the boot, and a small insect fell out

onto the ground. "That's why," Chad said. "That's a scorpion. They're night crawlers and like to hide in dark places, especially boots. Never put your boots on in the morning without shaking them out first."

"They're dangerous?" Christine asked, amazed that anything so small could be dangerous.

Chad read her mind, saying, "Remember what I told you about looks being deceptive down here? The scorpion is a good example of that. He may be small, but his sting is poisonous. It may not kill you, but it can make you damned sick."

Christine watched as Chad placed the heel of his boot on the scorpion. The insect's tail curled up, jabbing its stinger into the leather of Chad's boot. He ground the insect into the ground. Christine shivered.

Chad turned, saying, "All right. Get your stuff together, and let's get going."

They followed the muddy Rio Grande that day, Chad driving them just as hard as he had the day before. The scenery grew monotonous, mesquite brush, cactus, rock and sand, and an occasional clump of cottonwoods hugging the river. The sun beat down on them unmercifully, and soon Christine was drenched in sweat. The silence was almost as unbearable as the heat, the only sounds the rhythmical clopping of the horses' hoofs, the squeaking of the saddles, and an occasional coo-coo of the Mexican whitewings.

By the time they pitched camp that evening, Christine was almost as exhausted as she had been the day before. Only the thought of a bath kept her going. As soon as they had finished eating, she took her saddlebag and headed for the river.

"Where are you going?" Chad called.

"To take a bath," Christine called back over her shoulder.

"Wait a minute," Chad said, catching up with her easily. "You'd better let me check the spot you choose first. In some places, the Rio Grande's bottom is quicksand."

Christine picked her spot, a secluded area screened by thick, mesquite brush. Chad poked at the river bottom with a stick.

"It seems solid enough," he drawled. He turned and walked away, saying over his shoulder, "Don't wade out too far. There might be whirlpools." And then as he was almost out of sight, he called, "And watch out for snakes."

Quicksand? Whirlpools? Snakes? Christine stood on the riverbank, shivering with fear. But the overpowering smell of her own odor finally motivated her to undress and step into the murky water. She bathed hastily and washed her filthy clothes, tossing them over the mesquite brush to dry overnight.

When she staggered wearily back into the camp, Chad was already asleep in his bedroll. As Christine lay down and fell into an exhausted sleep, she thought bitterly, well, I could have been bitten by a snake or drowned in a whirlpool for all he cared.

Chapter Nine

Christine awakened the next morning and gazed sleepily around the camp. Then, seeing Chad, her eyes grew wide as she gasped loudly.

Chad was standing with his back to her, shaving. At her gasp, he turned and looked at her curiously. "Is something wrong?"

Christine stared at his broad, muscular chest, particularly fascinated with the vee of tight, dark curls that tapered to a fine line at his belt and seemingly pointed straight to his manhood. She blushed furiously at her own thoughts, and snapped, "You should be ashamed, exposing yourself like that."

Chad shot a quick look down at the fly of his pants. Seeing nothing wrong, he looked up saying, "Exposing myself?"

"Yes," Christine retorted indignantly. "No gentleman would stand in front of a lady half naked."

Chad looked down at his bare chest and

grinned. "Well I guess, technically, I am half naked." His deep blue eyes bored into hers. "And you're right, I'm not a gentleman. I've never claimed to be, and furthermore, I don't want to be one. The only gentlemen out here are six feet under the ground."

Christine looked at him wide-eyed, sputtering impotently.

Chad continued. "Besides, you're not a lady either. No lady would travel all over Mexico with a man who isn't her husband or a close male relative."

Chad turned around and calmly continued to shave. Christine couldn't think of an appropriate reply, so she sat watching mutely while he shaved, her eyes glued to the rippling muscles on his shoulders and back.

He turned, drying his face with a towel. "Now, lady," Chad said, "I should warn you to get out of here. Because in about one minute, I'm going to strip off my pants and take a bath in that river." He pointed to the river right beside them.

As Chad reached for his belt buckle, Christine lost no time scampering to her feet. She rushed away, blushing hotly and muttering indignantly, Chad's mocking laughter in her ears.

That morning, Christine was glad Chad rode ahead of her so she didn't have to look him in the eye. She followed behind him, thinking, he's not only arrogant, domineering and cold-blooded, but brazen too.

Chad rode ahead of Christine, brooding on his own dark thoughts. Despite his expectations, traveling on the trail hadn't distracted him from Christine's charms. He still wanted her. Knowing that she lay just a few feet away from him the past two nights had been sheer hell. And her accusation that he was no gentleman that morning had only served to remind him of his precarious position. What she had said was certainly true. What he was thinking and wanting wasn't in the least gentlemanly.

Well, one thing was sure. He had to get release from the sexual tension Christine had built up in him, the fire she had lit in his blood. Tonight, they'd stop at that little Mexican town up ahead, and he'd dump her and find a woman and a bottle. Once he had satisfied his hunger, he'd be in control again.

As they rode closer to the outskirts of the town, Chad pulled back and said, "Better put your serape on now, Chris. We'll stop for the night at the cantina ahead."

"A cantina?" Christine said, surprised. "I thought a cantina was a saloon."

Chad shook his head, saying, "Not always. In some places in Mexico, the cantinas are also hotels and local trading posts. We'll be able to get a couple of rooms for the night and restock our supplies."

As they rode down the hot, dusty street between a row of squat adobe buildings, Chad said in a firm voice, "Now remember to walk like a boy and keep your head down. If anyone asks you anything, lower your voice and say as little as you can. If they talk to you in Spanish, just say

177

'No español.' Okay?"

Christine nodded mutely, feeling a little twinge of fear. At the stable, she watched in silence as Chad gave instructions to the Mexican youth and paid him. Then carrying her saddlebags and carbine, she followed Chad across the street to the cantina, trying to imitate his long-limbed, swaggering gait.

Once inside the cantina, Christine's nose wrinkled with disgust. The big room, which apparently served as a saloon, restaurant and general store, was smoke-filled and reeked of stale cooking odors, liquor and unwashed bodies. The floor was packed dirt, and a thin coating of dust covered everything.

Christine glanced curiously at the occupants of the cantina. Several tables were already filled with men drinking and playing cards. Judging from their slouched hats, some were Americans. Others were Mexicans, wearing wide-brimmed sombreros, many with fierce mustachios. But regardless of their nationality, they all wore guns, and they all looked mean and dangerous. Christine remembered that Chad had said many outlaws hung out in the Mexican border towns. She inched closer to his big, protective body.

Chad motioned to the bartender and talked to him in Spanish. When the Mexican turned to pick up their keys, Christine whispered to Chad, "Ask if they have a bath."

Despite himself, Chad had to smile at her words. Now wasn't that just like her? he thought. A lady right down to her bones. Worrying about a bath instead of the danger she might be in surrounded by all these outlaws and murderers.

Christine followed Chad up the rickety stairs to the second floor and down the dim, musty hallway. Chad stopped at a doorway and slipped the key into the lock, saying, "This will be your room. I'll take the one next door."

As the door opened, Christine stepped into the room, eyeing it with revulsion. Thick dust rose and almost choked her. She looked at the sagging bed, the chipped dresser with its cracked mirror, the dirty, hand-smeared water pitcher and the lone straight-backed chair, listing precariously to one side on its broken leg. I'd rather sleep outside in my own bedroll, she thought.

Chad pulled Christine aside as a grinning Mexican boy pulled in a wooden tub full of water. "They would only give us this tub," Chad said. "Water is pretty scarce around here, so we'll have to share it."

"Share it?" Christine asked in a shocked voice.

Chad chuckled, saying, "I'll go next door while you bathe. When you're through, knock on the wall, and we'll exchange rooms while I bathe."

After Chad and Christine had bathed, they went downstairs to eat. Chad weaved through the crowded tables to a darkened corner, and Christine followed. Once they were seated, she watched as Chad motioned to a Mexican woman across the smoky room.

The woman approached them, her flimsy blouse hanging off her shoulder and practically baring one big breast, her broad hips swinging

179

provocatively. She stopped at the table, smiling down at Chad in open invitation.

No one had to tell Christine what the woman was. She knew she was a prostitute by her blatant actions and cold, calculating eyes. Christine was forced to sit by as the woman took every opportunity to rub against Chad, bending over to give him a good view of her breasts, smiling seductively all the while. But what infuriated Christine was that Chad smiled back, obviously receptive to her offers.

Christine sat through the meal and watched the sickening display with growing anger. And when she saw the woman's hand slowly sliding up Chad's muscular thigh, her control broke. Her head snapped up, and she glared at the woman, her green eyes spitting fire.

The prostitute was stunned by Christine's glare; then her look turned puzzled. Finally she shrugged and walked away, calling something over her shoulder in Spanish.

"Damn it! Chris," Chad snapped. "I told you to keep your head down. What are you trying to do, let the cat out of the bag?"

Christine dropped her head, thinking furiously, No, I'm trying to keep that cat out of your bed!

When they had finished eating, Chad rose, saying, "Come on, Chris. I'll take you back to your room and see that you're safely locked in."

"What are you going to do?" Christine asked suspiciously.

"That's none of your damned business," Chad replied in a hard, tight voice.

180

Christine's face registered shock at his blunt remark. Chad sighed in exasperation. "Look, Chris. For the past three days, I've been playing the role of guide and *pistolero*. Well tonight, I'm taking some time off. I'm going to get a bottle and relax. You'll be safe enough in your room."

Having been put firmly in her place, Christine had no choice but to follow Chad up the stairs to her room. She watched as he checked the lock on her door.

When he was satisfied that the lock was secure, Chad said, "Good night, Chris. I'll see you in the morning."

After Chad had left, closing the door firmly behind him, Christine sat on the sagging bed, fighting back tears. I know where he's going, she thought. He's going back to that horrible woman.

Christine would never have admitted to being jealous. To her, it was simply a matter of pride. She knew Chad wasn't attracted to her. Twice he had rejected her. But to think that he would choose a cheap prostitute—a woman who sold herself to any and every man—over her was more than she could bear.

She rose and went to her saddlebags, searching until she found the green nightgown she had accidentally packed the night before they left El Paso del Norte. At the time, the action had seemed innocent enough, but she wondered now if, in her subconscious, she hadn't already decided to seduce Chad.

Seduce Chad. The thought shocked her. Not because she felt it was wrong, rather because she

181

still doubted she could do it. After all, he had rejected her twice already.

While Christine would never have admitted to being jealous, she was brutally honest with herself when she admitted that she desired Chad. Furthermore, she didn't feel she would be compromising her vow never to trust a man with her heart if she seduced him. She wouldn't be offering him her heart or her love. No, all she would be giving was her body.

But something Christine couldn't admit to, because she wasn't even aware of it, was that Chad had awakened more than just desire in her. His fleeting moments of gentleness and tenderness had eroded her defenses and uncovered a deep-seated hunger for a profound, all-consuming love, a love she could return just as totally.

She stripped off her clothes and slipped on the gown. She stood before the cracked mirror and studied herself critically. Yes, the gown did make her look shorter and smaller, and the flowing skirt hid her long legs. Maybe, just maybe, she thought.

Christine walked to the bed and sat on it, her hands clasped tightly in her lap to keep them from trembling, her heart racing in her chest. Patiently she waited for Chad's return.

Downstairs, Chad sat at a table, a glass in one hand and a bottle of tequila at his elbow. The prostitute sat beside him, one arm around his neck, smiling up at him seductively and talking in Spanish.

Chad paid little attention to her words.

Conversation wasn't what he had come for. She rubbed her thigh against his suggestively and ran her finger around his ear and down his neck. She leaned forward, giving Chad a full view of her heavy, full breasts with the large, dark nipples. Her hand moved up Chad's thigh and cupped him intimately, her fingers moving with practiced expertise.

But Chad felt nothing. Absolutely nothing.

He looked down at the prostitute, puzzled by his lack of response. She was pretty enough, black eyes, long black hair, her skin a warm, dusky color. Then Chad looked at her eyes again, for the first time noticing the cold, calculating gleam in them. He glanced down at her mouth, hard-looking, despite its smile. His eyes dropped to her overly lush breasts, breasts that left him feeling strangely repulsed.

Chad shoved the woman's hand away from his groin and rose. "Forget it," he said in a disgusted voice, tossing a couple of coins down on the table.

The prostitute looked up in surprise. Then as Chad turned and walked away, her face twisted into an ugly snarl as she hissed, *"Bastardo!"*

Chad ambled up the stairs and down the dim hallway, feeling frustrated and disgusted with himself. His footsteps automatically slowed as he walked past Christine's door, a vision of golden-green eyes flashing through his brain. Then his footsteps quickened and he stormed into his room, muttering darkly and slamming the door behind him angrily.

Christine had recognized Chad's footsteps in

the hallway and had been surprised that he had come back so soon. She jumped at the violent slam of his door and then sat rigid, listening.

Through the thin walls, Christine could hear the protesting squeak of Chad's bed and the dull thuds as first one boot and then the other hit the floor. A minute passed before she heard the squeak of his bed again and then . . . silence.

She sat on her own cot, her heart pounding with both fear and anticipation. Then as if in a daze, she rose, went to the door, and opened it. Without even looking to see if anyone was about, she walked down the hallway and knocked softly on Chad's door.

The door was flung open, and Chad, seeing Christine standing there in her flimsy nightgown, gasped, "What the hell!"

Then recovering from his shock, he pulled her roughly into the room, looked down the hallway quickly, and slammed the door. He whirled, his look angry, and shook her shoulders, saying, "What in the hell is wrong with you? Wandering around this place in a nightgown! Are you crazy?"

All of Christine's expectations of seducing Chad evaporated. She had hoped that seeing her in her sheer nightgown would inflame his passion. But other than that, Christine had no earthly idea of how to go about seducing a man. She had never deliberately tried to attract a man or to entice one. Nor had she ever developed the art of flirtation, like other women. All of her energies had been expended on keeping men away, repelling them. Suddenly she felt awkward and foolish. Now she would have to offer an explanation for coming to his room. She searched for an excuse, any excuse.

"I'm afraid to stay by myself," she mumbled, hanging her head in embarrassment.

Chad saw her pale face and accepted her explanation. "Chris," he said patiently, "there's nothing to be afraid of. Your lock is good and sturdy. I checked it myself, remember? Besides, I'm right next door if you need me."

Christine looked up at him, her eyes pleading.

Chad sighed in exasperation, saying, "Chris, you can't stay in here with me tonight. It wouldn't be right. Outdoors, in the open, it's different. But a man and a woman . . . alone in a room . . . all night? Something . . . something might happen."

"But we stayed in the same room at night back in El Paso."

Goddamnit, Chad thought, doesn't she know what she's doing to me? Hell, I'm no saint. How much does she expect me to take?

"That was different!" Chad snapped.

Christine's head jerked up. "Why . . . why was it different?" she demanded.

Chad looked deeply into her golden-green eyes and felt the heat rise in him. Damn her, damn her, he thought.

"Because I didn't want you then!" he blurted.

Had Chad never made the admission, Christine would never have had the nerve to do what she did next. She leaned into his big body and slipped her arms around his waist, burying her head in his chest, whispering, "Make love to me, Chad."

Chad stood, his body rigid, his jaw clenched in

185

concentration, fighting with every ounce of his will for control.

Christine couldn't stand the thought of being rejected by Chad a third time. In desperation, she raised her head, her eyes pleading, unaware of the subtle change of her words or of their profound meaning. "Please love me," she whimpered.

Chad's control shattered. His mouth crashed down on hers in a bruising, demanding kiss as his arms pulled her into a fierce, savage embrace. Christine wasn't even aware of Chad's lack of gentleness. She was too excited by the realization that Chad hadn't rejected her after all, that Chad was holding her in his arms and kissing her. She was in a daze as he threw her roughly across the bed, himself on top of her. She lay staring at the ceiling as Chad covered her face and neck with urgent, almost brutal kisses, his hands searching frantically.

Slowly, awareness returned, and Christine pushed at Chad's chest, muttering, "No, Chad, no."

The words filtered through to Chad's passion-dulled brain. His white-hot passion turned to cold fury. He grabbed her hands, wrenching them over her head, and glared down at her, his blue eyes glittering.

"No?" he croaked in a hoarse voice. "What kind of crazy game are you playing, Chris?" he asked angrily. "First you practically beg me to make love to you, and now you tell me no?" Chad shook his head, saying, "No, Chris, it's too late to change your mind. I intend to have you!"

Tears welled in Christine's eyes. She whispered, "I didn't change my mind. But . . ." Her eyes darted around the room. "But not here. Not here in this awful room."

For the first time, Chad became aware of their sordid surroundings. He looked at the cracked, dirty walls, covered with cobwebs in the corners, and at the water-stained ceiling. Suddenly, he could smell the sickening odors that seemed to permeate the room, hear the sounds of glasses clinking and drunken laughter from the cantina below them. From somewhere on the second floor, he could hear the obscene sound of a bed rocking rhythmically.

He nodded curtly and rose from the bed, pulling Christine with him. He yanked the blanket from the bed, tossed it over her shoulder, pocketed his key, and strapped on his gunbelt. Then taking Christine's hand in his, he led her to the door and opened it, peering back and forth before he pulled Christine into the empty hallway.

Chad guided her to a door at the end of the darkened hallway and opened it. A small gust of sweet, fresh air rushed in. They crept down the old stairway at the back of the cantina, the steps creaking and shaking precariously under their weight.

Chad stopped at the bottom of the stairs and looked around. Then spying a small copse of mesquite trees a short distance away, he picked Christine up in his arms and carried her toward them.

The boughs of the trees hung low, some almost

touching the ground. Chad stooped as he carried Christine under one tree and then stood, still holding her in his arms.

"Is this better?" he asked softly.

Christine looked around her. The limbs of the mesquite hung almost to the ground, forming a small enclosure and protecting them from prying eyes. She glanced up. A beautiful full moon shone down on the delicate leaves of the tree. Why, it looks as though the tree is covered with silver lace, Christine thought, in awe.

"Oh, yes," she breathed.

Chad set her gently on her feet and took the blanket from her shoulders, tossing it on the ground. Then he unstrapped his gunbelt and placed it at one corner of the blanket. Christine stood watching him, trembling, not in fear, but at her own audacity.

When Chad rose, he noticed her trembling. He frowned and lifted her chin with one finger, saying, "Have you changed your mind, Chris?"

Christine ducked her head, mumbling, "No."

"Are you afraid?" Chad asked softly.

"No, not of you," Christine admitted in a small voice.

"Then why are you trembling?"

Tears of frustration stung Christine's eyes. "Because . . . because I don't know what to do," she whispered.

Chad smiled, pleased with her innocence and her honesty. He cupped her face in both of his big hands and raised it, kissing her gently on the forehead.

"Don't worry about that, Chris," he said softly. "When the time comes, you'll know what to do."

He pulled her down on the blanket, stretching his long body beside hers. Christine lay rigid, feeling suddenly shy and very awkward.

Chad sensed her feelings, and for the first time in his life, he wasn't concerned about his own satisfaction or pleasure. Tonight, with Christine, he wanted to give, not take. And now that the white-hot heat of his passion had cooled and the driving urgency for immediate release was gone, he was willing to be patient with her.

He lay on his side, propped on one arm, smiling at her. He gently stroked her long neck with his thumb, saying, "Did you know, Chris, that there are certain spots on a woman's body that are particularly sensitive to touch? They're called erotic zones."

He bent his head and kissed her just below the ear, whispering, "This is one of them."

Christine shivered in delight; Chad smiled knowingly. He nuzzled her neck, kissing the long column softly, lazily, enjoying her taste. His hands stroked her shoulders and arms, soothing and lulling her. He rolled and cradled her in his powerful arms, dropping light teasing kisses over her face and mouth.

Christine felt as if she were floating on a warm, soft cloud. Her arms slowly twined around his neck, pulling him even closer. Chad's mouth locked on hers in a long, searching kiss that left her reeling and feeling breathless. She wasn't even aware that Chad deftly stripped her gown from her and tossed it aside. Not until she felt the breeze on her heated skin did she realize she was totally naked. And then, before she could object, Chad was kissing her deeply, hungrily, and all thought fled.

Chad's kisses grew more fiery and demanding as his hands roamed over her body, stroking her back, her lips, her legs, marveling at the silky texture of her skin. One hand rose to cup her breast, his thumb gently coaxing the sensitive peak.

Christine's breath caught in her throat at the feel of Chad's fingers at her breasts. But if she had thought the feeling Chad's fingers were invoking was pleasurable, it was nothing compared to what she felt when his warm mouth replaced his hand, kissing, nipping gently, then rolling the tender nipple around his tongue. Christine tingled all over. She was whirling in a maelstrom of delicious sensations. She grasped his head, tangling her fingers in the soft curls, pulling him even closer, never wanting to let him go.

When he lifted his head and nuzzled her throat, Christine whimpered in protest and then gasped as Chad's slender fingers slid up her thigh and touched the soft curls between her legs. She was utterly shocked at the intimate touch. Her eyes flew open, her hand darting to pull his away. But then as Chad's fingers parted the soft folds, seeking and finding, then gently, sensuously stroking the small bud, her hand fell limply away. She clutched his broad shoulders weakly, feeling as if every nerve ending in her body was suddenly sensitized, as if she had turned into a fiery torch.

Wave after wave of exquisite pleasure washed over Christine, and she arched her hips to get even closer to those warm, tantalizing fingers. Then as the waves turned to spasms that rocked her body, she thought, I can't stand any more. I'll die. I'll simply die from the pleasure. And suddenly, Chad was gone, and a throaty moan of disappointment tore from her throat.

Then he was back, pressing his warm, naked body against hers. Christine's long arms locked around him, pulling him to her greedily, thrilling at the feel of his hard, muscular body against her soft one. She squirmed even closer into his embrace and felt the proof of his desire, hot and throbbing against her. In a primitive action, she arched her hips against his, her body seeking.

Chad's passion was thoroughly aroused, his need for possession urgent. His mouth descended to lock on hers in a fierce kiss, his tongue insistent, demanding a response. His hands roamed at will, exploring, caressing, exciting.

Christine was whirling in a tornado of pure sensation, lost in the ecstasy of Chad's kisses, the wildly exciting feeling his hands were invoking. She was barely aware of his knee nudging her legs apart, his trembling body moving over hers, his rock-hard sex pressing against her softness, slowly, insistently invading.

Not until she felt the sharp, stabbing pain as Chad plunged into her, did she become fully aware of the stage their love-making had reached. She gasped at the pain and tried to pull away, but

Chad held her hips tightly, groaning in her ear, "No, Chris, don't pull away."

Christine lay beneath Chad as the pain slowly subsided to a dull ache. But as Chad started to move inside her, at first slowly, and then more and more urgently, the discomfort increased and despite Chad's passionate kisses and ardent caresses, Christine couldn't regain those wonderful sensations she had felt before. She lay beneath him, holding tightly to his shoulders as their bodies rocked, feeling strangely detached. And she watched, fascinated by the changing expressions on Chad's face as he culminated his lovemaking. First, his look was one of intense concentration, then almost of pain, and finally, as he stiffened and shuddered above her, it became rapt.

Chad collapsed over her, his breathing ragged, groaning in her ear, "Oh God, Chris."

He enjoyed it, Christine realized with total amazement.

Chad rolled from her and pulled her into the crook of his arms, kissing her tenderly on the forehead. Christine nuzzled into his embrace, happy that he was still willing to hold her even though the love-making was over. For a few minutes, she puzzled over her new knowledge. What a strange act making love is, she thought. The woman enjoys the first part, the man the last. And although she had been uncomfortable in the end, Christine didn't feel she could deny Chad his pleasure. After all, he had given her all those wonderful sensations before, and turnabout was only fair. She moved closer into Chad's warmth and dozed off.

Several hours later, Christine awakened to find Chad kissing her. "Wake up, sleepy head," Chad muttered in her ear. "Are you going to waste a perfectly good night sleeping?"

Christine looked up at him with a surprised look. "Twice in one night?"

Chad chuckled and nuzzled her throat, saying, "Lady, you can sure play hell with a man's ego."

Christine smiled. "Lady," he had called her. But not in the hateful, mocking tone he had always used before. This time when he said the word, it had been soft, caressing, almost like an endearment.

"Don't you want to?" Chad asked, holding his breath for fear she would say no.

Christine well remembered all the wonderful sensations she had experienced only a few hours before. She shivered in anticipation. "Will it feel as good?"

Chad smiled knowingly. He knew that she had not reached fulfillment the first time. "Better, I hope."

Christine couldn't imagine how it could be any better, unless he was referring to his pleasure. She sighed and stroked his muscular shoulder in silent agreement.

Chad kissed her warmly, his hands caressing her slender back. Christine's hands wandered in turn, over his broad back, thrilling to the feel of the rippling muscles. How different our bodies are, she thought. I wonder . . .

"Chad?"

"Mmm," Chad muttered, engrossed in his exploration of her neck and shoulders, his head lowering with determined intent.

"Do men have erotic zones too?"

Chad's head snapped up, his heart quickening. He smiled at her, saying softly, "Yes, they do."

Christine couldn't meet his hot, searching look. She averted her head, blushing. "Where?" she mumbled.

Chad smiled, saying, "I should think that would be obvious, Chris."

He moved closer, deliberately brushing his erect organ against her thigh. Then he took her hand in his and guided it down to his pulsating heat.

Christine gasped, then blurted, "It's so big!"

Chad chuckled, saying, "Lady, are you trying to restore my damaged ego?"

Christine's eyesbrows rose in surprise. Are men proud of being big down there? Well, why not, she thought. Didn't all women long for big breasts?

Christine pulled her hand away, embarrassed at touching him that intimately. Besides, his large, hot manhood frightened her just a little.

Chad frowned and then said gently, "Chris, have you forgotten what I said about touching? Men like to be touched too."

Christine knew what he wanted. But she couldn't force herself to touch him there. Instead, her hands wandered over the powerful muscles of his shoulders and back and dropped to stroke his lean flanks. She trailed her hand over his broad chest, marveling at the soft, tight curls. Her hand brushed his male nipple, and Christine heard Chad's hiss of pleasure. She smiled, pleased that she had discovered one of his erotic zones on her own.

Feeling Chad's body was exciting Christine almost as much as Chad's exploration of hers. Gathering her courage, she reached down for him, thinking as she touched him, Is it my imagination or had he grown even bigger?

Chad groaned at her touch, whispering huskily, "Oh God, Chris, don't stop."

He's enjoying my touching him as much as I enjoy his touch, Christine realized. But that's not fair, she thought with a pang of resentment. He gets to enjoy it all.

Chad kissed her thought away with deep, hungry, demanding kisses. His hands and mouth and tongue caressed and teased her, doing wonderful, marvelous things to her, exciting her wildly and arousing her passion until Christine was twisting feverishly beneath him, her hands clutching his broad shoulders, her breath coming in ragged gasps, her body arching against his and begging for release. And when Chad entered her and buried himself deep inside her, Christine's long legs wrapped around him in her own urgent, demanding caress.

Chad felt her long legs lock around his hips as if to squeeze the life from him. He trembled, hissing in her ear, "Jesus, lady!"

Christine felt as if her blood were liquid fire, her senses reeling, as Chad moved against her with bold, powerful, masterful thrusts that sent her climbing dizzy heights. She matched him, stroke for stroke, her hands clutching and urging him on as she whimpered little animal sounds of pleasure. And then she was soaring, whirling, spinning through space, totally unaware of her cry of ecstasy and Chad's moan of pleasure.

They lay, gasping and still shuddering with aftershocks, their bodies drenched with sweat, his head buried in the soft crook of her neck. Chad wondered in his first lucid thought, where in the hell did I ever get that stupid idea that blondes weren't passionate?

He lifted his head and gazed down at Christine's face in wonderment. Then he frowned, seeing a small tear trickle down her cheek.

"My God, Chris, did I hurt you?" he asked.

"No," Christine said in a weak sob.

"Then what's wrong?"

"Nothing's wrong. It's just . . . it's just that I got it all," she mumbled.

Chad's brow furrowed. "Got it all?" he asked in a puzzled voice.

Christine jerked away from him and rolled over, her back to him. Chad's warm hand cupped her hip. He bent and kissed her shoulder, a soft, comforting kiss. "What do you mean, Chris?" he asked gently.

Christine was feeling a mixture of awe and embarrassment, not really sure that ladies were supposed to respond that way. Maybe there was something wrong with her, some dark, primitive side of her that she had never been aware of.

"Chris," Chad said firmly, "what did you mean, got it all?"

Christine was stubbornly silent. Chad rolled her over and looked into her face, his look demanding. "Chris?" he said in a low, threatening voice.

Christine chewed her lips nervously. She averted her eyes from Chad's face and muttered, "The first time we did it, I didn't like it all. Not that last part. But you seemed to enjoy that the most. So I thought the first part was for the woman, and the last part for the man. But . . ." She closed her mouth, refusing to say any more.

Chad suppressed a chuckle. "But women are supposed to enjoy all of it."

"Then there's nothing wrong with me?" Christine said in a relieved voice.

Chad smiled warmly, saying in a husky voice, "Lady, there is most definitely nothing wrong with you."

For a few minutes, Christine was pensive. Then she asked, "Will it be that way every time?"

Chad kissed her softly, saying, "Yes, every time, if I have anything to say about it."

A thrill ran through Christine. Did he mean that tonight wouldn't be the only time he would make love to her? she wondered. Was that a promise?

Chad lay down, pulling Christine with him. She nuzzled, kittenlike, into his warmth. She looked about their private, little hideaway, covered in silver lace, and thought, how perfect it had been.

Chapter Ten

It was still dark when Christine and Chad walked back to the cantina the next morning, the eastern horizon lined with a streak of silver light. A rooster crowed somewhere in the sleepy Mexican town as they climbed the dilapidated stairs at the back of the building, Chad's arm draped lazily over her shoulder.

When they walked into Christine's room, Chad said, "As soon as you change your clothes, we'll go across the border and see if we can find a safe place for you to stay until I get back from Mexico with your brother."

Christine whirled, her face ashen. "What are you talking about? Have you forgotten? I'm going with you. You promised me. Remember?"

Chad was stunned by her words. He stared at her, his look one of total disbelief. Chad had figured the only reason Christine was so determined to go along was that she didn't trust him, but after what they had just shared, it seemed impossible that that could still be the case. He shook his head, saying, "Surely after last night, you can't possibly not trust me, Chris. You gave yourself to me completely, totally, and you were a virgin to boot. Are you telling me that after that, you still don't trust me to bring your brother back?"

Trust him? Christine thought. Why, of course, she didn't trust him. She didn't trust any man. And she hadn't given herself totally and completely. She had only given her body. Nothing else. Did he think that because of what had happened last night, she loved him, had given him her heart too? Oh no! She might give away her body, but never her heart. No, no man would ever possess her heart!

"What does trust have to do with last night? What does last night have to do with anything?" Christine screeched hysterically. "No, you promised, and I'm going!"

Chad glared at her. He wasn't sure just what his feelings for Christine were, but after their shared intimacy of the past night, he felt fiercely protective of her. He couldn't take her with him on the rescue attempt. It was just too risky, too dangerous. "Why are you so determined to go along?" he asked in an exasperated voice.

"Why?" Christine asked as if the question were the most ridiculous she had ever heard. "Because my brother is down there. That's Charles they're holding! I have to go!"

"I can understand your concern for your brother, Chris," Chad replied, trying to be patient with her. "But this rescue attempt is just too dangerous. Any sensible woman would wait in Texas and let me go down and do the job they've hired me for. Just because your brother was foolish, is no reason for you to be too."

Christine's eyes flashed dangerously. "How dare you call Charles foolish!"

"Well that's what he is!" Chad retorted. "Hell, a greenhorn like him, wandering off into the wild Sierra Madre in the middle of a war, and then getting drunk in some cantina and blabbing about his inheritance. How stupid can you get?"

"Charles is *not* stupid! Why, he's the most intelligent man I've ever known. And he's kind and . . ."

Chad was at the end of his patience, for the only thing that Christine had talked freely of was her brother. She clearly idolized the man, and Chad was sick and tired of hearing, "Charles said, Charles did."

"Oh, Christ!" Chad interjected with disgust. "Don't tell me you're going to start praising your brother's virtues again. Well, you can save your breath. I've already heard it all. Hell, no one is that perfect!"

"And I suppose you think you're perfect?" Christine spat back. "Why, you're arrogant, cold-blooded, domineering, and crude. And you're a liar!"

"A liar?"

"Yes, a liar!" Christine glared at him, saying, "You promised me if I cut my hair, dressed like a boy, learned to ride and shoot, and kept up with you, I could go along. And now you're trying to leave me behind. You lied to me!"

Chad's anger turned to cold fury. "All right, Chris," he snarled, "you can go out and get yourself killed for that crazy brother of yours, for all I care. I don't give a damn what you do!"

Chad turned and walked to the door angrily, throwing over his shoulder, "Get your stuff together. We leave in an hour."

The next two days were emotionally traumatic for both Chad and Christine. As they followed the muddy Rio Grande eastward, they both remained furious with each other. They were two stubborn people, each refusing to give, Chad snarling, Christine snapping, both glaring. Even their silence was angry, each nursing hurts and resentments.

During the daytime, Chad rode ahead of Christine, pretending cold indifference and cursing the day he'd met her. Crazy bitch, he raged silently. Her and her stupid brother! Hell, he ought to turn around and go right back to Texas. To hell with both of them!

And he was right in his first estimation of her, Chad thought. She was just like Anne. She used people, except not even Anne had sunk low enough to use her body to get what she wanted.

For in Chad's mind, he had decided that Christine had offered him her body as an added enticement to take her along with him. The thought that she had had an ulterior motive when she'd let him make love to her infuriated him, ate at him. Honest lust, he could accept. But to use his

202

own passion against him? And she'd had the audacity to accuse him of being cold-blooded, Chad thought with disgust. Well, she'd never pull that stunt on him again. She could go down on her knees and beg him to make love to her, but he'd never touch her again!

Christine rode behind Chad, glaring at his back, brooding with her own dark thoughts. Does he think because I let him make love to me that he owns me, body and soul? That giving him my body gives him the right to dominate me? And calling Charles stupid and me foolish for wanting to go along to rescue him. How could he understand how I feel about Charles, that he's all I have in the world. Why that cold-blooded *pistolero* has probably never cared about anyone but himself, has probably never had an honest emotion in his life. He's nothing but an insensitive brute, Christine thought hotly, completely forgetting the remarkable sensitivity Chad had shown when he had initiated her into love-making.

But at night, under the cover of darkness, they both lay in their separate, lonely bedrolls, each still aching for the other, and both too proud to admit they still desired each other.

On the third night, Christine tossed her bedroll on the ground and lay down with her back to Chad, as she had done the past two nights. A few minutes later, an eerie, shrill scream brought her up and out of her bedroll, a terrified look on her face. Her eyes flew to Chad, who sat calmly propped against a tree smoking a cigarette.

Completely forgetting her anger at him, she asked in a weak voice, "What was that?"

Despite himself, Chad had to chuckle at her frightened look. "An owl," he answered.

"An owl?" Christine asked in disbelief. "I've never heard an owl make that kind of noise!"

"A screech owl does. He's probably up in that saguaro cactus over there."

Christine looked around at the different cactus plants in confusion.

"The one that looks like a candelabra," Chad explained.

The owl screeched again; Christine shivered. She sat back down on her bedroll, pulling her blanket around her tightly.

Chad laughed, saying, "From the way you're acting, anyone would think you're an Apache, afraid of owls."

"Apaches are afraid of owls?" Christine asked in disbelief. From what she had heard, she didn't think the fierce Apaches were afraid of anything.

"Yes. They believe that the dead return to the living as owls," Chad explained.

"The Apaches believe in ghosts?"

Chad chuckled, saying, "The Apache have an absolute horror of death and dead people, so much so that they never mention the names of the dead or go near their graves."

"I wouldn't think the Apaches were afraid of anything," Christine commented.

Chad shrugged, saying, "Why not? They're human too. They have their fears, their hates, their enemies, both red and white."

"Red enemies? You mean other Indians?"

"Yes, the Comanche."

"But why the Comanches?" Christine asked, her curiosity aroused.

"Because of the two tribes, the Comanche is the superior. But that's the Apache's fault. He brought on his own downfall. You see, the Apache were one of the first tribes to get the horse. They stole them from the Spanish. But they never learned how to appreciate the horse or use it to its full potential. An Apache would just as soon eat a horse as ride it. Now the Comanche, on the other hand, took to the horse like they had been born in the saddle. They became the most proficient horsemen of all the southern plains Indians and used the horse to conquer the plains and dominate the other Indian tribes. With their supremacy, they pushed the Apache out of the plains and down into this arid, mountainous area. For that reason, the Apache hate and fear them."

"Apaches eat horses?" Christine asked in a shocked voice, a horrified look on her face.

"Yes, they do. They eat cactus, roots, mesquite beans, rats, snakes—anything and everything they can get their hands on. Look around at this land, Chris. It's nothing but desert and mountains. With game so scarce, the Apache can't be particular about their diet."

Christine swallowed hard before asking, "And people? Do they eat people too?"

Chad gazed at Christine. At that minute, she looked like a frightened child. She was a puzzle to him. Sometimes she was so fierce looking she was almost awesome, and then at other times, she seemed as vulnerable as a newborn babe. She was undoubtedly the most complex woman he'd ever met. A strange mixture of part child and part warrior woman.

"Well, do they?" Christine persisted.

Chad smiled before answering, "No, Chris, Apache don't eat people. But I have heard that the Karahawa Indians down on the coast of Texas are cannibals."

Christine shivered.

Chad flicked his cigarette away and lay down. Rolling to his side, he said, "We'd better get some sleep. We've got a long day ahead of us tomorrow."

The next morning when Christine went down to the river to get the clothes she had washed the night before, she couldn't find her pants. She frowned down at the rock she had left them on to dry. The shirt was still there, but the pants had completely disappeared. She stood for a minute looking about her, perplexed. Then she remembered Chad talking about the Apache the night before.

She glanced around her, her heart racing and her eyes wide with fright. Then, utterly terrified, she ran back to camp, stumbling and falling several times in her wild flight.

Chad saw her running back to camp, and called, "What's wrong?"

"My pants . . . they're gone," Christine answered, gasping for breath. "Indians . . . Indians must have gotten them."

Chad laughed, saying, "Chris, Indians may steal your horse, but they won't steal your pants. No, a coon probably took them. They're night prowlers and notorious thieves."

"You mean some animal took my pants?" Christine asked, her fear quickly replaced with anger. "But that's the only change of pants I have!"

"Take it easy, Chris," Chad said, chuckling. "Once the coon discovered your pants weren't something to eat, he probably dropped them. Come on, we'll go look for them. More than likely, he didn't carry them too far off."

They found Christine's pants about a hundred feet from where she had left them. The pants were filthy from being dragged in the dirt. But Christine didn't get mad until she saw the ragged, chewed hole in the seat of the trousers.

Poking her finger through the hole, she glared at it and mumbled, "Why, that little bastard!"

Chad's dark eyebrows rose in surprise at her unladylike words. Would she never cease to amaze him? he thought. Then he threw his dark head back and roared with laughter.

Christine gave him a murderous look. She turned and flounced away angrily, thinking, If that coon had to chew on anything, why couldn't it have been the leg or waistband? Or better yet, why couldn't he have picked the big, arrogant Texan's pants?

Later that morning, Chad rode ahead of

207

Christine, as he had done in the days before. For the third time in the past thirty minutes, he glanced back over his shoulder at her. He was accustomed to riding alone for hours—even days—at a time over the desolate Texas frontier, with only his horse for company. The silence and seclusion had never bothered him before. In fact, he usually enjoyed the solitude. Even when he had ridden with the Texas Rangers, it hadn't been unusual for them to ride all day with only a word or two between them. But that morning, Chad felt the need for company, not just anyone's company, but Christine's.

He hesitated. He was still half angry at her for the way she had used him. But it seemed childish to continue ignoring each other. He still had no intention of ever letting her use him again, but that didn't mean they couldn't be civil to one another.

Having made his decision, he turned his horse back to where Christine rode and, pulling up beside her, said in a casual voice, "We're entering a narrow desert valley now." He nodded to the barren mountains north of them, saying, "Those are the Quitman Mountains over there."

Christine nodded in reply, then was surprised when he continued to ride beside her, instead of pulling ahead as he had done since their violent argument at the cantina. She was pleased, not because she was bored with the tedious ride, but because, as much as she hated to admit it, she had sorely missed his company the past few days.

He pointed to a snake sunning on a rock a few

208

yards away from them, saying, "That's a desert rattlesnake. Some people call them sidewinders because of their peculiar sideways movements."

Christine nodded, shivering with revulsion.

As they continued to ride, Chad pointed out things he thought might interest her: a peculiar bird he called a roadrunner, various species of cactus, unusual rock formations. Christine listened attentively and occasionally asked questions. Even when he was silent, she was content just to be in his company, her eyes greedily sneaking glances at him.

That night, Chad walked into the camp carrying several quail in each hand, announcing, "We'll have fresh meat tonight."

"I didn't hear any gunshots," Christine said in surprise.

Chad chuckled, saying, "No, I didn't shoot them. I snared them. I'm afraid if you put a .44 into one of these, you wouldn't have much left."

Christine looked down at the small birds with pity, convinced she couldn't eat a bite of the poor little things. But as the tantalizing aroma of roasting meat filled the air, she was forced to change her mind.

She ate hungrily, digging her small teeth into the delicious roasted meat. Her appetite matched Chad's, quail for quail, and when she had finished, Christine sighed deeply, contentedly, and lay down in her bedroll.

But Christine couldn't get comfortable, not because of the hard, rocky ground beneath her, for Christine had become accustomed to that discomfort. Unbelievably, she couldn't get comfortable because she was too cold. How can you be cold in the middle of a desert? she asked herself. She pulled her blanket closer, shivering, her teeth chattering.

Chad, lying in his own bedroll, saw Christine's shivers and felt the urge to take her in his arms and comfort her. The urge irritated him. What in the hell is wrong with you? he asked himself angrily. First you go and snare those damned birds so she can have fresh meat to eat, and now you want to comfort her? Have you forgotten that you want her to be miserable and uncomfortable so she'll change her mind about going along?

He said in a hard voice, "Better pull your bedroll closer to the fire, Chris. The air is dryer here in the desert and doesn't hold the heat. It'll get even colder later on."

Christine heard the hard tone of Chad's voice, a tone that told her he still resented her coming along. If she moved the bedroll closer, he would probably throw it in her face later on, reminding her she was just a weak woman. Well, she'd show him! Stubbornly, she stayed where she was.

But long after Chad had fallen asleep, Christine continued to shiver. She glanced over her shoulder at him, sleeping so comfortably by the toasty fire. Well, if he could do it, why couldn't she?

Taking care not to awaken him, Christine rose and pulled her bedroll closer to the fire. She lay down and pulled the blanket over her, sighing in contentment as the warmth enveloped her. She

210

rolled sleepily to her side, and then was suddenly wide awake, shocked at how close she lay to Chad, their bodies only a foot or two apart.

Had Chad been awake, Christine would probably have moved her bedroll farther away. But Chad was sound asleep, and Christine found herself studying him. His face was relaxed in sleep, his usual cynical look gone. Christine glanced at the stray lock of dark hair that hung over his forehead and smiled. He doesn't look so fierce and dangerous now, she thought.

Her eyes dropped to gaze with admiration at his broad shoulders and chest. She stared at his chest, mesmerized, remembering all too well what it had looked like naked the day he had shaved, the muscles rippling in the sunlight, the dark hairs tapering down, as if pointing to his manhood. Blushing furiously at her own thoughts, she jerked her eyes away from his body and back up to his face, locking on his mouth. Usually tight set, it was relaxed in sleep, and her eyes feasted on his sensual lips. The memory of the night he had held her in his powerful arms and made love to her came flooding back and, with it, all of those wonderful sensations she had felt. Suddenly she was warm, too warm. She pushed the blanket back down and quickly rolled onto her opposite side, feeling suddenly very lonely and miserable.

It was a long time before she fell asleep that night.

The next day, Chad was following Christine

211

through a narrow, rocky gorge. Preoccupied with his thoughts, he had fallen behind her without noticing it.

He glared at her back in frustration. Damn it, he would have sworn she would have begged off by now. But the last few days, Christine, instead of getting more exhausted and disgusted, had seemed to rally, and Chad wondered what source within her had provided her with the strength and determination to do so. Who would have thought that a greenhorn like her, and a woman to boot, would take to the trail the way she had, Chad mused with a mixture of admiration and disgust.

Chad's horse whinnied and pranced nervously beneath him, jerking on the reins. Alerted, Chad looked about him, trying to determine what had disturbed the horse. He glanced ahead and saw Christine struggling to control Diablo, the big stallion skittish and trying to rear.

All Chad's senses were sharp with alarm. "Chris, come back!" he yelled.

But Chad's warning came too late. The cougar, crouched on the ledge above them, sprung from the rock, snarling, his teeth bared, his long claws unsheathed, his yellow eyes intent on the woman and horse below him.

Chad's gun exploded, the loud noise reverberating off the walls of the canyon. The cat dropped limply, just short of his mark, as Diablo reared in terror, frantically pawing at the air. Christine was thrown hard to the rocky ground below her.

Chad ran to Christine's limp, crumpled form,

cursing himself for being every kind of fool. As he crouched beside her, she sat up, a dazed look on her face.

"What happened?" she muttered, her head spinning crazily.

"A cougar jumped you," Chad replied. He motioned to the ledge. "From up there."

Christine nodded and then looked up with anxious eyes. "Is Diablo all right?"

"He's fine," Chad answered. "I shot the cat before he got to you. But are you all right?"

Christine rubbed the back of her head and winced. "I think I hit my head."

"Here, let me look," Chad said, pushing her hand away. He parted her hair gently and saw the angry swelling. "That's a good-size goose egg you've got there." He sat back on his heels, looking at her with concern. "Are you hurt anywhere else?"

Christine was much more shaken by Chad's concerned manner than her fall. Besides, he was sitting far too close for comfort.

"No, I think I'm all right," she said, stumbling to her feet hastily. She took a step and gasped.

"You must have twisted your ankle," Chad said, bending to pick her up in his arms.

"No!" Christine cried in alarm. She well remembered what had happened the last time Chad had held her in his arms. "Just help me to that rock."

Chad frowned, then supported her as she walked to the rock. Christine limped, hardly feeling her pain, acutely aware of Chad's muscular thigh brushing against hers, his powerful arm around her shoulder, his heart thudding against her arm. She felt suddenly dizzy, and knew it had nothing to do with her fall.

She sighed with relief as Chad sat her on the rock and then became even more disconcerted as he slipped off her boot and gently probed her ankle.

"I don't think it's too bad," Chad said. "But we had better wrap it good and tight before we put your boot on."

Christine watched as he wrapped her foot and ankle, her heart hammering wildly in her chest. "I'm sorry I fell off my horse," she said, more to distract herself from the feelings his touch was arousing in her than anything else.

Chad looked up at her and frowned. "You didn't fall off, Chris. The horse threw you. And there aren't many people who could have stayed in the saddle with a horse as wild as Diablo was." He shook his head. "No, if it was anyone's fault, it was mine. I should have been watching closer."

Christine gaped at him in disbelief. She couldn't believe the arrogant Texan would ever admit to making a mistake or being wrong about anything.

Chad looked up from slipping her boot on and smiled. Christine looked at that smile and then into his deep blue eyes and caught her breath. Her heart raced even faster.

"Do you think you could ride another mile or two?" Chad asked. "I'd like to get out of this canyon."

"Yes, yes," Christine muttered, only too anxious to get away from his close proximity and the overwhelming sensations it was arousing.

When they stopped for their noon meal, Christine limped to a rock to sit down and then froze. A lizard at least two feet long, its scaly body covered with black, yellow, pink, and orange bands, moved toward her. Despite her fear, Christine stood, rooted to the spot as the lizard moved closer and closer on his short, squat legs.

"Don't move, Chris," Chad's voice, low and warning, came from behind her.

Then she heard the deafening roar of Chad's gun, saw the familiar orange-white smoke of the black powder.

Chad grabbed her arm roughly, yanking her around. "Why in the hell didn't you shoot it?"

Christine stood, trembling violently, her face pale. "I didn't know. You said . . . you said not to shoot. To ask first."

Chad was a little shaken himself. That was twice in the same day that Christine could have been killed. If anything should happen to her . . . His mind refused to complete the thought.

He looked over her shoulder at the dead gila monster and frowned, saying, "I'm afraid I gave you some bad advice, Chris. That's a gila monster and he's poisonous. And I'd say from the looks of him, he was pretty hungry too."

Christine refused to look back. "How do you know that?"

"Because his tail is flat," Chad replied. "A gila monster stores his fat in his tail. If he's well fed, his

215

tail is big and fat. If it's been awhile since he's eaten, his tail is flat."

Christine shuddered, and Chad led her away. As she nibbled at her lunch, she thought, I hate this country with its heat, its sand and rocks, its snakes, scorpions, cougars, and gila monsters.

But that evening as the sun set, Christine found herself watching in breathless awe. The mountains around them turned orange, then red, and as the shadows fell, they became violet and purple. The blue sky was tinged with delicate shades of pink and streaked with vivid reds and oranges. Christine had never seen such a beautiful sunset in her life. Reluctantly, she admitted that this strange land, harsh and inhospitable as it was, had a beauty all its own.

That night, Chad sat, his back against a tree, watching Christine as she stroked Diablo's neck and talked to him. Her and that damned horse, Chad thought irritably. She's spoiling him rotten, petting and pampering him, sneaking him sugar. Seeing them together now, no one would ever believe they had gotten off to a bad start.

And who would have thought she would take to the trail the way she had, Chad thought once again. He had to admit he'd badly underestimated her. She never complained or gave him any trouble, kept up with him on the trail, and carried her share of the camp chores.

Christine's laughter roused Chad from his thoughts, and he looked up. He watched as Diablo nickered softly and nuzzled her neck, and he felt a twinge of jealousy which irritated him all the more.

His eyes narrowed as he studied Christine. Now that her sunburn was gone, her face was tanned to a golden honey color, making her silver curls and beautiful green eyes even more startling. His eyes drifted down to her mouth, a wide, generous mouth that matched the rest of her to perfection, a mouth made for kissing.

Chad shook his head as if in a daze and jerked his eyes away from her mouth. He gazed at her body. God, she was a lot of woman, he thought. And what a magnificent, stunning woman. His eyes drifted down over her proud, full breasts, the gentle swell of her hips, to her long, graceful legs. Chad's breath caught in his throat, his mouth turned dry. Too well, he remembered what those long legs had felt like locked about his hips.

Chad felt the heat rise in his loins, his manhood hardening and rising in anticipation. "God damn!" he muttered, throwing himself to the ground and rolling over with his back to Christine.

Chad did a lot of twisting, turning, muttering, and groaning that night, before he finally fell asleep. And even then, he was plagued by a pair of beautiful golden-green eyes and a pair of incredibly long legs.

The next morning, Chad was in a foul humor. Having to admit that he still wanted Christine, wanted her desperately despite her deceptiveness, had been a low blow to his ego. Compounded with that was the realization that she wasn't going to change her mind, although the time had come for them to turn away from the Rio Grande. The Río Conchos was right ahead of them, the river he planned to follow into the heart of Mexico.

As far as Chad was concerned, he had only two choices: quit the job and go back to Texas or take Christine along with him. And Chad couldn't quit. Without the money, he'd never get his ranch back. Sure, the rescue attempt was still a crazy, hare-brained scheme, but without his ranch, what kind of a future did he have anyway?

Still risking his life was one thing. Risking Christine's was quite another. Damn the stubborn woman, he thought angrily as he grimly turned his horse southward.

Christine, having never realized that Chad had still clung to the hope that she would change her mind about going along, was bewildered by Chad's sudden turnabout. The last few days, he had almost seemed willing to overlook their argument at the cantina, but today he was snapping and snarling at her again. She watched as he rode ahead of her again, knowing that he was deliberately shunning her and wondering what she had done to revive his anger.

After they had eaten their lunch, Chad climbed beneath a ledge to lie down in the shade. He frowned as he watched Christine unsaddle Diablo and take off his bridle.

"You'd better keep him hobbled," he called in a hard voice, still angry with her. "Otherwise, he might wander off."

218

Christine heard the biting tone of his voice, and her own anger rose. "He can't get any grass if I hobble him!" she snapped back. "Besides, even if he does wander off, he'll come when I call him."

Christine's words only irritated Chad further. What she had said was true. All she had to do was call and Diablo came running. Of course, his own horse came when he whistled, but it had taken him months to train him. "Her and that horse of hers," Chad muttered, deliberately turning his back to Christine.

Because Chad had not slept well the night before, he and Christine dozed in the noonday sun longer than usual. The nicker of a horse roused Chad from his drowsy state. He sat up and looked at his horse and the packhorse grazing leisurely nearby. He glanced around for Diablo, but the black stallion was nowhere to be seen.

Christine was looking for Diablo too. She opened her mouth to call him, but Chad clamped his hand over it, motioning for her not to speak.

Christine watched as Chad silently and carefully climbed the hill behind them. Lying on his stomach, he inched the last few feet to the top of the hill.

Christine's curiosity got the best of her. She crawled up the hillside until she lay beside Chad and peeked over the rim of the hill, looking to see what he was watching with such intensity.

Christine's eyes widened with mixed surprise and fear. "Comanches?" she whispered.

"No, Apaches," Chad whispered back. "Be quiet, Chris. I don't think they know we're here."

Christine looked back down at the six Indians, her fear being slowly replaced with disappointment. In all of the paintings she had seen, Indians were clothed in intricately beaded buckskins and wore magnificent war bonnets, but the Apaches were naked except for brief loincloths, leggings, and moccasins. She looked at their hair in disgust, the left side cut above the ear, the right hanging in a long, greasy braid with dirty feathers tied to it. Christine squinted to get a better view of the Apache closest to her. Why his eyebrows were plucked and his ears are pierced, not once but many times, she realized with amazement. Well, they certainly don't look very impressive or fierce, Christine thought. In fact, it was hard to tell which were scrawnier and more pitiful looking, the Apaches or their horses.

Christine gasped, realizing for the first time that Diablo was down there with the Indians. She watched, her heart thudding in her chest, as one of the Apaches slowly approached her horse. Diablo shook his head nervously, his nostrils flaring.

"They're going to take Diablo," Christine said in a shocked voice.

"Sssh, Chris," Chad rebuked softly.

"But you can't let them take Diablo," Christine said in a horrified voice. "He's my horse, and you said Apaches eat horses."

"Calm down, Chris," Chad hissed. "I'm not going to let them take him. Now be quiet, so I can think."

What Chad had said was true. He had no intention of letting the Apaches take Diablo, but

220

not because Christine had become so attached to him or because Chad hated the thought of the animal being eaten. No, Chad's reasons were much more practical. Stuck out in these rugged, desolate mountains, fifty miles from the nearest civilization, they needed all of their horses badly for survival. Besides that, Diablo was a well-bred, valuable animal, a superior animal that any man who could appreciate fine horseflesh would hate to lose to horse thieves, red or white.

Chad's eyes narrowed as he watched the Apaches below them. Were the six Indians a hunting party or part of a larger war party? He scanned the small valley, but could see no signs of any other Indians.

He looked back down at the Apaches, wondering how he should attack them. If he stayed on the hill where he was, he could pick them off, but not before they got off a few arrows. And he couldn't take the chance of Christine being hit. That left only one other choice. He'd have to rush them so he could draw their fire away from Christine. Yes, with the element of surprise and the advantage his repeater carbine gave him, he'd have no trouble. Oh, they might get a few arrows off, but he could easily dodge them.

His decision made, Chad whispered to Christine, "I'm going down there. You stay here and keep your head down."

Christine watched as Chad crawled a few yards along the ridge, away from her, then she gasped, shocked, when she saw him stand and run down the steep hillside, for the first time realizing he intended to rush them. But he can't, she thought in horror. He's outnumbered six to one! She picked up her carbine and tore down the hill behind him.

As Chad raced down the steep, rocky hillside, he let out a blood-curdling rebel yell, a yell that stunned the Apaches and raised the hair on the back of their necks. Before they could recover from their surprise, Chad was firing his carbine, and three of the Apaches fell to the ground. As the remaining Indians began shooting their arrows back, Chad zigzagged, arrows whizzing through the air around him, his carbine roaring. He felt the sting of an arrow as it ripped across the side of his chest, then he heard the hiss of another as it flew past his ear.

Two more of the Apaches fell to Chad's deadly accurate fire, and Chad wheeled, intending to finish off the sixth and last Indian; then he froze. Christine stood directly in his line of fire, her carbine raised and pointed at the last Apache.

Chad watched in horror as Christine's gun jammed and the Apache lunged at her, throwing them both to the ground, where they rolled and grappled in the dirt just a few feet from where Diablo stood. Chad waited in tense expectation for an opportunity to shoot the Indian, but with their rolling and twisting, it was impossible to get a clear shot of the Apache without risking the possibility of hitting Christine—a risk Chad was not willing to take.

He tossed his carbine aside and ran to the wrestling couple, intending to pull the Apache from Christine. But before he could reach them, he saw the glint of metal in the sun as the Indian raised his knife, and then, unbelievably, Diablo savagely biting the hand which held that knife. Chad heard the Indian's scream of pain as the knife fell harmlessly to the ground.

When Chad finally reached the rolling couple, he discovered, much to his frustration, that he couldn't grab the Apache because Diablo was in the way. Chad had seen dogs come to the defense of their masters, but he had never seen a horse do it. It was the damnedest thing he had ever seen in his life.

Diablo stood over the Apache and Christine, trying to trample the Indian with his hooves. And it wasn't just the nervous pawing and rearing of a frightened animal either. Diablo's actions were coldly calculating. Only when the Apache rolled to the top, would he rear and slam his hoofs down on the Indian's body. And then when Christine's body rolled to the top, he would stand, patiently waiting for the Indian to emerge from the bottom.

But Diablo was seriously hindering Chad's attempt to rescue Christine. When Chad tried to push the big stallion away, Diablo snarled and painfully nipped him on his shoulder.

"Goddamn it, you stupid horse!" Chad roared. "I'm trying to help her too!"

He finally succeeded in shoving the horse aside and reached for the Indian. But as his hands descended, he heard the muffled sound of a gunshot.

Chad froze, his hands still extended. The

Apache reared back and froze too. Christine lay beneath him, perfectly still. The tableau only lasted for a minute, but to Chad it seemed a lifetime. He held his breath, acutely aware of the blood spilling onto the sand below Christine and the Apache, not knowing which of the two had been shot.

Then the Apache grunted and pitched forward over Christine. Chad grabbed his shoulder and roughly yanked him off, seeing the gaping hole in his chest. He squatted beside Christine, who lay stunned on the hard, rocky ground, her eyes blinking at the glaring sunlight. Gently, he took the still-smoking pistol from her hand.

"Are you all right, Chris?" he asked anxiously.

Christine sat up, dazed. She looked dumbly at the bloodstain on her shirt and then at the dead Apache lying beside her. Her eyes widened in horror.

"Are you hurt?" Chad repeated, his voice full of concern.

Christine looked back down at her body as if checking to see that everything was still there. "No . . . no, I don't think I'm hurt," she said in a shaky voice.

Chad felt a rush of relief so great it made him feel weak. She could have been killed, he thought. My God, he had almost shot her himself! His relief was quickly replaced with anger. He rose, his blue eyes flashing dangerously as he looked down at her. "Why in the hell didn't you stay where I told you to?" he yelled. "Don't you realize you could have been killed?"

"But you were outnumbered," Christine objected. "I only wanted to help."

"I didn't need your help!" Chad snarled. "I could have handled it."

Christine glanced at the dead Indians lying all around her, and realized the truth of Chad's words. He had been perfectly capable of handling the situation. He'd certainly proved that by the quick work he'd made of the other five Indians. She had never seen him shoot his gun before and had had no idea he was so deadly accurate or so lightning fast. But then, what did you expect, she berated herself. After all, he is a professional gunslinger.

For the first time, she realized how foolish her action had been. She might have been killed, or she might have distracted Chad so badly that he would have been killed. She looked up intending to apologize, and gasped, noticing the bloodstain on his shirt, just inches below his left armpit. She paled. "You've been shot," she said in a voice barely above a whisper.

"It's just a scratch!" Chad snapped.

Diablo took that inopportune minute to comfort Christine. The stallion nickered softly and bent his head, nuzzling her shoulder gently.

The act infuriated Chad. He slapped the horse's neck angrily. "Cut that out, you jackass! If it hadn't been for you, we wouldn't be in this mess in the first place."

Christine had seen Chad angry before, but never this furious. What made matters even worse was that she felt she deserved every bit of his anger. If she had hobbled Diablo like he'd wanted in the very beginning, none of this would have happened. And then she had foolishly rushed in, further endangering them both. She looked at the bloodstain on Chad's shirt. Just a few more inches to the right, and he would have been killed. The realization made her feel sick.

"Come on, Chris," Chad said. "We may not be out of this mess yet. Get up and go saddle Diablo. Bring the other horses back with you."

He turned and walked away.

"Where are you going?" Christine called.

He pointed to a high ridge off to one side. "I'm going to climb that ridge and look around."

Christine's breath caught in her throat. "You think there might be more Indians around here?"

"How in the hell should I know?" Chad snapped. "I can tell you one thing though. If these Indians were part of a war party, there's more of them around here for sure. Apaches never travel with less than a dozen men on a war party."

The thought of more Apaches being in the vicinity galvanized Christine. She stumbled to her feet and ran off, calling Diablo to follow her. When she returned with the horses, Chad was waiting for her.

Christine watched mutely as Chad shoved something into his saddlebags and swung on his horse.

"We just may luck out yet," he said. "I think this was just a hunting party that stumbled onto us. But just in case, let's get the hell out of here!"

Chad drove them harder that afternoon than he

226

ever had. And Christine didn't object. She was just as anxious to put as much distance between them and the Indians as he.

That night, Chad sat leaning against a tree and glaring at Christine across the campfire. Crazy bitch, he thought angrily. Just yesterday, he was thinking that she never gave him any trouble, and then she went and pulled a stunt like that. And every time he thought about how close she came to being killed, how close he'd come to killing her himself, his blood ran cold.

Christine was very much aware of Chad's anger. She felt foolish and very guilty. Summoning all of her courage, she said, "I'm sorry for what happened this afternoon."

Chad just glared at her, his jaw bunching in anger, his mouth taut.

"And I know it was all my fault," Christine added in a contrite voice. "I should have hobbled Diablo like you told me to."

Christine looked so miserable, Chad's anger evaporated. His disgust turning toward himself, he thought, Why can't I ever stay angry with her? Even when she deserves it, I can't stay mad at her.

"All right, Chris. We'll just forget it happened," Chad said in a tight voice. "But the next time I tell you to stay put, you'd better damned well do it!" he threatened. He sat up and winced, rubbing the wound where the arrow had glazed him.

Christine saw his movement and asked, "Does it hurt?"

"No, it's just sore," Chad answered. "I've had worse scratches than this from mesquite thorns.

227

But I'm going to have to get up and clean it before it gets infected."

As Chad started to rise, Christine said, "No, let me do it."

Chad's head snapped up, a look of surprise on his face.

"It's the least I can do," Christine explained. "Since it was my fault it happened."

Chad shrugged and sat back down, watching Christine as she poured water into a bowl and walked toward him.

"Where are the bandages?" Christine asked.

"Here in my saddlebag," Chad answered. "There's an antiseptic in there too."

Christine knelt beside Chad and waited while he removed his shirt. As he pulled the blood-crusted garment from his body, the laceration began to bleed again. Chad watched as Christine gently washed the wound. He smiled in amusement as she chewed her lower lip in concentration. When she leaned forward, her shirt gaped open, and Chad caught his breath at the sight of one perfectly shaped, rose-tipped breast. Feeling his desire rise, he jerked his eyes away.

"This is going to sting," Christine said as she poured on the antiseptic.

Chad welcomed the distraction of the burning liquid. But as Christine wrapped his broad chest, reaching behind him to roll the bandage around him, her soft breasts brushed against his bare chest, and Chad groaned.

"Did I hurt you?" Christine asked anxiously.

"No," Chad answered between clenched teeth,

228

thinking this was a mistake. He should have done it himself.

When Christine was finished bandaging his chest, she sat back on her heels, admiring her work.

"Thank you, Chris," Chad said softly.

Christine's head rose at Chad's soft words, and Chad felt himself drowning in those beautiful green eyes. That now-familiar urge came over him. Desperately, he clenched his teeth and fought it back down. Then he grabbed his shirt and rose, saying in a hoarse, strangled voice, "I'd better wash this."

Christine watched as Chad rapidly walked away and disappeared in the darkness, once again bewildered by his abrupt departure. When he returned later that night, she was in her bedroll, pretending to be asleep. She watched through half-closed eyelids as he lay down in his own bedroll and rolled away from her.

It was a long time before either of them slept that night.

Chapter Eleven

As Chad and Christine rode deeper into the heart of Mexico, the terrain became more rugged and torturous. The heat was oppressive, not a breath of air had stirred that entire day. Christine rode behind Chad and followed him down the twisting, narrow trail of a steep canyon. Sweat plastered her clothing to her body. She felt hot, unbearably sticky, weak, and a little giddy from dehydration.

She heard a low, ominous rumble and glanced up to see the sun blazing white-hot down on them. It must be the echo of a rock slide somewhere in the mountains, she thought.

Chad whirled his horse and yelled, "That's thunder! Let's get out of this ravine and up to higher ground."

Christine glanced up at the cloudless, blue sky. Thunder? Why, that's impossible, she thought.

"Come on, Chris, move it! Unless you want to stay down here and drown."

Christine looked at the baked, scorched earth below her, the ground laced with deep cracks. Drown? she thought. In what?

But she followed Chad who was already urging his horse up the steep side of the mountain, rocks scattering under the hooves of his horse. Christine hung on to Diablo's reins for dear life as he scampered up the slope, straining on the sharp incline, sliding precariously on the loose gravel several times.

Then seemingly from out of nowhere, dark, angry clouds appeared, and suddenly they were buffeted by slapping gusts of wind, first from one direction, then abruptly from the other. They rode higher and higher as thunder rolled and crashed around them and jagged, white-hot, blinding streaks of lightning lacerated the dark sky above them. The strong, penetrating odor of ozone stung their nostrils. Then it rained, pouring, drenching them to the skin in seconds, pounding down at them with a force that was almost painful.

Christine struggled to control her frightened horse as a flash of lightning tore through the sky and struck the ground near them. The wind-whipped rain lashed at her, stinging her face as she strained into the solid sheet of water, trying to see Chad's shadowy outline in front of her.

"Chris!" Chad shouted above the deafening noises of the storm, "I think I see a cave up there. Follow me!"

It seemed to Christine that nature was waging a personal vendetta against them. She labored to

232

follow Chad through the violent thunderstorm. At one point, she faltered, panic rising and her heart racing when she lost sight of Chad, only to get a brief glimpse of him just a few feet away as another flash of lightning illuminated the sky.

Chad led them beneath a rocky overhang that offered them partial protection from the raging storm. Christine watched as he dismounted and felt his way along the side of the mountain.

"Yes, there's a cave here," he called to her. "Wait until I check it out to make sure it's not some animal's lair."

Christine sat on Diablo, the wind still lashing at them. She expected to see a snarling mountain lion leap from the cave any minute. Instead she saw the brief flare of a match, heard Chad's muttered curse, and then saw another flare as Chad cupped the meager flame in his hand to protect it from the wind. For a moment Chad disappeared from her view.

Suddenly, he was back, standing at her side, saying, "It's safe, Chris. Come on, I'll lead you."

Chad guided Christine into the dark recesses of the cave. "Wait here," Chad said. "I think I might have seen some firewood."

Christine stood, shivering with cold, in an eerie total darkness that was almost as frightening as the violent thunderstorm had been. She sighed with relief as the kindling ignited and she saw Chad hovering over the small fire.

Chad rose and looked about the cave. "We're in luck, Chris," he said, pointing to a small pile of logs in one corner. "Someone must have used this cave before."

"But who would live in a cave?"

Chad shrugged. "Indians. Or perhaps a band of bandits used it as a temporary hideout. Whoever it was, I'm thankful they left us some firewood."

While Chad lugged in their saddles and supplies, Christine stood before the small fire shivering violently. How can I be so cold when less than an hour ago I was roasting? she asked herself.

"Our bedrolls are soaked," Chad said with disgust, throwing the soggy blankets down on the ground. "Fortunately, I packed a couple of extra ones in the pack."

He searched in the pile he had thrown in one corner and pulled out two dry blankets. He rose and frowned, for the first time aware of Christine's shivering.

"You'd better get out of those wet clothes before you get sick, Chris. Here, you can dry off with one of these," he said, tossing her one of the blankets.

Chad sat on the ground and removed his wet boots and soaking socks. He rose and stripped off his shirt, tossing it on a nearby rock. Then he looked up and scowled.

Christine stood in a darkened corner of the cave. She had her boots off, but she was shaking so hard, she couldn't manage the buttons on her shirt.

Chad walked to her, pushed her shaking hands away, and started to unbutton the shirt. Despite her chattering teeth, Christine managed a gasp and grabbed at his hands.

"Cut it out, Chris!" Chad said angrily. "You're freezing and shaking so hard you can't even get undressed." His eyes bored into hers. "I've seen you naked before, or have you forgotten?"

Christine was shaking too violently to offer him much resistance. He quickly stripped her and threw the blanket over her, drying her briskly, almost roughly.

Tucking her blanket around her, he led her to the fire, saying, "Sit here while I add some more logs."

Christine huddled in the warmth of the fire as Chad added more logs and made coffee. He handed her a cup of the hot brew saying, "Drink this. It will help warm you up."

Christine took the cup in her shaking hands and put it to her mouth, her chattering teeth clattering on the metal cup. She nursed her coffee as she watched Chad prepare their meal. By the time they had finished eating, Christine's shivering had stopped.

Christine looked across the fire at Chad. He sat cross-legged with a blanket thrown over his broad shoulders, moodily drinking a cup of coffee.

She held out her cup, saying, "May I have another cup of coffee, please?"

Chad rose, took the cup, and poured the coffee. Coming around the fire, he crouched beside her and handed her the cup. As Christine reached up for it, the blanket slipped from her shoulders and fell in a soft heap around her hips. Christine froze.

Chad's eyes locked on Christine's pink-tipped

breasts. His breath caught, his heart hammered. He raised his head to look into a pair of wide, golden-green eyes.

A growl escaped Chad's throat as he threw the cup aside, grabbed Christine's shoulders, and forced her to the ground. His mouth crashed down on hers in a savage demanding kiss that seemed to suck the breath from Christine's lungs and leave her reeling. He rained fierce kisses on her face and nipped at the long column of her neck.

Raising his head, he looked down at her, his eyes glittering like splintered blue glass, and said huskily, "I swore I would never touch you again! What kind of crazy spell have you cast on me, Chris, that I can't keep my hands off you?" He shook her roughly as if demanding an explanation. "Are you a *baja*? A sorceress? A witch?"

Christine didn't care what he called her. All that mattered to her was that she was in his arms again. Her long fingers tangled in his dark hair as she forced his head down and kissed him boldly, hungrily.

Their coming together was a fierce, wild union, the slow-burning embers of their suppressed desire suddenly igniting into a white-hot, consuming flame. There was no tenderness, no sweetness, no gentleness in Chad's love-making. His hands roamed roughly over her body, demanding a response, his lips nipping everywhere, his kisses fierce and searing.

But if Chad thought to dominate Christine with his body, he was mistaken. She bucked and twisted beneath him, returning every nip and bite, every savage, burning kiss, her own hands devouring him.

They were more combatants than lovers, each fighting for supremacy, each demanding the other's surrender. They rolled in the dirt, their long legs entwined, their animal groans and moans filling their ears, their breaths hot and ragged. The ground shook, and the air around them reverberated with the sounds of their frenzied love-making.

Chad felt an urgent, burning compulsion for total possession, a need to place his brand on her once and for all. His mouth crashed down on hers, his lips hard and bruising, his tongue thrusting, then plundering her mouth. And Christine met his savage kiss, her own scalding tongue ravishing him back.

Again they rolled, still locked in that sweet-savage kiss, before Chad pinned her to the ground. For a brief second he poised above her; then with a cry that was half exultant and half growl, he wrenched her legs apart and drove his hot, rigid flesh deeply inside her. Christine lurched, feeling as if a bolt of lightning had entered her, shock waves of electrical heat coursing up her spine until they burst into a white-hot flare in her brain.

Two demanding mouths sought and clung, two eager tongues met and devoured, two hearts pounded frantically against each other as their sweat-slick bodies strained and their hips pounded with feverish urgency. Then, suddenly, they were perfectly still, frozen on that lofty apex, both breathless and trembling with intense anticipation, before tumbling over into the shattering explosion that devoured them in a fiery shower of swirling, brilliant, flashing colors and then . . . total oblivion.

As they drifted back down, bodies still trembling, their legs still entangled, Chad muttered weakly in Christine's ear, "My God!"

Christine's only reaction to their shattering experience was a soft purr of utter contentment before she drifted off to sleep.

A few minutes later, Chad gently disentangled himself and rose, covering Christine with a blanket. He walked to the cave opening and leaned against the rocky entrance, smoking and watching the rain, deep in thought.

He didn't know how or when, but Christine had crawled under his skin. It was crazy, yet there was no denying he had fallen in love with her, despite his vow to never again succumb to that emotion. But it wasn't his vow that was bothering him. What disturbed him was Christine's emotion. Did she feel anything for him at all?

Chad sensed she felt something, at least a seedling of love. He couldn't believe that a woman like Christine could give her body so freely without feeling something more than just desire. But he didn't want just a part of her love. He wanted all of it. And he knew she was holding something back, some inviolable part of her.

Well, he'd have all of her, her body, her heart, her soul, everything, Chad vowed with fierce determination. He'd fight for her love. She wasn't like Anne, spoiled and selfish and shallow. No, Christine was worth fighting for!

Chad frowned. But how could he make her love him, give him all of herself? One thing he knew—this wasn't the right time to tell her of his feelings. A declaration at this point might frighten her off. No, he'd have to move slowly, and he'd have to work at it. He'd have to take that seedling of love and carefully nurture it, make it grow until she freely gave all of herself to him, completely and totally.

Christine stirred and gazed about the cave. She saw the dim outline of Chad standing in the entrance. "Is it time to leave?" she called in a sleepy voice.

"No, Chris," Chad's rich, deep voice came from across the cave. "It's still raining, and we won't be going anywhere today. There's too much danger of getting caught in a flash flood. You can go back to sleep."

Christine lay on the blanket, watching Chad's shadowy figure. Her eyes followed the arc of Chad's cigarette butt as he flicked it away. Then he turned and walked back into the cave.

The fire had burned down to red embers, bathing the cave in a subdued rosy glow. As Chad moved toward her, Christine realized he was naked. Her breath caught in her throat, and for a minute, Christine's eyes feasted on his magnificent male body. Then, guiltily, she turned away, closing her eyes in pretended sleep.

The blanket rose, and Chad slipped in under it

and beside her. Christine could feel the heat radiating from his body. His masculine scent filled her nostrils, exciting her. His muscular thigh pressed against her naked one, seemingly scorching her. Her heart pounded erratically, and her breath grew ragged. Slowly, she turned to him, and Chad was waiting for her.

Chad made love to her, slowly, lazily, tenderly, his sensuous, achingly sweet love-making a sharp contrast to the fiery union they had shared earlier. He didn't tell her he loved her, not in words, but his hands, his lips, his tongue spoke volumes, serenaded her with love songs.

They spent the better part of that day closeted in their cozy little cave, sleeping and making love alternately. Christine marveled at how the same act could be so different each time, and when they finally rose, dressed, and went outside, Christine was positively glowing.

They were feeding the horses when Christine first noticed the rumbling. Confused, she looked up at the blue, cloudless sky, and then remembering how suddenly the storm had come on them the day before, she asked, "Is that thunder?"

"No," Chad said in an ominous voice. "Come over here, Chris."

Christine walked to him, and Chad pointed, saying, "See that ravine down there?"

Christine nodded.

"Watch it."

Christine watched as the rumbling became louder and louder until it built to a roar. And then she saw it. A monstrous, fifteen-foot wall of water

240

thundered down the narrow ravine and swept past them. The muddy flood swirled and twisted, lashing at the walls of the ravine with greedy, grasping waves that ripped boulders from the mountainside, throwing and tumbling them as if they were mere pebbles.

"An awesome sight, isn't it?" Chad said as the water roared past them and down the ravine.

Christine was trembling from the experience, having never seen the powerful force and frightening destruction of a flash flood. To her, it seemed incredible that something as innocent-looking as water could be that rampant and devastating.

"But where did all that water come from?" she asked in a bewildered voice.

"From the mountains above us," Chad answered. "The ground is too rocky to absorb the rain so it all runs off. You never know how much water is going to collect, or what ravines or arroyos it will choose to drain in—or even when it's going to come. That's why when it rains in the mountains, you seek higher ground, even if it doesn't rain a drop where you are."

Christine looked down at the swirling, angry water in the ravine below them, the same ravine that she and Chad had been in when the storm broke. If they had been caught down there when the water had come, they would have been drowned without a doubt. An involuntary shiver ran through her.

Christine glanced around at the barren mountains. "But where does it go?"

241

"It will drain into the Río Concho somewhere below us and then into the Rio Grande."

Christine looked down at the swirling flood water again and felt a new fear. The ravine curved around them, trapping them on the mountainside.

"How long will it take to go down?" she asked.

"At this height and incline, it will drain off fairly fast. More than likely, it will be gone by morning."

True to Chad's prediction the flood waters were gone by the next morning. Crossing the ravine, Christine looked down at the small innocent trickle of water and wondered if the whole, frightening scene hadn't been just a bad dream. Then she saw a huge boulder, a boulder as tall as a man, a boulder that she knew hadn't been there the last time they had traveled down this ravine. She shuddered.

Traveling that day was difficult. The rain had loosened the ground, increasing the danger of rock slides, so that in many places they had to dismount and gingerly pick their way across. Several times, they found the trail blocked by large piles of rock and rubble and were forced to take long, tedious detours. The heat was even worse—steamy—as the moisture from the ground evaporated under the blazing sun. That afternoon, when they came across a ravine still swollen with flood waters, Christine almost sobbed from exhaustion and frustration.

"I thought you said all the water would be

gone," Christine said in a voice that was almost accusing.

Chad frowned and studied the flood waters. "I don't think this is a ravine, Chris. It's probably a creek and drains a much larger area." He looked up and down the swollen stream, saying with disgust, "Hell, it could take days for it to go down."

Days? Christine thought in alarm. Why, they couldn't afford to lose that much time. "Can't we go around it?"

"I doubt it," Chad said. "We'd probably lose just as much time trying to do that." He studied the curve of the creek. "And backtracking too."

Chad thoughtfully paced the bank of the swollen creek. He stood, scrutinizing the opposite side for a long time; then he tossed a stick into the middle of the stream, judging its current.

He turned, saying, "Well, I'm afraid we're going to have to ford it."

"You mean cross it?" Christine asked in disbelief.

"It's either that or sit here for several days and wait for it to go down."

Christine knew several days might make the difference in saving Charles's life. There really isn't any choice, Christine thought. She looked at the muddy, angry water, twisting and swirling dangerously, and shivered in fear.

"Come on, Chris," Chad said, his voice brisk and businesslike. "Help me transfer some of this stuff on the packhorse to our horses."

"Why are you doing that?" Christine asked.

Chad sighed in exasperation, saying, "Because that's too much weight for him to carry across that flooded creek."

"But then, where will we sit?"

Having met nothing but one obstacle after another all day, Chad's mood wasn't at its best. He whirled, but one look at Christine's pale face tempered his anger. "Chris," Chad said patiently, "our horses can't carry us across that flooded stream. They'll have all they can do to cross that stream without our weight dragging them down. We'll have to swim across it."

"Swim?" Christine squeaked, her eyes wide.

"You won't have to do much swimming," Chad explained. "We'll hold on to our horses' tails and let them tow us across. All you'll have to do is hold on and keep your head above water. Diablo will do all the work."

Chad didn't give Christine any time to contemplate her fate. Immediately, he started barking orders at her. His brisk, confident manner reassured Christine, and she scampered to obey his commands.

After they had distributed the supplies evenly among the three horses, Chad said, "Take off your boots and gunbelt and put them in a saddlebag. They'll only weigh you down."

But when Christine stood thigh deep in the muddy, swirling waters and watched Chad force the frightened packhorse into the flooded stream, her fear returned, stronger than ever.

Chad saw the look on her face and said, "It

244

won't be so bad, Chris. It will be over before you know it." Taking her hands, he said, "Here, twist Diablo's tail around your wrists like this. That will give you an even better grip. Now all you've got to do is hang on. I'll go first, so I can help you out when you get to the other side. Okay?"

Christine was too frightened to speak. She nodded mutely.

"See you on the other side," Chad called as he followed his horse into the twisting water.

Christine looked at the other side of the creek. It's not all that far, she tried to reassure herself. I'll close my eyes and just hang on until we reach the other side. "Go, boy!" she called to Diablo, urging him into the murky water.

Christine squeezed her eyes shut and held her breath, feeling herself sliding into the water. Then as they entered the strong current in the middle of the stream, the water twisted her body, tugging at her legs, threatening to pull her under. She opened her eyes, terrified. Her head bobbed and ducked in the murky water as the angry current swirled and rolled about her. She went down, then came up, spitting muddy water and gasping for air. She caught her breath, then saw a large, ragged limb racing toward her. Without thinking, she tried to pull her hand loose to push it away, but her wrist was too tangled in Diablo's tail. She kicked out at the limb and sent it veering away, but a branch of it scratched her cheek as it bobbed past.

Christine could hear Diablo's labored breathing and feel the rush of water against her body at each stroke of his powerful hind legs as the horse struggled to swim the flooded stream. How much longer? Christine sobbed to herself, and then gasped in horror when she realized they were going downstream instead of across. She closed her eyes, fighting back tears, thinking, I'll drown out here in the middle of this muddy Mexican creek.

Then suddenly, Christine felt Diablo's flank muscles bunch as he heaved to crawl up the muddy bank and powerful arms were about her waist, pulling her from the swirling, rushing water. Tears of relief spilled down her cheeks as she knelt on the bank, coughing and spitting muddy water.

"Are you all right?" Chad asked anxiously.

Christine huddled into herself, not wanting him to see her tears, and nodded silently.

Chad squeezed her shoulder gently, saying, "That's my girl."

Christine rallied at his praise and lifted her head, smiling weakly. Then, looking over his shoulder at the angry, swirling water, she almost fainted.

That night as they sat by their campfire, Chad turned and pulled something from his saddlebags. Handing it to her, he said, "I thought you might like this as a souvenir of sorts."

Christine looked down at the long, round, hollow object, its surface painted with bright, colorful designs. A single string ran down its length, and several small holes could be seen at one end. "What is it?"

246

"An Apache fiddle," Chad answered. "It's made from a hollowed yucca stalk. I found it on one of the Indians' horses that day we ran into the Apaches. It's what made me decide the Indians were just a hunting party. Somehow, I couldn't imagine an Apache taking his fiddle to war with him."

He handed her a small bow, and Christine took it and slid the bow over the string on the fiddle. She laughed at the high, squeaking noise.

"I didn't know Indians had musical instruments," Christine commented.

Chad nodded, saying, "Indians love music. The Apache have a flute they use to woo their women. They think it softens the woman's heart."

Christine tried to form a mental picture of a fierce, Apache warrior playing a love song on a flute. The thought was too preposterous, the picture ridiculous.

"You made that up," she accused, laughing.

"No, it's true," Chad said. "Apaches take their courting very seriously, and Apache men are noted for their fidelity to their women. Polygamy is rare, and an Apache is very protective and jealous of his wife. If he catches her committing adultery, he cuts off her nose."

Christine shivered, thinking, now that sounds more like an Apache. She looked back down at the curious object in her lap. When she looked back up, her breath caught. Chad had risen and was placing Christine's bedroll with his own, making one big pallet on the ground. She watched, her heart racing, as Chad walked lazily

247

across to her, his eyes warm and caressing.

He held his hand down, and Christine accepted it dumbly. He led her to the pallet and silently undressed her. Smiling, he lowered her to the pallet and undressed himself, joining her. He folded her in his arms, kissing her tenderly, then more urgently, his hands and lips and tongue rousing her to unbelievable heights with infinite care.

Chad set a precedent that night. From then on, he and Christine shared their bedrolls. Sometimes, they lay talking and gazing at the stars, Chad pointing out the different constellations to her. Most of the time, they would make love, but on the few occasions when they didn't, Christine was content. Just lying beside his big warm body, his powerful arms about her, made her feel safe and cared for.

Several days later, they found a pool of crystal-clear water surrounded by a copse of graceful, swaying water willows. The unusual and unexpected discovery prompted Chad to declare the afternoon a holiday.

"But can we afford to lose the time?" Christine asked in surprise.

"Yes," Chad answered firmly. "We've made good time, and I think we deserve a little relaxation for a change."

Christine was delighted. After she had rubbed down and fed Diablo, Christine headed for the pool, calling over her shoulder, "I'll take my bath first."

Christine luxuriated in the clear, deliciously

248

cool water. She soaped herself, not once, but three times, scrubbing the accumulated grime and dirt from her body and hair. Then she waded in, waist deep, enjoying the feel of the water around her long legs.

She glanced up and gasped, seeing Chad coming from the camp toward her. She crouched lower in the water to hide her nakedness and watched as he walked toward the pool with that lazy swagger that made her heart do crazy flip-flops in her chest. What a virile, lusty man he was, she thought, secretly glad she had him all to herself these few, brief weeks.

Christine's eyes widened in alarm when she saw him removing his boots and shirt. "Can't you wait until I'm through?" she asked irritably.

Chad's eyes rose and met hers evenly. Christine's breath caught at the sight of those deep blue eyes, her legs turned to rubber.

"Why? It looks big enough for two," he drawled, infuriatingly calm.

Chad grinned, unbuckling his belt, and Christine averted her eyes as he skimmed down his pants. She inched farther into the pool away from Chad, pretending deep interest in soaping her shoulder as the sounds of Chad's splashing invaded her ears. Christine was shocked by his total disregard for their nakedness. True, they had been intimate, very intimate. She blushed in remembrance. But still, that had been in the dark or in subdued light. And this was broad daylight!

She cowered, trying to hide in the water, feeling very self-conscious and acutely aware of Chad's nakedness just a few feet away. Despite herself, Christine couldn't resist sneaking glances at his body, the same powerfully muscled body that had brought her such ecstasy.

"Stop peeking, Chris," Chad said in a teasing voice. "Didn't anyone ever tell you it wasn't ladylike to watch a man bathing?"

Christine swiftly turned her back to him, mortified at having been caught in the act. She heard Chad's chuckle and splashing behind her, and then she gasped as Chad's long arms picked her up and flung her into deeper water.

Christine felt and saw the water close over her head. She thrashed wildly, trying to fight her way to the surface. Her head briefly surfaced, and then she sank again, fighting, struggling, her heart pounding in her chest, her lungs feeling as if they would burst as a roaring filled her ears.

Two powerful arms grabbed her and pulled her to the surface. Christine clutched frantically at Chad's broad shoulders, coughing and spitting water, as he swam toward shore and then waded into shallow water.

When Christine's feet were firmly planted on solid ground, Chad stopped and yelled, "Why in the hell didn't you swim?"

Christine's eyes burned with tears of outrage. She had never been so terrified in her life. "Because I can't swim. I don't know how!" she sobbed.

"Don't know how to swim?" Chad asked in a disbelieving voice.

"No!" Christine snapped. "Where would I learn

how to swim in New York City?"

"New York City is an island, surrounded by water. What about the beach?"

Christine felt a little calmer. She realized now that Chad was truly astonished at her inability to swim and that he would never have behaved as he had if he'd known that. "Charles and I were never allowed to go to the public beach."

Chad frowned. "A private resort then. Hell, there're resorts all up and down the Atlantic coast."

Christine shook her head, saying, "My uncle never took us to a resort. He said resorts cost too much money and were frivolous. Besides, even if we could have gone to one, he wouldn't have let me swim. He thought swimming was unladylike."

Chad's jaw bunched in anger; his fists clenched. There were times when he would have dearly loved to have her uncle's neck between his hands. This was one of them. Then he remembered the day they had forded the flooded creek and he recalled Christine's pale, frightened face. My God, he thought, and she couldn't even swim! She must have been terrified; yet, she never said a word. She had to be either the biggest fool in the world or the bravest woman he had ever met. But Chad knew his Christine was no fool. His heart swelled with pride.

He smiled, saying, "Well, Chris, I think it's time you learned how to swim."

Christine looked up, stunned. Was he offering to teach her? True, he had taught her to ride and shoot, but that had been necessary for the trip.

251

Would he be willing to take the time and trouble to teach her to swim?

Chad saw Christine's stunned look and mistook it for fear. "There's nothing to be afraid of. You won't even have to go into water over your waist if you don't want to. And everyone should know how to swim. You never know, it might save your life someday. Besides, swimming is fun."

Christine smiled and her eyes sparkled with excitement. "I would like to know how to swim."

"Okay. First, I'll teach you to float. The body is naturally buoyant. People drown because they panic, not because their bodies won't float. Now just lay back in the water, and I'll support you with my arms until you get used to it."

Christine started to do as Chad told her, but then she realized with horror that if she floated before him her whole body would be blatantly exposed to his eyes. She struggled to her feet and pulled away from him.

Chad frowned, saying, "What's wrong, Chris? Are you afraid I'll drop you?"

Christine cowered in the water, once again trying to hide, her face beet red with embarrassment. "No, but . . . but I'm naked."

Chad shrugged and said, "That's the best way to swim. Clothes would only encumber you."

"But . . . but . . ." Christine stammered.

Chad was exasperated. He'd seen her naked before. But if her nakedness was going to make her nervous, she wouldn't be able to concentrate on what he was trying to teach her.

"All right, Chris," Chad said. "Go and put on your shirt."

Chad watched as Christine hurried from the pool and quickly donned her shirt. Her modesty both amused and pleased him. After all, he thought, she's a lady, and a lady didn't go around flaunting her body before a man.

Christine started to walk back in the water and then froze. She could see Chad's long legs through the clear water and the black triangle between them. How can I possibly concentrate on learning how to swim with *that* distracting me? she thought.

"Now what's wrong?" Chad called in an irritable voice.

Christine's head snapped up guiltily. She smiled nervously, saying, "Would you mind . . . would you mind putting on your pants?"

Chad started to refuse and then decided against it. Knowing Chris, she'd argue, and then she'd be insisting he wear his shirt too. Better leave well enough alone, he thought, wading from the pool.

As he supported Christine in his arms while she floated, Chad had to suppress a chuckle. The thin, wet shirt hid absolutely nothing from his view. He could clearly see her full, proud breasts and the silver hair between her long, beautiful legs. God, how he ached to bury his head in those curls and taste her sweetness there. Christine was a passionate woman and growing more so each day under his careful tutelage. But he knew she would be utterly shocked if he kissed her there, the most intimate of all kisses. No, Christine wasn't ready

253

for that . . . not yet.

Chad felt his manhood rise in anticipation. Not now, old man, Chad chided himself. First things first. With supreme effort, he drew his mind away from the distraction of Christine's body and concentrated on the task at hand.

They stayed in the pool for hours as Chad patiently taught Christine. Finally he waded away from her into deeper water.

Standing in water up to his neck, Chad called, "Now try it, Chris. See if you can swim to me."

Christine frowned, saying, "Are you touching bottom?"

Chad nodded.

Christine remembered the terrifying experience she'd had just a few hours earlier. It took all of her courage to push off and swim toward Chad. But instead of getting closer, Chad was getting farther away, and Christine realized with horror that he was swimming away from her. She tried to touch bottom and, realizing she couldn't find it, became terrified.

"Don't panic, Chris," Chad said firmly, treading water just a few feet in front of her. "Your body floats, remember? There's nothing to be afraid of."

Christine swam, her long arms and legs thrashing, her eyes wild, following Chad's semi-circle around the deeper part of the pool.

Finally, Chad said, "You can touch bottom now, Chris."

Christine's feet lowered, searching and probing until she could feel the firm sand below her. Her feet firmly planted, she sobbed in relief.

Glaring at Chad, she said angrily, "You tricked me."

Chad grinned, a little, lopsided grin that tugged at Christine's heart. "That's right, I did," he drawled lazily. "But you were wonderful, Chris. Do you realize you swam the whole pool?"

Christine had been too terrified to know how far she had swum. All she had known was that she couldn't let Chad out of her sight. She looked around the pool in amazement and said, "I did?"

Chad led her from the pool, saying, "Now, remember, you know how to swim. It's something your body never forgets. Anytime you find yourself in water over your head, just remember that."

Chad lay down on the mossy ground by the side of the pool. Christine sat hugging her long legs to her body, feeling very proud of herself. Then she laughed, a sudden burst of joy.

"What's so funny?" Chad asked.

"I was just thinking. My uncle would never let me go swimming because he thought the bathing dresses women wore were immodest. Why, he'd have a stroke if he could have seen me swimming around that pool in a man's shirt."

Chad frowned. Christine had never told him much about herself, only a casual remark here or there. Chad, himself, had been close-mouthed about his own private life. But he knew enough to know that Christine had had an unhappy child-hood. True, she had had all of the physical comforts of life, but Chad knew in his heart that she had been denied something much more important, love. That damned cold-hearted uncle of hers, he thought angrily. And her father deserting her. Surely that must have hurt her too.

He felt a twinge of sadness, not pity, for Chad loved Christine too much for that. But knowing that she had been hurt, made him ache for her, so much so that he almost shared her pain. Maybe if she talks about it, exorcises it from her memory, he thought.

"Tell me about your childhood, Chris," Chad said softly.

Christine looked around at the serene pool and the blue sky above. She didn't want to remember her childhood and all its pains, her father's desertion, her uncle's hateful dominance, the cold indifference of her governesses and tutors. No, today had been too beautiful and special. She didn't want to spoil its perfection with those memories.

"I don't want to talk about that," she said tightly.

Chad frowned, feeling a sharp twinge of disappointment. So, she still didn't trust him, he thought, for Chad sensed that gaining Christine's trust was the key to her heart. Well, he'd just have to be patient, give her more time to gain confidence in him.

"All right, Chris," Chad said calmly, "we won't talk if you don't want to."

He pulled her gently down beside him and kissed her warmly, nibbling at her ear as his hands deftly unbuttoned her shirt. Christine realized his intention and was once again shocked by his boldness. No, she thought frantically. He can't make love to me now. Not here in the glaring sunlight! She caught his hand, muttering, "No, Chad."

"Oh yes, lady," Chad whispered in her ear, his teeth gently nipping the lobe, his tongue circling and probing. Christine shivered in delight.

Chad firmly shoved Christine's hand away and pushed the shirt open. He bent his head, placing kisses and little love bites over her soft flesh, then licking them as if to soothe the tiny hurts.

"You have such magnificent breasts, Chris," Chad said huskily, "so proud, so full. And these," he muttered, his tongue flicking erotically at one nipple, "like pink rosebuds."

Christine gasped, not only because of the marvelous feelings Chad's lips and tongue were invoking at her breasts, but from surprise at his words. Not once had Chad complimented her on her looks, much less her body. Her embarrassment fled, and in its wake, a newfound confidence in her womanly charms was born. Suddenly, Christine wanted to make love to Chad. She wanted to take the initiative. She pushed him away and rolled him to his back.

A seductive smile played at her lips as she looked down at him and said softly, "Let me make love to you."

Chad's heart thudded in his chest, his mouth suddenly dry. He managed a weak nod.

Christine's eyes swept over Chad, hungrily feasting on his muscular shoulders and his broad chest with its mat of dark curls. With one finger, she traced the corded muscle on his chest from one shoulder to one dark nipple, lazily circling it until she saw it harden. Leaning forward, she licked the hardened bud and heard Chad's ragged indrawn breath.

Encouraged by his obvious pleasure, she nipped and tongued at each rib, slowly descending down his chest, then following the fine line of hair that disappeared beneath his pants.

She frowned at the offending material and then, glancing lower, saw the huge bulge straining impatiently there. Boldly, she unbuttoned his pants and then sat back on her heels, openly admiring the proof of his masculinity. His sex jutted from the dark hair between his legs, long and full, standing proudly erect, the tip glistening with moisture in the bright sunlight.

Christine reached to softly stroke the velvety skin, tracing the long hot length from base to crown, then slowly circling the smooth tip.

Chad groaned, "Oh God, lady. Do you know what you do to me?"

Christine smiled at his words. That was one thing she appreciated about Chad's love-making. He never muttered endearments to her, not even in the heated throes of his passion. He never called her sweetheart, honey, or darling, and if he had Christine would have felt foolish. To her such endearments were more suited to small, dainty women. No, the only thing Chad ever called her, besides her name, was "lady." But when he said the word, with his deep, rich voice and lazy drawl,

Christine quivered all over, her toes curled. "Lady" was her own, very special endearment.

Suddenly she wanted to see all of him. She tugged impatiently at his pants, and Chad lifted his hips as she pulled them down and off. Tossing them to one side, she again sat back on her heels, her golden-green eyes smoldering, her look hungry. What a magnificent, perfect specimen of manhood he is, she thought.

Her hands lowered to caress him with soft butterfly strokes, slowly inching upward, lingering on the muscles of his thighs, brushing the dark hair at his groin, then deliberately, teasingly, skirting his manhood to trace the fine line of hair on his taut abdomen. Spying a small pool of water lying around the hollowed area of his navel, she bent and licked at it avidly, smiling in satisfaction when she saw Chad's stomach muscles jerk in response.

She lowered herself over him, provocatively brushing her nipples across his hard chest, then gasping at her own pleasure as his dark hairs rubbed against her sensitive peaks. She dropped light kisses over his shoulders and up the straining cords of his tanned neck, then nipped at his earlobe before circling it and probing its recesses with her tongue.

Chad clenched his fists and ground his teeth. He couldn't take any more of this delicious torment. He reached for Christine, pulling her length down over his and whispering huskily, "Now, Chris. Ride me now."

Christine was confused by his request. She

could feel his long hot length pinned between their lower abdomens, throbbing with a life of its own. Did he mean what she thought he meant? Tentatively she moved her hips, rubbing herself against him.

"Yes, Chris. Oh God, yes," Chad muttered, his hands pushing her hips upward.

Christine now knew what he wanted, but she was shocked by the unorthodox position. She hesitated.

"Please, lady," Chad groaned.

Chad's agonized plea gave her the courage she needed. She swung her long legs over him and, straddling his hips, slowly lowered herself, gradually enveloping his turgid manhood, surrounding him inch by inch. Christine felt him filling her, so deeply her breath caught in her throat. Then as her muscles contracted hungrily, she felt a wave of delicious sensations sweeping over her.

She needed no further urging. Her own pressing need took command. She gyrated her hips, swiveling, twisting, up and down, the movements exciting her unbelievably, driving her up that familiar ascent.

Chad lay beneath her, writhing in his own rapturous agony, his hands fondling and stroking her breasts. For one brief second, he remembered the wild mustangs he'd compared Chris to, and was grateful he hadn't broken her spirit after all. Then the thought was gone, drowned in sheer sensation.

At the last minute, feeling Christine's back arch and knowing she was on the brink of reaching her fulfillment, he pulled her head down, and with a little snarl, his mouth captured hers in a fiercely possessive kiss, his tongue demanding and ravaging the sweetness of her mouth. And then with one powerful thrust, he brought them both over that peak, shuddering and moaning in unison, as he exploded, his seed a hot searing jet deep inside her.

Christine lay over Chad, her body sprawled weakly over his, her head buried in the crook of his tanned neck. Chad caressed her back and hips, then bent to kiss the damp curls on her forehead. His arms tightened possessively around her, as he vowed silently, someday, my magnificent lady, you'll give me all of yourself. Not just your body . . . but your trust and your heart too.

Chapter Twelve

Christine wiped the perspiration from her brow and looked up wearily at the rugged mountains surrounding them. It seemed to her that they had been climbing up and down and around mountains for years instead of weeks. They had been on the trail for over three weeks now. Surely, they must be getting close to their destination. They had to be close, she thought frantically. They had only eight days left until the ransom date—only eight days to find and rescue Charles.

She twisted in her saddle to face Chad riding beside her. "How much farther is it to El Puma's camp?"

Chad shrugged, saying lazily, "The way I figure it, El Puma is somewhere in the mountains surrounding us. But we're about as close as we're going to get. From now on, whether or not we get into that camp is up to El Puma."

Christine looked about her in confusion. She didn't see any camp. She squinted at the rocky

263

mountains, studded sparsely with trees. She couldn't see anything unusual.

"We're not going to be able to find that camp, Chris," Chad said calmly. "The French have been combing these mountains for years trying to find El Puma's hideout without any success. El Puma will find us."

"Find us?"

Chad chuckled, saying, "You can be sure El Puma knows when there's anyone strange in these mountains. He'll have sentries posted all around watching for intruders. He knows we're here." His voice turned ominous. "Or at least, someone knows we're here. I don't know if it's El Puma's Juaristas or bandits."

"What are you talking about?" Christine snapped.

"I mean, we're being watched by someone, Chris. We have been for the past two days."

Christine felt a shiver of fear run up her spine. "How do you know?"

"Well, at first, I just sensed it. So I started watching more closely. Today, I've seen a couple of flashes of light when the sun hit their muskets. They're up there watching us right now. The question is, how much longer are they going to let us wander around down here, before they get curious enough to see why we're here?"

Chad's experienced eyes caught another brief glint of metal in the distance. "Better put your serape on now, Chris," he said tightly. "Company's coming."

Christine hurriedly donned the heavy serape,

and none too soon. The next turn they took in the twisted trail found them facing four, dangerous-looking Mexicans, some with fierce mustachios, all holding guns pointed at Chris and Chad. From seemingly out of nowhere, three more men appeared behind them.

Christine sat on Diablo, frozen with fear. The Mexican's hot, black eyes glared at them. She shivered despite the heat.

"*Buenos días, amigos,*" Chad drawled lazily. "I am looking for your leader, your *jefe*. Can you take me to him?"

The Mexicans sat on their horses scowling, their eyes boring into Chad and Christine. They don't understand English, Christine realized. Why doesn't Chad speak Spanish? she wondered.

"Your *jefe*," Chad repeated. "I want to see your *jefe*, El Puma."

Despite the men's sullen silence, Christine saw the flicker of recognition in their eyes at the mention of the name.

"Chris," Chad said, "they don't trust us. Do what I do." Chad slowly raised his arms and placed his hands at the back of his neck, suggesting voluntary surrender. Christine followed Chad's example.

Chad smiled, saying, "I'm a *tejano amigo*. El Puma's *amigo*."

The men glared at them suspiciously. Then one spat something to the others in Spanish. Two of the men urged their horses forward toward Chris and Chad.

"Don't move, Chris," Chad said in a low,

warning voice.

Christine sat on Diablo, her heart hammering in her chest, as the Mexican beside her jerked her pistol from her gunbelt and shoved it into his belt. He took her carbine and tossed it to another man. Then he roughly pulled her hands in front of her, tying them together, the rawhide biting painfully into her wrists.

Christine glanced at Chad. He was being disarmed in the same manner, only he was smiling as if they were pleasantly passing the time of day instead of cruelly tying him up. She gasped as she watched a Mexican throw a blindfold over his eyes and tie it, and then watched in horror as her own eyes were covered.

"Chris," Chad's voice came to her in the darkness.

"Silencio! No inglés!" a harsh voice snapped.

Christine was forced to hold on to her saddle horn as they moved forward. Riding in total darkness and feeling the sway of her body in the saddle made Christine feel strangely disoriented. The only sounds that reached her ears were the steady clip-clops of the horses' hooves. Knowing that she was totally surrounded by hard, dangerous men, perhaps even murderers, and not being able to see or speak, compounded the strange feeling until Christine was panic-stricken. The longer they rode, the more Christine's strange terror grew. She began to feel as if she were smothering, drowning in the darkness and silence, whirling in a deep, black vortex.

And then she heard a tune being whistled,

softly, lazily. How Chad had sensed her terror she had no way of knowing. She clung tenaciously to that comforting sound, seemingly her only touch with reality, her lifeline, and it didn't even matter that the tune was "Dixie," the hated rebel national anthem.

After what seemed to Christine hours of riding, she became aware of other new sounds. Chad apparently heard them too, for he stopped whistling. She heard a laugh, the clang of a pot, muted voices. She could smell wood smoke mixed with the tantalizing aroma of something cooking.

Diablo stopped, and Christine felt the blindfold being yanked away. She blinked at the sudden, bright light, trying to focus her eyes. She looked about her with amazement. They were in a camp in a deep woods that snuggled against a steep, rocky cliff. Rough lean-tos and tents sprinkled the area, and several campfires burned, their smoke drifting lazily into the sky.

A crowd of curious, excited Mexicans milled around her and Chad, and Christine was surprised to see women and children mixed among them. She looked at the large, crudely built log cabin in front of her, knowing that it must be the headquarters of this band, be they Juaristas or bandidos. A new shiver of fear ran through her.

She glanced at Chad. He smiled at her reassuringly and nodded slightly, motioning for her to keep her head down. Quickly, she ducked her head, hiding her face in the shadow of her hat.

The door of the cabin opened and a man stepped out. He was tall, broad-shouldered, his head covered with a thick mane of blue-black hair. He stepped into the light and Christine gasped. She had never seen such a dangerous-looking man. Even her first glimpse of Chad hadn't frightened her this much. Those eyes, Christine thought, black, boring, glittering. She felt as though she were facing the devil himself.

One of their Mexican captors said something in Spanish to the man and pointed to Christine and Chad.

The *jefe*'s black, bushy eyebrows lowered menacingly as he scowled at them. His mouth twisted into a mocking, cruel smile.

Christine shuddered and glanced apprehensively at Chad. The big Texan sat on his horse, one leg casually curled around his saddle horn, leaning forward leisurely, a small insolent smile playing at his lips. His blue eyes met the devil's eyes levelly. The two men seemed to be measuring each other carefully. Christine held her breath.

"*Buenos días, señor*," Chad drawled. "Are you El Puma?"

The Mexican *jefe* nodded curtly. He leaned against the porch post, crossing his arms across his broad chest, a seemingly casual gesture. But with his hot, black eyes boring into them Christine felt more as if he were a panther crouching in preparation for his leap. She swallowed nervously.

Chad lazily slung his leg back into his stirrup and sat up in the saddle. Arrogantly, with his tied hands, he pushed his hat back on his head and grinned down at the Juarista leader. "My name's

Chad Yancy, and this is my younger brother, Chris. We heard you might be interested in some hired guns."

El Puma sneered. "*Pistoleros?*"

"That's right," Chad said. "We're *pistoleros*. Damned good *pistoleros* too!"

The Mexican's look was one of pure disgust. "You have been misinformed, *señores*," he said in a cold voice. "I have no use for *pistoleros*."

Christine gasped, not at his hard, clipped words, but at his perfect use of the English language.

"Is that so?" Chad replied easily. "Well, maybe you ought to reconsider. From what I've heard you Juaristas aren't doing so hot right now. Seems to me, you could use all the guns you can get."

The Juarista *jefe* glared at them and pushed away from the post, saying, "Guns, *sí*." His eyes swept them in deliberate insult. "Mercenaries, no."

El Puma snapped an order to the Mexicans who had brought them to the camp, and then he said to Chad and Chris, "My men will take you back to where they found you. You have one day to get out of these mountains. Go back to your own country where you belong."

Christine's head snapped up, and Chad glared at him angrily.

But just as the Mexicans moved to tie on their blindfolds, El Puma whirled. He walked over to Chad and Christine, motioning the Mexicans away.

He looked up at Chad, his gaze a measuring one. "Just how much do you know about guns, *yanqui*? Besides their usefulness in killing people?" he added sarcastically.

Christine saw the hot flush of anger in Chad's face. Then he shrugged, saying, "If it shoots, I can shoot it."

"A repeater carbine?" El Puma snapped.

Chad nodded, saying, "Have one myself. Or rather, I did until your men took it away from me."

El Puma's look was penetrating. "Could you teach others to shoot this gun, this repeater carbine?"

Chad thought he was beginning to get the drift of El Puma's thoughts. Apparently, he wanted someone to teach his men how to shoot repeater carbines. He grinned, saying, "Sure, I taught my kid brother here how to use one. I reckon if I can teach him, I can teach anyone." Chad leaned forward and said in a confidential voice, "He's not too smart you know."

Christine's head jerked around; she glared at Chad.

El Puma looked thoughtful. Finally, he said, "Perhaps we can do business after all, *señores*. Stick around for a couple of days. I will discuss this with you later. In the meanwhile, you will have complete freedom of my camp." His voice turned hard and contained a warning. "Only, do not try to sneak away, *señores*. I have men watching all the exits and entrances to this camp."

El Puma said something to one of the Mexicans

270

standing by them. Then he turned back to Chris and Chad, saying, "Roberto, here, will show you where to sleep and where you can get something to eat."

The Juarista leader abruptly turned and walked back into the cabin, dismissing them arrogantly.

Christine watched with relief as the Mexicans untied her hands. She rubbed the chafed skin gratefully, and looked up in surprise as they handed her her pistol and carbine. Well, she thought, if we're prisoners, we're certainly unusual ones.

As they followed Roberto through the camp, Christine's heart quickened with anticipation. Hopefully, Charles was somewhere in this camp. They had managed to get into El Puma's hideout. Now all they had to do was find Charles and get out. She glanced around the crowded camp. There were at least forty or fifty Juaristas within view, not counting the women and children. And almost all of the men carried guns of some sort. For the first time, she realized how formidable their task was, and her heart sank.

Roberto pointed out an unoccupied lean-to, and Chad nodded his understanding. Then he led them to one of the campfires and barked an order to one of the women standing there. He gave Christine and Chad a sullen look and then walked away.

"I don't think he likes us too much," Chad drawled.

The Mexican women laughed, saying, "He is, how do you *yanqui* say? *Mucho* bear?"

271

Christine looked at the woman, surprised at her English. The woman smiled, openly appraising Chad's big body. Oh no, Christine thought in disgust, here we go again!

Chad grinned down at the woman, saying, "Well, now, I'm mighty glad to see someone around here speaks English. I was afraid the only one I'd have to talk to was my kid brother here."

The woman tossed her long, black hair flirtatiously, saying, "I am Juanita." She placed one hand on her broad hip provocatively and thrust out her large breasts. "You are *mucho* hungry, *sí*?"

Christine couldn't stand watching the hussy throw herself at Chad another minute. "We sure are," she said in a gruff, husky voice. "How about you stop that yapping and feed us?"

The woman's eyebrows rose in surprise. Her look became sullen. She turned, angrily filled two plates, and shoved them at Chad and Christine.

"Thank you, ma'am," Chad said politely, tipping his hat.

Christine felt like kicking him. She whirled and walked away. Chad, with his long strides, quickly caught up with her.

"What in the hell's wrong with you?" Chad mumbled angrily. "Didn't I tell you to keep your mouth shut?"

"I don't like her!" Christine snapped.

"That's irrelevant!" Chad said in a low voice. "Hell, we've got enough problems without you going around antagonizing these people."

They sat in their lean-to and ate, Chad glaring

272

at Christine, and Christine pretending indifference. After they had finished, Chad took their plates back to the Mexican women. Christine was forced to sit and watch while Chad and the woman laughed and talked.

When Chad returned, he plopped down beside her. He glanced around them before saying, "Now listen to me, Chris. I'm deliberately pretending not to know much Spanish in the hope that one of the Mexicans will let something slip in front of me. By the same token, be careful what you say to me when others are within hearing distance. Two can play that game. Understand?"

Christine nodded.

"All right, I'm going to take a leisurely stroll around the camp and see what I can find out. You stay here."

"Why can't I go along? I can be looking too?"

"Damn it, no!" Chad said angrily. "I want you to stay out of sight as much as possible. Now you stay here and keep out of trouble."

Christine glared at his back as he walked away. He treats me like a child, she thought resentfully. For a short while, she seethed, but then her attention was drawn to the camp itself.

She was still surprised that there were women and children present. She had imagined a guerrilla band to be solely male. After all, weren't they soldiers of some kind? She observed the women washing and cooking, occasionally stopping to scold a particularly unruly child. And when the men drifted back that evening, they didn't look fierce and dangerous to Christine

273

anymore. Most of them looked weary, much like average men returning from daily toil. She watched in amazement as the men greeted their families warmly, one swinging his little daughter high into the air while the child squealed in delight.

Not all of the men had families. That became obvious as more and more of them returned to camp. And it also became clear to Christine that not all of the women were attached to one man. There were several women who were greeted by many different men. Juanita was one of these. Apparently Juanita was one of those women called camp followers, Christine thought as she watched a big Mexican man openly fondling the woman.

Christine looked up in surprise when Chad sat down beside her, a worried look on his face.

"Well?" Christine asked anxiously.

Chad glanced around him cautiously before he answered. "Well, they're holding someone all right, but it's not your brother. I found an old, dilapidated shed back deep in the woods. I could see a man tied up in it through one of the windows."

"How do you know it wasn't Charles?"

"Because he had black hair," Chad replied.

He stared moodily into space. At this point, Chad was reasonably sure El Puma wasn't holding Christine's brother after all. The whole damned trip had been nothing but a wild-goose chase. The realization made him feel sick. And now what? he asked himself. Knowing Christine, she'd insist he keep looking and trying to find her brother somewhere in these damned mountains. But without a clue to go on, that would be like looking for the proverbial needle in the middle of a haystack. And with only one week left to find him, the whole thing was impossible!

He wondered if he should tell her what he suspected. Chad looked down at her anxious, drawn face. His heart twisted. No, he couldn't tell her, not now at least. And not in the middle of the Juarista camp. What if she got hysterical and blew their cover? He didn't think El Puma would take kindly to them entering his camp under false pretenses. And El Puma was one man Chad didn't want to aggravate.

"After I've eaten, I'll search the other side of the camp," Chad said, playing for time.

Later that night, Chris stood beside their lean-to, watching for Chad's return. The light from several campfires bathed the entire center of the camp. She strained her eyes to see the man emerging from the trees on the opposite side of the clearing, then, recognizing Chad's lazy swagger, she sighed in relief.

"The big *tejano*, he is not here?" A sultry, feminine voice startled Christine.

Christine looked at Juanita, standing beside her, and ducked her head to hide her face, muttering, "No."

Juanita looked at the youth, nervously shuffling his feet. His rudeness that afternoon had made her angry, and she still had not forgiven him his insulting manner. He looks shy and nervous now, she thought. He's just a boy, and I could easily put him in his place. No, she thought, smiling maliciously, I can think of an even better revenge. He's just an inexperienced youth. I'll tease him, excite him, and then tell him to go to hell!

Christine gasped as Juanita ran her hand over her cheek, saying, "No whiskers? How old are you *muchacho*?"

"Fourteen," Christine croaked nervously.

"*Sí, sí*, just a *muchacho*." Juanita pressed her lush body against Christine's, wiggling suggestively. "You are, how do you say? Cute?"

Christine looked down at Juanita's big breasts pressed against her chest and felt like gagging. My God, Christine thought, she's trying to seduce me! Christine had no idea of how to handle the awkward situation. She backed away and found herself trapped against the lean-to.

"Tell me, *muchacho*," Juanita said in a husky, seductive voice, her body pinning Christine against the lean-to. "Have you had a woman yet?"

Christine shook her head jerkily and then froze in horror. Juanita's hand was slowly, deliberately moving up her thigh, closer and closer to her groin.

Suddenly, Juanita's body was whirled away from Christine's. Chad stood, holding the Mexican woman in a tight embrace, grinning down at her.

"What do you want a boy for, sweetheart, when you can have a real man?" he drawled.

Juanita completely forgot Christine. She wiggled even closer to Chad's big body, her pelvis grinding into his, saying, "Oh *sí*, you are *mucho hombre*."

"You're damned right I am," Chad replied. "Come on, sweetheart, I'll show you just how much of a man I am."

Totally ignoring Christine, Chad and Juanita strolled off, Chad's arm around the woman's waist possessively. Christine, trembling with shock, was left behind to deal with a mixture of emotions. She was relieved at being rescued from an awkward, almost dangerous situation. But she was angry at Chad for taking the woman away, obviously to make love to her, and she was hurt by his rejection and the knowledge of what he was going to do.

She stumbled into the lean-to and collapsed in one corner, fighting back tears. She knew that Chad had gone to other women before her. She had also known that as soon as there were other women around, he would go to them again. After all, Chad was a man, she thought. But what hurt was that he had done it so openly, almost insultingly, like a slap in her face, without a backward glance or any concern for her feelings.

You have no claim on him, Christine reminded herself firmly. Nor has he made you any promises. You know he doesn't love you. You were just a willing partner who would satisfy his needs. And he didn't just use your body, either. No more than you used his. Besides, you don't love him. What you feel for him isn't love. It's just physical attraction. You shouldn't care what he does. You don't care about him.

But if I don't care about him, Christine thought, then why do I feel so hurt, so miserable? Suddenly Christine was racked with soul-tearing sobs, tears streaming down her face. She huddled in a tight ball in a corner of the lean-to, trying to muffle the sounds of her crying, thinking, I'm only crying because I'm worried about Charles, not because I care about that damned, big Texan.

Christine emerged from her lean-to the next morning, drawn and exhausted. She had been tormented all night by visions of Chad making love to Juanita, and knowing only too well how beautifully Chad made love, those visions had been very vivid. Seeing him crossing the camp and striding lazily toward her, Christine panicked. Despite her anxiety over whether or not he had any news about Charles, she couldn't face him, not yet. She turned and ran into the deep woods behind her.

Christine ran through the woods, stumbling and half sobbing, with Chad following and calling her name. Hearing his voice, she ran even faster, not even noticing when she lost her hat. She raced, twisting and turning blindly, not caring where she was going, knowing only that she had to get away from him. Finally, when she was deep in the woods, she leaned against a tree to catch her breath.

Hearing no further sounds of pursuit, she collapsed on the ground, thinking, he'll never find me here. Her breath still came in ragged gasps and her body was drenched with sweat from running in her heavy serape. She stripped off the offending garment, relishing the feel of the cool air on her overheated skin and wiping the sweat from her face and neck with the serape.

His tracking abilities made it easy for Chad to follow Christine's erratic flight through the woods. He entered the clearing where she sat just minutes later. "What in the hell is wrong with you, Chris?" he asked in irritated voice. "Didn't you hear me calling you?"

Christine whirled, shocked that Chad had found her. She flew to her feet, panting, "Go away! Leave me alone!"

Chad frowned, saying, "Chris . . ."

Anger came to Christine's defense, blind, unreasoning anger. "Go back to your whore!" she hissed.

So that was what was bothering her, Chad thought. Then she does care about me after all. At least enough to be jealous. A slow grin spread over his face. "You're jealous," he accused.

"Jealous?" Christine screamed. "Don't be ridiculous! Why should I care what you do? Why, you . . . you can make love to every damned whore in Mexico for all I care!"

Chad heard the hurt in Christine's voice. He sobered, saying, "I didn't make love to her, Chris. Nothing happened. I only kissed her a couple of times. And the only reason I did that was to keep her from getting suspicious."

Christine was so hurt and incensed that she didn't even hear Chad's words. She glared at him, her look murderous.

What in the hell is the matter with her? Chad thought. Doesn't she believe me? Hell, he'd only gone with Juanita to protect Christine's true identity. He'd seen the camp follower's hand on Christine's thigh and knew it was just a matter of seconds before the woman would discover Christine wasn't the boy she was pretending to be. Hell, he hadn't wanted Juanita. After experiencing the supreme ecstasy and total fulfillment of making love with Christine, just the thought of the act with another woman disgusted him. No, he belonged to Chris now, body and soul. And now she was accusing him of infidelity. His own anger rose.

"For Christ's sake, Chris," he snapped. "Do you actually think that after what we've shared, I could make love to any other woman?" He stepped closer, saying, "No, Chris, I . . ."

Christine still didn't hear his words or realize that he was on the verge of making a declaration of love. But she did see him reaching for her. "Don't touch me!" she screeched. "Do you think I'd let you touch me after that woman, that whore? No, you'll never touch me again!"

Chad wasn't paying any attention to Christine's tirade. His sharp ears had caught the sound of a twig cracking. He swung his head around, quickly scanning the woods behind them.

Chad saw nothing, but all of his senses were sending out warning signals. He whirled back to Christine, hissing, "Sssh, Chris. Keep your voice down." He bent, picking up her serape and saying, "Here, put this on, and hurry!"

Christine's eyes flashed. "Don't tell me what to—"

Chad's hand clamped over Christine's mouth, and she struggled against him. "Be still, you little wildcat," Chad whispered urgently. "Someone's out there in the woods behind us."

Looking over Chad's shoulder, Christine froze, her eyes widened with surprise. Seeing her look, Chad's hand flew to his gun.

"Don't try it, Señor Yancy," a deep male voice said. "I have you covered."

Slowly Chad turned to face El Puma. The Mexican *jefe* stood with his six-shooter pointed at them, a mocking smile on his face.

Instinctively, Chad moved in front of Christine.

"If you are trying to hide the señorita's charms, I am afraid it is too late, *señor*. Now, move aside!" El Puma snapped. "I want to see both of you."

As Chad reluctantly moved away from Christine, El Puma said, "You, *señorita*, throw away your gun."

Her hand trembling badly, Christine drew her pistol from its holster and tossed it to the ground.

"Now his!" El Puma barked.

Christine fumbled in Chad's holster for his gun and dropped it beside her own. Chad stood rigid, angrily glaring at the Mexican.

"And now my friends," El Puma said sarcastically, "I think we will go back to my cabin and have a little talk."

281

Chapter Thirteen

Tight-faced and grim-lipped, Chad walked back to the Juarista's camp, wondering what El Puma had in mind for them. Christine walked beside him, feeling sick with remorse, knowing El Puma's discovery of her true identity was her fault and that she had ruined their chances of rescuing Charles and had placed their lives in jeopardy.

As they walked up to El Puma's cabin, several astonished-looking Mexicans joined them. El Puma snapped an order to one of the men who nodded and trotted off, saying, "*Sí, sí, jefe.*"

El Puma led them into the dark cabin, and for a minute, Christine couldn't see anything. Then as her eyes adjusted to the sudden change of light, she saw that they stood in a large, sparsely furnished room. El Puma motioned them to a door at one side and pushed the door open with his foot.

"You wait in here, *señorita*," the Mexican said gruffly.

Christine moved toward the room, and Chad stepped forward protectively, his look murderous.

"Not you, *señor*!" El Puma barked. "You and I are going to have a little talk. The *señorita* will wait in here."

Christine looked at Chad anxiously and then walked into the room. The door closed behind her with a soft click as it locked.

El Puma looked up at Chad after locking the door, and said, "Now, *señor*, suppose you walk over there to that big chair, and you and I will have a little chat."

Chad walked sullenly over to the big overstuffed chair, its material torn and badly worn, and sat down. El Puma sat on the edge of a battered desk a few feet away, one leg swinging lazily.

For a minute, the two men, both very dangerous and deadly, looked at each other. Blue eyes and black eyes met and clashed in a show of stubborn wills. Neither wavered. Both thought, I've met my match in this man.

El Puma broke the silent confrontation. His voice was hard, his look angry. "You are not the *tejano pistolero* you pretend to be. I do not like being tricked, *señor*." He looked at Chad thoughtfully. "I might think you were a French spy, except not even a Frenchman would be stupid enough to bring a woman into an enemy camp." He leaned forward, the gun pointed menacingly at Chad's head, saying, "Now who are you, *señor*, and why were you so determined to get into my camp?"

Chad looked into the muzzle of the gun and thought, It won't do any good to lie. Not that he had a convenient lie handy, he thought ruefully. He might as well tell him the truth.

He sighed, saying, "My name is Chad Yancy. The lady," he motioned toward the room where Christine was, "is Miss Christine Roberts. About two months ago, Miss Roberts's brother was captured by someone in these mountains and is being held for a twenty-five thousand dollar ransom. She couldn't raise the money, so she hired me to bring her down here to find her brother."

"And you think the brother is here in my camp?" El Puma asked, his voice incredulous.

Chad nodded.

El Puma's look turned thunderous. "Señor Yancy, these mountains are crawling with bandidos. Why do you think I am holding her brother?"

"Miss Roberts's brother is a reporter for a New York newspaper. In the last letter she received from him, before the ransom note arrived, he said he was going into northern Mexico to find a Juarista named El Puma. He wanted to interview you for a story. The ransom note said the money was to be delivered to Sarita, near here, so we figured it might be you that held him." Chad shrugged. "It was the only clue we had."

El Puma's black eyes glittered with anger. "Her brother is not here!"

"I know that now," Chad drawled lazily. "I've

already looked."

El Puma glared at him. Chad shrugged again.

"Señor Yancy," El Puma said in a biting voice, "I do not take hostages and hold them for ransom. I am not a criminal, a common bandit." He raised his dark, handsome head proudly, saying, "I am a soldier, a Juarista!"

Chad was frustrated and angry himself. He threw caution to the wind. "Oh hell, get off it! You damned Juaristas aren't above a little thievery yourselves! Look at some of your own generals, Díaz for example."

The Mexican's body was stiff with outrage and indignation.

"All right," Chad conceded. "So maybe you wouldn't sink to lining your own pockets with blood money, but the French have you Juaristas backed into a corner, and everyone knows the Mexican government is flat broke. You're desperate, and when a desperate man is cornered, personal principles have a way of going down the drain."

El Puma frowned. What the *tejano* said was true. Desperate people did do desperate things. And the Juaristas were desperate. His body relaxed.

The Mexican cocked his head to one side, a curious look on his face. "Tell me, Señor Yancy, if you had found her brother here, what would you have done?"

"Try to rescue him and escape," Chad replied evenly.

The Mexican's dark eyebrows rose in astonishment. "Rescue him? Escape? In the middle of a Juarista camp with over a hundred armed men? With only one woman to help you?"

El Puma threw his head back and laughed. Chad glared at him.

When he had controlled himself, his black eyes still twinkling with amusement, El Puma said, "Señor Yancy, you are not only crazy, you are stupid! Only an idiot would try such a crazy stunt. With men like you, no wonder the South lost her war."

The jibe infuriated Chad. He sneered, saying, "Don't be so smart, El Puma. You haven't won your war yet either."

The look of amusement on El Puma's face disappeared. He glared at Chad, who glared back. If looks could kill, both men would have been dead.

Finally Chad said, "Look, I've got better things to do than sit around here exchanging insults with you. I'll just get about my business and leave you to yours."

He started to rise, then froze at El Puma's words. "I'm afraid not, Señor Yancy. You see, I'm not through with you yet. Sit down!"

Chad sat back down, stunned, wondering what in the hell to do. Even if he rushed the Mexican and managed to get the gun away without getting killed himself, he wouldn't have a ghost of a chance of getting him and Christine out of the camp alive. He sat back and waited, his face inscrutable, his nerves crawling.

A minute later, one of El Puma's men entered

and handed El Puma a carbine. The Juarista leader dismissed the man and placed the gun on the desk beside him.

Pointing to the gun, El Puma said, "Tell me about your gun, *señor*."

"What do you want to know?" Chad drawled lazily.

"Everything, *señor*."

Chad shrugged, saying, "That's a Spencer carbine. It's a seven-shot, tube-fed, fifty-four-caliber, lever-action repeater. With two loaded single shots, it can be fired nine times without reloading. Fully loaded, it weighs ten pounds and eight ounces."

"And the ammunition?" El Puma asked.

"It uses a fifty-six/fifty-six Spencer rimfire metallic cartridge that holds between forty to forty-five grains of powder with a three hundred fifty-grain lead bullet."

"Is it accurate?" El Puma asked, his look intent.

"At short range, yes," Chad replied. "But if you want accuracy for over a thousand yards, you'd want a Sharps. But that's a single-shot rifle."

El Puma nodded and gazed at the gun thoughtfully. He looked back at Chad, a small smile playing at his lips. "Is it a good gun to fight a war with?"

Chad's eyebrows lifted. So that was why he was so interested. "Yes. It's been said that if the North had used it from the beginning of the Civil War, it would have shortened the war by a year or more."

"How fast can you fire it?" the Mexican asked, his eyes glittering with excitement.

"When the army was testing it, Spencer himself was present. He fired it nine times in one minute. Of course, he was an expert."

"And you, *señor*, how fast can you fire it?"

"I've never timed myself," Chad answered sarcastically.

"Guess, *señor*," the Mexican said with an ugly snarl.

Chad shrugged. "With accuracy, maybe seven times a minute," he said indifferently.

El Puma was impressed with both the *pistolero*'s expertise with a gun and the gun itself. He looked at Chad intently, saying, "Do you realize, *señor*, that the Mexican army has been fighting with single-shot rifles, many of them not even breech loaded? Do you know what a difference a gun like this Spencer carbine could make in our war against the French?"

"Sure," Chad replied. "Look, El Puma, if it's Spencers you want, all you've got to do is go to the border and help yourself. The American army leaves wagonloads of them sitting around at night, deliberately unguarded so that the Juaristas can sneak over the border and take them."

"The border is over two hundred miles away, *señor*," El Puma replied. "And the Juaristas are not the only ones taking those guns your army leaves unguarded at night."

Chad frowned. He had never thought of it before, but anyone could take those guns, not necessarily just Juaristas, but bandits, Apaches or gunrunners too. He knew there was a lot of gunrunning going on, mostly to the French since the Mexican government was broke. Hell, if the gunrunners were stealing those guns from the army, no wonder gunrunning was such a lucrative business.

As if reading his mind, El Puma said, "*Sí, yanqui* gunrunners."

El Puma laid his pistol on the desk beside Chad's carbine and paced thoughtfully. Chad eyed the gun, wondering.

"Don't try it, *señor*," El Puma said, again reading his thoughts. He pointed to a darkened corner of the room. "He would have to shoot you."

Chad glanced into the darkened corner of the room and, for the first time, realized another Mexican sat there, his face impassive, his gun aimed right at Chad.

Chad sat back, feeling even more frustrated.

El Puma continued to pace. He walked with an easy catlike grace, and Chad could sense the unleashed power in that tall, lithe body. No wonder they call him the mountain lion, he thought with reluctant admiration.

El Puma broke the silence. "Yesterday, before you came into my camp, some of my men had just returned from an encounter with the enemy. They had come across a French patrol. A civilian rode with them. The French, my men killed of course. The civilian, they brought back as a prisoner."

Chad remembered the man he had seen tied up in the old shack. Well, that settled that mystery, but he still didn't know what El Puma was leading up to.

El Puma continued. "It turned out that the man was a *tejano*, like yourself. A mercenary hired out to the French. He and the French patrol were on their way to pick up a wagon of Spencer carbines and ammunition from *yanqui* gunrunners. It seems the French sent the *tejano* along because he spoke English. He carried a French letter of credit."

Despite his promise to himself to act disinterested, Chad asked, "A letter of credit?"

El Puma chuckled softly, saying, "*Sí, señor*, the French know better than to send money with all the *bandidos* in these mountains. Bandidos will kill for money, but a letter of credit is of no use to them. For years, the French in these parts have used this method of paying for the supplies they buy. It has cut down on the bandidos attacking their patrols drastically."

Chad nodded. He supposed if the bandits knew the French didn't carry money, there would be no gain in attacking them.

El Puma continued, "The French and the gunrunners were supposed to meet late tomorrow in a pass about a day's ride from here." El Puma continued to pace, then whirled suddenly, his look fierce, saying, "I want those guns!"

Chad was wary. He knew the Juarista wasn't telling him all this just to pass the time of day. He had a very uncomfortable feeling.

"What's all this got to do with me?" Chad asked suspiciously.

El Puma smiled smugly. He sat back down on the corner of the desk and folded his arms over his chest, saying, "I think that you and I might make a . . . how do you *yanquis* say? A deal?"

"A deal?" Chad asked warily.

"*Sí, señor*. You see, I happen to know who is holding Miss Roberts's brother. I make it my business to know everything that goes on in these mountains." El Puma leaned forward, saying, "I know what bandidos are holding him and where their hideout is. So you see, I have the information you want. And me? I want those guns."

"Wait a minute," Chad said in a hard voice. "Are you suggesting that I impersonate this mercenary?"

El Puma grinned. "*Sí, señor*. You and the mercenary look remarkably alike. And of course, you both talk with a Texas accent. I propose that you take the mercenary's place. Some of my men will dress in the French uniforms and accompany—"

"You're crazy!" Chad interjected. "Did it ever occur to you that the French may have done business with these gunrunners before? That the gunrunners might know this man I'm supposed to impersonate personally? Then what?"

El Puma shrugged, then said, "Then you will have to fight for the guns."

"Fight?" Chad yelled, jumping to his feet. "Hell no! Not me! I just got through with three long years of fighting someone else's war. I'm not about to get involved in another one. It's your war, El Puma. You fight it!"

The Juarista seemed totally unperturbed by Chad's outburst. "As you wish, *señor*." He rose and walked across the room, saying over his shoulder. "You and the *señorita* are free to leave." He stopped at the door and said meaningfully, "Good luck in finding Miss Roberts's brother, *señor*. You're going to need it."

Chad knew El Puma had him just where he wanted him. The realization infuriated him. "What happened to the noble El Puma, the man whose principles wouldn't let him sink to holding a hostage for ransom?" he scoffed, adding, "but you're not above a little blackmail are you?"

El Puma turned, his eyes glittering with anger. "I prefer to think of it as a business agreement, *señor*," he said tightly.

"Business agreement?" Chad asked sarcastically. "An innocent man is being held by a bunch of cutthroats, who are going to murder him in cold blood if a ransom isn't paid. You can prevent that murder by telling me where that man is. But you won't do it, unless I do some dirty work for you first. You call that a business agreement?"

El Puma glared at him. Chad looked at him with contempt.

El Puma's proud shoulders slumped. He walked back into the room and sat down behind the battered desk. He leaned forward, his head cupped in his hands, staring moodily at the desk top. Then slowly he raised his head, a sad look in his eyes, and said, "You are right, *señor*. Desperate men *do* do things that are against their principles. And I am desperate. In ordinary times, I would abhor what I am forced to do now. But I have seen too many of my people killed, many just

293

as innocent as Miss Roberts's brother. I have seen whole villages burned and totally wiped out by the French, women and children included. I am sick of killing and death, and yet I know there is so much more killing ahead of us before we push these damned French dogs out of our country. If blackmail can possibly keep any more of my people from being needlessly killed . . . then, yes, I will do it."

Chad looked down at the man with empathy. He knew just how he felt. He, too, was sick of killing and death. The Civil War had been a long, bloody, bitter struggle, but it had never been a war against civilians as this war in Mexico was. Chad had heard stories of entire villages being wiped out, of hundreds of men, women, and children shot before French firing squads as reprisals for some meaningless Juarista victory.

Chad sat back down and faced the Juarista leader, all animosity gone. His look was penetrating as he asked, "Who are you, El Puma? I mean, who are you really? I know you're a Creole. Your skin coloring, your aristocratic air, your fluency with English tell me that. So what's a man like you doing out here in these mountains leading a motley bunch of mestizos and Yaqui Indians?"

El Puma's dark eyebrows lifted, and then his eyes met the Texan's levelly across the desk. "Who am I, you ask? My name is Ramon Carlos Estaban de Vega. And *sí*, I am a Creole. My family was an old and respected one in Mexico." He lifted his head proudly. "But first and foremost, I am a Mexican, *señor*, just as those mestizos and Indians out there are Mexicans. And for the first time in our long history, all the social classes in Mexico are fighting a common enemy, the French."

El Puma rose and walked around to the front of the desk. Leaning on it casually, he said, "I am also a Juarista, as was my father. I happen to believe in what Juárez wants for Mexico, social changes and equality for all men. The day of feudalism is gone. It is time, *señor*, that Mexico belong to the Mexican people, instead of a select few."

Chad nodded. He knew enough about Mexican politics to know that many Creoles supported Juárcz. But those men were in the higher echelons of his government or army.

Again, El Puma seemed to read his mind. "I could have been an officer in the Mexican army, *señor*. A major or a colonel perhaps," he said with a sneer. Then his face broke into a wide smile, his white teeth flashing against his tanned face. "But I am not a man to take orders from some stupid burro who happens to outrank me, *señor*. I prefer to fight with the true soldiers in this war, the common Mexican people, my people."

Spoken by anyone else, these words might have seemed melodramatic to Chad. But he was impressed with El Puma's sincerity. Despite himself, he found himself liking and respecting the proud Mexican. He had also had time to calm down. He knew his only chance of rescuing Christine's brother lay in accepting El Puma's deal. He still disliked his tactics, but he had to admit that if he was in El Puma's situation, he'd do the same thing.

Chad sighed, saying, "All right, you've got me over a barrel, and we both know it. But before I agree to this crazy scheme of yours, there're several things I want to get straight."

El Puma grinned, saying, "*Sí, amigo.*"

Amigo, Chad thought ruefully. Suddenly, I'm his friend. Clever bastard, too, isn't he?

Chad looked the Juarista straight in the eye, saying, "In the first place, I refuse to call you by that ridiculous name, El Puma."

The Mexican's dark eyebrows rose, then he shrugged. "Call me *Ramón*."

"Okay, Ramón," Chad drawled lazily, "now what about her?" He motioned to the room Christine was locked in. "What happens to her while I'm gone?"

"She will wait here for you. She will be perfectly safe," El Puma answered smoothly.

"Safe? With that randy bunch of desperados out there you call an army? Hell, you marched her right through your camp. I'm sure every man out there knows she's a woman by now. The least you could have done is let her put her serape back on."

El Puma chuckled, saying, "*Señor*, do you really think that short hair and serape would have fooled anyone for long? No, *señor*, there is something about the way she walks that . . ." He shrugged, then added, "That is what made me suspicious in the first place. Then when I saw you both rushing from the camp this morning, I was

296

even more suspicious. So I followed you."

Damn, Chad thought, I warned her about that walk of hers.

"But, *señor*, you are right about some of my men. There are a few that are a little unruly. She will stay here in my cabin as my guest."

Chad glared at him.

El Puma's face flushed with anger. "*Señor* Yancy, despite what you may think of me, I am a gentleman," he said indignantly. "I do not ravish women. Also, my younger sister lives here with me. If you prefer, she can be your woman's companion. No one in this camp would dare accost your woman as long as she is in my sister's company."

Chad nodded in agreement. He hadn't missed Ramón's reference to Christine as his woman. Apparently the Juarista had been eavesdropping in the woods for longer than Chad had realized.

"But, *Señor* Yancy," El Puma said stiffly, "I must insist that if we involve my sister in this, we tell her Miss Roberts is your wife."

"My wife?" Chad asked, surprised.

"*Señor* Yancy, my sister is young and impressionable. I have tried to protect her innocence and, despite our unsavory surroundings, bring her up to be a young lady of quality as my mother would have wished. She has been taught that men and women do not live together and travel together unless they are married."

Chad jumped to his feet, his eyes blazing. "You-son-of-a-bitch! Do you think Christine is any less a lady than your sister?"

"*Señor*, please, calm down. I do not mean any insult to Miss Roberts. I am not that foolish. Apparently you love her very much, or you would not be so fiercely protective. And quite frankly, *señor*, you are one man I wouldn't like to tangle with. But as my sister's guardian, I am only trying to protect her too."

Typical stiff-necked Creole, Chad thought with disgust. Them and their obsessive protectiveness of their women's virtue and innocence. El Puma might be clever and a brilliant strategist, but he was downright stupid if he thought he could shield his sister from the world and the facts of life living in this camp. Hell, Chad thought, I don't really care what Ramón tells his sister about me and Chris. The only important thing is that Chris will be safe while I'm gone.

"Tell your sister any damned thing you want!" Chad snapped. He leaned forward, his big body menacing, saying, "But if anything happens to Chris while I'm gone—"

"*Señor*, I promise you, she will be safe here."

"One more question," Chad said firmly. "What happens to her if we are forced to fight for those guns and I don't come back?"

El Puma's face paled slightly. "Then, *señor*, I shall personally escort Miss Roberts back to the border."

Chad nodded and then relaxed in the big chair. "When do we leave?"

"Tomorrow morning before dawn. I sent some men yesterday to strip the dead Frenchmen of their uniforms. I will send eight of my best men with you, including Miguel, one of my lieuten-ants. He is young, but he is one of my best fighters. He also understands and speaks En-glish."

"That's not necessary for my sake," Chad replied. "I speak fluent Spanish."

"I guessed that, *señor*," El Puma said, his smile mocking.

"Then you still don't trust me? Hell, you've got Chris. You know I won't try anything."

El Puma shrugged, saying smoothly, "I have not managed to survive all these years in these mountains by trusting others, *amigo*."

Chad glared at him. El Puma chose to ignore him, saying, "I would go with you, but I have already made plans for tomorrow. You see, I have recently received word that the French are sending reinforcements to Fort Andreas, south of here. I have planned a little welcome for them."

The diabolical look on El Puma's face sent a shiver down Chad's spine. Then another realiza-tion took hold. "You mean you aren't going to be here either?"

"*Amigo*, please, your woman will be safe. Would I leave my own sister if I was not sure of this?"

Chad sat back, feeling uneasy. All his senses were sending out warning signals. But was the impending danger he sensed a threat to him or Christine? To me, I hope, Chad thought. He looked up, saying, "Any of those men you're sending with me particularly good with a gun?"

"*Sí*, that would be Miguel again."

"Do you think he and I could get together this afternoon? I was thinking he could carry Chris's Spencer. I'd feel safer with at least two repeating carbines on our side. I thought I could show him how to load it and give him some pointers on firing it."

"That is an excellent idea, *señor*. And if you don't mind, I would like to join you and learn also. Then when we get our new carbines, Miguel and I can teach the rest of my men."

"Don't count your chickens before they hatch," Chad replied sourly.

The Texan rose, holding out his hand. "Now I'll take that key to that door over there. I imagine Chris is frightened half out of her wits."

"*Sí, amigo*," El Puma said, handing him the key. He grinned, saying, "You and your wife will be my honored guests."

Sanctimonious son-of-a-bitch, Chad thought as he walked to the door. He bent, turned the key, and stepped into the room. Christine sat huddled in one corner of the room, her eyes wide with fear.

"You can relax now, Chris," Chad said softly. "El Puma isn't going to harm us. As a matter of fact, he knows who's holding your brother and where we can find him. He'll tell us . . . for a price."

Christine cried out with joy and flung herself into Chad's arms, saying, "Oh, Chad, that's wonderful! I'm so happy I could cry."

Then the last of Chad's statement penetrated Christine's consciousness. Her look turned anxious. "What do you mean, for a price? Chad, I didn't bring any money with me!"

"I wish it was that simple," Chad replied. "Here, sit down on the bed while I tell you about it."

After Chad had explained, Christine sat on the bed, staring at her hands in her lap, a worried look on her face. "How long will you be gone?" she muttered.

"Two days. Don't worry, you'll be safe here," Chad said misinterpreting her worried look.

Christine hadn't even considered her safety. She was too worried about Chad's. The plan sounded dangerous to her. And if anything happened to the big Texan . . .

Chad interrupted her dismal thoughts, saying, "By the way, Chris, I told El Puma we were married." I'll be damned if I'll let her know that stiff-necked Creole suggested it to protect his sister's innocence, Chad thought, feeling his anger rise again.

"Married?" Christine asked in a shocked voice.

"Yes," Chad replied. "I figured if the men in this camp thought you were my wife, they'd think twice about trying anything with you."

Well, Christine thought, there certainly wasn't any point in trying to resume her disguise. She had seen the men looking at her breasts when El Puma marched them through the camp. And now she was to be Mrs. Chad Yancy. The thought sent a thrill through her. She frowned in puzzlement at it. She had sworn never to marry.

"El Puma has a sister who lives here with him," Chad said. "She'll keep you company. But promise me you'll never go out into the camp without her."

Christine nodded, still distracted by her puzzling feelings.

That afternoon after Chad had left, a soft knock sounded on Christine's door. She opened it to see a petite, very pretty girl standing in the hallway, her black eyes twinkling with excitement.

"*Buenas tardes, señora*," the girl said. "I am María, El Puma's sister."

"Oh yes," Christine said, moving aside for the girl to enter. "I'm Christine Roberts." Christine blushed, saying, "I mean Yancy. You see, we've only been married a short time, and I'm not used to my new name yet," Christine added nervously.

The girl smiled knowingly. She was not so easily fooled. "I thought you might like to have a bath and some clean clothes."

"The bath sounds wonderful," Christine replied. "But I'm afraid I'll have to put these clothes back on. I didn't get a chance last night to wash my dirty pair."

María tossed a long, black curl over her shoulder and moved her head from side to side thoughtfully. Then she cried, "I know! We'll ask Rita if we can borrow some clothes from her. She's shorter than you are, but I think they will fit."

"Oh, I couldn't borrow clothes from anyone," Christine said in a shocked voice.

"Of course you can!" the vivacious girl replied. "You don't want to go around looking like that!"

302

She looked at the boy's clothes and wrinkled her nose in distaste.

Christine flushed hotly. But before she could object any further, María had whisked her away, ignoring her objections completely, and before Christine fully realized what had happened, she was sitting in a tub of water in María's room, her dirty pants and shirt carried away by the Mexican girl.

Sitting in the hot water, still a little stunned, Christine thought, goodness, she must have learned that tactic from her brother. What do they call it? Storming the fortress?

Christine's bath was interrupted briefly when María discreetly tossed some clothes through the door, saying, "Here, *señora*, see if these fit."

Christine tried to work up some resentment toward the girl's domineering attitude, but found it very hard to be successful. María was just too cheerful, too lively not to like. But imagine, Christine thought, a tiny girl, who couldn't be much over sixteen, bossing me around as if I were a three-year-old. Why, I'd make two of her!

Christine dried off and slipped on the white blouse, petticoat, and long, red skirt. The blouse, embroidered with tiny flowers around the neckline, fit perfectly, but Christine was disturbed at its low cut. It revealed entirely too much of her full, generous breasts. While the skirt fit perfectly at the waist, it was, naturally, too short on Christine's tall body. Instead of reaching her ankles, the skirt hit her at mid calf. Christine looked down at herself with disgust. Well, at least they're clean, she thought, as she slipped on the crude sandals María had left her.

But that night, when Christine joined Chad, María, and El Puma for their evening meal, Chad thought she looked lovely. The Mexican *jefe* saw the warm, loving look that came into the Texan's deep blue eyes when he looked at Christine. El Puma looked at her thoughtfully. Yes, she was quite a remarkable-looking woman. But then, they were both magnificent specimens, both so tall and well proportioned, him so dark and her so fair. Ah, what children those two would produce, their own race of handsome giants.

Later that night, as their bedroom door closed behind them, Chad lost no time in taking Christine into his arms. He didn't know if she was still angry with him over Juanita, but if she was, he wasn't going to give her any time to remember. Tonight, he needed her badly.

His mouth claimed hers in a deep, hungry kiss as his hands roamed over her soft hips, her back, her thighs. He cupped her buttocks, arching her hips into his, pressing her softness into that hot, aching part of him that strained painfully at his tight pants.

Impatiently, with trembling fingers, he undressed her and then himself, pulling her down on the narrow bed, molding their naked bodies together. His mouth and hands were urgent, demanding, and seemingly everywhere—her face, her throat, her breasts, her stomach and thighs— as Chad made tempestuous, almost violent love to her.

At first, Christine was stunned by Chad's sudden, intense love-making. But soon, she was whirling and gasping, her blood coursing hotly through her veins, as Chad covered her with fiery kisses, his hands invoking, demanding response.

"Oh God, lady, I need you," Chad muttered thickly in her ear as he rose over her, his body covering hers.

He took her fiercely, with deep, bold, powerful strokes, his mouth claiming hers in a hot, devouring kiss. The intensity of his thrusts increased to a feverish pitch, driving them higher and higher, until they finally convulsed in a white-hot eruption that seemed to rock the earth around them.

Chad made love to Christine over and over that night, sometimes fierce and demanding, sometimes achingly tender. He was driven by a desperation to satisfy his hunger for her completely, as if he were trying to cram a lifetime of loving into one night.

When he rose the next morning, Christine was still asleep, exhausted by their marathon love-making. Chad dressed and then sat on the narrow bed beside her. He tenderly stroked her jawline, and Christine stirred in her sleep.

"Just in case I don't ever see you again, my magnificent lady," he whispered huskily, "I loved you with all my heart. Just remember that!"

Chad had not shaken his feeling of impending doom.

Chapter Fourteen

Chad glanced back over his shoulder at the Juaristas following him down the narrow, twisted ravine. For all practical purposes they looked like any other French patrol. The uniforms had been washed of their bloodstains and carefully mended, so no telltale signs might reveal that they had once been worn by dead men. Even the saddles and equipment were French. Chad had to hand it to El Puma. He had thought of everything.

He turned and looked at the young Juarista riding beside him, thinking that Miguel looked quite handsome in his French lieutenant's uniform. Chad was impressed with the young man. The youth couldn't be over nineteen or twenty, and yet he showed a maturity far past his years. His keen intelligence, self-assurance, and steely strength of character already set him above most men, even at his young age. Chad remembered the youth's skill at handling the Spencer the day before. Given a few more years of experience, he would probably surpass both himself and El Puma in marksmanship. He watched in admiration the way the young Mexican sat his horse. If he didn't know better, he'd think he was part Comanche.

Of course, Chad knew Miguel was part Indian. His dusky coloring and high cheekbones clearly revealed his heritage. But more than likely, in this part of Mexico, he was part Yaqui. The Texan was curious to know more about the young mestizo.

"Have you been with El Puma long, Miguel?" he asked in Spanish.

"*Sí, señor*, I have been with him three years," the young Mexican replied, switching to English. "I joined him after my family was killed and our village burned by the French," he added, his voice taking on a hard, bitter tone.

Chad frowned; bitterness in one so young disturbed him. Unfortunately, it was all too common here in Mexico.

"Tell me, Miguel. Do you by any chance know what happened to the rest of El Puma's family? Yesterday, he said that his father *was* a Juarista. I assumed that meant his father is dead."

"*Sí, señor,*" Miguel replied. "He was arrested and shot before a firing squad, back when General Zuloaga took over the government and declared himself *presidente*."

Chad remembered the overthrow of the Mexican government by General Zuloaga and his bully-boy army. It had marked the beginning of a series of military coups that threw Mexico into a civil war that lasted three years. It wasn't until 1861 that Juárez was finally returned to his rightful place as president. A year later, the French invaded. Yes, Chad thought sadly, Mexico's history was a long, bloody, violent one. He wondered just how long it would be before the nation would know peace, if ever.

"I assume El Puma's father was one of those who objected to General Zuloaga's takeover," Chad commented.

"*Sí, señor*, he and many other influential hidalgos. They were shot and their lands confiscated."

"So El Puma and his sister lost their land too?"

"El Puma lost much more than that, *señor*," Miguel said sadly. "His mother was a fiercely proud woman. She refused to give up the land. General Zuloaga, the butcher"—Miguel spat contemptuously—"sent his army to force them out, and El Puma's mother and four older brothers were all killed. El Puma and María barely escaped with their lives. Had it not been for his promise to his mother to see his sister to safety, El Puma would have probably fought to the death also."

Chad nodded. He had figured something like that. He and the Juarista *jefe* had one more bond. Besides being sick of war and killing, they had both lost their families and land.

Chad's thoughts drifted back to the young man riding beside him. He was amazed at Miguel's fluency with English, no small accomplishment for a mestizo who had never received any formal education.

"Your English is remarkably good, Miguel. Where did you learn it?"

"María is teaching me," Miguel said proudly.

Chad's head snapped around. Miguel's dusky face flushed under the Texan's close scrutiny. So, Chad thought, El Puma's sister has been secretly meeting with Miguel, and Chad guessed from the young man's blush that more than teaching English had transpired. And after all the stiff-necked Creole's talk about protecting his sister's innocence? It serves him right, Chad thought, suppressing a chuckle.

He knew what El Puma would think if he knew about the young couple. He'd be furious, of course. Despite all his talk about equality of men, Chad knew El Puma would never consent to a match between his high-born sister and this mestizo, regardless of his admiration for the young man.

Chad looked at Miguel. The young Mexican's eyes met his levelly, unflinching, his jaw set stubbornly. No, Chad thought, this youth isn't going to back down for El Puma, despite his hero worship for his *jefe*. Ramón was going to have a fight on his hands. Chad regretted that he wasn't going to be around for the confrontation between the two men, both fiercely proud and deadly dangerous. That would be something to see.

"We are getting close to our meeting place, *señor*," Miguel announced. "It is just past this next bend in the trail."

Chad tensed, his heart racing in anticipation.

310

"All right, Miguel, let me do the talking."

"*Sí, señor,*" Miguel replied gravely.

When they rounded the next corner of the narrow trail, Chad saw a wide clearing. In the middle of it sat a wagon, surrounded by eight, well-armed, dangerous-looking men.

As Chad rode up to them, one of the men stepped forward, his eyes squinting in the glare from the hot Mexican sun. Seeing Chad, the gunrunner tensed, his hand going to his pistol, saying, "Hey, wait a minute! You ain't Tony Peters!"

With lightning speed, the gunrunners pulled their guns out, pointing them at Chad and the disguised Mexicans.

God, this is it! Chad thought, feeling his heart slamming in his chest, beads of perspiration breaking out on his brow. But much to the Juaristas's credit, they played their role to the hilt, pretending confusion instead of drawing their guns and precipitating a shoot-out, that would have caught Chad in the cross fire.

Chad raised his hands slowly, saying, "Hey, wait a minute, fella. I'm Tony's replacement."

The gunrunner glared at him suspiciously.

"Look," Chad said, "I don't blame you for being careful. But I can prove who I am. I have the French letter of credit right here in my shirt pocket."

The gunrunner motioned to one of his men to search Chad. The man pulled the letter of credit out of Chad's pocket, saying, "He's right, Joe. It's the letter of credit all right."

Chad grinned his most engaging grin and said, "Name's Yancy, Chad Yancy. And how about pointing that gun someplace else, friend. You're making me a mite nervous."

The man named Joe lowered his gun slightly, his look still skeptical. "How come Tony didn't come?"

"Tony had a little accident," Chad lied smoothly.

"What kind of accident?" the gunrunner asked, frowning.

"Well, you see, old Tony got himself shot," Chad drawled.

The gunrunner's bushy eyebrows rose. "That right?" Then he leered, saying, "Don't tell me. I bet I can guess what happened. He got caught messing around with some other man's woman, right?"

"That's right," Chad said, grateful for the explanation. "I heard some French officer caught him in bed with his wife."

Joe nodded, saying, "That sounds just like Tony, all right." He slipped his gun back into its holster and turned to the other gunrunners, saying, "Put your guns up, boys. He's okay."

Chad sighed with relief and dismounted.

"Come on, Yancy," Joe said. "Got me a bottle of tequila over here. We'll have a drink."

"Now that sounds good," Chad drawled.

Joe pulled a bottle from his saddlebags and offered Chad a drink. Chad lifted the tequila and pretended to take a long swig of the fiery liquor, then handed it back to Joe.

Joe took a couple of big gulps of tequila, the liquor dribbling down his dirty beard; then he looked suspiciously at Miguel, who had casually followed them. He leaned forward, saying in a low voice, "He's kinda dark for a Frenchie, ain't he?"

"He's one of those black Frenchmen," Chad lied smoothly. "You know, like the black Irish."

Joe had heard of the black Irish. He had no idea what it meant, but he supposed if there could be black Irish then there could be black French. At any rate, he wasn't going to let on to this stranger that he didn't know what he was talking about.

Miguel and one of the other Juaristas had walked to the wagon and were untying the tarp that protected the guns. Seeing them, Joe swung around to Chad, saying, "What in the hell do they think they're doing?"

Chad shrugged, saying, "Checking to see if everything is there I guess."

Joe's ugly face contorted with anger. "The Frenchies never checked the guns before."

"Take it easy, Joe," Chad said smoothly. "He's just a shavetail lieutenant. He's still green behind the ears and scared to death he's going to do something wrong to get him in trouble with his superior officers. Come on, if he wants to do all that work, let him. Let's you and me go sit under that tree over there."

Joe trudged behind Chad reluctantly. He slumped down beside him, glaring resentfully at Miguel. Then he turned, spitting a mouthful of tobacco juice on the ground beside him, and said with a disgusted voice, "Never did like officers. Had me one when I was in the army that was a real smart aleck, always ordering me around and trying to tell me what to do. I finally got tired of it and bashed his skull in. Then me and several other fellas took off and joined Quantrill's Raiders."

"You were with Quantrill's Raiders?" Chad asked, trying to keep the disgust out of his voice.

Joe tipped the half-full tequila bottle and drank greedily before answering. "Sure was."

"How did you get down to these parts then?"

"Quantrill sent a bunch of us down to raid a silver mine in Mexico," the gunrunner answered. "Didn't like the bastard that was running the show, so when we got to Texas, I took off on my own. Just as well I did too."

"How's that?" Chad asked.

Joe took a bite of chewing tobacco and jawed it noisily. "Met me one of them other raiders in a saloon back in El Paso a couple of months ago. He said they found that mine and raided it. Came back with a whole bunch of silver bars." Joe guffawed, saying, "Silver wasn't the only thing they picked up in Mexico. That fella said they got across the border, in that part of Texas that juts out into Mexico, and got sick as dogs. They picked up typhoid fever too. Said they all damned near died out there. Anyways, he said they were so sick and weak they just buried that silver right there. Never did go back for it either. It's still buried out there someplace." Joe's look turned ugly. "Tried to get him to tell me where they buried it, but he said he was too sick to even

314

remember. That dirty son-of-a-bitch! I know he was lying!"

Chad was amazed at the story. He had never known that Quantrill had raided that far south.

Joe guzzled the tequila and then said, "Figure when this gunrunning plays out, I'll just go over there and see if I can't find me that silver. Hell, there must be a fortune buried out there!"

Chad knew the part of Texas Joe was talking about. Some people referred to it as "big bend." It was one of the most desolate and dry areas in the world, nothing but sand, rocks, and rattlesnakes. Many a seasoned, experienced man had gotten lost in that country and never come out alive. Besides that, the trail the Comanches used on their raids into Mexico ran right across that area. Chad wondered if he should warn the gunrunner. Then he remembered what Joe was, a murderer, a deserter, Quantrill Raider, and gunrunner, and he decided against it. Chad thought it would be God's justice if the man died out there searching for that silver.

Joe's face was flushed from the tequila. "Frenchies pay pretty good?"

"Not bad," Chad replied. "Sure is a hell of a lot better than our army."

Joe grinned, a silly, drunken grin, saying, "Say, fella, you ought to go into gunrunning like us. We sure got us a sweet deal going." He threw his arm around Chad's shoulder and said in a low, confidential voice, "You know we don't even have to buy them guns. We steal them."

"Who from?" Chad asked.

"From the army. Those stupid asses leave them right out in the open, all up and down the border, for the Meskins to take." He hiccuped loudly before he continued. "Hell, we just put on sombreros and serapes and just ride in and help ourselves."

So, Chad thought, El Puma had guessed correctly. For the first time, Chad had to agree with Joe. The army was stupid. If the United States ever did fight the French in Mexico, they'd find themselves facing their own guns.

Miguel said something to Chad in Spanish.

"The lieutenant says we've got to get going," Chad said as he stood up.

"Going? What for?" Joe asked, reeling slightly. "Hell, it's gonna be dark in a couple of hours." His look turned suspicious again. "The Frenchies always spent the night with us before."

"I know, but the lieutenant has orders to get these guns back in a hurry," Chad lied easily. He leaned over and whispered, "I think the French are getting ready for a big push."

"That right?" Joe grinned. "Well, I'll be glad when these Frenchies kick them Meskins clean out of Mexico. Heard me a couple of fellas talking about how they was going to get them a plantation down here after the Frenchies take over. That's what I think I'll do after I find me that silver. I'll buy me a plantation and get me a parcel of these Meskin Injuns for slaves."

Chad saw Miguel's back go rigid with anger.

"Say," Chad said as the gunrunner stumbled to his feet. "I just might take you up on that gunrunning offer. But I've got to finish this job

316

with the French first. Where could I get in touch with you?"

"When we ain't running guns, we stay at the Plaza hotel in El Paso. Just ask for Joe Gibbons."

Chad nodded and joined Miguel, thinking if he ever got back to El Paso, he just might pay a visit to the commandant at Fort Bliss. The officer just might be interested in what Joe had told him about stealing the guns.

Chad and Miguel mounted. Then they and the other Juaristas followed the wagon loaded with carbines from the clearing. Chad turned in his saddle, calling, "See you in El Paso, Joe. Be my turn to buy the drinks."

"Yeah, sure, fella," Joe replied, stumbling to a tree. "Be seein' ya."

As they rode away from the clearing, Miguel turned to Chad and said, "There is a well-hidden cave about two hours ride from here. We will spend the night there."

Chad grinned, saying, "What's the matter, Miguel? Don't you trust our gunrunning friends?"

"There were a few times there, *señor*, when I would have loved to kill that *bastardo*," Miguel said tightly.

"I know. He made me ashamed to call him a fellow countryman," Chad said with disgust.

Miguel smiled, and then said sadly, "Every country has it's *bastardos* and butchers. Mexico has had her share too. Remember General Zuloaga?"

Chad looked back at the gunrunners. It didn't look to him like they had any plans for jumping them. One man was already building a fire; the others were settling down with their individual bottles.

An immense wave of relief swept over Chad. We pulled it off, and I'm still alive, he thought with amazement. He threw his dark head back and laughed lustily.

Miguel looked at him in surprise. "Is something funny?"

"Yes," Chad replied. "Don't ever believe in premonition, Miguel. That's a bunch of crap!" He grinned widely, saying, "Come on, let's get these damned guns back to El Puma."

Christine slept until afternoon on the day Chad left, having been given very little time for sleep the night before by Chad's desperate, almost continuous love-making. She was awakened by María gently shaking her shoulder.

"*Señora, señora,*" María cried softly. "Are you ill?"

Christine looked up at the Mexican girl and then around the room, disoriented. She started to rise, and the sheet fell away to reveal her nakedness. Blushing, she quickly pulled it back up.

"No, María, I'm not sick. I guess I was just tired, that's all," Christine replied.

"*Sí, señora.* My brother told me that you and your husband had traveled all the way from Texas."

"Husband?" Christine asked dumbly. Then remembering that she and Chad were supposed to be married, quickly added, "Oh yes, I'm sorry,

María, I must still be half asleep."

María smiled smugly, then said, "If you like, after you have dressed and we have eaten, I can show you around the camp this afternoon."

"That would be nice," Christine replied.

"Then hurry and dress," María said. "I am starving."

After María had left the room, Christine rose and dressed, her mind occupied with thoughts of Chad and his intense love-making the night before. What in the world had gotten into him? Christine wondered. Never had his love-making been so fierce and demanding, or so prolonged. Christine had sensed an urgency in him that disturbed, almost frightened her, something she could not put a name to.

A knocking on the door interrupted her thoughts. "I'm coming María," she called.

As they walked through the camp that afternoon, Christine was amazed at María's easy, friendly manner with the other Juaristas, men and women alike. They called and waved and joked back and forth with one another, María's pretty face beaming with a broad smile, her black eyes twinkling.

"I'm surprised to find so many women and children here," Christine commented.

"*Sí, señora*, after their villages were attacked and their homes burned down by the French, there was no place for the men to leave their families. So they bring them with them."

Christine frowned and said, "Was your home burned by the French also, María?"

María's smile faded; her eyes took on a haunted

319

look. "*Sí*, my home was burned, but not by the French. It was burned by General Zuloaga."

Then María told Christine the same story that Miguel at that very minute was telling Chad. Christine ached for the Mexican girl who sadly related the shocking tale.

"And so Ramón and I fled to the mountains for safety and have been in them ever since," María finished. "Ramón fought with Juárez's guerrillero army during the civil war and now he fights against the French."

"And you've lived in this place all that time?" Christine asked, her hand waving over the camp.

"No, *señora*, we have had camps all over northern Mexico, but always in the mountains."

"You must miss your home and the life you had before you came here," Christine commented.

"*Sí, señora*, I miss the rest of my family and our beautiful hacienda," María said sadly. Then her face brightened, "But I do not miss my way of life."

Christine looked at the Mexican girl, shocked.

"Oh, *señora*, you cannot possibly know what the life of an hidalgo's woman is like in Mexico. You yanqui women have so much more freedom. Our men have this strange compulsion to protect us from the world, a holdover from our Spanish forebearers. We are not allowed to go out of the hacienda without them or some male protector. Otherwise, we are confined to our house and our patio, which itself is walled. They love and protect us, *señora*, so fiercely, so possessively that we are smothered. We are more prisoners than wives and daughters."

María looked up at Christine, her pretty little face intently serious. "Before I came to the mountains, I used to think I would die of boredom. As the daughter of a wealthy hidalgo, I had servants to do everything for me. I didn't even dress or bathe myself without their help. The only thing I could do was embroider and read. And still, I was more fortunate than the other girls I knew. My father was one of the rare hidalgos who believed in educating women. At least, I had my studies. And when my friends came to visit we were expected to sit sedately and talk. Talk? About what, *señora*?"

María's black eyes twinkled, her mouth curved in a smile, two dimples winked. "But then I came to the mountains, and it was like being reborn. I was only ten, and Ramón was away much of the time fighting. I went barefoot and learned to ride a horse bareback, climb trees, shoot a gun, plant corn, make tortillas, and cook. I even swam naked in the creek with the other children. I was like a bird who had escaped her cage. I was free and soaring. No, *señora*, I did not miss my way of life."

María sighed deeply. "But then when my womanhood came on me, Ramón returned to being the overprotective male. He found a Yaqui Indian woman to watch over me, and she watched me like a hawk. Ah, *señora*, she was a formidable woman, as tall as you, with shoulders like a man and fierce black eyes." María giggled. "I had a terrible time sneaking away from her."

"What happened to her?" Christine asked curiously.

"She returned to her tribe after her husband was killed in one of our raids on the French. Then my brother decided I should go and live with some Creole friends of ours. He said I should learn to be a lady of quality, a proper Creole woman, but I refused to leave. He argued that I would wear beautiful clothes, go to parties, be waited on hand and foot. I knew that I would not be allowed out of the house and would have a duenna to watch my every move. Even my *novio*, my intended husband, would be chosen for me." María lifted her head defiantly, her black eyes flared. "No, *señora*, I will not go back to that! I told Ramón if he sent me to our Creole friends, I would run away and he would never see me again." She nodded her head firmly. "And he knew I meant it." Then she giggled, saying, "Poor Ramón, he does not know what to do with me."

"But he has let you stay," Christine pointed out.

"*Sí*, but I am not supposed to go out of the house at night or when he is gone," María replied. "But as you see, I do not obey." Her black eyes implored Christine's understanding. "Don't you see, *señora*, that is so stupid. No one here in this camp would hurt me. They are my family, my friends."

Christine could understand María's reluctance to return to her former position in life. She, too, had been sheltered, although not to the extreme María had. And after the last two months of independence, she knew she could never return to that life again. But still, María was much younger, pretty, and very vulnerable.

Christine chose her words very carefully. "I

322

think I can understand your need for freedom, but you must be very careful."

"You mean I must protect myself from men's lust?"

Christine was shocked by María's blunt statement.

María laughed, saying, "Ah, *señora*, you are as naïve as Ramón, who thinks I am so innocent. I know what goes on between men and women, how babies are made." She raised her head proudly. "I already have a *novio*."

Christine's eyes widened in surprise. "Who? Someone in this camp?"

María's look turned dreamy. "*Sí, señora*. Miguel. He is one of my brother's lieutenants. Ah, *señora*, he is so handsome . . . so *macho*!"

"*Macho?*"

"*Sí, señora*. It means manly, all male, very masculine." María giggled. "You know what I mean. Your man, he is *macho* too."

My man? Is she referring to Chad? Christine wondered. Yes, and he is most definitely all male, Christine thought, blushing at her thoughts.

María read her mind and giggled. "*Sí, señora*. Are they not wonderful, our *macho* men?"

Christine hardly knew what to say. Instead, she answered, "Please don't call me *señora*."

"You would prefer *señorita?*"

Christine's face turned pale, her look totally stunned.

"*Sí*, I know you are not married," María said calmly.

"How . . . how did you guess?" Christine stammered.

"Because every time I mentioned your husband you looked confused. Besides, you are not wearing a ring."

Christine flushed hotly, feeling both embarrassed and foolish. What must this young girl think of her? That she was Chad's mistress, or worse yet, just some cheap tramp.

"Do not be embarrassed because of me, *señorita*. Remember I told you I have a *novio*."

Christine gasped, "María, you haven't!"

María smiled knowingly. "No, *señorita*, we are not lovers. Not yet. But we love each other, and someday we will be married."

Christine frowned. Is that what María thought, that she and Chad were lovers? But to Christine, the word lovers suggested love and future marriage. And she didn't love Chad and had sworn never to marry. Her subconscious mind asked, Don't you love him? No, Christine violently denied the thought. We're just . . . friends, good friends.

"Ah, *señorita*," María said, snatching Christine from her troubling thoughts, "when Miguel kisses me, I don't think I can stand to wait one minute longer. I ache for him all over." She sighed deeply, saying, "Making love must be wonderful, *sí*?"

Christine was shocked at María's frank question. Did women talk so openly about something as intimate as making love? Well, how should she know? Up until just a few weeks ago, she had been even more innocent than María. Propriety told her that as an older woman she should discourage the girl. But María had been so candid and open

324

with her that Christine couldn't find it in her heart to lie to the girl.

"Yes, María," Christine said softly, "making love is a wonderful, beautiful experience."

"I knew it!" María cried. She looked at Christine, her black eyes sparkling with excitement, saying, "Do you know, *señorita*, that you are the first to be honest with me? All the other women I asked presented it as something dirty or distasteful. But when Miguel holds me in his arms and kisses me, I feel so warm, so good. I knew they had to be lying to me."

All the barriers were down. Christine was no longer the older, experienced woman, María the young innocent. Their minds met as equals with no subterfuge between them. The two smiled at each other in perfect understanding.

"Please call me Christine."

"Christine," María said softly. "Such a pretty name. I wish I had such an unusual name."

"But María is a lovely name," Christine objected.

"*Sí*, but do you realize that practically every third woman in Mexico is named María? I would like something different, more unusual, a name that would set me apart."

Come to think of it, Christine mused, she had never known another girl named Christine. There seemed to be innumerable Janes, Marys, and Margarets, but she had never known another Christine. She smiled with a new appreciation of her name.

"María, what will happen when your brother

finds out about you and Miguel?"

"He will be very angry. Absolutely furious! Oh, Christine, my brother is just a hypocrite," María said with disgust. "He preaches equality of all men, but that does not include his sister. For me, only another Creole will do." María lifted her head, her chin set stubbornly, saying, "But I shall fight him for what I want. And he will give in eventually." She giggled. "When it comes to me, El Puma is . . ." Her pretty, little face screwed tightly in intense concentration. Then she smiled, saying, "A pussycat."

Christine laughed.

"Poor Ramón," María said. "He loves me and tries to do what he thinks is best for me. But he must learn that no one can dictate to my heart, not even me."

Christine frowned. María's words were strangely disturbing.

As they continued to walk around the camp, María stopped and introduced Christine to her friends. The longer they strolled, the more aware Christine became that the camp was almost deserted of men. She commented on this to María.

"Ramón and most of the men are gone on a raid today," María replied.

"But isn't there anyone left to protect the camp in case of an attack?"

"Oh, *sí*. There are fifteen or twenty men left to guard the camp. But do not worry, Christine. The French have never discovered any of our camps. We are perfectly safe."

Chapter Fifteen

The sun was just rising, tinting the horizon with soft pinks and brilliant oranges, when María and Christine crept through the Juarista camp the next morning. The ground was still wet with dew as they walked through the sleepy camp, most of its occupants still rolled up in blankets on the ground or under their lean-tos. A lone fire, it's smoke curling lazily in the morning air, burned on the other side of the camp.

Christine and María had talked into the late hours of the previous night, exchanging their life stories. Christine had opened to the younger girl, telling her things that she had never divulged to any of her friends back in New York: of her father's painful desertion; of her lonely, loveless childhood; of her uncle's cold domination and recent treachery. The result was an outflow of words, a healing purge of Christine's soul that was long overdue. And by the time the night was over, Christine's and María's friendship was firmly sealed.

Christine's story about Chad's teaching her how to swim had prompted María to suggest this adventure. They had decided to go for an early morning swim before the camp awakened and the pool was crowded with other women and children.

After making their way through the thick woods at the back of the camp, they stepped into a clearing, and Christine gasped at the beauty of the crystal-clear pool, its surface glittering with silver in the early morning light. The banks of the pool were lined with graceful weeping willows, the dewdrops on the branches reflecting the sunlight and winking teasingly at them. For a minute, Christine stood, awed by the arresting sight and acutely aware of the birds trilling a greeting to the new day and the soft breeze ruffling her hair.

"It's beautiful, María," Christine said softly.

"*Sí*, it is," María answered, her voice almost a whisper, as if she were afraid the sound of her voice would shatter the magical scene before them.

Suddenly, the sound of gunfire and screaming pierced the air, and the two women looked at one another in stunned surprise. then María's face blanched, totally drained of all color.

"*Madre de Dios,*" she muttered. "We are being attacked."

She whirled and ran back toward the camp. Christine followed, stumbling to keep up with the tiny girl's amazing speed, her heart pounding in fear at the Mexican girl's words.

The sight that met them at the Juarista camp was a scene straight from hell itself, one that would be forever etched in Christine's memory and would haunt her the rest of her life. Total pandemonium reigned as the French rode through the camp, shooting indiscriminately at men, women, and children. The Juaristas ran in every direction, stumbling over the dead and wounded as they tried to escape the bullets and flying hooves of the horses. The air was filled with smoke, its acrid odor burning Christine's nostrils as the sounds of gunfire, pounding hooves, women's screams, whinnying horses, and the moans of the dying assaulted her ears.

She watched in stunned horror as a woman and her infant were run down and trampled beneath the hooves of a French soldier's horse, and as a toothless, old man, his hands raised in supplication, was clubbed to death with the butt of a French rifle.

"*Bastardos*," María hissed and ran to one of the fallen bodies that were scattered all over the camp. Picking up the ancient musket beside it, she aimed at the French soldier riding down on her and Christine. The musket fired with a deafening roar, and the man's chest seemed to explode, blood spurting everywhere. Christine barely had time to move aside as the Frenchman's limp body pitched from the horse and landed with a sickening thud beside her.

María struggled, frantically trying to reload the clumsy musket, her hands trembling violently.

329

"Let me help you," Christine said, holding the awkward, long-barreled gun while María tried to ram home the ball. If I only had my Spencer carbine, Christine thought.

She looked over María's shoulder and froze in terror as a French soldier rode down on them. The Frenchman's fist balled and cuffed María's head, and she slumped into Christine's arms as the horse and man thundered past them. Christine knelt and clutched the unconscious body of the tiny girl protectively to her chest, sobbing, "Oh my God, no," tears running down her cheeks.

And then as suddenly as it started, the shooting stopped. Caught by total surprise in their sleep, the Juaristas's brief, but bloody resistance was ended.

María moaned and struggled to sit up, reeling dizzily. The French were already rounding up the survivors, shoving and pushing them forward into the center of the camp, many of them pulled dispassionately from the bodies of their dead loved ones. Two wagons lumbered into the center of the camp, driven by men of the victorious French force.

Christine was rudely prodded by the muzzle of French soldier's rifle. The man's eyes still glittered with blood lust. She struggled to her feet, trying to support the dazed Mexican girl in her arms. Stumbling, they were pushed forward by the impatient soldier.

A line of Juarista prisoners had already formed at the two dilapidated wagons, and Christine and María had to wait their turn to climb in. Other soldiers ran through the camp setting fire to El Puma's cabin, the lean-tos, and the storage shed that held the Juaristas's meager supplies. Christine looked down at María. A large, ugly bruise was forming on her temple. The girl stood mutely, watching her home burn to the ground with dull, listless eyes. This is the second time she has been through this, Christine thought, her heart twisting with compassion.

A French soldier, leering obscenely, reached over and fondled one of María's breasts. The act infuriated Christine.

"Take your damned hands off of her, you filthy swine," Christine hissed in French, slapping the man's hands away.

The soldier's leer twisted into an ugly snarl as he raised the butt of his rifle. The sharp command of an officer standing behind him was the only thing that saved Christine from being clubbed to death on the spot.

They were shoved impatiently into the wagon, already overcrowded with Juaristas, many of them wounded. Christine and María huddled off to one side as more of the prisoners were crammed into the small wagon. One Juarista was still struggling, trying to fight the three soldiers that held him. Christine watched as the man was beaten senseless and his limp, unconscious body tossed into the wagon as if he were a sack of corn. When the prisoners were finally loaded, the wagons, squeaking loudly in protest at the heavy weight, were driven from the clearing the Juaristas knew as their home.

For several miles, the captives sat in stunned silence, the only sounds the muffled sobs of a little girl huddled in her mother's skirt. And then drawing from some unknown source of strength, the Mexicans rallied and began to comfort one another and attend to the wounded. Petticoats were quickly stripped and torn as the heads, arms, and legs of the injured were bandaged. One man with a severe chest wound was avoided. The women didn't even attempt to treat him. Everyone knew, by unspoken agreement, that his wound was hopelessly fatal. Instead, his head was cradled in the lap of one of the women, her fingers stroking his cheek, her voice muttering soothing words to comfort him in his death throes.

When all the wounded had been cared for, Christine and María slumped back wearily against the side of the wagon. For hours, they rode in silence as the wagons bumped over the rocky, twisted trail, the hot sun beating down on them unmercifully. Their lips were cracked and their throats parched from lack of water. Not once did the French offer to appease their thirst. Not once did the Juaristas beg. They sat mute in the scorching sun as the flies, drawn by the smell of blood, buzzed around them and the death rattle of the dying man filled their ears.

Christine finally broke the silence, asking, "Where are they taking us?"

"To Fort Andreas, about twenty miles south of our camp," María answered. Suddenly her eyes flared with hate. "Filthy pigs! French *bastardos*!"

Christine glanced around in alarm at the

French soldiers riding beside the wagon. "Ssh, María, they'll hear you. There's no need of agitating them any further. There's no telling what they will do."

"Do?" María snapped. "What does it matter what they do! I would just as soon die here as before a firing squad."

"A firing squad?" Christine asked. "What in the world are you talking about?"

"We are being taken to the fort to be shot," María said in a cold, hard voice. "Tomorrow morning we will be lined up in front of a firing squad."

Christine's look was one of total disbelief. "You can't be serious, María. These women and children are not combatants. Why, even the men shouldn't be shot. They're prisoners of war."

"No, Christine. Have you not heard of our beloved emperor's infamous decree?" María asked, her voice heavy with sarcasm.

"Emperor? You mean Maximilian?"

"*Sí*. Last October, he signed a decree stating that anyone continuing to resist, regardless of political affiliation, is an outlaw, and if caught bearing arms against the emperor, will be shot before a firing squad within twenty-four hours, without appeal."

"But not women and children!"

"*Sí*, women and children. Are we not aiding and abetting outlaws? That makes us outlaws too," María answered bitterly.

Christine sat back, her mind reeling. They were going to be killed? Shot in the morning?

María saw Christine's pale face and horror-filled eyes. "Not you, Christine," María said softly. "You are an *americana* woman. They would not dare shoot you, not with your army sitting poised on the border just waiting for an excuse to invade. As soon as we reach the fort, you must demand to see the commanding officer and tell them who you are."

"I couldn't desert you!" Christine cried.

"Don't be silly, Christine," María said in a firm voice. "How would dying with us be of any help to us? No, it would be a total waste of life, and there has been too much of that already."

"But won't El Puma try to rescue you?" Christine asked, feeling hope rise.

"I pray that he won't be so foolish," María answered fervently. "Fort Andreas is surrounded by twenty-foot walls, five feet thick and armed with cannons. Inside, there are over three hundred French soldiers." María shook her head sadly, saying, "No, it would be hopeless for El Puma to attack it. It would be suicide."

Christine's mind was whirling with the enormity of all María had said. The Juaristas would be shot in the morning. There was no hope of El Puma rescuing them. She should reveal her true identity to the French to keep from being shot along with them. But I just can't stand by and watch them be shot, she thought. I'll have to do something. But what?

"I am not afraid to die, Christine," María said softly. Her eyes glittered with unshed tears. "But I am sorry for one thing. I regret that I did not give

334

myself to Miguel. Now I will never know . . ." Her voice broke with a small sob.

Chad, Miguel, and the disguised Juaristas rode into camp early that afternoon with the wagon of Spencer carbines. As they cantered into the clearing, each man came to an abrupt halt, stunned by what he saw before him.

Bodies lay scattered over the clearing. A few Juaristas ran from one corpse to the other checking for possible survivors. Another group of Juaristas was extinguishing the multiple, small fires that still smoldered in the lean-tos. Off to one side of the camp, men were already digging graves in the hard, rocky ground. The sickening smell of smoke, blood, and death filled the air. Chad glanced to his right and saw the body of a little girl lying crumpled face down. She had been shot in the back.

Miguel was the first to recover. Dismounting, he ran to the group of Juaristas throwing water on a lean-to. After a brief conversation, he returned to Chad, his look pale and drawn.

"What happened?" Chad asked.

"They were attacked by the French this morning." He pointed to two women huddled under a tree, sobbing hysterically. "Those women managed to escape and hide in the woods. They said the French surprised them at dawn when everyone was still asleep. El Puma and his patrol just returned an hour ago themselves."

Chad looked across the clearing at the black-

335

ened, smoldering shell that had once been El Puma's cabin, the cabin where Christine had been staying. Icy fingers clutched his heart.

"Chris?" The word came out with an odd, choking sound.

"Her body was not found, nor María's," Miguel replied. "It is presumed they were taken prisoner with the other survivors."

"Prisoner?"

"*Sí, señor.* The French are probably taking them to Fort Andreas. That is the closest fort."

No one had to tell Chad what the French did with their prisoners. They were quickly and efficiently disposed of, shot before a firing squad at dawn. And Christine was with them. Eyes the color of blue steel swept over the area and locked on El Puma who was helping two other Juaristas put out a fire. The anger that had been smoldering in Chad broke into a white-hot rage. He dug his spurs into the flank of his horse, and the surprised animal lurched forward crossing the clearing at a gallop.

Chad was out of the saddle before the horse even stopped moving. He grabbed El Puma by the shoulder, swinging him around, and slammed his fist into the Mexican's jaw. El Puma staggered at the sudden, violent attack. Chad would have swung again, except that the two Juaristas helping El Puma put out the fire had grabbed the Texan's arms and were wrestling him back.

"You son-of-a-bitch! You promised me she would be safe!" Chad roared, struggling to free himself from the two men holding him in an ironlike vise.

El Puma wiped the blood from his mouth with the back of his hand, saying, "If you had done that at any other time, I would have killed you, *señor*. But you have every right to hate me." He raised pain-filled eyes to meet Chad's furious ones. "But, *señor*, you cannot possibly hate me as much as I hate myself." His hand swept the camp. "These were my people." He turned to the men holding Chad and said in Spanish, "Release him."

The two men hesitated and then reluctantly dropped their arms, stepping back. Chad stood glaring at El Puma through a red haze, his breath rasping in his throat, his fists still clenched. He knew if he made one move toward the Juarista *jefe*, the men would kill him. And yet he wanted to slam out at something, anything to ease his pain and frustration.

"I know how you feel, *amigo*," El Puma said sadly. "You want to hit out at something. But killing me won't change anything."

Reason was slowly beginning to return. Chad turned and kicked viciously at one of the buckets lying on the ground, sending it skittering across the camp. The act drained Chad of the last of his blind rage. Only a cold anger and a determination to seek revenge on the French remained.

He turned to El Puma, saying, "What are you going to do?"

Ramón sighed wearily, saying, "First, bury my dead. Then move what is left of my camp to a safe

337

place." His eyes burned with fierce determination and met Chad's levelly. "Then get my people back."

"How?" Chad asked.

"By attacking the French."

Chad frowned, saying, "Miguel said they were probably taking them to a fort near here."

"That is correct," El Puma answered calmly.

"You think you can catch them before they get the prisoners to the fort?"

"No, *señor*. I intend to attack the fort."

Chad stared at the Juarista in disbelief for a minute. Then he spat, "With what? This pitiful, little group of men you've got left?" Chad looked around the camp, saying, "How many do you have left? Seventy, maybe eighty men?"

"Closer to sixty, *señor*."

"Sixty?" Chad exclaimed. "That's all that are left out of a hundred men?"

El Puma shrugged, saying, "There were never a hundred men."

"But you said—"

"I exaggerated, *señor*," El Puma interjected.

Chad glared at him, saying, "You're going to attack a fort with only sixty men? And you accused *me* of being crazy to think I could sneak one person out of your camp? Mister, you're the craziest damned fool I've ever seen."

Ramón flushed, saying, "We have the new repeater carbines now."

"So what?" Chad yelled. "They have them too. Plus cannon and walls to protect them. How many men and officers are inside that fort?"

338

"The full complement is three hundred men," Ramón replied. "But as I told you they were expecting reinforcements that will not—"

"Damn it, Ramón!" Chad cried in exasperation. "Stop hedging! How many?"

"About two hundred fifty men."

"You're going to attack a fort that has two hundred fifty men in it with only sixty men? You're crazy!"

"I am going to get my people back," El Puma replied resolutely.

"It would be suicide!"

"I am going to get my people back!"

Chad turned away from the Mexican in frustration and paced restlessly for a few minutes, thinking. Then he turned and asked, "Is there some way you could get inside that fort?"

"I am afraid that is impossible, *señor*. The only way we could do that would be if someone from the inside opened a gate for us. The French do not allow any Mexicans inside the walls of their forts. No, *señor*, we will just have to storm it."

Chad grinned, saying, "How about Americans? Would they allow an American inside that fort?"

El Puma looked at him, frowning with puzzlement.

Chad laughed and said, "Come on, *amigo*. Let's go someplace and sit down. We've got some plans to make."

El Puma grabbed Chad's arm, saying, "What is this *we* business, *señor*?"

"I'm going to help you get them out," Chad replied casually.

"Why?" Ramón asked bluntly.

"Simple, they've got my woman."

El Puma shook his head saying, "No, *señor*, it is not that simple. You know as well as I do, that all you have to do to get your woman back is ride into that fort and tell them who she is. They would not dare kill an *americana* woman."

Chad shrugged.

El Puma cocked his head and studied the big Texan thoughtfully. "What happened to the man that told me he was not going to fight anyone else's war for them? This is not your war, *señor*. I repeat, why?"

Chad looked at the bodies littering the camp, mostly women's and children's. His eyes darkened with anger, his jaw bunched. "Let's just say," he said tightly, "that killing women and children goes against my grain."

El Puma smiled and said, "We welcome you and thank you, *amigo*."

The Juarista *jefe* and the Texas *pistolero* strolled across the camp. One man walked with a lithe, animal-like grace, the other with a long-legged, lazy swagger. Both men exuded power and self-confidence. The Juaristas watching them felt their spirits lifting, convinced that all was not lost after all.

When they were seated beneath a low-hanging tree, Ramón said, "Now tell me your plan."

Chad deftly rolled two cigarettes and handed one to Ramón. After lighting them, he said, "I'm thinking our friend Tony Peters may come in handy again." Chad looked about the camp

340

curiously. "By the way, what happened to him?"

Ramón sighed deeply, saying, "I'm afraid he was still locked in that shack when the French fired it. We found a charred body in the ruins."

Chad nodded, thinking that burning to death was a terrible way to die. He shook off his gloomy thoughts and said, "Where do you suppose the French were taking those guns we intercepted?"

"Probably to Fort Andreas," El Puma answered.

"That's what I figured," Chad said. "Look, this is my plan. I'll ride on to the fort this afternoon while you're finishing up here. They're probably expecting the guns to arrive any minute. I'll tell them I'm this Tony Peters, that the French patrol was wiped out by El Puma and his men, and that you have the guns now. If I can, I'll try to convince them to send out another patrol after you. That might cut down on the odds a little. I figure as an American in their employ, they'll at least let me stay the night."

"Do you still have Peters's identification papers?"

"Yes, right here," Chad replied, patting his shirt pocket.

"What if they have done business with this Peters before?"

"I'll just have to bluff my way through like I did with the guns."

El Puma nodded in silent agreement.

"Do you know anything about the inside layout of that fort?" Chad asked.

"*Sí*, it was a Mexican presidio before the

French captured it."

"Draw me a map of the inside," Chad requested.

El Puma tossed his cigarette aside and squatted on the ground. Using a stick, he drew a quick sketch of the fort, showing walls, gates, buildings, and the positions of the cannons.

"So the prison is in the left-hand corner, and there's a gate near it," Chad said half to himself. "What's over here?" He pointed to the opposite side of the fort.

"A blacksmith shop and the stables."

Chad nodded thoughtfully. "If I set fire to the blacksmith shop, they'd probably be pretty frantic to get their horses out before the stables caught fire. That ought to keep them distracted while I overpower the sentry and open that gate by the prison. Hopefully, you can sneak your people out before the French realize what has happened."

El Puma bristled. "Sneak them out? No, *señor*, we will fight!"

"Don't be a damned jackass," Chad snapped. "You don't want to risk your women and children do you? Hell, first get them out of there. You can get your revenge later. Besides, I doubt if we'll get away without a fight anyway. With that many French around, someone is bound to see us and sound the alarm. But there's no need to go looking for a fight. How do you intend to take your people away? By wagon?"

"No, *señor*, as you said, the French will probably pursue us. I figure there are about thirty prisoners, so that means that some of us will have to ride double. But wagons would be too slow."

"How does between three and four in the morning sound to you?" Chad asked. "That way, everyone would have had time to get to sleep. Being awakened from a sound sleep will only add to the confusion."

"*Sí, amigo*. Also, we will have the cover of darkness for our escape if we are pursued. Once we reach the mountains, we can easily lose them."

"Agreed," Chad said, rising from the ground. "As far as I'm concerning any more talking would just be a waste of time. How do I go about finding this fort?"

"I will send a man with you to show the way. It will save time. But I am afraid I cannot send Miguel. I will need him here to help me teach the men how to use the new guns."

El Puma turned and called a command to one of his men. The man nodded eagerly and mounted his horse, waiting for the yanqui to join him.

Chad started to swing up into his saddle and then stopped, watching as a Mexican led a horse from the woods across the camp. He grinned, relieved that the big black stallion had survived the attack. He knew if anything had happened to Diablo, Christine would be inconsolable.

He turned to El Puma, saying, "Do me a favor, will you? See that that ornery horse of Christine's is taken care of. She's gotten kinda attached to him."

El Puma chuckled, then nodded.

Chad swung into his saddle and looked down at

El Puma. The *jefe* raised his hand to Chad, saying, "*Vaya con Dios, amigo.*"

Chad grinned lazily and grasped the man's hand firmly, saying, "See you tonight, *amigo.*"

The Texan spurred his horse to follow the Juarista leading his way out of the smoky camp. The other Mexicans continued doggedly with the grim business at hand. The first body was just being lowered into its shallow rocky grave.

Chapter Sixteen

The wagon squeaked and groaned as it clam-
ored through the massive wooden gates of Fort
Andreas. The thick adobe walls towered above it,
casting long, deep shadows along one side of the
interior of the fort. Christine squinted in the sun's
glare and looked curiously about the enclosure,
seeing the parade ground, a long line of barracks,
and a large adobe building in the center that
apparently served as the headquarters.

Through the long, hot, grueling drive, Christine had pondered on what to do when they
reached their destination. She had decided that
María was right. Dying with the Juarista prisoners would serve no purpose. And despite what
María had said, she couldn't help but believe that
the fierce El Puma would make some rescue
attempt. Perhaps all the Juarista leader needed
was time to rally aid, and if so, maybe she could
help buy him that time. Regardless, she could be
of no help either to the prisoners or El Puma if she

was locked up with them.

"María," Christine said in a low voice, "you were right. I can't help you if I am locked up with you. I'll tell the French who I am, but don't think I am deserting you. If there's any way I can, I'll try to help you."

María smiled at the American woman and nodded. How naïve she is if she thinks there is anything she can do to help us, María thought bitterly. What could one lone woman do to change the fate the French had planned for them in the morning?

The wagons were driven to a building at one corner of the fort. The iron bars on its meager windows clearly proclaimed it a prison. The weary Juarista prisoners were unloaded impatiently, the French soldiers seeming to take sadistic pleasure in being particularly rough with the wounded. The Juarista who was seriously injured had died hours before. His stiff body, covered by a petticoat, was left in the wagon.

After they had been unloaded, Christine stepped away from the line of prisoners that was being prodded into the dark, musty building. A burly French soldier tried to shove her back into line.

Christine whirled away from him, her green eyes glittering dangerously. "Take your filthy hands off me, you pig," Christine said in French.

The private jerked his hand back, surprised at the use of his native language.

"You fool, I'm not a Mexican. I'm an American. I demand to see the commandant," she said in her haughtiest voice.

The private, not too bright, blinked in confusion. Usually, he obeyed his orders blindly, but something about the woman's haughty manner and her tone of voice reminded him of the aristocrats back in France. His instincts told him to beware. He motioned to a lieutenant standing a few feet away.

The officer walked up, saying impatiently, "What's the trouble here? Get that woman back in line."

Christine raised her chin defiantly. "I think not, Lieutenant. Not unless you want to make a very bad mistake. My name is Christine Roberts, and I'm an American, not a Mexican. I demand to see your commandant."

The lieutenant was just as surprised at Christine's use of French as the private. He also recognized Christine's American accent. He frowned, saying, "An American? What are you doing with these Juaristas?"

Christine drew herself up to her full height, which happened to be two inches taller than the Frenchman. Looking down her nose at him, she replied, "I'll explain everything to the commandant. Now stop dawdling and take me to him."

"Colonel Le Blanc is not at the fort at present, *mademoiselle*," the officer replied stiffly.

"Then who is in charge?" Christine retorted.

"Major Renault, but he is ill."

"Lieutenant," Christine said coldly, "are you trying to tell me there is no one in charge here?

That there is no one in temporary command of this fort?"

The lieutenant flushed, saying, "No, *mademoiselle*. Of course there is someone in temporary command. Captain Dubert—"

"Then take me to him!" Christine snapped indignantly.

The officer resented the woman's imposing size and arrogant manner. He had hoped to fluster her and see her break down in tears, but obviously, the stubborn woman had no intention of doing something so feminine. Well, he'd be more than happy to pass her off to Dubert. He had always hated the ambitious captain anyway, being one of many who had been stepped on during the captain's unscrupulous climb to the top.

The Frenchman's eyes glittered with revenge. He smirked, saying, "As you wish, *mademoiselle*."

Christine followed the officer across the dusty parade ground to the large adobe building in the center. The lieutenant walked ahead of her in hurried, angry strides, but Christine, with her long legs, had no trouble keeping up with him, which only infuriated the man more. It seemed the only way he could force her to run after him was to run himself, an act that would certainly be demeaning to a French officer.

Leading her into a small office, he said abruptly, "Wait here, *mademoiselle*."

He turned to leave, but Christine stopped him, saying, "Just a minute, Lieutenant."

The officer whirled, his face white-lipped with anger. Christine had to suppress a smile. She knew full well why the man was angry. Since she was a woman, he had meant to intimidate her. Instead, she had the upper hand.

"Tell me, Lieutenant. I once met a Colonel Le Blanc at the French embassy in Washington," Christine lied easily. "Which Colonel Le Blanc is this?"

The officer frowned. There were a lot of Le Blancs in the French army, but as far as he knew, there was only one Colonel Le Blanc. "Why, Maurice Le Blanc, *mademoiselle*."

"Thank you, Lieutenant," Christine replied, turning her back on him and dismissing him.

The young Frenchman glared at her rigid back angrily. Bitch, he thought as he stomped from the room.

Christine waited apprehensively for the appearance of Captain Dubert. She realized that the captain was probably inexperienced in administrative decisions, and that would be a decided advantage for her. If she could use his insecurity against him, she might be able to get him to delay the execution of the Juaristas until the colonel returned. That way, she might buy time for El Puma, time for him to reorganize and hopefully plan a rescue of the prisoners.

When Captain Dubert entered the office, Christine quickly appraised him. He's one of those cocky, little men, obviously overly impressed with his own importance, she thought. And more than likely, he's overly ambitious. She watched as he strutted toward her arrogantly. She decided the quicker she could confuse him the better.

"When will Maurice be back?" Christine demanded in French.

Captain Dubert came to an abrupt halt, stunned not only by Christine's question, but by her size too. *Mon dieu*, he had never seen such a large woman! And how did she know the colonel's first name?

"Are you speaking of Colonel Le Blanc?" he asked stiffly.

"Of course," Christine replied impatiently. "How many Maurice Le Blancs do you have in the French army?"

"Do you know the colonel, *mademoiselle*?"

"Yes, I do. I met him at a party at the French embassy in Washington several years ago. He's a very charming man, keen minded, a true gentleman. My father was so impressed with him that he invited him to dinner several times while he was in Washington."

The captain frowned. The Colonel Le Blanc he knew was a hard, stern, arrogant man, a man who could be harsh, even cruel if necessary. As a matter of fact, he had tried to fashion himself after the colonel's example. Of course, the colonel did come from an aristocratic family and traveled in high circles. He imagined if it suited the colonel's purpose, he could appear very charming. But still, this bedraggled woman standing before him, dressed in simple peasant clothes, didn't look like the kind of woman who would know the colonel personally.

"*Mademoiselle*, I will be the one who will ask

the questions here," Dubert snapped.

Despite her trembling knees, Christine managed an appropriately indignant look.

"Who are you, and what are you doing with the Juaristas?" Dubert demanded.

"I'm an American. My name is Christine Roberts—"

"You're lying," the captain interrupted rudely. "Look at the way you're dressed. Just like the other Mexican women. No, you're only lying to escape your punishment."

Christine laughed sharply. "Don't be a fool, Captain. How many Mexicans do you know that speak French with an American accent? Besides, look at me. Have you ever seen a blond-haired, green-eyed Mexican?"

The captain's doubts returned. Her accent was decidedly American, and he had seen a few green-eyed Mexicans, but never that shade of green. In fact, he had never seen such strange green eyes on anyone.

"What were you doing with the Juaristas?" he asked, switching abruptly to English.

"So, you speak English?" Christine replied in her native tongue. "Good, I feel much more comfortable with it."

Christine's mind searched frantically for a suitable story. She didn't want the captain to know about Chad. He might want to know where he was at the time of the attack, and Christine could hardly tell the captain he was out stealing French guns. She also didn't want to let the Frenchman know her brother was being held by bandits. He mustn't think she was completely alone in Mexico without someone to protect her, for then he might decide to ignore the fact that she was American.

"Answer my question, *mademoiselle*!" Dubert snapped.

"Well, you certainly could learn some manners from Colonel Le Blanc, Captain," Christine retorted indignantly. The captain had the grace to flush.

"I was traveling to Chihuahua, when the man I had hired to escort me deserted me in the mountains when we were attacked by bandits," Christine lied smoothly. "For two days, I wandered around out there, and if it had not been for the Juaristas finding me, I would probably have died. Naturally, my clothes were in tatters. The Juarista women were kind enough to loan me something to wear."

"How long were you in the Juarista camp?"

"For only one day," Christine answered calmly. "They told me that they would escort me to the outskirts of Chihuahua as soon as there was someone available to take me."

The story sounded strange to Dubert. What was a woman doing traveling in Mexico? Didn't she know there was a war on? But then he'd always heard Americans were a little crazy.

"Why were you going to Chihuahua?" he asked.

"To join my brother. He's a newspaperman covering the French-Mexican war. He wrote me that Chihuahua was a beautiful city and suggested I visit him. I thought it would be a wonderful opportunity to see Mexico. We Roberts always were adventuresome."

Dubert sat on the corner of his desk and stroked his black mustache thoughtfully. She must be telling the truth, he thought. Surely, no one could make up a ridiculous story like that. If her brother was expecting her, questions might be raised about her disappearance. Newspapermen were a damned nosy, persistent bunch. And if she turned out to be a personal friend of Colonel Le Blanc, he'd better watch his step. He had worked too long and hard to impress the colonel to have everything ruined by one arrogant, Yankee woman.

"Excuse my manners, Mademoiselle Roberts, but you can see why we must be very careful. The Mexicans have many clever spies among them."

Christine hid her sigh of relief, saying, "Of course, Captain Dubert. I can understand why you have to be careful. I must remember to tell Maurice how efficient you were. I'm sure he'll be pleased."

The captain could not hide his smug smile.

"Now, about the prisoners," Christine said.

Dubert's head snapped up, his look wary. "What about the prisoners?"

"I want to know when they will be released?" Christine said calmly.

"Released?" Dubert asked, his look incredulous. "No, *mademoiselle*, the Juaristas will not be released. They will be shot at sunrise."

"Shot?" Christine exclaimed, her look horri-

353

fied. "Surely, you can't be serious Captain Dubert? Why, most of the prisoners are women and children, not prisoners of war!"

"*Mademoiselle*, we have very explicit orders from the Emperor that all Juaristas, women and children included, are to be executed within twenty-four hours after their capture," Dubert said, his words coldly measured.

"The Emperor? Are you speaking of that pompous fool, Maximilian? Since when does the French army, the most powerful army in the world, take orders from a stupid Austrian?"

Dubert colored. Christine had hit a sore spot. Most of the French officers did resent taking orders from the arrogant Hapsburg, who showed absolutely no military sense or skill. Why the crazy fool actually believed he was the Mexican's savior, and his interference in behalf of the Mexican people was a source of agitation to the French military command. Still many officers, Colonel Le Blanc for one, had been glad when Maximilian finally had signed his death-to-resisters decree. It had been the first positive action he had taken against the Mexicans.

Captain Dubert rose from behind his desk and said stiffly, "*Mademoiselle*, those are our orders. Do not try to interfere!"

"Don't interfere?" Christine replied indignantly. "I'm afraid not, Captain Dubert. There's no way I'll stand by and watch women and children murdered. I thought you French were supposed to be civilized. Surely, Colonel Le Blanc doesn't approve of such barbarism?"

Captain Dubert flushed with anger. "*Mademoiselle*, the Mexicans are not people. They are animals. And you are wrong. Colonel Le Blanc does approve. The orders will be carried out. The Juaristas will be shot!"

Christine glared at him and, her words measured, said, "I think you had better reconsider, Captain Dubert. You don't seem to realize who I am. My father owns over forty newspapers in the United States, powerful newspapers. If the story should get out that the French are murdering innocent women and children, the American people will be outraged. They will demand war!"

Dubert was furious. How dare the woman threaten him! Then he remembered what she had told him about her brother. "You're lying! You told me your brother was a newspaperman covering the war. If your family is so powerful and influential, why is your brother a mere reporter?"

Christine thought fast and then laughed harshly. "You are the one that is a fool, Captain. Do you think my father would turn over forty newspapers to a man who doesn't know a thing about newspapers? No, my brother is being trained from the bottom up. He started by learning how to set type and run the presses. Then he was a copy boy and now a reporter. When he returns to the United States, he will be an assistant editor, then an editor, before he is allowed to take over. Tell me, Captain, does the French army make a private a general?"

Dubert looked doubtful, and Christine pushed

for an advantage. "Relations between our countries are already strained, Captain. A large army of well-armed, battle-seasoned Americans stands poised on the border. This story, combined with my father's political influence, could well be the fuse that lights the powder keg. Are you willing to take that risk?"

"Do not threaten me!" Captain Dubert yelled.

Christine rammed home her attack. "I feel it only fair to warn you, Captain, that Secretary Seward and my father are personal friends."

Dubert's face paled. He had no knowledge of American newspapers or who owned them, but everyone in the French army had heard of the American Secretary of State, William Seward. He was the man who had issued the ultimatum to Napoleon to get out of Mexico or else. Imagine everyone having the audacity to threaten Napoleon! Still, since then, the French army had had orders not to advance any farther than Chihuahua, and he had heard rumors that the French might pull out of Mexico.

Dubert was reeling with indecision. If he didn't execute the prisoners as ordered, he could be court-martialed. On the other hand, if what the woman told him was true and she followed through with her threats, he would lose his commission at the very least. Either way, his head was on the chopping block.

Christine smiled smugly, well aware of the Frenchman's dilemma. "Don't you think, Captain Dubert, in view of the extraordinary circumstances, that it would be wise to rescind the order at least until Colonel Le Blanc returns? I think when I present the facts to him, he'll appreciate the delicate, if not impossible, position you were in."

Dubert frowned and turned away, pondering over his awkward position. He had worked very hard over the years, conniving and scheming to get where he was. He had been persistent and merciless in his climb to the top, and now it was all being threatened by this American woman. Dubert was no fool. He knew Le Blanc wasn't going to like having this problem dumped in his lap. He would much rather have a scapegoat to blame it on, and who better than he? Dubert wondered how he could keep from losing his standing with the colonel. The answer came to him with shrewd cunning. Of course, give the colonel another scapegoat, Major Renault. Dubert smiled in self-satisfaction. He would tell the colonel he had consulted with the major and had been told to wait for further orders. The major was so ill with fever, delirious half the time, that he would never remember not issuing the order. That would get the responsibility off his back. But still, being forced into this position by the woman's ultimatum rankled. To be bested by a mere woman, even if she was an amazon, stung his considerable male ego.

He turned, his eyes boring into Christine's, and said tightly, "Very well, *mademoiselle*, I will consult with Major Renault on this. In the meanwhile, you will be given a room. You are not to leave it except for meals. Under no circum-

357

stances, are you to leave this building."

Christine was stunned. She would have sworn the vain captain wouldn't go to his superior officer. And she knew nothing of this Major Renault. He might be one of those officers who obeyed orders regardless of possible repercussions.

"I would prefer to talk to the major myself," Christine said haughtily.

"You will talk to no one!" Captain Dubert answered angrily, his black eyes glittering dangerously. "I have had all of your interference I will tolerate!"

He turned and walked to the door, snapping a command to a soldier standing there. "This man will show you to your room. You will be summoned for meals. Otherwise, you will not leave that room until Colonel Le Blanc returns."

Christine was infuriated by the captain's arrogant, overbearing attitude. The way he shouted orders at her reminded her of her hated uncle. She walked across the room stiffly and turned at the door. Raising her head proudly and towering over the short Frenchman, she said in a cold voice, "Very well, Captain. See that a bath is brought to me." Her eyes glittered with reckless maliciousness. "I seemed to have picked up a little dirt . . . not all of it Mexican."

Christine turned and walked away regally. To the frustrated captain she looked like a queen, despite her dirty, blood-splattered peasant clothing and ridiculously short hair.

Captain Dubert clenched his fists, sputtering

with impotent rage. He walked to his chair and slumped in it angrily. Damned bitch, he thought, furious. She was jeopardizing everything he had struggled for. When the patrol had ridden in that afternoon and reported that they had discovered the Juaristas's hideout and destroyed their camp, Dubert's spirits had soared. True, he was disappointed that the notorious El Puma had not been captured also, but the discovery of the hideout and the taking of the Juaristas as prisoners would be a feather in his cap. Naturally, since he was in command at the time, he would take credit for it. He had entertained fantasies of Colonel Le Blanc returning and praising him, perhaps even promoting him on the spot for the extraordinary coup. Had not the French been looking for El Puma's hideout for years with no results? And now all of his dreams had been shattered by this damned Yankee woman. Instead of being a prize catch, the Mexican prisoners were an awkward problem.

Dubert toyed with the idea of the hated American woman meeting with an accident. But then he remembered the woman had also talked to Lieutenant Dupont. How much of the story had she told him? he wondered. Did the lieutenant know her true identity? No, it would be too risky to kill the woman, he realized. Lieutenant Dupont was just waiting for him to make a fool mistake like that. Had the men under him been loyal to him, it might have been different, but he had stepped on too many toes on his ambitious climb up the ladder.

Damn the woman and damn this stupid war! Dubert thought in angry frustration. The French army had been in Mexico for over three years and still the Mexican people resisted. They seemed to be impossible to beat down. But how could you fight against men who refused to stand still? The damned Mexicans attacked and then ran and hid. Whoever heard of fighting a war by shooting from behind rocks and cactus, and ambushing your enemy in narrow mountain ravines? He and most of the other French officers longed to be back in Europe in a war with conventional military tactics, a war where two enemies confronted each other on an open battlefield and the victory belonged to the best-equipped and best-trained of the two. *Mon dieu*, he hoped the rumors were true and the French would withdraw. The longer they stayed, the more demeaning and embarrassing this war was to his proud army, as yet unbeaten by any other. And why in the world did Napoleon want this miserable, godforsaken country anyway? He had been here three years and had yet to see any of the gold and riches Mexico was supposed to have.

Captain Dubert's thoughts were interrupted by a scuffling noise at the door. He raised his head to see a big, tall, dark-haired man struggling to throw off the hands of three French soldiers trying to hold him back. The captain jumped to his feet in alarm.

The stranger looked at him, his blue eyes glittering with anger, saying, "I hope to hell you speak English."

"Who are you?" the French officer asked in astonishment. Two Americans in one day? he thought. *Mon dieu*, what was going on?

"My name is Tony Peters. I'm an American in the employ to the French. If you'll tell these damned apes to let go of me, I'll show you my identification papers!" Chad yelled indignantly.

Captain Dubert snapped an order to the French soldiers. They withdrew their hands from Chad reluctantly and left the room, casting distrustful looks over their shoulders. Chad glared at them resentfully as they withdrew.

He turned to the French captain and threw Powers's identification papers on the desk, saying irritably, "I thought you were supposed to know about the shipment of guns we were bringing you."

Guns? What guns? the captain thought. Then he remembered seeing a letter on the colonel's desk saying something about a shipment of guns to be delivered soon.

He relaxed and smiled, saying, "I am sorry, *monsieur*. I am Captain Dubert. The colonel has been called back to Chihuahua, and Major Renault was taken ill last night. I'm in charge now, but things have been rather confused today. I'm afraid I forgot to tell my men we were expecting a shipment of guns. But where is the lieutenant assigned to the patrol? I can't believe he would let my men manhandle you that way."

As the Frenchman spoke, Chad suppressed a smile. So, the commandant and next-in-command were not present? How lucky could he be? They might well have known Tony Peters personally, and then he'd have some tall bluffing to do. Now if he could just get this Frenchman to swallow the rest of his story.

"I guess that was my fault," Chad replied. "I came riding in like a bat out of hell. I was in such a hurry, I didn't even stop to think. All I wanted to do was ride to the fort and report what had happened as quickly as I could."

"Report what?" Dubert asked apprehensively.

"We were attacked by El Puma and his Juaristas about five miles north of here. He hit us right out in the open. All of a sudden they were just there, like out of nowhere," Chad said, shaking his head in a dazed manner. "Before I realized what had happened, six of our soldiers were lying on the ground."

Dubert sat weakly in the chair, his face pale. "The whole patrol was wiped out?"

"Hell, I don't know," Chad snapped. "When I realized what was happening, I took off. Barely escaped with my life. Bullets were flying everywhere. Look at my hat," Chad said, showing the officer the gunshot hole in the top of his hat, a hole he himself had shot in it before entering the French fort.

Captain Dubert ignored the hat. His face flushed angrily as he jumped to his feet. "You deserted?"

Chad's own look turned angry. "Look, I was hired by you French to fight. When the odds get six to one that ain't fighting. That's suicide! Besides, someone had to get to the fort to warn

362

you. My God, man, don't you realize what a disaster this is? El Puma and his men armed with repeating carbines!"

Mon dieu, Dubert thought, sinking back into his chair, what a terrible day this was. First Juarista prisoners he didn't dare execute, and now El Puma had succeeded in capturing a shipment of repeating carbines. Colonel Le Blanc will have my head for sure, he thought bleakly.

"What are you going to do?" Chad demanded.

"Do?" Dubert asked, dazed. "What can I do?" he asked resignedly.

"Go after them!" Chad retorted angrily. "Hell, man, I told you, they're right out there in the open! Couldn't have been over twenty of them. You've got three hundred men here. Hell, you can spare fifty to go after El Puma and those guns."

Dubert didn't want to tell the American he didn't have three hundred men. The reinforcements that were supposed to come yesterday had not arrived either. That was probably something else he'd be blamed for, he thought, his spirits sinking even lower.

"Look," Chad said, "you can easily catch up with them before they reach the mountains. If you hurry, you can even catch them before dark. They can't travel very fast with that heavy wagon. The horses pulling it were already exhausted. We were having to travel at a snail's pace ourselves."

Dubert looked up, confused by the barrage of Chad's words.

Chad threw down his trump card. "Hell, are you crazy? This is your chance to finally catch

El Puma!"

Catch El Puma? Was it possible? Dubert wondered. If he managed this remarkable feat, captured the notorious El Puma, the man who had been a thorn in the French's side for years, Colonel Le Blanc would forgive him anything. Why, he'd be a hero and receive a promotion, be a major, or maybe even a colonel, himself.

Dubert's monumental ambition overruled his good sense. "Do you think we can catch up with him?" Dubert asked, his eyes glittering with excitement.

"Hell yes," Chad answered. "That's why I rode like a madman to get here and tell you."

Dubert made his decision. Rising from the desk, he said, "I will dispatch a patrol immediately. Will you ride with them, *monsieur*, to show them where you were attacked?"

This was something Chad hadn't expected. His mind searched for a quick excuse. He turned and limped in an exaggerated manner to the door, saying, "I sure will. This is one piece of the action I want to get in on. Imagine, being able to say I was in on capturing the famous El Puma himself. I could sure use some of that reward money!"

Dubert frowned. He had no intention of sharing the glory or the reward money with this Yankee. Feigning concern, he said, "*Monsieur*, you are injured!"

"Huh?" Chad replied in pretended surprise; then, looking down at his leg, he said, "Oh, this ain't nothing. Sprained my leg a little when my horse stumbled on a rock and threw me. Guess

I'm lucky the horse didn't break his leg."

Dubert drew himself up, saying, "*Monsieur*, I cannot possibly allow you to travel with my men, injured as you are."

"Hell, I can ride!" Chad retorted.

"But you might slow my men down, *monsieur*. We can't take any chances on catching El Puma."

"Now wait a minute," Chad began in an ugly voice.

"*Monsieur*," Dubert said in a soothing voice, "I can assure you, you will still share in the reward money. And I shall personally tell Colonel Le Blanc that it was your warning which led to the capture of El Puma. Believe me, you will be adequately rewarded."

Chad hid a smug grin. Damn right, you'll tell him who it was that put you on El Puma's tail, he thought. Only it won't be to share the glory, but the blame. It's a good thing you're dead Tony Peters, because after today, your name will be mud with the French.

Chad smiled, saying in an amiable voice, "Well now, Captain, that's right wide of you. To tell you the truth, my leg is smartin' a bit."

Dubert walked to the door hurriedly, wondering what "right wide" and "smartin'" meant. These Yankees could sure bastardize the English language, he thought.

While the captain was dispatching the patrol after El Puma, Chad sat in a chair, thinking, So far, so good. He wondered if he could convince the captain to let him see the prisoners the French had taken that morning? He had been tortured all afternoon by visions of Christine being wounded. He had to reassure himself that she was all right. But then, maybe that wouldn't be such a good idea after all, he thought. What if the Juaristas unknowingly gave him away? He was still puzzling over that problem when Dubert returned to the room, strutting like a peacock.

"Ah, Monsieur Peters," the cocky captain said, "now we shall have a drink to celebrate."

Chad sat in silence while the captain filled two glasses with French wine and handed one to him. Then sitting in his own chair and smiling with self-satisfaction, Dubert raised his glass in a salute, saying, "To the success of our venture."

Chad grinned and returned the salute.

After taking a sip of the wine, the Frenchman said, "You have no idea how opportune your arrival was."

"How's that?" Chad drawled.

"This morning my men discovered El Puma's hideout and destroyed it. They brought back over thirty prisoners."

"Say, this has been your day," Chad said in mock admiration.

"Yes, one would think so," Dubert replied tightly. "But unfortunately, taking prisoners didn't turn out to be such a good thing after all."

"What do you mean?" Chad asked with sincere curiosity.

The captain scowled, saying, "There was an American woman with them. Seems she was deserted by her escort when they were attacked by bandits. The Juaristas found her in the mountains

366

and befriended her. If she is to be believed, she comes from a rich and influential family in your country. She has threatened to expose our execution of the Juarista prisoners to the newspapers." Dubert leaned forward, his look penetrating, saying, "Tell me, *monsieur*, have you ever heard of a man in your country named Roberts, one that owns a large number of newspapers?"

Newspapers? He thought Christine's uncle was in manufacturing. Then Chad chuckled to himself, thinking, Why the little hellion! She's made the whole story up to scare the Frenchman off.

Frowning with consternation, Chad said, "You know, I have heard of a Roberts family that owns a string of newspapers. Powerful people, very powerful. They have a lot of influence in Washington too."

Dubert sighed, saying, "I was afraid of that."

"You say she's been threatening you, huh? I can sure see where that would put you between a rock and a hard place," Chad said, trying to sound sympathetic.

Dubert frowned in horror, thinking, "rock and a hard place"? *Mon dieu*! But he had to admit that certainly described his position accurately.

"Yes, my position is awkward to say the least," Dubert sighed. His anger at Christine returned. "Ah, *monsieur*, you should see her! I have never in my life seen such an arrogant, demanding woman. And she's the biggest woman I have ever seen. *Mon dieu*, bigger than most men. Why, even her hair is cut short like a man's. She's disgusting!"

367

Despite himself, Chad's jaw bunched angrily. His eyes flashed dangerously. No one called his magnificent lady disgusting!

Dubert saw the big Texan's look and shuddered in fear. "I am sorry, *monsieur*," he quickly apologized. "I did not mean to insult one of your countrywomen, but . . ."

Chad realized he was about to give himself away and interjected, "That's all right, Captain. I guess we've all got some women we ought to lock away in a closet."

"*Mon dieu!*" Dubert cried, throwing his hands up in disgust. "This one you could not lock up even in the bastille! I have never seen such a fierce, strong-willed woman in my life!"

Chad smiled to himself. Yep, that's my magnificent lady, he thought. And apparently Chris wasn't injured if she was throwing her weight around and issuing ultimatums.

"Well, after you capture El Puma you won't have to worry about her and her threats," Chad soothed. "With El Puma a prisoner, no one's going to pay any attention if you let a few, miserable Juaristas go. Hell, without him to lead them, they couldn't do anything anyway."

"My sentiments exactly," Dubert said, smiling smugly.

A French enlisted man appeared at the door. Seeing him, Dubert said, "Ah, I see it is time for dinner. Bring your glass with you. We will have more wine with our meal."

Chad picked up his glass and limped after the captain. But when he stepped into the dining room, he froze. Christine stood, staring back at him, her look stunned.

"Ah, Mademoiselle Roberts," Dubert said smoothly, "I see you are surprised to see another of your countrymen here. May I introduce Tony Peters? He works for the French, mademoiselle. You see, not all of your fellow Americans support the Juaristas. There are those who support us too."

Oh, my God, Chad thought. What if she gives me away? He gave her a hard, warning look.

Christine was stunned. Chad? What was he doing here still impersonating Tony Peters? Why was the captain acting so friendly to him? And why was he looking at her like that, so hard?

Captain Dubert gave Chad a conspiratorial wink, an act not missed by Christine. "I am most fortunate, mademoiselle. Monsieur Peters just brought me word that El Puma was trying to steal a shipment of guns from us. Already, a detachment of men are on his trail, and soon, he, too, will be my prisoner."

Christine stared at Chad in shock. He had betrayed El Puma, had come to tell the French of the Juarista's plan to intercept the guns. But why was he still posing as Tony Peters? Had he decided to join the French? Become one of their hateful mercenaries? But why would he do that?

Captain Dubert was enjoying Christine's reaction to his news. He smiled maliciously, saying, "Yes, soon Monsieur Peters and I will be sharing the reward money my government has posted for El Puma. We will both be wealthy men."

That's why, Christine thought with sudden, sickening realization. The reward for El Puma was more than she was paying him. And that explained his hard look when he first saw her. He hadn't expected to find her here. He had walked out on her and assumed the mercenary's identity, betraying both her and El Puma. And all for money!

But what could she expect? Christine asked herself bitterly. She had always known she couldn't trust men, particularly some cold-blooded *pistolero* who hired out his gun to the highest bidder. And to think that she had begun to think that Chad was different from other men, that she might be able to trust him. What a fool she had been! Tears of anger and deep hurt stung Christine's eyes as she glared at Chad.

Chad saw her look and thought, my God, she believes him! She actually thinks I've betrayed El Puma. But why does she look so hurt? Anger I can understand. But hurt?

And then it dawned on him. She thought he had walked out on her, abandoned her. But surely she knew he wouldn't do that to her, surely she trusted him more than that? Chad felt a sharp twinge of hurt himself.

But then he remembered that Christine had no way of knowing of his and El Puma's plans. She could probably think of no logical reason for him to be impersonating Tony Peters, except for the one Dubert had given her. And he had to admit that the captain had sounded very convincing. For a minute, he considered trying to send her some secret message with his eyes, some silent message that would reassure her. But then he thought better of it. No, for the time being it was better that she believed Dubert's story, since he couldn't tell her the real one yet. Otherwise, she might unwittingly give him away. But still, he wished she hadn't been so quick to condemn him.

Christine raised her chin stubbornly. Her shoulders set, she waited for Chad to reveal her true identity to the captain. But as he stared back at her, she realized that he couldn't expose her without exposing himself as an impostor. The realization gave her little comfort, the hurt of his betrayal overpowering all.

Raising her head proudly, Christine said haughtily, "You'll have to excuse me, *monsieurs*, but I find my appetite has suddenly disappeared." She looked with pointed disgust at the captain and then at Chad with open contempt. "There seems to be a stench of something rotten in this room." She turned and walked toward the hallway, her bearing majestic.

Captain Dubert's face turned red with anger. His fists clenched and unclenched in frustration. "Damned bitch!" he snarled.

Chad found it very hard to keep his admiration for Christine's spirit from showing on his face. Not trusting his voice, he managed a shrug, hoping to show casual indifference to the Yankee woman's opinion of him.

Chapter Seventeen

Chad squirmed restlessly in the big overstuffed chair and groaned to himself. It seemed he had been sitting for hours and listening to Captain Dubert brag about his military exploits, half of which Chad thought were out-and-out lies, the other half exaggerated beyond any recognition. What a conceited bastard he is, Chad thought with disgust, a frozen smile on his face. I wish I could be a fly on the wall when Colonel Le Blanc comes back and discovers Dubert has let the Juarista prisoners escape. I'd love to see the arrogant French captain trying to squirm out of that one.

Chad watched as Dubert drained another glass of wine. The Frenchman had been drinking steadily since dinner and was well on the way to being drunk. That's good, Chad thought. He'll be all the more confused when he's awakened suddenly in the middle of the night. But, unfortunately, the wine was making the man more talkative, and Chad was anxious to get away and find Christine. He had a lot of explaining to do, and knowing how obstinate she could be, Chad knew he had a formidable task on his hands.

Chad sat and impatiently listened to Captain Dubert's long, boring monologue, smiling in satisfaction as the man's speech became more and more slurred and his eyes became more glazed. When the captain's head finally lolled backward on his chair and Chad heard a loud snore, he grinned. He rose and walked to the chair, shaking Dubert's shoulder roughly. The captain slumped over, one arm dangling limply to the floor, his mouth gaping open.

Chad smiled smugly and walked from the room. When he stepped into the dim hallway, the same enlisted man who had summoned them to dinner stepped forward and motioned for Chad to follow him.

As he followed the Frenchman down the long hall to the room he had been assigned, Chad studied the row of doors lining the hallway. He had no idea which room Christine was in. And even if he had spoken French, he wouldn't have dared asked the man he was following for such information.

After making a big show of yawning before he closed his door on the enlisted man, Chad waited for a few minutes for the Frenchman to go back down the hall. Then he cautiously opened the door and peered down the dimly lit corridor. Grateful that the hall was empty, he stepped back

374

out into the hallway and crept to the first door. For a minute, he listened with his ear against the wooden panel. When no noise came from the room, he opened it and looked in. It was empty. The next two rooms were also empty. At the fourth door, Chad heard loud snores through the wooden panel and moved on. The fifth door was locked.

Chad smiled to himself. Only Christine would lock her door in a barracks full of officers. Judging by all of the open doors he had found, the Frenchmen did not expect the privacy of their rooms to be intruded on. Now Chad's problem was getting into Christine's room without alerting the French or Chris. He didn't dare break the lock for fear Christine would hear him and start screaming, thinking she was about to be attacked. Damn, for once, he wished she hadn't been so careful.

Chad looked up and down the hallway in frustration. Then he remembered that every room he had looked in had had a window in the back. That was it, Chad thought with relief. Surely, Chris wouldn't have her window down and locked in this heat.

Chad hurried back down the hallway to his room, counting the doors as he passed. He closed the door behind him and looked out of his window. The back of the barracks was dark and screened with low shrubbery. He twisted and squirmed until he managed to get his big body through the narrow window.

Landing lithely on the ground outside, Chad

crouched and crept down the back of the barracks, ducking lower at each window he passed. Before he even reached Christine's window, he realized that she had left her light burning. He peered through the window and saw her, still fully clothed, sleeping on the narrow bed. Thank God, she's asleep, Chad thought. Otherwise, she'd raise the roof before he had a chance to get through the window. But damn it, he wished she had put out her light. Now as he crawled in, he would be clearly silhouetted in the light from the window. He could only hope that the French sentries on those walls were looking in the direction they were supposed to be watching.

Chad's climb into Christine's window was even more awkward than his exit from his own. I'd make a rotten thief, Chad thought wryly, as he scraped his elbow on the window sill painfully, his gun making a loud, metallic noise as it bumped against the wood. Christine stirred at the noise, and Chad held his breath. When he was sure she hadn't awakened, he finished crawling through the window.

Standing safely inside the room, Chad quickly drew the flimsy shutters. He wasn't sure how well anyone could see into this room from the walls, but he wasn't going to take any more chances than he had to.

Christine had returned to her room after finding out about Chad's betrayal and had cried herself to sleep. Now she was awakened by feeling a hand placed over her mouth. She sensed someone on the bed beside her. With pure animal instinct for survival, she began to fight and claw even before she opened her eyes.

"Chris, cut it out!" a deep, familiar, masculine voice said.

Christine saw Chad leaning over her. The realization that it was him only made her fight harder. Her long legs thrashed and kicked wildly, and Chad was forced to pin them down with his own long, muscular legs. Her hands clawed at his face and neck, and Chad had a hard time catching them in his free hand. He finally subdued her, his big hand holding her wrists above her head, his body lying half over hers. She looked up at him, her green eyes spitting hate, her body still twisting and bucking beneath him.

Chad grinned down at her, saying, "Lady, you'd better stop that bucking, or you're going to make me forget what I came here for."

Christine's body froze at the implication. Then she sank her sharp teeth into the flesh of Chad's hand over her mouth.

"Goddammit!" Chad swore, jerking his hand away.

Christine glared up at him, a smug smile on her face.

Realizing she wasn't going to scream, Chad took her shoulders and shook them roughly. "You crazy, little hellion, will you listen to me?" Chad snarled. "I didn't walk out on you. And I didn't betray El Puma. I only pretended to be Tony Peters so I could get in this fort. Someone had to get inside to open the gates for El Puma. How else could he possibly hope to rescue the prisoners?"

"But you told Captain Dubert about El Puma's plan to steal the guns!" Christine retorted.

"Chris, El Puma has the guns back at his camp. I only told Dubert that story so he would send his men out on a wild-goose chase."

Christine was reeling in confusion. "You mean, everything Captain Dubert told me was a pack of lies?"

"Yes, lies I told him."

Briefly, Chad told Christine of his and El Puma's rescue plans, ending with how he had rushed into the fort that afternoon and what he had told Captain Dubert. As he talked, Christine began to relax.

When he had finished, she said, "Then it was all an act on your part?"

Chad grinned, saying, "Yes, and that stupid Dubert fell for it, hook, line, and sinker."

Suddenly, Christine felt very foolish. She blinked back tears of happiness and shame that she had doubted him. Tracing an angry scratch on Chad's face with one finger, she said, "Oh, Chad, I'm sorry for doubting you. But you didn't say anything to deny it and Captain Dubert sounded so convincing."

"Yeah, I know."

A sudden thought occurred to Christine. "Chad, what if the captain should come looking for you for some reason. You'd better go back to your room."

Chad chuckled, saying, "Don't worry about him, Chris. He won't be looking for me or checking up on anybody tonight. He's passed out, dead drunk. I doubt if even an earthquake could rouse him right now."

Christine laughed softly from relief. Chad looked down at her, remembering how terrified he'd been when he'd returned to El Puma's camp and found his cabin burned to the ground. Then all afternoon, he'd worried about her being wounded or hurt. He found it hard to believe that she was really safe and here in his arms. Suddenly he wanted to make love to her, *had* to make love to her. Only by loving her, could he satisfy his need to confirm she was really and truly alive and whole.

His mouth lowered, and his lips traced the pulsebeat on her throat up to her ear. He nibbled at the delicate lobe, his tongue probing gently. Shivers of pleasure ran down Christine's spine.

"Chad," she said, a little breathlessly, "tell me more about the rescue plans."

"Later," Chad mumbled against her ear, his mouth trailing teasing kisses down her temple and across her jawline.

"No, tell me now," Christine objected weakly, trying without success to ignore the warm hand that cupped and stroked her tender breasts with tantalizing skill.

Christine gasped as Chad's hand slipped between her naked thighs, his fingers sensuously brushing the sensitive skin. She had never even been aware that he'd inched up her skirt.

"Chad!"

"Hush, lady," Chad muttered against her ear,

his voice husky with desire. "We've got more important things to do than talk."

His lips nibbled and teased the corners of her mouth before his mouth claimed hers in a deep, passionate kiss that left her breathless and robbed her of any further resistance. Before Christine fully realized what he had done, Chad had deftly stripped her and disposed of his own clothing. Lying beside her, his eyes feasted on her body, the proud breasts, the soft curve of her hips, the silver nest of curls between her legs. Christine lay, flushing under his warm gaze. His eyes rose to meet hers, his look hungry.

"I've missed you, lady," he muttered hoarsely before his mouth covered hers in a fierce, penetrating kiss that left her whirling, her blood coursing hot through her veins.

Chad broke their searing kiss and dropped small kisses down her neck and shoulders to her breasts, where he dallied, his tongue lazily tracing ever-decreasing circles around the aching flesh until his mouth closed hungrily over a rosy tip. Christine's heart pounded in her ears as she clutched at him, trying to pull him even closer.

His head descended, his tongue licking erotically over her rib cage and taut abdomen, stopping to circle and explore her navel. Trembling, Chad shifted his weight over her, cupping her buttocks and drawing her to him, and Christine arched in anticipation of his thrust. She gasped in surprise as Chad buried his head between her legs, his mouth searing, his tongue seeking, probing, stroking the core of her femininty. For a minute, Christine struggled, shocked by his action, but Chad held her hips firmly, not allowing her to squirm away from the hot demand of his mouth and tongue. And then the waves of pleasure began, first sweet, rippling sensations and then hot, searing undulations, rocking her with their intensity. A low throaty moan escaped her lips.

Christine opened her eyes to see Chad's blue eyes shimmering above her. "Did you like that, lady?" he asked in a thick voice.

"Oh, yes," Christine breathed, still feeling deliciously languid.

Chad smiled knowingly. He bent to kiss her mouth softly, and Christine tasted herself on his lips.

Then she felt the moist tip of his hardness brushing against her thigh, probing. "No!" Christine cried, tearing her mouth away from Chad's.

Chad stared down at her in bewilderment.

Christine's emotions were confused at that moment. She didn't know exactly what her feelings for Chad were. She only knew that she wanted to return all of those marvelous feelings he had just given her, to give him some special gift. She was just a little shocked at herself, at what she wanted to do. She blushed furiously and then, for lack of better words, said, "I want to taste you too."

Chad had thought that there was nothing Christine could do or say that would surprise him anymore, but he was stunned by her words. When she rolled him onto his back, Chad lay rigid with shock. He had been made love to in this manner before, had found it wildly exciting, but those women had been whores. And Christine was a lady! But then as Christine began kissing and licking his inner thighs and the bush of tight curls on his groin, her hands sensuously stroking his hips and outer thighs, all thought fled. His heart pounded in his ears. His blood turned to molten fire. And when Chad felt her kissing his engorged flesh, her tongue tracing its length from base to tip, then swirling around the crown, flickering like a fiery dart, he clenched his teeth and groaned in rapturous agony, every muscle in his big body quivering.

And then, when he felt he was about to burst, Chad threw her to her back and plunged into her fiery, throbbing center, burying himself deeply, filling her completely as his mouth smothered her cry of pleasure. Two hearts thudding wildly, bodies straining, mouths locked in a passionate kiss, Chad carried her up those spiraling heights with bold, masterful strokes, ever increasing in tempo. Not until Christine was shuddering in her own climax, did Chad allow himself his own release, his body stiffening and shuddering above hers, emptying himself into her.

When his trembling had subsided and his breathing had slowed, Chad rolled from Christine, carrying her possessively with him to lie in the crook of his arm. He lay staring at the ceiling, deep in thought. Christine had always been passionate, but she had always seemed to hold some part of herself back. Tonight, she had opened to him completely, her surprisingly erotic love-making spontaneous and totally voluntary.

He couldn't believe that a woman like Christine, a lady to the core, could make such intimate love to a man unless she felt something much deeper than desire. Was she finally offering him a part of her heart and soul as well as her body? Her love? The thought sent his heart racing even faster than it had at the height of his passion.

Christine snuggled into Chad's warm embrace. She licked the livid scratch on his neck where she had scratched him when he had first awakened her. "I'm sorry I did that," she mumbled.

Chad chuckled, saying in a voice that was still a little shaky, "Lady, you'd better believe I'll never come into your bed uninvited again. I thought you were going to tear me to pieces. And you've got a kick like a mule."

Christine laughed. Chad didn't bother to tell her about the scratches she had inflicted on his back in the throes of her passion. He didn't want to risk inhibiting her responses.

Christine rose on her elbow and looked down at Chad, saying, "Chad, when you were at El Puma's camp after the attack, did you by any chance see . . ."

"Diablo?" Chad interjected. He grinned, saying, "Yes, I saw your ornery horse. He's safe."

Christine sighed with relief and lay back down. "Oh, I'm so glad. I was worried he might have been hit by a stray bullet."

Chad nodded, saying, "I figured you'd be worried about him. No, believe me, he's alive and kicking. As a matter of fact, when I was riding out of the camp, he was giving some poor Juarista hell." He chuckled, then added, "The man made the mistake of trying to mount him."

Christine laughed, then said, "Now tell me about the rescue plans."

"There's really not much more to tell. It's really a very simple plan. I'm going to start a fire in the blacksmith's shop to distract the French. While they're busy trying to put it out, I'm going to open the gate for El Puma."

"What can I do to help?"

"Nothing. Just stay safe where I hide you."

"But I just can't stand around doing nothing! Surely there must be something I can do to help."

Chad really didn't want Christine to get involved in the rescue attempt, but he knew she would keep persisting until he agreed to let her help in some way. He sighed, saying, "All right, you can cover me while I start the fire. Only I hope your aim has gotten better."

Christine frowned, knowing what Chad said was true. She still wasn't very good with a gun. "Maybe I can open the gate while you're starting the fire."

"I doubt it," Chad replied. "I got a good look at those gates when I rode in this afternoon. Those crossbars look heavy. In fact, it will probably take both of us to lift them."

They lay for a few minutes in silence, each lost in thought.

"When do we leave?" Christine asked.

"Not until about two-thirty in the morning. No sense in going out there any sooner. It would only increase our chances of being discovered."

Christine snuggled against Chad's warm, naked body, her head pillowed on his hard chest. Her hands played over the damp, dark curls there, tracing the planes of his broad chest and taut abdomen. Her eyes drifted in open admiration, following the line of dark hair down his abdomen until it flared again at his groin. She gasped, her stare locked on his aroused sex standing boldly erect.

Chad chuckled and hooked one long leg over hers, pulling her closer. "I just figured out how we can pass the time," he mumbled huskily in her ear. "Unless, you'd rather sleep?"

Christine blushed and then eagerly squirmed closer to that hot, throbbing part of him, mumbling, "No, I'm not sleepy."

But Christine did manage to sleep for several hours. Chad lay, forcing himself to stay awake and wondering if he was doing the right thing. He wanted to help El Puma, but hated to take the risk of something happening to Christine. He knew the rescue attempt was dangerous, and he seriously doubted if they could sneak the prisoners out without being discovered. Then all hell would break loose. His forehead broke out in perspiration as he protectively pulled Christine closer. Lady, he thought furiously, why couldn't you have waited in Texas where you would have been safe? The more Chad thought about it, the more worried he became. By the time he wakened Christine and waited for her to dress, he was tense and irritable.

"Come on," he said gruffly as he led her to the door, his hand closing over her arm roughly.

Christine looked up at him in surprise. It seemed impossible that this was the same man who had made such tender, passionate love to her only a few hours before. Now he seemed almost angry at her. She shook her head in dismay, thinking, Will I ever understand this man and his quicksilver moods?

Chad looked down the deserted hallway and motioned for Christine to follow. She crept behind him, her heart pounding in her chest, her own breathing sounding like a roaring in the deep silence of the night. She sighed with relief as they stepped out of the door, the darkness covering them in a welcoming blanket.

"Stay low," Chad warned, as he crouched and moved along the side of the barracks.

When they reached the end of the building, he looked both ways before darting across the open area to another low building. Quickly, Christine followed. And so they progressed, moving from one building to the other, until they stood beside the stable.

"Wait out here while I go in and saddle my horse," Chad whispered. "If you see anyone coming, give a low whistle."

Christine nodded, and Chad disappeared behind the stable door. Crouching in the darkness, it seemed to Christine that Chad had been gone an eternity. Her eyes strained into the black night. And then she realized with sudden horror that her mouth was dry. She wouldn't be able to whistle if she had to! Frantically she tried to wet her lips.

She jumped nervously at the squeak of the stable door when Chad opened it and led his horse outside. Standing on trembling legs, she followed him as he led the animal around to the back of the stable and then across the fort, hugging the shadows of the back wall.

Christine looked down at the horse's hooves, surprised to see that Chad had covered them with a thick wad of material to muffle the sound they made on the hard, packed dirt. She peered closer, trying to make out the material, and almost fainted when she recognized the swaddling as pieces of a French uniform. Somewhere in that dark stable, Chad must have run into a French sentry, and she had not heard a whimper. She wondered if Chad had knocked out the unfortunate man or killed him. She shivered, deciding she preferred not to know the answer.

When they reached the opposite wall of the fort, Chad led the horse behind a pile of water kegs and motioned Christine down beside him. Chad crouched with her, the sounds of the sentry's footsteps above them pounding in their ears.

Only when the steady cadence of the footsteps diminished to a bare tapping noise, did Chad whisper, "You wait here, while I start the fire. Here's my carbine. You can cover me, but don't shoot unless you're positive I've been discovered."

Christine nodded, as sudden tears burned her eyes.

"See you, lady," Chad muttered, pulling her into a bone-crushing embrace and giving her a quick, fierce kiss.

And then he was gone, swallowed up by the darkness.

Christine huddled behind the water kegs and blinked back hot tears, her heart in her throat.

She strained her eyes in the darkness and tried to catch some glimpse of Chad, but she could see no sign of him. The sentry's steps sounded above her again, and Chad's horse moved restlessly. Christine stroked his neck in an effort to quiet him. Then she heard the gasp of the sentry above her, followed by his cry of alarm. For one brief moment, she froze in terror, convinced he had discovered her. Then, as she heard him running away, she looked and saw the fire across the fort.

Already, men were running and calling the alarm. The barracks' doors flew open as half-dressed, barefoot soldiers poured from the buildings. Men swarmed in confusion all over the parade ground, some running to the fire, others to nearby stables, a few moving aimlessly as if in a daze.

But where was Chad? Christine thought. Her eyes scanned the area, but suddenly he was crouching beside her, gasping from his mad dash across the grounds.

"Where's the sentry?" he whispered, pointing above them.

"He ran to the other end when the fire started," Christine whispered back.

"Good. Come on, Chris, let's get that gate open."

Chad and Christine crept to the gate and reached for each end of the crossbar holding it shut. Chad silently blessed Christine's height. A shorter woman wouldn't have been able to reach the bar. When he lifted the heavy beam, he wondered if Christine could handle the weight. Christine wondered herself, feeling her muscles pulling painfully.

"Don't drop it," Chad warned as the bar slid over the braces. "Just hang on to your end until I can lay mine down."

Christine clung to the bar, her muscles screaming in protest, until Chad was beside her, taking the heavy beam and placing it on the ground. Chad moved to the door and pulled it open, its hinges creaking loudly. Christine looked around anxiously for fear someone would hear the noise. But she had no need to worry about that. No one could have heard the squeaking over the roar of the fire and the yelling of the soldiers.

She turned and gasped in surprise as El Puma and Miguel stepped through the gate, grinning broadly and hugging Chad in comradeship. Quickly and as quietly as mice, the other Juaristas moved through the gate, fanning out and melting into the darkness.

"Let's get to the prison," Chad whispered.

"No, you stay here with your woman and cover us with the rest of my men," El Puma replied. "Miguel and I and several others will go to the prison."

Chad nodded and pulled Christine back behind the water kegs. They watched as the French formed a bucket brigade. But by now, the fire in the blacksmith's shop was totally out of control. Men were leading frightened, rearing horses from the stables, the animals' shrill whinnies adding to the clamorous noise of the scene. Sparks from the fire fell onto the stables, and the men beat at them wildly in an effort to keep another fire from starting. Seeing the impending danger, the bucket

389

brigade quickly forgot the blacksmith's shop and began pouring and splashing water on the sides of the stables nearest the fire. Christine smiled with satisfaction as she saw several sentries desert their posts to help with the fire.

"Christine," a soft feminine voice said behind her, and Christine turned into María's happy embrace.

"My God, I didn't expect you back that soon," Chad said to a grinning El Puma.

"We were lucky," El Puma replied. "Most of the guards had left to fight the fire. There were only two left, and we quickly overpowered them. Look, *amigos*." He pointed to the gate.

Silently, the Juaristas were guiding the prisoners along the dark walls of the fort and out the gate. Several of the women and children were sobbing quietly in relief. One male prisoner, supported by a Juarista compatriot, limped badly. Another more seriously injured man was carried on the burly shoulder of his rescuer.

Chad could hear the whinnying and nervous pawing of the Mexicans' horses outside the wall as the prisoners mounted them. His own mount stirred restlessly and snorted, alarmed by the smell of smoke in his nostrils.

"Go, María," El Puma commanded, pulling Christine and María apart and pushing María toward the last of the prisoners going through the gate.

"You too, *señora*," El Puma said to Christine.

Christine raised her chin stubbornly, saying, "No, not until Chad goes."

El Puma chuckled and said, "Then both of you go."

A loud noise from across the fort drew their attention back to the fire. A large blackened beam supporting the roof of the blacksmith's shop had collapsed, sending red cinders flying into the sky and all over the stable roof. Almost instantly, multiple small fires ignited on that building. The fort was in chaos as the men rushed to fight the new fire. Christine sighed with relief when she saw that all of the animals had been removed. But several horses had broken loose and were racing wildly across the grounds seeking escape, only adding to the confusion.

El Puma turned and motioned to the rest of his Juaristas to leave. Silently, the men crept from their hiding places and disappeared through the gate.

"You, too, *señor*," El Puma said to Chad.

"What about you?" Chad asked.

"I'll be right behind you."

Chad nodded and turned to his horse. El Puma walked to the gate to open it farther for Chad's horse to pass through. Christine looked up and froze in horror. Three French soldiers were running toward the water kegs where they stood. Upon seeing them, the soldiers also froze briefly in surprise. Then Christine saw one of the soldiers raise his gun and point it directly at Chad's back.

"No!" Christine screamed, throwing her body in front of Chad's.

Chad whirled as the Frenchman's gun roared and caught Christine, the impact of the bullet slamming her body against his. At that same moment, El Puma ran from the gate, his carbine spitting bullets. The French soldiers crumpled to the ground, either dead or seriously wounded.

"Chris!" Chad cried, supporting her and staring in horror at the gaping hole in her left shoulder, the wound already pouring blood over her blouse and breasts.

"Hurry, *amigo*," El Puma urged.

"She's been hit!" Chad yelled.

"I know, *amigo*," El Puma said in a soothing voice. "But the French have been alerted and know we're here now. Get on your horse. I will help you put her up behind you. Then ride like hell. As soon as we make it to the mountains, we can bandage the wound."

Chad mounted and helped as El Puma lifted Christine behind him.

"Can you hold on, *señora*?" El Puma asked.

Christine nodded weakly, biting her lips to keep from moaning in pain. Her shoulder felt as if it were on fire. She reeled with dizziness; her vision blurred. She leaned against Chad's broad shoulder and, with supreme effort, put her arms around his waist, wincing as a darting pain shot through the injured shoulder.

"Hold on to her hands tightly, *amigo*, in case she faints," El Puma told Chad.

Then he slapped the rump of Chad's horse. Startled, the animal bolted through the gate and rushed into the sweet, clean air of the darkness beyond.

Chapter Eighteen

Chad raced his horse across the dark, gently undulating plain, following the escaping Juaristas before him, the noise of the gunfire between the remaining Juaristas and the French in his ears. He clutched Christine's hands as they slumped limply around his waist, and heard her moan.

Careening around clumps of cactus and up and down arroyos, the ride seemed an eternity to Chad. He knew that each jarring gait of the horse must be causing Christine excruciating pain.

"Hang on, Chris," he said, trying to reassure her. "We'll reach the mountains soon."

At the sound of hoofs behind him, Chad turned and looked over his shoulder. He could barely see El Puma and two other Juaristas rapidly gaining on him.

"Hurry, *amigo*. The French are mounting a patrol to follow us," El Puma yelled, as he galloped up beside him.

Chad spurred his horse. The animal was

already blowing hard from carrying double at breakneck speed. Chad rode like a demon out of hell through the night, acutely aware of Christine's blood soaking the back of his shirt. My God, she'll bleed to death before we even reach the mountains, he thought. When he felt her body go completely limp, he pulled back on his reins, slowing his mount.

El Puma, riding beside him, called, "No, *amigo*, you can't stop here. The French will catch us."

"I've got to," Chad yelled back. "She's fainted, and I can't hold on to her this way."

As Chad brought his mount to a stop, Ramón called to the other two Juaristas riding with them in Spanish, "Drop back and cover us."

The two *guerrilleros* obeyed immediately, reining in and whirling their horses about. Soon, they had disappeared into the darkness.

El Puma helped Chad lift Christine's limp body from the back of the horse. Lying her on the ground, Chad knelt and started to take off his shirt to use as a bandage.

"No, *amigo*, use mine," El Puma said, stripping off his shirt and handing it to Chad. "Yours is already soaked."

The two men formed a pressure bandage over the wound in Christine's shoulder. The sounds of gunshots not far behind were a warning that the French patrol had caught up with the rear guard El Puma had sent back.

"Quick, *amigo*, get back in the saddle. I will lift her up, and you can hold her in front of you."

Chad nodded and leaped into his saddle. El Puma lifted Christine's unconscious body up to Chad. Chad cradled her across his lap, her injured shoulder against his chest.

"Hold her tightly against you, *amigo*, so the bandage will stay in place," El Puma said as he mounted his own horse.

"How much farther to the mountains?" Chad asked.

"A couple of miles, and then we can slow down."

Those few miles turned out to be a harrowing ride. It wasn't easy for Chad to ride at breakneck speed while trying to hold onto Christine's limp body with one arm. To make matters worse, his horse was nervous and difficult to handle because of the bullets whizzing through the air around them and the noise of the answering fire from the Mexicans riding beside him. Chad was greatly relieved when they finally began to climb upward through a narrow, twisting ravine.

But then he realized with horror that the French had not given up their pursuit. Not accustomed to riding through the mountains at night as the Juaristas were, they had dropped behind, but they still followed too closely to permit the Juaristas to slow down.

"I thought you said we'd lose them in the mountains," Chad called angrily to El Puma riding ahead of him.

The Mexican *jefe* grinned back over his shoulder, saying, "Soon, *amigo*, soon."

After the next turn in the trail, El Puma called,

"You can start slowing down now, *amigo*."

"But," Chad began and then froze in his saddle, hearing the low rumbling noise that built to a deafening crescendo. Chad looked back over his shoulder at the ravine they had just passed through. He couldn't see a thing in the darkness, but the rising dust watered his eyes and choked him. He grinned when he realized what had happened. The Juaristas had started a rock slide in the narrow passage behind them and had blocked the trail to the French patrol following them. The pursuit was over.

After another few twists and turns, they emerged from the ravine to follow a steep trail that hugged the side of the mountain. Traveling at a slow pace, they inched their way up the precarious path, rocks and gravel breaking loose beneath the horses' hooves and tumbling down the mountainside. Finally, the trail widened and leveled out.

El Puma dropped back, saying, "How is she?"

"Bad," Chad answered, his throat dry with fear. "She's lost a lot of blood and is still bleeding. How much farther to the camp?"

"About an hour's ride," El Puma answered.

Then a terrible explosion rocked the earth beneath them, and the four riders turned and looked down the mountainside to the fort below. A large red-and-orange ball of fire rose over the fort, illuminating the night sky and the surrounding area with its brilliance as tons of debris and rock were thrown high in the air. Chad and the Mexicans sat in stunned silence as another, and yet another, explosion roared and the earth trembled.

"What the hell," Chad muttered, staring at the awesome sight.

El Puma turned in his saddle and said in a quiet voice, "I had completely forgotten that the arsenal was on the same side of the fort as the blacksmith's shop and stable."

Chad looked down at the fort below him. The stable was still burning, and through the billowing smoke, he could see the gaping hole in the ground where the arsenal had once stood. Most of the wall on that side of the fort had been destroyed by the explosion and now lay in rubble.

"I'm afraid the French will have to abandon it," El Puma said, smiling smugly. "What good is a fort with only three sides?"

Chad nodded in agreement, thinking the French had paid a heavy price for their raid on the Juarista camp. And then he remembered the woman in his arms and thought the price not large enough.

The rest of the ride to the Juarista camp was agonizing for Chad. The bandage on Christine's shoulder was soaked with blood that dribbled down Chad's chest and pooled in a sticky mess on the saddle. Even in the darkness, he could see how frighteningly pale her face was. He held her to him fiercely, acutely aware of her shallow breathing and weak, thready heartbeat.

Chad was not a deeply religious man, but that night he prayed fervently, begged God to spare her life. Fear and frustration, because he couldn't do anything to help her, led to anger. He rode, clutching her to his rock-hard chest, alternately praying to God and cursing her. Please, dear God, don't let her die, he prayed silently. And then, with the next breath, in an anguished voice he muttered, "Damn it, don't you die on me, lady. Do you hear me? Don't you dare die!"

When they finally reached the Juarista camp, Chad lost no time in lifting Christine off his horse and carrying her into the small cabin. As they entered the door, María gasped at the sight of her injured friend and then quickly took command of the situation.

"Back here, *señor*," she cried, leading Chad to a small bedroom at the back of the cabin.

Chad gently laid Christine on the narrow bed as María quickly shredded a sheet for bandages and ordered El Puma to build a fire and bring tequila.

"Is the bullet still in?" María asked.

"Yes," Chad replied in an odd, choked voice, his face almost as pale as Christine's.

El Puma returned with the tequila and Miguel. The young Mexican's dark eyes flicked to Christine, and then he nodded gravely to Chad. Turning and leaving the room, he said, "I will start the fire."

"We have to get that bullet out," María said calmly as she removed the bloody shirt that had served as a bandage. "Give me that tequila, Ramón," she said in a commanding voice.

El Puma frowned, but handed her the bottle.

"Hold her tight, *Señor* Yancy. This will burn," she said as she poured the fiery liquor into the bullet hole.

Christine moaned and twitched. Chad's face turned ashen.

El Puma moved forward, a knife in his hands, saying, "Move aside, María. I will remove the bullet."

María's head snapped up. "No, I will do it. And not with that knife. That will only push the bullet in farther and cause more injury. I will use my fingers. They are small and nimble."

El Puma looked shocked and then said in an authoritative voice, "This is no place for you, María. You will please leave the room. We will do this."

María's eyes glittered with anger. "No, Ramón, I will not leave. *I* will do this."

El Puma's face turned a shade paler than either Chad's or Christine's. He stiffened; the muscles in his jaw jerked. He said in a tight voice, "This is no place for a delicate, young lady like you, María."

"Madre de Dios!" María spat. She glared at El Puma, saying, "Why don't you grow up and stop treating me like a child? Do you think this is the first time I have bloodied my hands? No! I have helped deliver babies, which is much bloodier than this. And this will not be the first time I have dug out a bullet with my fingers either. Many times, the women in the camp have called me to help with bullet wounds because my fingers are so small. Only, you never knew it. Because of your silly ideas about ladies and propriety, I had to sneak behind your back to do it!"

El Puma stood, stunned by María's revelation.

She ignored his reaction and liberally poured tequila over her hands.

Bending over Christine, she said to Chad, "Hold her very tightly, *señor*. The more she moves, the more it will hurt."

Chad nodded and held Christine's body in a fierce grip. María's tiny fingers probed at the edges of the bloody wound gently, and then one small finger began to search for the lead ball. Chad's brow broke out in perspiration as Christine moaned and twisted.

"Lay still, Chris," Chad mumbled in her ear. "We'll have it out soon."

María's pretty face contorted with intense concentration. Then she smiled as she found the lead ball embedded in the soft, fleshy part of Christine's shoulder. She deftly nudged it forward until she pulled it from the wound. Smiling at her success, she held the ball up and showed it to the three men.

Chad and El Puma sighed deeply, relieved. Miguel smiled proudly at María and grunted in approval. Then he turned and walked from the room.

Chad watched, grim-faced, as María washed the wound out again with tequila. This time, Christine didn't even move when the liquor touched the raw wound, having slipped into an even deeper level of unconsciousness. From the corner of his eye, Chad saw Miguel approaching with a red-hot poker in his hand. His heart leaped in his chest as he realized the young Mexican's intention.

Chad jumped to his feet, his face pale. "No, not that!" he rasped.

"*Señor*," María said patiently, "it is necessary. The bullet must have torn a big blood vessel. She is still bleeding."

Chad looked at the glowing poker. The thought of that burning Christine's flesh was more than he could bear. "No!" he yelled, his look fierce.

El Puma moved forward and said firmly, "María is right. She will die if we do not sear the wound. She has lost too much blood already."

Chad realized what they said was true. Searing the wound was the only way to stop the bleeding. Feeling sick, his knees weak, he finally nodded with mute resignation.

"If you like, I will hold her," El Puma said compassionately.

"No! I'll hold her!" Chad retorted.

He sat on the narrow bed and pulled Christine back into his arms, pinning her arms down firmly at her sides, bracing himself.

María took the poker from Miguel and said calmly, "Someone hold her legs." El Puma bent and laid his weight against Christine's legs.

María looked up into Chad's anguished eyes, saying softly, "I will try to be as gentle and quick as I possibly can."

Chad swallowed hard and nodded. María plunged the red-hot poker into the gaping wound, and Christine's body lurched in shock. Her eyes flew open as she screamed in pain, and then her body went totally limp.

The big Texan holding her clenched his teeth

and squeezed his eyes shut, wishing feverently that there was some way he could take the pain for her. The seconds seemed like an eternity of hell to Chad. He could hear the sizzling noise and smell the nauseating odor of burning flesh.

And then he heard María saying, "It is all over, *señor*."

Chad opened his eyes and looked down at Christine. The wound was puckered and blackened, but no longer bleeding. He glanced up at her deathly pale face and for a terrible second thought she had died.

María saw his horrified look and said in a soothing voice, "No, *señor*, she is not dead. She has just fainted."

The Mexican girl looked down at Chad. His face was pale, and he was trembling from the ordeal. "Now you men must go so I can clean her up and make her more comfortable."

Chad looked up at her, his jaw set stubbornly. "No, I'll stay."

María drew herself up to her full five feet and said sternly, "No, you will not stay. Not now. Your clothes are filthy and soaked with blood. You will change clothes and eat something. Then you can return."

Chad glared at her.

María smiled and said softly, "I know how you feel, *señor*, but I will need your help much more when the fever starts. Now go and freshen up, eat something, and drink some coffee."

Reluctantly, Chad gently laid Christine down. He rose and walked wearily to the door with El

Puma and Miguel beside him. He turned at the doorway. Tears glittered in his eyes as he said, "*Gracias, María, gracias.*"

María smiled and nodded in return. Then she turned back to her patient.

Chad was back within the hour. When he returned, he found María had stripped Christine's bloody clothing from her, bathed her, and wrapped her shoulder in a neat bandage. Christine lay on the bed, deathly pale, her face almost as white as the sheet that covered her.

An hour later, the chills began, first a bare shivering and then deep tremors that rocked her entire body. Chad piled blankets on her as María slipped warm rocks under the blankets to provide extra heat. But still Christine shivered, her teeth chattered. Chad rose, a determined look in his eyes, and started to strip off his clothes.

María looked at him wide-eyed. "*Señor!*" she cried in a surprised voice. "What are you doing?"

"I'm going to climb in that bed with her, María. Give her the heat from my body."

María was much too practical and wise to object. "*Sí, señor.*" She turned her back modestly, saying, "Hurry, *señor.*"

Chad slipped his naked body beneath the blankets beside Christine. He pulled her cold, shivering body full length next to his, his hands massaging warmth into her back and hips. María continued to slip warm rocks under the covers as Chad cradled Christine and gave his body's heat to her. Slowly, the tremors subsided, became mere shivers, until she finally lay quietly in

403

Chad's arms.

"It is time for you to get out now, *señor*," María said. "The fever will begin soon. I will go and get cool water and clean sheets while you are dressing." She turned and hurried from the room.

Chad looked down at Christine. An unnatural flush was already spreading up her neck and face. Quickly he climbed from the bed and dressed. He bent and removed the blankets, knowing that the worst was yet to come.

For the next several hours, Chad and María worked frantically over Christine's feverish body. They took turns sponging her with cool water in an attempt to keep the dangerously high fever down. Christine twisted, turned, and clawed at her bandage in delirium. Chad held her hands down and talked constantly in a soft voice, trying to sooth and calm her. She mumbled as she thrashed, mostly a jumble of incoherent words. But once she called out clearly, "Charles!" To Chad, the anguished call was like a knife being twisted in his heart. Finally, Christine settled into a peaceful sleep, a thin sheen of perspiration glistening on her forehead.

María smiled across the bed at Chad, saying, "It's over, *señor*. She sweats. The fever has broken. She will be fine now."

Chad nodded. Having seen many gunshot wounds himself, he knew the battle was won. Christine's sleep was a healing one. She would live. For the first time since the shooting occurred, the terrifying fear he had been living with left him. Its exit left him feeling totally exhausted.

María looked at him compassionately. She had been worried about her friend, but she knew she had not been under the tremendous emotional pressure Chad had experienced. She wondered who had suffered the most, Christine or the big tejano?

"Go and get some sleep, *señor*," she said gently. "I will stay with her."

Chad started to object, but María stopped him, saying, "I slept last night before the escape. But you have been up all night and today too. I will take a nap when you return."

Chad smiled gratefully at the Mexican girl. He had marveled at her cool, efficient manner and her gentle, deft ministrations to Christine. It seemed impossible that anyone that small and childlike could be so determined and self-assured.

"Chris has found herself a very good friend," Chad said softly.

María's black eyes twinkled. "So have I, *señor*."

Chad turned and stumbled wearily from the room. No one was in the big room that served as a kitchen and living room when he entered it. Seeing a blanket in one corner, Chad walked over to it and collapsed in exhaustion. He was asleep almost as soon as his head hit the blanket.

When Chad awakened, it was evening. He rolled onto his side and saw a lamp burning on the table. Drowsily, his eyes scanned the room until he spied El Puma standing by the fireplace.

The Mexican smiled and poured coffee from a big pot into a tin cup. "I see you are awake, *amigo.*"

Chad rose from the blanket, saying, "I didn't mean to sleep so long. María must be exhausted."

El Puma handed him the cup of coffee. "You have time to eat first. I looked in a few minutes ago, and your woman was sleeping soundly. María says she is much better."

Chad sat and ate heartily of the beans and tortillas. El Puma joined him at the table, sipping on a cup of coffee.

"I received some interesting information a little while ago," El Puma said. "The French are withdrawing from Fort Andreas."

"That shouldn't surprise you," Chad replied. "You said a fort with only three walls wasn't much use to the French."

"*Sí,* but my informant also told me that three other northern forts have been abandoned this past week."

Chad's eyebrows rose. "You think the French are pulling back?"

"It's possible, *amigo.* But that happened once before, last fall. We thought they were withdrawing. They abandoned Chihuahua, and Juárez returned to the city for a big celebration. But then suddenly, the French turned around and advanced again. Juárez was almost caught."

"But that was before Seward gave Napoleon his ultimatum," Chad pointed out.

El Puma nodded, his look thoughtful. "I hope

406

this time they are leaving for good."

Chad rose from the table, saying, "Well, even if they aren't, you know the French will never use Fort Andreas again. What were our losses, anyway?"

"Only two wounded, your woman and one of the men that rode back with us. I had no idea we'd be able to pull the rescue off at all, much less with such success."

Chad frowned. He had been concerned about Christine and hadn't even been aware that one of the men had been shot. "Was he wounded seriously?"

"No, just winged." El Puma smiled. "Even the prisoner that was seriously injured is much better today."

"I'm glad," Chad said, walking to the door of the room where Christine lay.

He turned the knob and stepped into the room. María, sitting next to the bed, smiled up at him. She was glad he was back. Christine had been restless during the past hour and had called for him in her sleep several times.

"How is she?" Chad asked anxiously.

"Much better, *señor*."

Chad looked down at Christine. Some color had returned to her face, and the dressing on her shoulder was dry. Her breathing was deep and even as she slept peacefully.

Assured that all was well, Chad said, "*Gracias, María*. I will stay with her tonight."

"*Sí, señor*," María said, rising from the chair. "I have managed to spoon a little water down her,

407

and I would like to give her some more jimson weed before I leave. I know the wound must be very painful, and she is beginning to get restless again."

Chad nodded, being familiar with jimson weed and its narcotic effect. They had used it back in Texas too. He lifted Christine gently and held her as María slowly spooned the bitter brew to her, her swallows mere reflex actions.

After María had left, Chad sat on the chair beside the bed and picked up Christine's hand. He pressed it to his lips and kissed it, whispering, "Lady, don't you ever scare the hell out of me like that again."

Chad admitted to himself that he'd never been as terrified as he had been last night and earlier that morning. Oh, he had known fear before. Having grown up on the wild Texas frontier and having fought three years of war, he would have been an out-and-out liar to claim he had never been afraid. But Chad had always been able to control that fear. He was known and respected for his coolness under fire. Yet the fear he had felt for Christine had left him feeling completely defenseless. The realization that he had almost lost her still made him feel weak. He smiled wryly, thinking, You've brought me to my knees, lady.

He remembered her calling out for her brother. The memory still caused him pain. It had hurt him deeply that she had turned to another in her pain and anguish and not to him. At that minute, he had known that he had lost his battle for her. Oh, he knew she cared for him, maybe loved him a little. But his love for Christine was too intense, too overpowering, too passionate to accept anything less than an equal, total love from her. For him, it was all or nothing. And Christine wasn't prepared to offer him her all.

Now what? Chad asked himself morosely. Well, first he'd rescue her brother and bring him back to her. And then what? Go back to Texas and get his ranch back? But somehow, the ranch didn't seem so important anymore. He knew, without Christine, his life would always be empty and barren.

When María returned the next morning, she found a haggard man sitting next to Christine's bed. Chad looked as if he had aged ten years overnight.

Alarmed, María cried out, "Is she worse?"

Chad smiled, a smile that never reached his eyes. "No, María. In fact, I think she's much stronger. Do you mind staying with her while I talk to Ramón?"

"No, of course not," María answered, wondering what was bothering the big *tejano*.

El Puma was sitting at the table when Chad entered the big room. He motioned to a place across from him, saying, "Have some breakfast, *amigo*."

Chad sat down and filled his plate with eggs and tortillas. El Puma poured a cup of coffee and handed it to him.

"How is the *señora* this morning?" El Puma asked.

"She hasn't regained full consciousness yet, but

her color is much better," Chad replied.

Chad had to hide an amused smile. El Puma still persisted in calling Christine his wife. He wondered what the stiff-necked Creole would have thought if he had walked into the room yesterday and found him naked in bed with Christine, with María still in the room? He probably would have had a stroke, or worse yet, had me bullwhipped, Chad thought wryly.

"Ah, *señor*," El Puma said, "the *señora* is a very brave woman. She must love you very much to risk her life for you and deliberately take the bullet that was meant for you."

Chad frowned at El Puma's words, "love you very much." Had Christine deliberately thrown herself in front of him to save his life out of love for him, or had it been a spontaneous reflex action? He remembered her calling for her brother and decided it was the latter.

"*Sí amigo*, she is some woman, your woman. She saved your life. The bullet that hit her in the shoulder would have penetrated your heart. You must be very proud of her."

"Yes, I'm proud of her," Chad remarked honestly. Then he thought, but she's not my woman. The pain of his loss welled up in him again.

Chad sat silently eating while Ramón watched him curiously. The big Texan looked unusually preoccupied and despondent.

When Chad had finished eating, he looked across the table at Ramón and said, "I'm going after her brother."

El Puma nodded, saying, "I thought you would, *señor*."

"Who's holding him?"

"A bandit *jefe* named Juan Gonzales. He is one mean *hombre, amigo*."

"How many men do you figure he has?" Chad asked, pushing his plate away.

"Eighteen or twenty," El Puma replied.

Chad looked thoughtful, then said, "Where can I find his hideout?"

A small smile played on El Puma's lips. "Why go to his hideout, when you can make him come to you?"

"And how am I supposed to do that?" Chad asked sarcastically.

El Puma shrugged his shoulders casually, saying, "With the ransom money of course."

Chad was in no mood for playing games. "Goddammit, Ramón, you promised me you'd tell me where the hideout was. You know I haven't got that ransom money. I don't have twenty-five thousand dollars."

El Puma grinned and said lazily, "No, *amigo* . . . but I do."

Chad looked stunned, and then he became angry. "Are you telling me that you've had twenty-five thousand dollars all this time? You let me risk my neck to steal those guns for you, while all the time you had enough money to buy ten wagonloads of guns?"

"Calm down, *amigo*. I did not say I had money to buy guns. I only said I had twenty-five thousand dollars."

Chad glared at him across the table, his look murderous.

El Puma was enjoying himself immensely. His black eyes twinkled mischievously. "Come, *amigo*, I will show you."

Chad followed El Puma out of the cabin, fighting the urge to throttle him. They walked around the cabin to the back where an old, dilapidated shed stood. Chad looked at the small building, leaning precariously to one side, with disbelief. Why, one good puff of wind would totally collapse it, he thought with disgust.

"This is where you keep your money?" Chad asked with disbelief.

El Puma laughed, saying, "None of my people would steal this money, *señor*.'

El Puma bent and pulled a small metal trunk from the shed. Chad looked down at it curiously. The trunk was blackened with soot, and Chad assumed it must have survived one of the fires at the old Juarista camp a few days ago. El Puma took a rag and wiped off the soot to reveal ornate etchings over the top and on the sides of the trunk. In the sun the metal gleamed with bluish-silver highlights.

"It's made from a finely tempered metal of some sort and double lined," El Puma said. "For its size, it's amazingly light."

El Puma unlocked the trunk and flipped open the lid. Chad stared down at five piles of neatly stacked paper money. Then the Texan's brow furrowed as he bent for a closer look.

Chad rose, laughing harshly. "I hate to tell you

this, Ramón, but that's Confederate money. It's totally worthless. Hell, it's not worth the paper it's printed on!"

El Puma looked totally undaunted at Chad's announcement. "I know that, *señor*. And you know it. But the question is, will Gonzales know it's worthless?"

Chad cocked his head to one side in a silent question.

El Puma smiled smugly. "*Amigo*, Gonzales is a common *bandido*, totally illiterate. He cannot read Spanish, much less English. Now, he will know this is not Mexican money. We Mexicans do not print paper money. And he will know it is not French money. The French in Mexico use only gold coin. So he will know it is American money. And I am willing to bet that he does not know much about your Civil War, much less that the South printed its own money." The Mexican's eyes twinkled. "No, *amigo*. I do not think Gonzales will know the money is worthless."

Chad stroked his chin thoughtfully. "Do you really think I can pull it off?"

"Why not? Did you not fool the gunrunners and the French?" El Puma grinned, saying, "You must be a good poker player, *amigo*."

"I don't know," Chad said doubtfully. "It might be time for my luck to run out."

"*Sí*," El Puma replied, his mood suddenly very serious. "But I think your chances are much better with the money than trying to sneak the man out of the *bandidos*' camp. That would be suicide."

"I'm afraid you're right there," Chad answered.

"When is the ransom to take place?"

"The day after tomorrow, at a cantina outside of Sarita."

"Ah, then I think we had better leave this morning. Sarita is a two-day ride from here," El Puma said.

"We?" Chad asked suspiciously.

El Puma laughed, saying, "I seem to remember we had this conversation before. Except, I was the one who asked that question. Yes, *señor*, Miguel and I plan on going with you."

"Why? Because you feel you owe me something for helping you rescue your people?"

"That's part of it," El Puma admitted. "I will always be indebted to you for your help in that rescue. But it is much more than that, *amigo*. I would not be able to live with myself if I stood by and watched an innocent man be murdered." He grinned sheepishly, saying, "It seems I still have some principles left after all."

"And Miguel? Does he know what he'll be getting into, or did you order him to come along?"

"No, I did not order him," El Puma replied. "In fact, I would prefer he stay here and take command in my absence. But he insists upon going along." El Puma grinned. "Miguel is quite impressed with you, *señor*. I think I might be just a little jealous."

Chad laughed, feeling as though a tremendous load had been removed from his shoulders. "Well, I won't deny I'm glad to have both of you. Frankly, I don't trust those bandidos not to take the money and then kill me. But they said only

414

one man should bring the ransom."

"Ah, *señor*, they were afraid you would bring other *yanquis*. But they would never suspect two Mexicans of helping you. We will be there just in case something goes wrong. Like you, I do not trust Gonzales and his cutthroats."

El Puma closed the lid on the trunk and picked it up. "Now, I think if we are going to leave this morning, we had better get packed and go."

As the two men walked back to the front of the cabin, Chad said, "I'd like to check in on Chris one more time before we leave. You know, she's going to be awfully mad when she wakes up and finds out I've left without her. All this time, she has insisted upon going with me. I'm afraid she's going to give María a hard time."

"Don't worry, *amigo*, María can handle her," El Puma assured Chad. The handsome Mexican smiled and said ruefully, "Look at how well she handled me."

Chad allowed himself a chuckle.

El Puma frowned, thinking how much his sister had changed. It seemed she had gone from a pretty child to a self-assured, confident woman overnight. He was still a little angry to know she had disobeyed him. After all, Creole women were expected to obey their men, and that obedience included brothers as well as fathers and husbands. Yet, he found himself secretly admiring her spirit and determination.

When Chad and El Puma stepped into the small room where Christine lay, María looked up in surprise. "Ah, *Señor* Yancy," she said, "I was not expecting you back so soon. She was awake a little while ago and asking for you. But I did not see you in the other room and thought you had gone to bed. She was in pain, so I gave her some more jimson weed. Now, she is asleep again."

"It's probably just as well, María," Chad answered. "I'm leaving this morning to go after her brother. She won't like being left behind. Her being asleep just saves me the trouble of arguing with her."

"Miguel and I are going with *Señor* Yancy," El Puma told his sister. "We should be back within the week. Garcia will be in charge while I'm gone, but I don't think there should be any trouble. The French are pulling out."

María nodded, not surprised at the announcement. She had heard Miguel and her brother talking about joining the tejano on his rescue attempt the night before when she was preparing to go to bed.

"Is there any message you wish me to give Christine, *señor*?" María asked softly.

Chad glanced down at Christine. For one brief minute, his love and pain were blatantly exposed, and then he quickly hid his emotions from María and El Puma. "No, just tell her I've gone after her brother," he said coldly as he turned and walked from the room.

María and El Puma exchanged puzzled frowns.

Chapter Nineteen

The hot Mexican sun beat down unmercifully on the three men riding through the tortuous mountain arroyo. The riders appeared oblivious to the excruciating heat as they rode their horses with the casual ease of men born and bred to horseback riding. Their bodies swayed gracefully with the movement of their mounts as they rode in companionable silence, the only sounds the slight moaning of the wind and the clattering of the horses' hooves on the rocky ground below them.

Riding with El Puma and Miguel reminded Chad of his days with the Texas Rangers. In many ways the Juaristas were like the rangers, experienced, self-assured, minds intent on their mission—hard and dangerous men. Just the kind of men Chad needed to back him up when he confronted the sly Mexican bandidos. He would have been taking a big risk to attempt this ransom without them. And without El Puma's Confederate money, the ransom would have been impossible. Chad glanced back over his shoulder at the metal trunk tied to the back of his horse and grinned.

He urged his mount forward and trotted up to El Puma. The Mexican *jefe* looked across the gap between their horses and smiled, his teeth flashing white against his deeply tanned face.

"Tell me, Ramón," Chad said. "I've been curious all day. Where did you get that confederate money?"

"Ah, *amigo*," El Puma answered, "that is an interesting story. Miguel and I found it in a deserted Apache rancheria two years ago. It seemed the Apaches had suffered a disaster of some sort. We found several freshly dug graves nearby. And typical of the Apache and their fear of ghosts, they had abandoned their rancheria and moved elsewhere. We found that trunk tucked into one of their wickiups."

"Apaches? I didn't think there were any Apaches in this part of Mexico," Chad said.

"*Sí amigo*, you are right," El Puma answered. "But I have not always been in this area. I have been all over northern Mexico, depending on where the fighting was taking place. At the time we found the money, I was headquartered in the mountains outside of Monterrey."

"But how did the Apaches get the money?" Chad asked in a puzzled voice.

"We had to piece that part of the story together," El Puma replied. "As you know, toward the end of the Civil War in your country,

418

the South was desperate for guns and ammunition. The Union naval blockade prevented them from getting guns from Europe, so they turned south to their French friends in Mexico. More than one Confederate patrol was sent down here to buy guns from the French. Apparently, the patrol that was carrying this money"—he pointed to the trunk—"ran into an Apache war party." The Mexican shrugged, leaving Chad to form his own conclusion.

"And they were wiped out by the Apaches," Chad said thoughtfully. "But why would the Apaches keep the money? They have no use for money."

El Puma grinned, saying, "I think they probably kept it for the same reason I did, not for the money, but for the unusual trunk itself."

Chad nodded, saying, "Look, Ramón, if you want to keep the trunk, I can transfer the money to my saddlebags."

"No, *señor*, I am hoping that Gonzales might feel the same strange attraction to the trunk as the Apaches and I felt. It just might serve as an added enticement to accept the unfamiliar paper money."

Well, the trunk had certainly been circulated, Chad thought ruefully, from the Confederate patrol to the Apaches, then to the Juaristas, and now to the Mexican bandidos. And so far, no one had attempted to use the money inside. He wondered what the bandidos would do when they discovered the money was useless paper. He pitied the unfortunate man who broke the news to them.

The next day, Chad and his two Mexican friends gazed down on the small mountain valley below them where the Los Gallos Cantina sat. The cantina, its adobe walls crumbling in places from neglect, was the largest of several adobe buildings that lay scattered over the small valley. Even with his keen eyesight, Chad could barely see the sign swinging lazily in the breeze over the cantina door, a crude picture of a fighting cock.

Chad scanned the surrounding mountains. Somewhere among those majestic peaks, Juan Gonzales was holding Christine's brother, and if things didn't go smoothly today, Charles would be murdered and buried in a shallow grave in those Mexican mountains. Chad glanced at El Puma and Miguel, again grateful for their presence.

El Puma leaned forward in his saddle and studied the valley intently for several minutes. Then he sat back, the leather of his saddle squeaking in protest, saying, "Ah, *amigo*, this is perfect. If Gonzales agrees to accept the money, you can demand he bring the prisoner into the open for the exchange. Miguel and I can cover you from here with our new carbines." He patted his Spencer lovingly. "We would easily be in range in case something went wrong."

Chad nodded in agreement.

El Puma said, "We will go down first, *señor*. No

sense in letting the bandidos know you have brought help until absolutely necessary. You wait a couple of hours before you come down, and then no one will connect us with you."

Chad turned sideways in the saddle and shook both El Puma's and Miguel's hands, saying, "Here's hoping my luck still holds."

"*Sí, señor*," Ramón replied gravely. Then his black eyes sparkled. "But if it doesn't, the bandidos are going to find themselves in one hell of a fight."

Chad watched as El Puma and Miguel rode lazily down the mountainside and into the valley. Only when the door of the cantina closed behind them, did he dismount and pull his horse back into a concealing clump of brush. Then he sat and waited.

When Chad rode down into the valley it was almost evening. Deep shadows from the surrounding mountains lay across most of the valley floor. He dismounted casually in front of the cantina, acutely aware of eyes watching him. With seeming indifference, he untied the trunk from the back of his saddle. Then he slung his saddlebags over one shoulder and slipped his carbine from its saddle scabbard. Leisurely, he ambled into the cantina.

For a second, Chad stood just inside the cantina door, waiting for his eyes to adjust to the dimly lit room. He glanced about and saw El Puma and Miguel sitting at one of the tables in the corner. Miguel's body was slumped over the table, giving the appearance of a man passed out

421

from drunkenness. El Puma sat in a chair across from him. As Chad stepped farther into the room, El Puma looked up at him curiously and then away with seeming indifference.

They're not bad actors themselves, Chad thought with admiration as he walked to an empty table at the back of the room. He set the trunk pointedly on the table top, his carbine next to it, and then sat down facing the doorway.

Only two other tables in the cantina were occupied besides the one at which El Puma and Miguel sat. At one, three Mexican peons sat staring at the *yanqui* curiously and then, seeing the dangerous glint in his eyes, averted their own and squirmed nervously in their seats. The other table was occupied by a heavily armed Mexican, who slouched insolently in his chair and, for all practical purposes, seemed to ignore Chad. Instinctively, Chad knew he was the man Gonzales had sent to watch for his arrival.

The bartender approached Chad nervously to ask what he wanted to drink. Chad waved the man away, saying in Spanish, "Later, *amigo*. I didn't come here to drink. I've got business to attend to first."

The Mexican looked at him suspiciously and then scurried behind the protection of the bar. Many years of living in the mountains surrounded by fierce bandidos had sharpened the Mexican's instincts. He knew when trouble was brewing.

Chad looked up and noticed the lone Mexican had disappeared. He wasn't surprised. He had expected that. He sat waiting, his eyes glued on the door.

About ten minutes later, the cantina door opened, and a big, beefy Mexican with a fierce black mustachio strutted across the room with three other Mexicans. Chad's nose wrinkled as the strong, sickening odor of the man proceeded him. He must not have bathed for years, Chad thought with disgust, looking at the filthy clothing the bandit *jefe* wore.

Juan Gonzales stood before Chad, his ugly face grinning obscenely, his thick, short legs spread apart arrogantly. His big hairy hands rested on the guns strapped to both hips.

Chad looked at the double gunbelts and almost laughed. He had always thought it ridiculous for a man to wear guns at both sides, unless the man was ambidextrous, and few men were. No, he knew that men who carried two guns used them as a form of subtle intimidation to hide their own insecurity. All of the really good gunslingers Chad had ever seen wore only one gun.

Chad looked at the bandit's paunchy stomach with obvious disgust and then up at his face. "You got business with me?" Chad asked in Spanish, his voice hard.

Gonzales was taken aback by the *tejano's* cool attitude. Most people were terrified of him, like those Mexican peons who had scurried out of the room in fear when he walked in. Even his own men were afraid of him. Did they not call him El Toro, the bull? And yet, this arrogant *yanqui* looked at him as if he could easily squash him, as if he were a mere cockroach. For a minute, the big *bandido* hesitated, unnerved by the *tejano's* cold stare.

Then Gonzales remembered the three bandidos who had accompanied him. It wouldn't do for them to think he was afraid. Besides, this man was outnumbered four to one. His bravo returned.

Gonzales smiled slyly, saying, "*Sí, señor*, we have business. Providing of course, you brought the ransom."

"It's right here," Chad replied, motioning to the trunk on the table.

Gonzales's eyes glittered with greed as he reached for the trunk. Chad calmly pulled it from his reach, saying, "Where's the prisoner?"

The bandido's eyes flared with anger. Then he quickly covered his look and said smoothly, "He is in the mountains. We will bring him to you as soon as you have paid the money."

Chad's steely eyes bored into the bandido. "No deal. I want to see the prisoner first. I'm not paying money for a dead man."

Gonzales made no further attempt to hide his anger. His face suffused with blood and twisted into an angry snarl. "*Bastardo!*" he cried as he and his three companions reached for their guns.

"Freeze!" El Puma's command echoed across the small room.

The bandidos looked about them in stunned disbelief. El Puma and Miguel stood, their looks fierce, their guns aimed at the four men.

Gonzales' face had totally blanched of all color. He looked at Chad indignantly. "You have tricked us," he said in an accusing voice.

Chad laughed at the bandido's ridiculous accusation. Here just minutes before, the man was prepared to kill him in cold blood. "The pot calling the kettle black," Chad remarked lazily.

El Puma and Miguel chuckled; Gonzales flushed angrily.

Gonzales turned and said to Chad, "You are making a mistake to kill us, *señor*. I have over thirty men in the mountains surrounding this valley. You will never get out of here alive."

Chad shrugged, saying, "I don't doubt that, Gonzales."

The bandit *jefe* looked shocked at the mention of his name.

"Oh, I know who you are, Juan Gonzales," Chad said calmly. He pointed to Ramón, saying, "El Puma told me all about you and your cutthroats."

"El Puma!" The bandit *jefe* and his men turned to look at Ramón in disbelief.

"My pleasure, *señors*," El Puma said sarcastically, making a slight mocking bow.

For a minute, Gonzales looked as if he might faint. His men shuffled their feet nervously.

Chad allowed them a few minutes to stew, and then he said, "We didn't come here to kill you, Gonzales. We came to ransom a man. But like I said, I'm not paying money for a dead man."

Gonzales looked at the three dangerous-looking men, two Mexicans and one *tejano*. Nervous perspiration glittered on his brow. "The prisoner is alive, *señors*."

"Fine. Then we can do business," Chad said. "But on our terms."

Gonzales expression became hopeful. "But how do we know you have the money?" he asked in a whiny voice.

Chad flipped open the lid on the trunk. The bandidos shuffled forward and looked down at the money.

"Paper money?" Gonzales asked in disbelief.

"You didn't say anything about how to pay the twenty-five thousand dollars," Chad said irritably. "Hell, that much money in gold is hard to carry. Do you have any idea of how much it would weigh? I'd have to bring a pack horse just to carry it."

Gonzales stared down at the currency, still stunned.

"All right!" Chad snapped, slamming the lid on the trunk back down. "If you won't take paper money, then I'll just have to go back to the border and get it exchanged for gold. Damn it, if I see what difference it makes. Money is money!"

He picked up the trunk and headed angrily for the door, saying, "It will take me another two months to get back down here. In the meanwhile, you'd better hold on to that prisoner and make sure nothing happens to him."

Chad was moving too fast for the bandit *jefe*, and Gonzales was reeling with indecision. He knew the *americanos* had paper money. He didn't understand how it worked, but he didn't like the idea of that money getting away from him. Hell, the *tejano* might not make it down here the second time. These mountains were crawling with Indians and other bandidos. He also didn't like the idea of holding the *americano* prisoner for two more months. The man was arrogant and demanding. He reminded him of the hidalgos he hated so much.

"Wait a minute, *señor*," Gonzales called to Chad.

Chad turned at the door, his look impatient. "Now what's wrong?"

"Nothing, *señor*," Gonzales said in a soothing voice. "But how does your paper money work?"

Chad sighed in exasperation and walked back to the table. Placing the trunk on it, he raised the lid and said, "Each of these five stacks holds two hundred fifty bills, or pieces of paper. Each bill is worth twenty American dollars. That's twenty-five thousand dollars in all. If you like, you can take this money to the bank in Mexico City, or to any bank in the United States, and they will give you gold dollars for it."

Gonzales picked up one of the bills and said in awe, "They will give me twenty gold dollars for this piece of paper?"

"That's right," Chad said.

"But why does your country use paper money, *señor*?" one of the other bandits asked in confusion.

"Because it's easier to carry," Chad replied. "Like I said, a lot of money in gold is heavy and awkward."

Gonzales looked at El Puma for confirmation of what Chad was saying. He trusted another

427

Mexican, even if he was a Juarista, more than he did a foreigner.

"It's true, Gonzales," El Puma assured the bandido. "Soon, even Mexico will be printing paper money."

Gonzales grinned. He liked the idea of being one of the first men in Mexico to have paper money. It would add to his prestige. Besides that, he fancied the trunk, and if the *tejano* brought back gold coins, more than likely, he would bring it in sacks. "We will take the money, *señor*," he announced.

Chad, El Puma, and Miguel hid their relief behind inscrutable faces.

"All right," Chad said. "Now for the terms of exchange."

"Terms?" Gonzales asked suspiciously.

"Yes," Chad answered in a firm voice. "When you bring the prisoner down from the mountains, we will give you the money. We'll meet at noon tomorrow, right out in the middle of the valley. You bring the prisoner down yourself, Gonzales, and I will meet you. Bring him mounted. We didn't bring an extra horse for him. You hand over the prisoner, and I'll hand over the money. Then you go your way, and I'll go mine."

"But, *señor*, horses are valuable here in the mountains," Gonzales objected.

"With twenty-five thousand dollars, you can afford to be generous," Chad replied sarcastically.

"Why should I trust you?" Gonzales said sullenly. "You might give me a trunk full of rocks."

Chad grinned and pulled out the key to the trunk. He bent and locked the trunk and then handed the key to Gonzales. "Now only you can open the trunk. You have the only key, but we still have the trunk. Bring us the prisoner, and you get the money."

"*Sí, señor*, but we cannot bring the prisoner tomorrow. It will take us two days to bring him down from the mountains."

So, they didn't bring the prisoner with them, Chad thought. They never had any intention of exchanging Charles for the money. Again, he blessed Miguel and El Puma for coming along.

"All right," Chad said in a hard voice. "Three days from today, at noon."

Gonzales grinned as he slipped the key into his pocket. He and the other bandidos turned and walked toward the door.

"Just a minute, Gonzales," El Puma said in a hard voice.

The bandidos turned and looked at the Juarista leader, the man who was a legend all over northern Mexico. The common bandidos regarded him with mouth-gaping awe. Gonzales glared at him resentfully.

"Just so you don't get any stupid ideas about pulling something funny, I'd like to warn you about the guns we carry," El Puma said. He held up the Spencer carbine proudly, saying, "This is a repeater carbine. It fires nine shots without reloading, and it's loaded with one of these." He held up a tube of cartridges, and then with lightning speed, he slammed the tube through the trap in the butt of the gun.

The Mexican bandidos gasped, their eyes wide with wonder.

El Puma smiled smugly, saying, "You may have us outnumbered, but we think these guns even up the odds." His look turned fierce, his eyes glittered dangerously. "And I warn you, *señors*, we are all excellent marksmen."

Gonzales paled at the threat, his eyes shifting nervously. He swallowed loudly before answering, "We will not try anything, *señors*."

The bandidos turned and left the room in a hurried, undignified exit. Chad, El Puma, and Miguel exchanged knowing grins. The Mexican bartender crawled from behind his protective barrier, smiling sheepishly.

Chad's horse snorted impatiently and moved restlessly beneath him. Chad patted the animal's neck soothingly, his eyes scanning the mountains around him. He had been out here, sitting in the hot noonday sun, for over thirty minutes. The valley was deserted except for him. The few Mexicans who inhabited it had fled to the mountains for safety until the confrontation between the three dangerous- and fierce-looking strangers and the wily bandidos was over.

Chad shifted his weight in the saddle and looked behind him. He had no idea from which direction the bandidos would approach them. But he wasn't worried about being caught from behind. He knew El Puma and Miguel were up in the mountains, their carbines drawn and ready in

430

case the bandidos decided to ignore their warning.

Chad's eyes narrowed as he saw two figures moving down the mountainside. The flash of sunlight on a gun barrel behind them told Chad the bandidos were keeping their own watch on the exchange. As the figures moved closer, he recognized the thick, short body of Gonzales. His eyes moved past him indifferently to lock on the tall, silver-haired man who rode several feet behind the bandido.

So that's Christine's brother, Chad thought, the man she had traveled halfway across Mexico to rescue, risking life and limb. He remembered all of the hardships she had gone through on the trip down and all of the times she had almost been killed. And all because that stupid brother of hers couldn't keep his big mouth shut! Chad's blood came to a slow boil, and he glared angrily at Charles who approached him.

As he and Gonzales rode across the valley floor, Charles Roberts had been staring at Chad, naturally curious about the man his uncle had sent to ransom him. He saw a dark-haired fellow, taller and more broad-shouldered than he, sitting his horse with the ease of a born horseman. Charles looked into a pair of steely blue eyes and shivered. This man is dangerous, he thought, and then laughed at himself. Of course, his uncle would send a hard, dangerous man to rescue him. It would take just that sort of man to deal with these Mexican cutthroats. Charles smiled at the Texan, a dazzling smile that had always worked to his advantage before, a smile that disarmed both men and women alike.

Chad glared at him even harder, and Charles felt that hot, angry look as if it were a slap in the face. Charles sat back, stunned.

"Are you Charles Roberts?" Chad asked in a demanding tone of voice.

Charles's pride fought to the surface. Just who in the hell did this bastard think he was anyway? he thought angrily. He raised his head proudly and thrust out his chin, saying, "Yes, I am."

An involuntary smile teased at Chad's lips. Yes, he thought, this is Christine's brother all right. He has that same defiant, stubborn look about him.

"My name's Yancy. Chad Yancy," the Texan drawled in an almost civil tone of voice.

Charles was totally confused by Chad's abrupt turnabout. Just a minute ago, the arrogant man had looked as if he would gladly murder him, and now he had almost smiled at him. Charles was wary and said cautiously, "Well, Mr. Yancy, I can't deny I'm damned glad to see you. I'd shake hands but . . ." Charles looked down at his hands tied to the saddle.

Suddenly a knife appeared, seemingly from out of nowhere, and the bonds were quickly severed. Charles sat and watched with mute admiration. He had never seen such swift, deft expertise with a knife. He looked up to thank the Texan, but Chad had turned away to face Gonzales, who was sputtering angrily.

"Take it easy, Gonzales," Chad said in Spanish. "I'm not going to try anything. You just hand me

432

those reins, and I'll pass the trunk of money over to you."

Gonzales handed the reins to Chad, his look still sullen. Chad grinned and passed the trunk to him, saying, "Don't spend it all on tequila, *amigo*. If you do, you'll have one hell of a hangover."

The bandido's eyes glittered as he grasped the trunk greedily. Then he grinned, a silly, lopsided grin that made his ugly face even more grotesque. "*Sí, amigo, sí.*"

Charles watched the exchange and frowned. Hell, he thought irritably, it looks like the Texan enjoys giving the money away.

Chad turned and tossed the reins to Charles carelessly. "Come on," he said in a cold voice. Indifferently, he whirled his horse and trotted off in a casual, easy gait.

Charles glared at him and then followed. He looked nervously over his shoulder. He suspected the bandits might take the money and then shoot them in the back. But Gonzales was totally ignoring them, already scrambling off his horse. Charles glanced up and caught his breath. The other bandits were riding at breakneck speed down the mountainside.

Charles called to Chad, "The other bandits are coming. I think we'd better make a run for it."

Chad ignored his warning, his manner totally unconcerned, his horse still trotting at the same lazy speed.

Charles rode up to him and glared across at him. Chad acted as if he didn't even know he existed. Charles considered spurring his horse

433

and leaving the man behind, but he knew he'd get lost in these mountains. Besides, he didn't even have a gun. He was forced to ride beside the silent, stubborn Texan, thinking, My God! Does he have nerves made of steel? His own nerves were taut as he fought the urge to look back to see if the bandits were following. At any minute, he expected a bullet in his back.

They left the valley floor and climbed up the mountainside, following a narrow, twisted trail. Halfway up the trail, Charles looked up and gasped, seeing two fierce-looking Mexicans mounted before them, their carbines drawn. Then miraculously, the Mexicans grinned and slipped their carbines back into their saddle scabbards.

"Congratulations, *amigo*," El Puma said to Chad.

Chad grinned back, saying, "*Gracias, amigo*." He turned half around in his saddle, saying, "Ramón, this is Charles Roberts."

El Puma leaned forward in his saddle, his hand extended, saying, "My pleasure, *Señor* Roberts. Ramón de Vega at your service."

Miguel rode up and introduced himself, both he and Charles shaking hands warmly. Well, Charles thought, these two Mexicans were a hell of a lot friendlier than his own countryman.

"I assume you're with Mr. Yancy, here, *señors*," Charles remarked. Then he laughed a little nervously, adding, "Since I still have my head."

Chad had ridden off while the introductions were taking place. He sat on his horse along a ledge overlooking the valley below. "Come and look at this, *amigos*," he called.

The three men nudged their horses forward and looked down into the valley. Juan Gonzales was kneeling in front of the open trunk and pulling the money out of it by the handfuls, throwing it over his head and into the air, laughing gleefully. The bills fluttered in the air and skittered across the ground as the other bandidos, laughing hysterically, ran after them.

Chad, El Puma, and Miguel threw their dark heads back and roared. Charles glared down at the bandidos below him. He didn't see anything amusing about it. Hell, that was his money those damned Mexicans were throwing away. And knowing his uncle, he'd charge him an outrageous interest on it too. The least the stupid bandits could do was show a little respect for it.

"I don't see anything so funny," Charles snapped irritably.

El Puma turned, his black eyes still twinkling with mirth. "But you see, *señor*, the bandidos are happy because they think they are rich. Wait until they find out that money is worthless. That's what we are laughing at."

"Worthless?" Charles asked, hardly believing his ears.

"*Sí, señor*," El Puma said, smiling smugly. "That is Confederate money."

"Confederate money!" Charles exclaimed. "My uncle ransomed me with Confederate money?" he asked incredulously.

"Your uncle didn't pay any ransom at all,"

Chad informed Charles in a hard voice. "It seems your father's will stipulated that if anything happened to you before you came of age, your money would revert back to your uncle. Your uncle was hoping the bandits would kill you."

Charles was shocked. He knew his uncle had no love for him, but he never dreamed he'd go that far. "But if my uncle didn't send the ransom, then who in the hell are you?"

"I'm a *pistolero*," Chad replied. "Your sister hired me to rescue you when she couldn't raise the ransom money."

"Where in the hell did Chris ever find a *pistolero*?" Charles asked.

"In El Paso," Chad drawled lazily.

"Chris is in Texas?" Charles asked with surprise.

"No, she's here in Mexico at El Puma's camp," Chad answered calmly.

"Chris is here in Mexico? And did you say El Puma? Are you talking about the famous Juarista leader, El Puma?"

Chad was thoroughly enjoying Charles's confusion and frustration. "Yes, none other than the famous El Puma." Chad's eyes twinkled mischievously as he motioned to Ramón. "May I present, El Puma."

Charles' mouth gaped open in shock. "You're El Puma?" he sputtered in awe.

Ramón grinned sheepishly. "I'm afraid so, *señor*."

Charles sat back, stunned by what he had learned. His uncle had refused to pay the ransom.

Chris had hired this Texas gunman to rescue him. She was here in Mexico at El Puma's camp. Then he thought of a million questions. What in the hell was Chris doing in Mexico? How did she get into El Puma's camp? How did the Juaristas get involved in his rescue? And where in the hell did they get that damned Confederate money?

Chad knew what was going through Charles' mind. Let him stew, he thought smugly. "Come on, let's get the hell out of here before those bandidos change their minds."

He whirled his horse and galloped up the steep side of the mountain. El Puma and Miguel followed close behind.

Charles, already reeling in confusion, stared at their rapidly retreating backs in disbelief. Then he yelled, "Wait a minute! I've got some questions I want answered!"

"Later!" Chad yelled back.

Charles was forced to spur his horse and gallop after them. It was either that or be left behind. And following the three men at breakneck speed through the tortuous, rocky mountain trails turned out to be no easy task. Charles had always considered himself a fairly good horseman, but compared to the three men riding before him, he was a novice. Long before they finally pitched camp that evening, Charles was aching and exhausted from the harrowing ride. He could almost swear the Texan had set such a hard pace on purpose, to punish him for something. But what?

Despite his exhaustion that night, Charles was

determined to get some answers to some of his questions. After they had finished eating, Charles leaned forward and said to Chad, "Now let me get all this straight. My uncle refused to pay the ransom because he wanted me to be killed. He wanted to claim my inheritance?"

Chad nodded.

"Christine wasn't able to raise the ransom, so she traveled to Texas and hired you to rescue me?"

"That's right," Chad replied.

"Where did she get the money to pay you?"

"She's using the money she inherited from her mother."

"And my uncle knew she was planning on hiring someone to rescue me, and he let her go?" Charles asked, his voice full of disbelief.

"Your uncle thought she was playing into his hand," Chad replied. "He wanted her out of New York, someplace where too many questions wouldn't be asked. He hired an assassin to kill her. You see, your father's will also stipulated that if anything happened to her, your uncle would inherit her money too. Your uncle is a very greedy man."

"That son-of-a-bitch!" Charles swore.

"I agree," Chad remarked.

"What happened to the assassin?" Charles asked.

"The last I saw of him, he was wandering around lost in a canyon outside of El Paso de Norte. He may still be there for all I know."

Charles sighed with relief, saying, "Then he

438

didn't get a chance to try to kill Chris?"

"To the contrary," Chad said in a hard voice. "He tried three times, once on the steamer and twice in El Paso. Fortunately, he didn't succeed."

Charles turned pale at this piece of information. But there was one question that was foremost in his mind. "But what is Chris doing here in Mexico? Why didn't she wait back in Texas? Surely, there must have been some safe place to leave her."

Chad didn't like the accusing tone of Charles's voice. God only knew how hard he had tried to discourage her himself. His anger rose. "If you think it was my idea, you're crazy! She insisted on coming. I even threatened to quit the job, but she said she'd hire some cutthroat that would have murdered her the first night out!"

"She insisted on coming?" Charles asked. "But why?"

"How in the hell should I know why? I never did figure that one out! All she would say is that you were her brother and she had to come."

Suddenly all of Chad's old anger at Charles rose to the surface. He slammed to his feet, saying, "Look, I'm not answering any more of your damned questions. If you want to know why, then ask Chris." He leaned forward menacingly, his eyes glittering dangerously, his fists clenched at his sides, saying, "But I'm warning you, if you ever do anything to endanger her or cause her pain again . . . I'll kill you!"

Chad whirled and walked angrily away. Charles sat, stunned by the Texan's sudden, violent

439

reaction to his questions. Endanger Chris? Charles thought, whirling in confusion. What in the hell was he talking about? And how had he caused her pain? Why, he wouldn't hurt Chris.

Charles kept his distance from the big Texan after that night. It wasn't difficult to do. Chad made a point of ignoring and avoiding him also.

Charles managed to piece part of the story together with the information El Puma and Miguel gave him. The Mexicans explained how Chris and Chad had come to their camp, thinking they were holding him prisoner. Then they told him of all the other events that had happened since. Charles had been deeply disturbed to hear of Christine being wounded, but the Mexicans had assured him she would be fine, that it was only a flesh wound.

The only thing the Mexicans didn't tell Charles about was the relationship between Chad and Christine. Both men had been very careful to drop no hint that Chad was in love with Christine, much less that they had shared intimacies. So while Charles had been amazed to learn of all the events that had transpired while he was a prisoner, he still had no inkling of why the big Texan had taken such a strong dislike to him.

He was still struggling with this puzzle when they rode back into El Puma's camp.

Chapter Twenty

Christine stared out of the window of her small bedroom. But she didn't see the trees swaying gracefully in the breeze, nor hear the soft rustle of their leaves or the birds singing joyously in their boughs. In fact, Christine didn't see or hear anything. Her thoughts were elsewhere.

Where were they? she asked herself. María had said El Puma had told her they would be back within a week. Today, the week was up, and still, they hadn't returned. Had something gone wrong? Had El Puma received the wrong information so they hadn't found Charles after all? Or had they found him, and then been killed in the rescue attempt? Oh God, she couldn't stand this waiting any longer. The suspense of not knowing what was going on or what had happened was tearing her nerves apart. María said she was used to waiting and worrying. But how could she stand it?

Christine had not known much for the first two days after Chad had left. María had kept her well sedated, and at the time, Christine had been grateful for the release from the raw pain in her shoulder. But when María had finally told her that Chad had left to rescue her brother, Christine had been furious. She had ranted and raved until María had taken her firmly in hand and rebuked her.

"Stop acting like a two-year-old, Christine," María had said. "You know you couldn't possibly have gone along with him, injured as you were. And he certainly couldn't wait for you to get better."

Christine had felt foolish, and then greatly relieved when she learned that El Puma and Miguel had gone along with Chad to help with the rescue.

Her recovery from the injury was remarkably fast; Christine knew the special herbs María had used on the wound had been responsible for that. After the first several days, there had been very little pain, only a stiffness in her arm that María quickly attacked with massages and hot packs. The scab had fallen off yesterday, and all that was left was a red, puckered area on her left shoulder. Christine found it hard to believe that she had actually been in danger of dying, of hemorrhaging to death. True, her color was a little paler under her tan, but if she had felt any weakness from her loss of blood, Christine had been too busy worrying about Chad and the others to notice.

Totally lost in her thoughts, Christine never noticed the sound of horses galloping into the camp or the excited greetings of the Juaristas. Not until María shook her and called her name, did she tumble back to the present and become aware of her surroundings.

"What?" Christine asked dumbly.

María's eyes twinkled with happiness. "Silly goose, I said they're back."

"They're back?"

"Yes, they just rode in a few minutes ago," María answered.

Christine whirled and ran from her bedroom. As she ran through the door, Charles tore into the small cabin and caught her, twirling her around, both of them laughing. When he sat her back down, he hugged her and kissed her soundly, saying, "God, I'm glad to see you, Chris."

"You're all right?" Christine asked, her eyes sweeping over him in quick appraisal.

"I'm just fine. Thanks to you, sis," Charles assured her.

Christine glanced about the room and saw María hugging El Puma and Miguel standing behind him, grinning. But where was Chad?

Charles had been studying his sister curiously. "Gosh, Chris, you've changed. I almost didn't recognize you."

"What?" Christine asked, her mind preoccupied.

"I said you're different."

"Oh no, it's just the haircut," Christine answered in a distracted voice. "You see, I had to cut it to come down here. Also, I'm afraid my skin is terribly burned from the sun."

Charles looked at his sister closely. The short

443

haircut and tan were becoming, but it was something much more than that. No the difference was something much deeper, for Charles knew Christine as well as he knew the back of his hand. The difference came from within, a glow, a radiance of soft femininity that changed her face, a face that Charles had always considered pretty rather than beautiful. Charles was awed by this change in her and wondered what had caused the transformation.

While Charles was puzzling over what could have caused this difference in Christine, she was twisting and standing on tiptoe, trying to see around his big shoulders. Where is he? she thought, her nerves taut. Has something happened to him? A terror like none Christine had ever known clutched at her heart. She looked at El Puma and Miguel grinning at her. No, surely if anything had happened to him, they wouldn't be smiling like that. But where was he?

Then she saw him.

Chad leaned lazily against one wall, his arms crossed over his broad chest, an arrogant smile playing on his lips.

Christine felt weak as an immense wave of relief washed over her. She looked back at him, at that insolent smile that always infuriated her and yet made her heart do strange flip-flops. These last days of waiting had seemed an eternity to her, a hell. She had worried, agonized, suffered mental torture; yet he stood there calmly smiling. A strange, irrational anger engulfed her. How dare he smile at her like that!

She pushed away from Charles and flew at Chad. She pounded on his chest with her fists and wildly kicked out at him, screaming, "You lied to me! You promised I could go along!" Her hands clawed at his face. "Damn you! You son-of-a-bitch!"

Charles was surprised at Christine's sudden attack on Chad. Hell, he didn't like the Texan himself, but he had never seen his cool, composed sister so violent. And her language! My God, he had no idea she even knew such words, much less knew how to use them.

Chad had grown more adept at handling Christine's temper tantrums. Calmly he ducked her swinging fists and twisted away from her kicks. He caught her flailing arms and pinned them behind her back, pulling her to him and up off the floor, her legs dangling helplessly.

Christine glared at him, and then her look turned anguished. "You damned fool! Don't you know you could have been killed?"

Her head dropped to his chest weakly, tears streamed down her cheeks, harsh sobs racked her body.

Charles had been surprised at Christine's attack, but he was shocked by her tears. Why, he hadn't seen his sister cry since she was five years old. Chris wasn't the type to display her emotions. She kept them locked deep within her.

Chad had been shocked by Christine's tears also. But the reason for Chad's shock was why she was crying. He knew her anger and tears were a release from the tremendous mental anguish she had suffered. But she had anguished over him! She was crying over *him*! With sudden clarity, Chad realized that he had won his battle for Christine's love after all. His heart soared. He was sitting on top of the world. He wanted to shout with happiness. For a minute, Chad savored the sweetness of his exhilarating victory. And then he dropped Christine's arms at her back and pulled her into a tight embrace, his lips closing over hers in a fierce, possessive kiss.

Charles was totally stunned, his mouth gaping, as he watched the Texan passionately kissing his sister. Even more shocking was Christine's reaction to his kiss. Her hands had slipped around the man's neck. She was kissing him back, arching her body even closer to his, their bodies seeming to blend together. Despite his shock, Charles blushed furiously.

Chad broke the kiss and swept Christine up in his arms. He walked casually to her bedroom door and then turned, carefully standing to one side, his long legs spread arrogantly.

Chad's steely blue eyes locked on Charles's gaze in open challenge. "Any objections?" he drawled.

Charles looked through the open door at the bed and then back at the man holding his sister possessively in his arms. His intention was shockingly clear. Charles's eyes flicked to Christine. She lay snuggled against the big Texan's chest, a dreamy smile on her face. At that minute, Charles couldn't have uttered a word if his life had depended on it.

Chad's dark eyebrows rose. "No objections?"

446

he asked. Then he smiled mockingly, saying, "It's a good thing. Because if you had, I would have told you to go to hell!"

Chad turned and walked into the bedroom, slamming the door behind him and Christine with the heel of his boot.

Charles stared at the closed door for a minute before reacting. He stepped toward the door, but El Puma grabbed his arm firmly.

"No, *señor*," El Puma said softly. "Didn't you say your sister has changed? She has blossomed, *sí*? The big *tejano* is the reason for that change. She is in love. She belongs to him now."

Charles's look was incredulous. "They're married?"

"No, *señor*," El Puma said and then shrugged lazily. "But I think that is only a matter of time."

"That son of—" Charles said angrily, stepping forward.

"No!" El Puma cried, pulling him back.

"That's my sister!"

"*Sí, amigo*, but . . ." El Puma stopped in midsentence. What had he just said about the reason for the change in Charles's sister? She was in love. The reason for María's transformation suddenly came to him with the swiftness of a bolt of lightning, for El Puma was not quite as blind as everyone thought he was. He whirled and shot a hot, penetrating look at Miguel, leaning casually against the doorjamb. The young Mexican was stunned by the older man's heated look. Then just as suddenly, El Puma smiled broadly, only adding to Miguel's confusion.

447

El Puma turned back to Charles, who was struggling against his iron grip. "No, *amigo*," El Puma said firmly. "There comes a time when a brother must yield to the man his sister chooses to love. It is not easy, but it is the natural order of things."

"But . . . but," Charles sputtered.

"*Amigo*, do you love your sister?"

"Why, yes, of course, I love Chris," Charles answered.

El Puma smiled and said, "Then do not stand in the way of her happiness."

Charles looked at the door, torn by indecision.

"Come, *amigo*. Did you not say you had some questions to ask El Puma? Well, I am in the mood for talking."

El Puma firmly guided Charles toward the front door. The tall, blond-headed man looked back over his shoulder at the bedroom door. If there had been any sound from behind that door, even a whimper, he would have torn loose from the Mexican's grip and barged in. But there was no sound.

Chad stood in the middle of the small room, still cradling Christine in his arms and kissing her leisurely, lovingly. He walked to the bed and sat on it, with her in his lap. He looked down at the tears staining her cheeks and tenderly brushed them away, saying, "No more tears for you, lady."

Christine was speechless with happiness. She could only nod as she basked in the warm circle of his arms. Chad was back, and that was all that mattered.

Chad rolled her gently to the bed and lay beside her. Softly, he kissed her eyelids, her nose, her mouth. His lips trailed down the frantic pulse of her throat to her shoulder, and then he froze, seeing the reddened scar the bullet had left. His heart twisted in remembrance of the pain and suffering she had experienced, knowing now that she had deliberately shielded his body with hers because of her love for him.

He softly kissed the still-tender flesh, saying, "Your badge of courage."

Why was it, Christine thought, that he could make her feel so beautiful? He even made her proud of that ugly scar on her shoulder. Her arms crept around his tanned neck, and her fingers tangled in his dark, thick hair. "Oh, Chad," she whimpered.

Gently, almost reverently, Chad undressed her, kissing each inch of skin as he exposed it to his warm gaze. His lips were worshiping and adoring as he kissed her breasts, her taut abdomen, her thighs, even her toes.

Christine felt warm and tingled all over. Suddenly, she couldn't stand his clothing between them one second longer. She wanted to feel his body naked against hers. She tore at his clothing with shaky hands.

Chad chuckled softly at her urgency. "My, but you're greedy today, lady."

"Yes, yes," Christine sobbed, struggling with the awkward belt buckle.

Chad smiled and rose, undressing quickly, and then lay back down beside her. Christine pressed herself into the warmth of his naked body, savoring the feel of his hard muscles against her and his heady masculine scent. Her hands, mouth, and tongue caressed him hungrily, roaming at will over his entire body. She reached for him, encircling the rigid, hot flesh with her hand.

Chad trembled and groaned in pleasure, and then gently removed Christine's hand. He wanted to delay this love-making, savor it to its fullest. "No, lady," he muttered.

"But I want you. I want you now!" Christine cried.

Chad smiled softly down at her, his eyes warm with love. "There's no hurry, lady," he drawled huskily. No, Chad thought, there's no hurry. We have the rest of our lives for loving.

He made slow, leisurely love to her, refusing to be hurried by her frantic clutching and urgent sobs. His hands caressed, teased, and tantalized as his mouth and tongue played at her, searching, arousing, carefully stoking the fires of her passion. He worshiped her proud breasts, his mouth hot and hungry, his tongue flicking erotically over the taut nipples, mumbling thickly, "My little rosebuds."

Christine was writhing beneath his artful ministrations, her body on fire, her breath rasping in her throat. She couldn't stand this delicious torment one second longer. "Take me, Chad. Please, now!" she cried, her voice weak with desire.

450

Chad smiled knowingly and rose over her. Christine felt the promising brush of his hot, throbbing manhood against her thigh and sobbed with relief, lurching frantically toward it.

Chad caught her hips in his big hands, whispering, "Easy, lady, easy."

If Christine thought Chad's hands and mouth had teased and tormented her before, it was nothing compared to the exquisite torture he was subjecting her to now. He held her long legs firmly apart to keep her from wrapping them around him, because Chad knew once she had enclosed him in that sweet vise there would be no holding back. He teased and taunted her, brushing against her sensuously with the hot, moist tip of his sex. He entered slowly, deeply, and Christine felt the electrifying heat of him inside her. She gyrated her hips, desperate to relieve the terrible throbbing ache inside of her. But Chad stilled her with his hands and stroked her with long, lazy, expert thrusts, bringing her to the trembling brink. And then suddenly, he withdrew.

Christine moaned with frustration, rolling her head from side to side, begging, "Please, Chad, please."

"Look at me, Chris," Chad said in a low, husky voice. "Open your eyes and look at me. I want to see your eyes when I make love to you."

Christine looked up into Chad's deep blue eyes and felt herself drowning. She watched as their warm, loving look flared with hot, naked desire.

Suddenly, Chad's need for release was just as urgent as Christine's had been. He plunged into her silky softness, a fierce bolt of flame, thrusting with bold, powerful, demanding strokes. He nibbled hungrily at her breasts, her shoulders and throat as if to devour her. Finally his mouth locked over hers in a deep, searing kiss as he swept them both up the breathless, spiraling heights to the crest, held them quivering at the zenith, and then plunged them over in an explosion of brilliant, flashing lights. They were hurled into space, bodies locked, souls merging and melting into one, in that perfect, ultimate union that only those deeply in love can ever hope to experience.

Chad drifted slowly back from the rapturous heights, his head buried in the soft curve of Christine's throat. He nuzzled her and kissed her tenderly, thinking as he drifted off to sleep, what a delightfully passionate woman she was, his magnificent lady.

Christine glanced out the window. The sky was just beginning to lighten with the new day. She lay cradled in Chad's arms, her head pillowed on his hard chest, her shapely thigh nestled between his legs.

She raised up on one arm and looked down on him as he slept. Her finger traced the outline of his ear and then down across his strong jawline. Tenderly, she brushed a dark lock of hair back over his brow. Her eyes drifted down to his thick dark lashes, rugged nose, and sensual mouth. She trembled, remembering the ecstasy that mouth could bring her. Her eyes continued to roam, feasting on him hungrily. God, how I love him, every wonderful, powerful inch of him, she thought fiercely.

The thought shocked her. She jerked her hand away as if she had been burned. She stared down at him in disbelief, and then her mind screamed, No! No, you can't love him!

Christine eased away from Chad's warm body and she rose from the bed, dressing frantically. She had to get away from his overpowering presence. She had to think.

Opening the door cautiously, she peered into the big room beyond. Two men, one blond, one dark-haired, lay sleeping in one corner of the room, rolled up in blankets. Silently, Christine crept across the room.

Once outside, she ran as if all the demons in hell pursued her until she reached the secluded spot, her own private little place. No one would find her here, deep in the woods by the narrow, gurgling stream. She was safe here. She could think.

How had it happened? Christine wondered. She had given her body freely, but Chad had stolen her heart. Somehow, he had slowly, insidiously torn down her defenses, and then like a thief in the night, he had taken that which she had sworn to give to no man.

When had it happened? Had she already loved Chad that night she had begged him to make love to her? Was that what had motivated her bold invitation? Had he already woven his silky web around her heart then?

What difference does it make how or when it

happened? Christine asked herself bitterly. What about your vow never to fall in love with a man, never to give away your heart? You're a fool, Christine. A silly little fool. You've given your heart to a man who doesn't love you, who's made no promises. Yes, he took your body. What man wouldn't take what was so brazenly offered? But he's never told you he loves you, much less asked you to marry him. Pain such as Christine had never known tore through her. Bitter tears glittered in her eyes.

She froze, hearing footsteps behind her. She recognized those footsteps. She squeezed her eyes and visualized Chad walking toward her with that lazy swagger that was so much a part of him. Oh, why had he followed her, and why did he have to find her? Not now, when all of her defenses were down, when she was so vulnerable. Defiantly, she kept her back to him, so he couldn't see her tears.

"Chris?" Chad said. "I woke up and found you gone. Is anything wrong?"

Christine walked closer to the stream, pretending interest in a leaf on a branch hanging low over it. "No. It was such a beautiful morning, I decided to come out here."

Chad frowned, noting her stiff stance and the trembling in her voice. Something was wrong. But what? Well, he decided, he wouldn't push her. Let her tell him in her own time. "Yes this is a pretty spot," he commented casually.

The silence hung heavy in the air between them. Say something, Christine thought frantically. Anything. Just don't let him know how much he's hurt you. If nothing else, salvage your pride.

In desperation, she said the first thing that came to her mind. "What will you do now, Chad?"

"Go back to Texas and get my ranch back," Chad answered. "You see, I lost it while I was away fighting in the war. With the money you're paying me, I can pay off the back taxes and rebuild."

A rancher? Christine thought. She smiled. Yes, with his sensitivity and love for the land, that fit Chad much better than a cold-blooded *pistolero*.

She heard him step closer and said quickly, "Tell me about your ranch."

Chad stopped, his frown deepened. Then he shrugged, saying, "It's beautiful, Chris. Not large, but not small either. The grass is lush and thick, and there's a small stream of crystal-clear water running through it. It's spring fed, so it never dries up, not even in years of drought. My house sits, or rather will sit when I rebuild, on a hill overlooking the ranch in a cluster of huge pecan and oak trees. It's a nice ranch, and I'm looking forward to settling down to a peaceful life."

Christine had been thinking while Chad talked. Perhaps there was more that she didn't know about him. Was there a woman back in Texas waiting for his return? She hated herself, but she had to know.

"And is there a woman to share that life?"

Chad smiled and relaxed. So that's what's bothering her, he thought. "Yes, there is, a very special woman," he answered. "But I haven't asked her to marry me yet. In the first place, I didn't think I had the right to ask until I got my ranch back and had something to offer her. And then, I wasn't sure until just recently that she loved me."

I should have known, Christine thought with renewed bitterness. All this time there had been a woman waiting patiently for him back in Texas. Oh, yes, she could just see her, Chad's woman. She would be dainty and docile, beautiful and, undoubtedly, a lady right down to her bones. *She* wouldn't have cut her hair and dressed as a boy and gone into Mexico with a strange man. *She* wouldn't have grappled in the dirt with a filthy Apache or thrown her weight around trying to intimidate a French officer. And *she* wouldn't have given her body to a man, brazenly begging him to make love to her. No, undoubtedly, *she* was still a virgin, waiting for the ring before she gave away her most precious gift. Fresh tears stung at Christine's eyes. Oh, God, why did it have to hurt so much?

Chad moved closer, and Christine's body went rigid. Don't let him see you cry, she admonished herself firmly. Say something!

Swallowing hard, Christine said, "What's she like, this woman?"

Chad smiled, saying warmly, "She's wonderful, Chris. She's spirited, brave, proud, warm-hearted, fiercely loyal, and deeply passionate. She's a woman any man would be proud to have for his wife." Chad's blue eyes twinkled mischievously. "But I have to admit, sometimes she's pretty hard-headed and stubborn."

Dainty and feminine and all that too? Christine felt sick. Why, she could never possibly compete against such a paragon. But strangely, Chad hadn't mentioned the one attribute men usually listed first, beauty. Could it be that she wasn't particularly pretty? She couldn't resist the urge to ask. "What does she look like?"

"She's beautiful, Chris." Chad's eyes caressed her hair as he said in a soft voice, "Her hair is like moonlight on the desert sand, soft and silvery. Her eyes are the color of mesquite leaves in the spring. She has a generous mouth, just made for kissing." His eyes drifted down her body as he said, "Her body is magnificent and her skin is like silk. And she's got the damndest, most beautiful pair of long legs I've ever seen."

Christine only heard Chad's first words, "She's beautiful." Misery surrounded her, totally engulfing her. And even if she had heard all he'd said, she wouldn't have recognized herself from his almost poetic description.

Chad stepped closer, and Christine froze. She could smell his heady male scent, a scent that always sent her senses reeling. She felt the heat radiating from his body and his warm breath fanning the nape of her neck. She clenched her teeth and dug her nails into her hands. Oh, God, no! she thought. Please, don't let him touch me now. I couldn't stand it, knowing he loves another woman.

Christine felt the warm brush of Chad's lips against her shoulder and then heard his husky voice saying softly against her ear, "Her name is Christine. I call her Chris, but I think of her as my magnificent lady. And I love her with all my heart and soul."

It took a long time for Chad's words to penetrate Christine's pain-dulled mind. When they finally did, her eyes widened with disbelief. And then she whirled, saying, "I am not stubborn!"

Chad laughed and pulled her into his arms, saying, "You're impossible, Chris. Here, I've given you more compliments than I've ever bestowed on all the women I've known, and all you heard was the part about being stubborn."

"Did you mean it? Do you really love me?" Christine asked in a wondering voice.

Chad smiled, his look tender. "Yes, I meant it. I love you, Chris. I love you deeply, passionately, with all my heart and soul."

Christine saw the expression of immense pride and deep love in Chad's eyes. His look overwhelmed her. Then she did the most ultra-feminine thing. She collapsed in his arms, crying, her body racked with sobs, her tears flowing in torrents.

"For Christ's sake, what are you crying about?" Chad asked in exasperation.

"Because I'm so happy . . . because I'm the luckiest woman alive . . . because I can't believe it's true . . . because I love you so much," Christine sobbed.

Her last words touched Chad deeply. It was the

first time he had heard Christine admit she loved him. He felt a burning sensation in his own eyes and pulled her into a fierce embrace, saying in an emotion-choked voice, "You're crazy, lady. Just plain crazy."

For a while, Chad gently rocked Christine while she cried with happiness. Then he lifted her chin and tenderly wiped the tears from her cheeks, saying, "Will you marry me, Chris? Share my life and dreams?"

Christine nodded, afraid to trust her voice for fear she would start crying again, and she didn't dare do that. Chad's shirt front was already soaked with tears.

"Ranch life isn't an easy life, Chris." He smiled wryly. "A month ago, I'd never dreamed of asking a city-bred woman to be my wife. But you're strong, Chris. You've got what it takes."

Christine smiled up at him proudly.

Chad continued. "But there's something I want to get straight from the very beginning. I won't touch your inheritance from your father. I don't care what you do with the money, bury it, give it away, will it to the grandchildren. But I don't want anything to do with it. It's never brought you any happiness."

Christine was thoughtful. What Chad had said was true. So far, being rich had never brought her any happiness. And greed over her inheritance had almost cost her her life and Charles his. She nodded in agreement.

"And another thing," Chad said firmly, "I want

459

our first child to be a daughter, just like you."

Christine started to object, "No, I want our first—"

Chad silenced her by laying his finger against her lips. He grinned, saying, "That's an order, lady."

She beamed with happiness and snuggled closer. "Chad, do we have to wait until we get back to Texas to get married? I'd like to be married here in Mexico among all of our new friends."

"That's just fine with me. The sooner, the better, as far as I'm concerned." Chad dropped his arms and took her hand, intending to lead her back to the camp. "And now I think we should go talk to your brother and tell him about our plans. I know he's worried." A wry smile played at his lips. "I don't think he particularly approves of me."

"Well, that's just too bad!" Christine snapped.

"No, Chris, it's my fault. You see, I haven't been very nice to him. Hell, I wasn't even civil. But every time I thought of all you had gone through to get to him, of how many times you had almost been killed, my blood boiled. I still think he was foolish to get himself into that situation, but I realize now that it was unfair of me to blame him for everything that had happened to you. I owe him an apology." Chad grinned, adding, "And an explanation for yesterday. I think it's time he knows my intentions."

"But, can't it wait? I want to enjoy my happiness for a few minutes before we share our

460

news with the others."

Chad agreed. This was a special time in their lives, and he, too, wanted to savor his happiness. They sat on the soft, mossy bank next to the small stream for a long time and talked. Christine told Chad all the things she had kept close to her heart. Then Chad opened to Christine. He told her about his infatuation with Anne and her treachery, how he had come home from the war to find his family killed, the ranch house burned to the ground, and his ranch confiscated for back taxes. He told her his plans for restoring the ranch, and then they discussed their future life together. And finally, for a long while, they sat in silence, enjoying just being together.

Eventually, Christine looked about her secret hideaway and said, "Isn't this a pretty place, Chad? I found it a few days ago. I'd come out here with Diablo when I wanted to be alone and think." She looked him deliberately in the eye, saying, "No one ever comes here."

Chad's look was expectant, his heart already pounding in anticipation.

"It reminds me of that beautiful, private place where you first made love to me," Christine continued in a soft voice. "Do you remember? Under the mesquite tree, in the moonlight?"

"I remember," Chad answered in a husky voice.

Christine traced Chad's sensuous lips with one finger and then said, "Don't you think this would be a beautiful place to start our family?"

Chad smiled, a slow lazy smile that sent Christine's heart racing. A warm look came into

461

his eyes. Then he pulled her back on the soft, mossy ground and nuzzled her neck, whispering, "I'm always happy to oblige my magnificent lady."

The hot Mexican sun beamed down its blessing.